CAPTURE THE CROWN

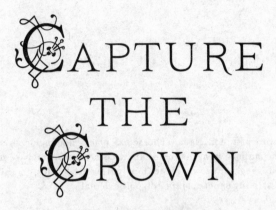

Capture the Crown

A GARGOYLE QUEEN NOVEL

JENNIFER ESTEP

HARPER Voyager

An Imprint of HarperCollins Publishers

CAPTURE THE CROWN. Copyright © 2021 by Jennifer Estep. Excerpt from TEAR DOWN THE THRONE copyright © 2021 by Jennifer Estep. All rights reserved. Printed in the United States of America. No part of this book may be used or reproduced in any manner whatsoever without written permission except in the case of brief quotations embodied in critical articles and reviews. For information, address HarperCollins Publishers, 195 Broadway, New York, NY 10007.

HarperCollins books may be purchased for educational, business, or sales promotional use. For information, please email the Special Markets Department at SPsales@harpercollins.com.

Harper Voyager and design are trademarks of HarperCollins Publishers LLC.

FIRST EDITION

Designed by Angela Boutin
Map designed by Virginia Norey
Title page and chapter opener art by Angela Boutin

Library of Congress Cataloging-in-Publication Data has been applied for.

ISBN 978-0-06-302303-1

21 22 23 24 25 LSC 10 9 8 7 6 5 4 3 2 1

To my mom and my grandma—for your love,

your patience, and everything else that you've given

to me over the years.

To readers who wanted more stories in my Crown of

Shards world—this one is for you.

And to my teenage self, who devoured every single

epic fantasy book that she could get her hands on—

for writing your very own epic fantasy books.

Spy the storm brewing, and you won't get struck by lightning. Ignore the clouds, and you'll get burned to a crisp.

—LADY XENIA RUBIN, FAMED SPYMASTER

Lords and ladies
go 'round and 'round,
laughing and playing
capture-the-crown.

Some are clumsy,
or foolish, or weak.
Some rightly fear
the power they seek.

But for those who conquer
their fear and capture the crown,
that lord or lady has the power
to tear their enemies down.

—ANDVARIAN SONG, BASED ON THE CHILDREN'S GAME

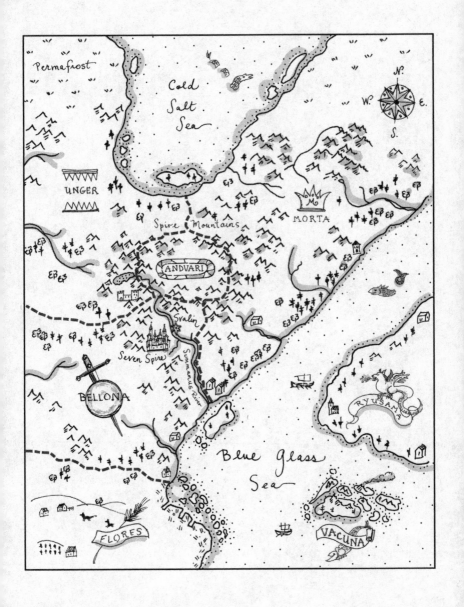

PART ONE

PRINCESS

CHAPTER ONE

I love being a princess.

The beautiful gowns. The sparkling jewels. The scrumptious food. And of course shopping for balls, dancing at balls, and flirting at balls. Oh, yes. I love all those things and many more.

Perhaps I shouldn't feel this way. After all, most royals have horrible reputations. Queens are cold, kings are cruel, princes are pompous. If you asked, most people would say that I was a pampered princess. Why, I would probably top the list of the *most* pampered princesses, both on the continent of Buchovia and the ones beyond, something that fills me with an inordinate amount of pride. If you're going to be known as something, then you should be known as the very best at it. And I bloody *excel* at being Gemma Armina Merilde Ripley, crown princess of Andvari, known far and wide as a fashion trendsetter, excellent dancer, and skillful flirt.

But there is one thing I love more than being a princess—being a spy.

"Are you ready, Gemma?" a voice asked.

I looked over at the fifty-something woman standing along the wall. Several strands of silver glimmered in her dark brown hair, which was pulled back into a bun, while lines were grooved into her bronze skin, especially around her hazel eyes, as if she had spent years perpetually squinting in worry. With me as her charge, that was exactly what she'd done.

The woman was dressed in a dark gray tunic, along with black leggings and boots. No crests or symbols adorned her clothes, but the silver sword and matching dagger hanging from her black leather belt hinted that she was far more than the commoner she appeared to be.

I smiled at Topacia, my longtime personal guard. "Almost. Just double-checking my disguise."

I studied my reflection in the freestanding mirror in the corner of the living room. As soon as we had secretly arrived in Blauberg last week, I had packed away my gowns and jewelry. Then I had chopped off my long dark brown hair to shoulder level and dyed it black, so that I would look slightly different from my normal self, although I hadn't bothered changing the curve of my cheeks or the shape of my nose with a beauty-glamour ring. There was no point, since my pale skin would be covered with grime the second I stepped into the mine.

My now-black hair was pulled back into a low ponytail that was tucked underneath the gray, ridged metal helmet that topped my head. Like Topacia, I was also wearing a dark gray tunic and black leggings, although they were currently hidden beneath my light gray coveralls. Sturdy black work boots covered my feet.

The thread masters at Glitnir, the Andvarian royal palace, would probably faint if they saw my miner's outfit, which was a far cry from the silks, satins, and velvets I usually wore. I didn't mind dressing down, although I did wish that the coveralls were softer and that the heavy-duty canvas didn't scratch the back of my neck. Perhaps I could lobby for more comfortable uniforms for my kingdom's miners once I was back in Glitnir.

Everyone at the palace would probably snicker, thinking that such a proposal was the height of foolishness, but I had spent enough time in heavy tiaras, constricting corsets, and pinching shoes to know how important it was to be comfortable, especially when working. And dancing at balls and hobnobbing with nobles *was* work. Besides, such a seemingly ridiculous idea would fit in perfectly with my carefully crafted persona.

To most people, Princess Gemma Ripley was a pretty decoration, another jewel among the scores that glittered, glistened, and gleamed at Glitnir, and I had no intention of disabusing anyone of the notion that I was all sparkle and no substance. Being underestimated had helped me more than once, especially on my secret missions, and this undertaking was far more important than most.

Topacia studied me. "Cutting and dyeing your hair certainly helped, although perhaps you should reconsider wearing a glamour ring and change your eye color too." A smile tugged up her lips. "Especially since you have the bluest eyes in all the kingdoms. Isn't that how the song goes?"

I groaned at her joke. A few years ago, for my twenty-fifth birthday, a potential suitor and music master had composed "The Bluest Crown," an admittedly catchy, fast-paced tune about how the blue of my eyes matched the sapphires in one of the Ripley royal crowns. To my horror, the song had spread like wildfire through Andvari and all the other kingdoms. Now people almost always sang the song, or at least performed an instrumental version, whenever I made an official appearance as Princess Gemma. I had enjoyed the song—the first few times I'd heard it. But now, hundreds of screechy, off-key renditions later, the mere thought of it made me grind my teeth.

Topacia chuckled at my sour look. I ignored her laughter, unlocked my jaw, and gestured at my helmet, coveralls, and boots.

"No one is going to recognize me dressed like this. Besides, as far as the public knows, Princess Gemma is currently on a frivolous shopping trip in Svalin, not engaged in an adventure in Blauberg."

Topacia arched an eyebrow. "*Adventure?* Is that what we're calling it now? And here I thought that working in the mine was hard, dirty, sweaty labor."

"Oh, it is most definitely that." I grinned. "But that's part of what makes it an adventure. And I do so love a grand adventure."

Topacia snorted.

"It *is* an adventure," I repeated in a firmer voice. "And even better, you and Grimley are here to join in the fun. Right, Grims?"

I glanced over at the gargoyle stretched out on the rug in front of the fireplace. He was roughly the size of a horse, although his dark gray stone body was much thicker, stronger, and lower to the ground. Powerful muscles rippled in his short, stocky legs, while black talons perfect for ripping into, well, everything protruded from his large, wolflike paws. His broad wings were currently tucked into his sides like the closed folds of a lady's fan, but two curved horns jutted up from his head, and an arrowlike point tipped his long tail.

The gargoyle cracked open his bright sapphire-blue eyes, which had also been memorialized in the cursed song. He yawned, revealing a mouth full of razor-sharp teeth.

Grimley was my best friend, and the gargoyle had been my constant companion ever since I had come across him in the Spire Mountains when I had been fleeing from Bellona after the Seven Spire massacre. Back then, I had desperately needed a friend, and Grimley had seemed like a gift from the gods. He had saved my life more than once during those dark, frantic, dangerous days, and we had been inseparable ever since.

Grimley lifted his head and peered at me. He must have been sensing my turbulent thoughts through our mental bond. I shoved away the unwanted memories of the massacre and its aftermath, walked over, and crouched down. Grimley rolled over so I could rub his belly, which had the same rough, weathered texture as the rest of his flexible stone skin. Thanks to the heat blasting out of the fireplace, he was as warm as a rock baking in the summer sun.

You lazy lout, I thought, using my magic and directing my silent, affectionate words at him. *You could at least* pretend *to be excited about our mission.*

I'm much too comfortable to be excited about anything. Grimley's deep voice filled my mind, sounding like bits of gravel crunching together. *Besides, working in the mine is* your *mission. Mine is to make sure that you return home safely, as per your father's orders. In between naps, of course.*

Even though I was twenty-nine and fully capable of taking care of myself, Dominic Ripley, the crown prince of Andvari, would have preferred that I remain in Glanzen, the capital city, and engage in courtly tasks there, as well as fritter my days away with shopping trips, teas, and balls. That would have also greatly pleased my grandfather Heinrich Ripley, the current king of Andvari. Both of them would have been *ecstatic* if I never set foot outside the royal palace ever again, rather than be a traveling ambassador for our kingdom, a position I had created to help facilitate my spy missions.

But to their credit—or they might say detriment—my father and grandfather had instilled a strong sense of duty in me, one that demanded I do everything in my power to protect my people. Which, in my mind, meant slipping away from the proper places people expected me to be, going on adventures, and putting myself in mild to moderate danger, from time to time.

People tended to either babble or brag in Princess Gemma's presence, and usually, all it took was a few kind words and a couple minutes of my attention to convince someone to share all the news and gossip they knew. I then used that information to thwart plots large and small, everything from stopping merchants from overcharging for their goods to getting nobles to pay their taxes to tracking down bandits who had been terrorizing a town. My seemingly innocent travels had also let me build a network of sources all across Andvari and beyond, many of whom were happy to write and keep me informed about the goings-on in their part of the continent.

Grimley wiggled around on the rug, getting even more comfortable. *I fully intend to follow your father's orders, should the need arise. But until then, I will leave you to fend for yourself, which you are quite capable of doing, and you will leave me to my nap, which I am quite capable of enjoying. Are we agreed?*

I stuck my tongue out at the gargoyle, just like I had done ever since I was a child. He grunted with amusement, closed his eyes, and returned to his nap, with his stubby legs still sticking up in the air.

Grimley was right. I *could* take care of myself, despite my pampered princess persona. As a mind magier, I had the ability to move objects with just a thought, hear people's private musings, and walk through dreams, among other things. I was far more powerful and much more dangerous than most folks realized—when my magic actually worked.

An old, familiar worry throbbed like a jagged splinter embedded deep in my heart, and I stood up, grabbed the silver chain around my neck, and pulled it out from underneath my clothes.

A pendant dangled from the end of the chain. The base was

silver, while the small pieces of black jet arranged on top formed a snarling gargoyle face—the Ripley royal crest. Tiny midnight-blue tearstone shards made up the gargoyle's horns, eyes, nose, and teeth, turning the design into Grimley's face.

The pendant had been a gift from Alvis, the Andvarian royal jeweler and metalstone master. Alvis was one of the few people who knew all the terrible things I could do with my magic, and he had crafted the pendant years ago to help me harness my power. The pieces of black jet helped me block out people's mundane thoughts, while the blue tearstone shards would deflect others' powers, if I was ever attacked. The blue jewels could also absorb and store my own magic, giving me an extra boost of power should I ever need it, although I had never used the shards in that way.

I *always* wore the gargoyle pendant, and I didn't take it off for anything or anyone, no matter how many times Yaleen, my thread master, complained that it clashed with her designs.

I was too afraid of what would happen—of what I might do—if I ever removed the pendant.

I rubbed my thumb over the tearstone shards embedded in the gargoyle's face. The soft pricks of the jewels against my skin eased my throbbing worry, and I tucked the necklace back underneath my coveralls. The light touch of the silver chain around my neck and especially the heavier pendant close to my heart further steadied me.

Think of the pendant like a miniature version of Grimley protecting you, Alvis's voice rumbled in my mind. That had been his kind, evasive way of saying the dark truth we both knew—that the pendant was more for everyone else's protection than it was for mine.

I went over and grabbed a dagger from a nearby table. The weapon was made of light gray tearstone, with Grimley's snarling face inlaid in black jet and blue tearstone in the hilt. Another gift from Alvis. A matching sword and shield, each boasting the same crest, also lay on the table, but those weapons were far too large and obvious to take into the mine.

I slid the dagger into a black leather sheath and tucked it into the side of my right boot. Then I grabbed a gray tin lunch box from the table and looked at Topacia again. "Let's go. It's time for Miner Gemma to report for work."

Topacia and I left Grimley snoozing by the fireplace and stepped outside. The cottage Topacia had rented for me under a false name stood off by itself in a patch of woods, but I still reached out with my magic to confirm that we were alone.

Everything had its own energy, a layer of power that surrounded it, whether it was an assassin skulking through the woods, a butterfly fluttering its wings on a tree branch, or a rock hidden in the grass. As a mind magier, I could mentally reach out and manipulate that energy, whether it was tripping an assassin, flicking a butterfly off its perch, or prying a rock out of the ground and sending it careening down a hill.

When I was younger, and first learning how to control my power, I used to pretend that I was a puppeteer, with invisible strings attached to my fingertips that connected to everyone and everything around me. All I had to do was grasp or release, or push or pull on those strings to make things happen—for better or worse.

I didn't sense anyone lurking in the woods, and the smallest thought was all it took to make the front door swing shut behind us. I waved my hand, manipulating the invisible strings of energy connected to the door, and the lock turned as well.

We stepped onto a dirt trail that led to a gray cobblestone road teeming with foot, carriage, and wagon traffic. It was just after seven o'clock, and people were streaming into the city to go to work.

As was the case in much of Andvari, mining was the main industry in Blauberg, a moderate-size city located a scant three miles from the Mortan border. Most people walking along the road wore gray coveralls and ridged helmets, marking them as miners, while the wealthier nobles and merchants rolled by in carriages and wagons.

Everyone's breath steamed in the cool late-September air, and the horses pulling the carriages and wagons snorted out thick clouds of frost that fogged the road. Given Blauberg's high elevation and the fact that the city had been built into the side of the mountain of the same name, autumn had already taken hold here, and brilliant gold and scarlet leaves adorned the trees lining the main thoroughfare.

Above the road, gargoyles sailed through the air, heading away from the people and buildings. Some of the gargoyles were bigger than Grimley, with wings so wide that they seemed to stretch from one side of the thoroughfare to the other, while others were almost as small as caladriuses, the owlish birds known for their snow-white feathers and the vast amounts of magic they possessed. Every morning, the gargoyles flew out into the surrounding forests and mountains to hunt for rats, rabbits, and more. Then, at night, they returned to roost on the city rooftops.

Topacia and I rounded a bend in the road, and the trees fell away, revealing the city itself. Blauberg boasted several different levels, each one steadily climbing higher and higher up the mountain. Stone steps shot straight up between the levels, while the streets zigzagged back and forth, gradually rising and falling with the terrain.

Many of the shops and homes were tall, slender structures comprised of gray stone, and their steep, pointed black-slate roofs made them look like towers, as though the entire city were a fairy-tale castle that had sunk deep into the mountain, and the towers were the only parts still visible.

Adding to the sunken-castle illusion were the intricate carvings and other artistry that embellished the buildings. Vines, leaves, and flowers flowed up many of the wooden shutters on the shops, while thick stone columns chiseled to look like blooming trees supported some of the finer homes. Bronze weather vanes shaped like gargoyles adorned practically every rooftop, creaking back and forth in the breeze.

Blauberg wasn't nearly as rich and prosperous as Glanzen, the capital, but spying a silver moon glinting on a column or a sapphire pansy glimmering on a door was an amusing game I could play with myself as I walked along.

Even better, it helped me block out some of the thoughts of the people around me.

Butchers, bakers, and other merchants were already hawking their wares from their shop doorways and freestanding carts, while customers were haggling over the prices of everything from cuts of meat to bags of cornucopia to bolts of cloth. The loud, cheery commotion was bad enough, but the steady stream of internal thoughts was almost deafening to me.

People thought *all the time*. Every bloody second of every bloody day. And being around so many people meant multitudes of thoughts flying through the air like hundreds of invisible bees incessantly buzzing in my ears.

My gargoyle pendant grew warm against my skin, like a hot stone pressing against my chest. The pieces of black jet were blocking and absorbing as many thoughts as they could, but there were simply too many people for the jewels to silence all the mental chatter.

Gotta sell this meat before it spoils . . .

This cornucopia is stale . . .

I can find a better price for this blue silk . . .

Those silent thoughts and dozens more assaulted me as I hurried through one of the plazas. Hearing all those murmurs in my own mind was *exhausting*, like being forced to listen to music that never slowed down, took a break, or stopped. Even worse, I could also sense people's emotions, which added to the perpetual cacophony in my head and my heart.

At times like these, I didn't feel like a puppeteer with strings attached to my fingertips, skillfully manipulating everything around me. No, right now I was a tiny, fragile ship caught in a raging storm, with waves of thoughts slapping me to and fro in a sea of emotion, and everything from icy disdain to lukewarm interest to sizzling anger cascading over my battered deck.

Topacia and I stepped onto a less crowded street. The incessant buzzing in my ears faded away, my pendant cooled against my skin, and my internal ship slowly righted itself as the storm of chattering people receded. I sighed with relief.

We circled around to the back side of Blauberg Mountain. This area was mostly shops, all designed to serve the workers heading toward the mine. The street opened up into an enormous plaza, which was lined with merchant carts. A gray stone fountain shaped like a gargoyle with its wings spread out wide stood in the center of the plaza, and several miners stopped to throw a penny into the bubbling water. Andvarian mines were among the safest on the Buchovian continent, but it never hurt to ask the gods for a little bit of luck before going down into the dark.

Beyond the fountain, a low stone wall cordoned off the rest of the plaza from the mine, and a black hole dominated this side of the mountain, as though it were a kraken's mouth frozen open in an enormous yawn. Carts filled with jagged chunks of raw ore rolled out of the main opening, along with the surrounding side shafts, and skated along metal tracks toward a large building in the distance.

Inside the refinery, miners would carefully chisel the tear-stone, gemstones, and anything else of value out of the surrounding mundane rock. Then the tearstone, gemstones, and the like would be further processed, cut, shaped, and polished, until the final products were ready to be shipped out to their buyers.

I jerked my head at Topacia, and we slipped into an alley that ran between two bakeries.

Topacia eyed the people moving along the street. "I've heard rumors that some Mortans are in Blauberg. Not just common merchants, but wealthy, high-ranking nobles, along with their guards, although I haven't seen them for myself—yet."

While I was staying at the cottage and working in the mine, Topacia had been renting a room in one of the city's inns, as well as visiting shops and taverns. In addition to being a fearsome warrior, my friend also *loved* to talk to people. Topacia had never met a stranger, and she excelled at picking up gossip and casually asking all the questions that I wanted answered. Her news about Mortans being in Blauberg increased my own suspicions.

Andvari and Morta were old, bitter enemies, and the Morricone royal family had long coveted the Ripley mines, which were full of precious metals, gems, and more. But one of the most defining moments in the centuries of hostilities between the two kingdoms was the Seven Spire massacre.

Roughly sixteen years ago, King Maximus Morricone of Morta had sent his bastard sister, Maeven, to assassinate the Blair royal family of Bellona. Even worse, Maeven had blamed the attack on my uncle, Prince Frederich Ripley, and a group of Andvarians who had been visiting Seven Spire palace in Bellona at the time.

I was one of a handful of people who had survived the horrific tragedy.

I had been twelve back then, but sometimes, it seemed like only yesterday that Crown Princess Vasilia Blair had plunged a dagger into Uncle Frederich's heart during a luncheon on the royal lawn, then killed Lord Hans, an Andvarian ambassador, with her lightning magic. After that, I'd hidden under a table like a coward and watched the turncoat guards slaughter everyone around me.

Screams and shrieks rattled around inside my mind, punctuated by softer but even more agonizing whimpers of pain and fear, along with choked, tearful pleas for mercy.

But there had been no mercy—only death.

I would have died too, if Everleigh Blair hadn't yanked me out of my hiding spot, dragged me across the grass, and handed me off to Lady Xenia Rubin, a powerful ogre morph.

I still remembered the exact moment when Xenia's arm had closed around my waist, tighter than a coldiron vise, and she had hoisted me into the air as though I weighed no more than a baby gargoyle. Maeven had blasted Xenia with her purple lightning, trying to stop our escape, but Xenia had kept going, and eventually, we had made it inside the palace.

From there, Alvis, who had been the Seven Spire royal jeweler at the time, had helped us escape through some old mining tunnels that ran underneath the palace, although it had taken us weeks to make it home to Andvari.

After the massacre, Andvari and Bellona had been on the brink of war—until Everleigh had exposed the Mortans' plot, killed her treacherous cousin Vasilia, and taken the Bellonan throne for herself.

King Maximus was long dead, but Queen Maeven ruled now, so tensions between Andvari and Morta remain high to this day, and the two kingdoms were always little more than a whisper away from war.

But lately, those whispers had grown into much louder, far more ominous rumblings.

"Gemma?" Topacia asked, breaking into my dark thoughts.

"What do you want me to do about the Mortans? If they knew you were here, especially one of the Morricone royals, then they would stop at nothing to kidnap you—or worse."

Screams wailed in my mind again. I was well acquainted with how much *worse* things could get when dealing with the Morricones. Still, I forced myself to be logical. Acting on assumptions could easily get Topacia and me killed.

"There are always a few Mortans in Blauberg, given how close it is to the border," I said. "After all, this is one of the few cities where trade between the two kingdoms is actually necessary and encouraged, due to the surrounding mountains and wilderness."

"But what about your theory that the Morricones are plotting something?" Topacia asked. "At least, something more dastardly than usual?"

Over the past two months, through my network of sources, I'd learned of several disturbing incidents in Andvari, all of them close to the Mortan border. A caravan of merchants murdered by bandits. A cave-in at a small mine that had claimed the lives of several workers. A group of royal guards who'd been swept away by a violent thunderstorm and the resulting flash flood.

On their own, each tragedy had seemed like an unrelated incident, but when considered all together, they had roused my suspicions. So as part of my ambassador duties, I had spent the past few weeks visiting the site of every attack and mishap. Along with offering my condolences to the victims' families, I'd discreetly conducted my own investigations, and I'd discovered one common thread between all the incidents—tearstone.

The merchant caravan, the mine, and the guards had all had hundreds of pounds of tearstone in their possession—ore that had never been recovered.

Tearstone was often used for jewelry and art, but it could also be crafted into weapons, like the dagger in my boot. My theory was that someone was stockpiling tearstone—someone in Morta, given that all the incidents had occurred within just a few miles of the border. Of course, the most likely suspects were the Morricones, specifically Queen Maeven, although a few Mortan noble families were also wealthy and powerful enough to make all that tearstone vanish without a trace.

As for what that person wanted with the ore, well, I doubted their plans included anything as benign as making necklaces or statues, given the dozens of people they'd already killed. My fear was that Maeven was going to somehow use the tearstone to try to assassinate my father and grandfather—again.

Several months after the Seven Spire massacre, the Bastard Brigade, a group of Morricone bastard-born royals, had tried to murder my father and had dosed my grandfather with amethyst-eye poison. Thanks to Queen Everleigh's intervention, Father and Grandfather Heinrich had both survived, but just barely.

I had already lost Uncle Frederich to Maeven's machinations, and she wasn't going to take anyone else from me.

But I'd grown even more worried two weeks ago, when a forewoman named Clarissa had sent a letter to Glitnir, to Grandfather Heinrich, saying that several shipments of tearstone had disappeared from the Blauberg mine—much larger shipments than what had vanished so far.

Things went missing all the time in mines, since they were literally dark holes in the ground, so my grandfather and father hadn't thought much of the letter. But to me, it was another suspicious incident in an increasingly long and alarming chain of tragedies—especially since Clarissa had died in a mining accident three days later.

Clarissa's death had struck me as entirely too *convenient*, so I had rushed to Blauberg to investigate. I had been too late to gather much intelligence at the other sites, but I was hoping this time would be different.

"My theory is just a theory—until I find proof that it's not," I said, finally answering Topacia. "Go back into the city, and see if you can pick up any more gossip about the Mortan nobles. I'll work my shift and try to figure out who is smuggling tearstone out of the mine."

Topacia nodded, slipped out of the alley, and left.

I started to head toward the mine when something brushed up against my mind. The new, unexpected presence was as soft as a feather tickling my skin, but I still froze. No thoughts buzzed in my ears, but my gargoyle pendant grew warm against my chest again, and my fingertips tingled as though I were clutching a lightning bolt. The tingling sensation meant one worrisome thing—that someone or something around here had magic.

Very powerful magic.

My gaze swept over the street, the plaza, and the mine entrance, but everything was the same. Miners trudging to work, merchants hawking their wares, carts of ore rattling along the metal tracks.

A shadow zoomed by overhead, momentarily blotting out the sun, and that faint presence brushed up against my mind again. Who—or what—was that?

I grabbed the dagger out of my boot and walked to the opposite end of the alley. Then I reached out with my magic, searching for that faint presence. It was over . . . *there*.

I slipped from one alley to the next like I was chasing a feather drifting along on the breeze. Eventually, the last alley opened up into a wooded area, and I darted into the trees and crept forward, peering around a maple to find . . .

A strix standing in the clearing beyond.

The hawklike bird was similar to Grimley in that it was roughly the size of a horse, only with a much thicker, stronger body. The strix's feathers were a vibrant amethyst-purple, and onyx tips lined its broad, powerful wings, each point as hard, sharp, and deadly as the arrow it resembled. The bird's big, bright eyes were the same amethyst as its feathers, while its pointed beak and curved talons were a shiny black. A beautiful if dangerous creature.

Many strixes lived in the surrounding Spire Mountains, and the wild birds often zoomed over Blauberg, although they tended to fly high and fast to avoid the gargoyles, since the two species didn't much care for each other. I didn't see a saddle or any reins on this strix, but it didn't seem like a wild bird. So where was its owner?

"See, Lyra?" a deep, masculine voice sounded, as if answering my silent question. "I told you the ride over the mountains wouldn't be too bad."

"Know-it-all," the strix chirped in a high, singsong voice, although her tone was full of affection.

A man stepped around the side of the strix. He looked to be a year or two older than me, thirty or so. His longish hair was as black and glossy as the onyx points on the strix's wings, while his eyes were a deep, dark amethyst. He had sharp, angular cheekbones, along with a straight nose, and his skin had the tanned look of someone who spent a fair amount of time outdoors.

He wore black leggings and boots, along with gloves and a long black riding coat. A black cloak topped his coat, and the layers of fabric outlined his tall, muscled body and gave him a commanding presence. A light gray tearstone sword and matching dagger dangled from his black leather belt, but I got the sense that the weapons weren't nearly as dangerous as the man himself was.

He turned toward me, and I spotted a crest done in silver thread on his coat, right over his heart—a fancy cursive *M* surrounded by a ring of strix feathers.

Shock jolted through me. Topacia had been right. There *was* a Mortan in the city.

Prince Leonidas Luther Andor Morricone, the son of Queen Maeven Morricone, second in line for the Mortan throne.

My mortal enemy.

CHAPTER TWO

Out of all the Mortans who could have been in Blauberg, the idea that Prince Leonidas could be one of them had never even crossed my mind.

A Mortan prince on Andvarian soil. I couldn't even *imagine* the last time that had happened. Probably not since my ancestor Queen Armina Andromeda Aster Ripley had founded our kingdom by raising an army of gargoyles and ripping our land away from the Morricones and their strixes. But the proof that it was happening now was right in front of my eyes.

Prince Leonidas cocked his head to the side, then whirled around, his hand dropping to his sword. I tensed, thinking that he had spotted me, or had at least felt my presence.

After all, he was a mind magier just like I was—and we had met before.

Memories crackled through my mind, the images so vivid and intense I was certain he would sense them. But instead of focusing on the area where I was hiding, Leonidas turned in the opposite direction.

Footsteps scuffed, along with some faint humming, and a

girl skipped into the clearing, swinging a tin lunch box back and forth in one hand in time to her quick, cheery movements.

The girl, who was around seven or eight, looked up. Her humming abruptly cut off, and she skidded to a stop. The girl froze, her eyes fixed on the strix, which peered at her with a curious expression. At least, I hoped that it was curiosity, and not hunger.

I had been so shocked by the sight of the prince that I hadn't sensed the girl approaching. I cursed my inattentiveness. The Mortan and the strix could both easily kill her.

Leonidas studied the girl, whose eyes slowly grew wider and wider, as though she were a fawn that had just realized it was in the presence of a greywolf. No one in Blauberg rode strixes except for the Mortans who visited the city, so she knew exactly what he was, if not his royal rank.

Several seconds ticked by, all marked by tense, silent contemplation on both sides.

Then Leonidas leaned down and plucked an ice violet out of a patch of them on the ground. He twirled the green stem back and forth in his gloved fingers and approached the girl.

I remained behind the tree, still clutching my dagger. If the flower was a trick, and he attacked the girl, then I would rush into the clearing and gut him.

Part of me longed to do that anyway, given all the horrible things that had happened between us as children, but I squashed the murderous urge—for now.

Leonidas stopped in front of the girl, who was clutching the lunch box in front of her like it was a gladiator shield that would protect her. Leonidas slowly lowered himself down onto one knee so that his face was level with hers. Then, just as slowly, he held the violet out toward the girl, as though she were a princess that he was offering a courtly token of his affection.

"Hello, there," he said in a surprisingly gentle voice. "A pretty flower for a pretty girl?"

The girl swayed forward, as transfixed as a bunny by a coral viper's hypnotic gaze. With her free hand, she plucked the violet out of his fingers, then scuttled back. The motion made the lunch box *bang-bang-bang* against her knees like a minstrel's drum. She giggled, but the high, nervous sound was more squeaky fear than genuine amusement.

"Why don't you run along?" Leonidas suggested in that same gentle voice.

The girl giggled again, then hurried into the woods, going back the way she'd come.

I kept a firm grip on my dagger. The girl might be gone, but I knew *exactly* how dangerous and duplicitous Leonidas Morricone truly was—concerned one moment, then cruel the next.

He climbed to his feet. "That was close."

"Too close," Lyra agreed in her high, singsong voice.

"You'd better find someplace to hide for the day. I'll nose around the city, and see if I can gather any news or gossip. We'll meet back here at sunset."

News? Gossip? It almost sounded like he had come here on a spy mission, just like I had. But why? Blauberg was a busy, prosperous city, but it wasn't terribly important in the grand scheme of things. Several platoons of Andvarian royal guards were stationed here to keep law and order, as well as to discourage thieves, bandits, and the neighboring Mortans from attacking citizens, but there was nothing of any real strategic value in Blauberg—except for the mine.

My eyes narrowed. Perhaps *he* was the reason those shipments had gone missing. Perhaps Prince Leonidas was the one who had been murdering my people in order to steal and stockpile tearstone. But why?

I would have to ask—before I killed him.

Leonidas's back was to me, and he was scanning the far side of the clearing, as if making sure the girl was gone. I could probably sneak up on him before he realized I was there.

But no doubt his strix would launch herself at me the second I attacked her rider. Even though I had trained with my stepmother, Captain Rhea Hans, along with Serilda Swanson and other deadly warriors, I was still wary of a full-grown strix, especially one that had probably been schooled in aerial combat and other warfare.

So as much as it pained me, I held my position in the trees.

Leonidas scanned the clearing again, then went over and stroked Lyra's side, smoothing his hand over her purple feathers much the same way I had rubbed Grimley's tummy earlier. The eerie similarity and his obvious love for the creature made me shift on my feet. I had always hated how very much alike the prince and I were.

"Be safe," he said.

"You too," Lyra chirped back.

Leonidas adjusted the cloak around his shoulders, draping the black fabric so that it hid the Morricone crest on his coat. I held back a derisive snort. That was even less of a disguise than my short, dyed hair and miner's coveralls. So he was arrogant, as well as duplicitous.

He disappeared into the woods, heading in the same direction the girl had gone. Lyra spread her wings and shot up into the sky, quickly climbing higher and higher until she too disappeared from sight.

A tense breath escaped my lips, although worry continued to hammer through my body, beating in time to my pounding heart. Suspecting that a Mortan noble was in Blauberg was bad enough, but knowing that a Morricone prince was here was even worse.

Especially *this* prince—a boy I'd met a lifetime ago, one who had grown into an even more dangerous, powerful man.

I had first encountered the bastard prince years ago in the Spire Mountains when Alvis, Xenia, and I had been fleeing from Bellona after the Seven Spire massacre. Leonidas had found me in the woods and offered me a chance to escape from the turncoat guards who had been chasing us.

Like a fool, I had believed him. But the second I had lowered my guard, he had handed me over to those same men.

I had learned a valuable, if painful, lesson that day—the only thing that truly mattered to Leonidas Morricone was his own survival.

Images flooded my mind, and my own screams echoed in my ears, but I pushed them all away, just as I had the memories of the massacre earlier. Someday, I was going to silence the screams and shove the horrific memories so deep down into my mind and heart that they would *never* bubble back up to the surface.

Someday—but not today.

Still, the prince and the strix were gone, so I left the woods and headed back toward the mine. If Leonidas Morricone was here to pilfer more tearstone, then I needed to figure out who was helping him. Once I had identified his source, then I could take steps to keep the precious resource out of the prince's clutches.

And maybe, just maybe, I could finally take my revenge on Leonidas for how he had betrayed me all those years ago.

I doubled back through the alleys and over to the plaza. I paused a moment to dig a penny out of my pocket and toss it into the gargoyle fountain for luck, then fell in line with the other workers trudging toward the mine entrance.

A woman smiled when she caught sight of me. Her long dark red hair was pulled back into a braid that was partially tucked underneath her helmet. Her eyes were a light blue, and freckles dotted her milky cheeks. She was also wearing gray coveralls, and a lunch box dangled from her hand.

"Hey, Gemma," she said in a soft, lilting voice. "Running late too?"

I might have cut and dyed my hair and stuffed myself into a miner's uniform, but I hadn't bothered to change my name. *Gemma* was very common, thanks to, well, *me*.

After I had been born, the name had become quite popular in Andvari, just as *Everleigh* had taken on a frenzied popularity in Bellona ever since Everleigh Blair had been crowned queen some sixteen years ago. All the royals' names were in vogue to some extent, so I had felt safe enough using my real name in Blauberg. Besides, not having to remember to answer to another name made my spying much easier.

I smiled back at the other woman. "Yeah, I'm still finding my way around the city, and I went down the wrong street. Why are you late, Penelope?"

I had met Penelope when I'd started working in the mine two days ago. There weren't many women here, so she had come over and introduced herself. I had liked her immediately, especially given her inherent cheerfulness, and Penelope had been showing me around ever since. A few butterflies of guilt fluttered in my stomach that I was using her to gather information on the other miners, but I swatted them away. As a princess and especially as a spy, I couldn't afford to indulge in such a treacherous emotion as guilt.

Penelope smiled again. "Oh, my daughter needed some extra help getting ready for school."

We reached the mine entrance, and she fell silent and faced forward.

Going from the morning sunshine into the darker confines of the mine was like stepping into a different realm, as though I had traveled through a Cardea mirror, an enchanted glass that let people see and talk to each other over great distances, as well as move from one place to another. In an instant, the crisp mountain air turned ten degrees cooler, and the natural sunlight gave way to black iron lanterns filled with round fluorestones. The lanterns hung on the walls like strings of popcorn on a yule tree, while the glowing fluorestones inside ranged in shade and intensity from cool, moody blue to bright, piercing white. The combined lights and colors painted the inside of the mine a pale, muted gray.

This first, topmost level was called Basecamp, since it was the base for all the mine's operations, both aboveground and below. The front part was an enormous hollow dome, with a hard-packed dirt floor, curved walls, and a ceiling that soared several hundred feet overhead. Carts filled with chunks of ore and buckets of tools squeaked, creaked, and rattled along the metal tracks that crisscrossed the ground. Adding to the commotion were the miners loading carts, hauling empty buckets away, and calling out directions to each other.

I drew in a deep breath to steady myself. Then I exhaled, reached out with my magic, and carefully skimmed the thoughts of everyone around me.

When I was first learning how to use my magic, Alvis had told me to picture my mind magier power as some task that I could complete, that I could *control*. Skimming thoughts was like leaning over the deck of my tiny internal ship and dipping my fingers into the sea of emotion that constantly ebbed and flowed all around me.

In some ways, skimming thoughts was much harder than moving objects: I could easily ignore the strings of energy surrounding people and objects, but once I dipped my fingers into that endless, churning sea, anything could happen.

Oh, I could hear people's whispered thoughts easily enough, but dealing with their emotions was much more difficult. Alvis had told me to treat other people's feelings as things that I could experience for a moment, then set aside. Like someone's seething jealousy was only a pinprick of pain, as though a thread master had accidentally poked me with a needle. Or boiling anger was nothing more than heat from a fireplace warming my face. Or bitter rage was merely an icy rain pelting my skin before dropping away. Brief discomforts that I could brush aside as quickly as I could close a book I had finished reading.

But try as I might, I couldn't always close that book.

Sometimes, people's thoughts and feelings were so strong, so vivid, so *intense*, that they completely overwhelmed me. Sometimes, if enough people were thinking and feeling the same things all at once—like fear, panic, dread, and terror—then my internal ship capsized in that raging sea of emotion, and my own magic crippled and paralyzed me, rendering me as useless as a fountain that had frozen over in the winter.

Just like I had been useless and frozen during the Seven Spire massacre.

A familiar combination of guilt and shame bubbled up inside me, burning like acid in my throat, but I shoved it down and focused on the people around me.

Gotta get back down into Shaft 3 . . .

Need to replace this cracked bucket . . .

Hope the baker has raspberry tarts for lunch . . .

The usual chatter whispered through my mind, and no strong emotions jumped out at me. Everything was normal.

I shuffled along behind Penelope and the other miners, heading toward the main checkpoint. The domed ceiling tapered down, morphing into a much smaller square shaft that was only about thirty feet high. Before they reached the shaft entrance, every miner stopped at a table where a man was sitting and shuffling through documents.

He was a large, bulky man, with thick arms and a round stomach that was slowly giving way to fat as he advanced into middle age. He wasn't wearing a helmet, and his dark brown hair was oiled and slicked back from his forehead. His eyes were also a dark brown, as was the bushy mustache that adorned his upper lip like a trapped fuzzy, woolly worm, but his skin had the unnaturally pale look of someone who had spent more time underground than above it. The Ripley snarling gargoyle crest was stitched in black thread over his heart on his gray coveralls, marking his importance—Conley, the head foreman, and my top suspect.

Conley was one of the few people who had access to the entire mine, as well as the neighboring refinery, and if anyone could make shipments of tearstone disappear, then it was him. Especially since Clarissa—the second, or under, forewoman, the one who had died in that supposed accident—hadn't been replaced yet.

Conley checked each person's name off on his master list and handed them a small paper map indicating which section they would be working in. As I neared the table, I reached out with my magic again, this time focusing solely on Conley.

Gotta get more production out of Shaft 5 . . .

Can't believe that idiot Horace broke another pickaxe . . .

Wonder if Wexel will be pleased with the latest shipment . . .

That last thought caught my attention. Who was Wexel? On the face of things, there was nothing truly incriminating about Conley's musing. Sending out shipments was one of the foreman's responsibilities, and it was only natural that he would be concerned about what his customers thought about their goods.

That thought skipped away in Conley's mind and sank like

a stone in a pond, but others sprang up like weeds to take its place, mostly about what he wanted for lunch—grilled pumpernickel bread piled high with red-pepper-crusted turkey, melted Swiss cheese, crunchy kale coleslaw, and extra onion dressing. He even pictured the bulging sandwich in his mind, and the image was so tempting that my own stomach rumbled with anticipation.

I could have probed a little more, but Conley might have sensed my magic. Most people didn't notice when I skimmed their surface thoughts, but trying to hear someone's deeper, more serious and private musings took much more power, skill, and control, and the person could sometimes feel that something was wrong, like the difference between a mild spring breeze ruffling their hair versus a cold winter wind chapping their cheeks. So I decided not to take that next step into Conley's mind. I needed to keep a low profile until I was certain that he was the thief.

Penelope stepped up to the table and jerked her thumb at me. "Okay if Gemma and I stick together again today?"

Conley's gaze slid down Penelope's body, even though she was covered from head to toe with her helmet, coveralls, and boots. He leered at her before giving me the same slow, disgusting once-over. His lust bloomed in my mind like a sickly sweet rose, each lascivious thought scraping against my skin like a sharp thorn, and I had to grind my teeth to keep from snarling at him.

"Yeah, sure," he drawled in an obnoxious baritone, and slid a map across the table. "You're in Shaft 4 today."

Penelope reached for the map, but Conley covered her hand with his much larger, beefier one. He leered at her again, then started stroking his index finger over her skin.

Penelope tried to smile, although her expression twisted into a grimace, and her anger, frustration, and fear sliced into my mind like daggers. Conley had done this same thing to her every time we'd gone down into the mine. When I had asked her about it yesterday, Penelope had said that she needed her job too badly to tell Conley to stop.

"Shouldn't we get to work?" I said in a loud, pointed voice, trying to pry Penelope out of his clutching grasp.

Conley's bushy eyebrows shot up. "*I* decide when you get to work, girl."

This time, my own anger sizzled in my heart, and my tongue itched with scathing words just begging to be let loose like arrows from an archer's bowstring. I wanted to growl that I was nobody's *girl* and to keep his fucking hands to himself, but I was Miner Gemma right now, not Princess Gemma.

Conley smirked at my stone-faced silence. He pulled his hand away from Penelope's and gave an airy wave, telling us to move along.

Penelope scuttled away from the table. I followed her, and we stepped into the smaller square shaft, which was lined with gray metal lockers and wooden benches. Several miners were stuffing their lunch boxes into the lockers, while others were sitting on the benches, tying their bootlaces.

Penelope opened her locker, stowed her lunch box inside, and pulled on a pair of thick gray canvas gloves. I did the same with my own lunch box and slipped on my own gloves. Penelope waited until the other miners left before she faced me.

"You shouldn't talk back to Conley," she said. "He can make your life very difficult, both here in the mine and out in the city."

"More difficult than he's making yours?"

She grimaced. "Things can always be worse."

Penelope was right. I should have kept my mouth shut, but sometimes, despite my best efforts to keep her contained, Princess Gemma got the better of Spy Gemma. After all, what was the good of being a bloody princess if I couldn't help people?

My father and grandfather had drilled that duty into me ever since I was a child, and seeing and hearing about all the amazing deeds that queens like Everleigh Blair of Bellona and Zariza Rubin of Unger had done over the years made me want to live up to their fine examples.

But I couldn't fix this situation—at least, not as Miner Gemma. Once I discovered who was stealing the tearstone, though, Princess Gemma would return to the mine and put Conley in his proper place—and out on his lecherous ass.

"You're right. I'm sorry. My mouth has a mind of its own. It gets me into trouble."

That much was *always* true, whether I was Miner Gemma or Princess Gemma.

Penelope smiled, leaned over, and bumped her shoulder against mine. "All is forgiven. Now let's get to work."

She shut her locker. I did the same and followed her into another, even smaller shaft where several miners were standing beside a large metal cart fitted with wooden seats. The cart was sitting on metal tracks that ran for a few feet before dropping down into what looked like a round, deep well filled with blackness.

Penelope and I climbed into the cart with six other miners. The driver released the hand brake, and the cart rolled forward, then started its descent down a steep slope into that waiting well of blackness. No one spoke as the cart creaked along the tracks, and the darkness was so absolute that I felt as though I were dead and buried six feet under. Only it was worse than that, since we were going much, much deeper.

Even though I couldn't see anything, my magic let me sense Penelope shifting in her seat beside me, as well as the movements of the other miners, and the rigid tension that radiated off them all, as though their arms, legs, and spines had transformed into stiff, unyielding boards. Most of the miners were veterans who had been working in these shafts for years, but there was always a bit of uncertainty going so far underground. Only a fool wouldn't be afraid of a mountain that could so easily crush them to dust.

Still, we Andvarians were sturdy stock, and this was how we had made a living for generations on end. I was just as proud of my countrymen and -women's heritage as Bellonans were of their gladiators, or Ungers were of their complicated dance routines. It took a whole lot of heart and even steadier nerves to venture this far down into the dark. Some legends claimed that Andvarians had liquid ore running through our veins, right alongside our blood, a sort of magnetic energy that compelled us to dig deeper and deeper into the Spire Mountains.

I had always loved those old fairy tales, and I had begged my mother, Merilde, to read them to me over and over again as a child. My favorites had been the stories about Queen Armina Ripley, who was supposedly the first person to ever befriend a gargoyle by chipping it out of a wall in a mine near Glanzen. The gargoyle had been so grateful to be free of its stone prison that it had vowed to protect Armina and her family for all time.

The cart skated over something on the tracks, loose rocks probably, and the jerking motion made me bump shoulders with Penelope. She tensed again, as did the other miners, but I remained calm and relaxed. I selfishly loved being this deep underground.

Hundreds of miners might be toiling away inside the mountain, but the thick stone walls blocked their thoughts, leaving me in relative blessed silence, certainly far more silence than I ever experienced at Glitnir, with its scores of servants, guards, and nobles roaming the halls, not to mention the gargoyles perched on the rooftops. I didn't often get such a prolonged, quiet reprieve, and I was going to enjoy every moment, no matter how dangerous the journey and the work itself was.

The driver leaned on the hand brake, the slope flattened out, and the cart rolled to a stop at the bottom of the shaft. Strings of lanterns lined the walls and low ceiling, while the fluorestones inside bathed the area in that familiar pale gray glow, as if someone had bottled up rays of moonlight.

I blinked my eyes several times, helping them adjust to the sudden influx of light, then climbed out of the cart. Penelope showed her map to the mine steward, who directed us to the appropriate section.

We walked through the shaft, following the strings of fluorestone lanterns like they were arrows pointing us toward our destination. The other miners split off and disappeared into different tunnels, but Penelope and I kept moving forward until we reached the end of this shaft.

We were in a different part of the mine than yesterday. This tunnel opened up into a large round chamber that had been chiseled out of the surrounding rock, and the jagged, dome-like shape reminded me of an uneven soap bubble that had somehow been trapped underground. Dozens of fluorestone lanterns had been rigged up in here, and the chamber was actually quite bright, although the light wasn't warm, like the sun's rays would have been.

Several miners were already using their pickaxes, rock hammers, and other tools to chisel chunks of tearstone out of the walls. Some of the tearstone seams were a light, bright, starry gray, while other sections were a deep, dark midnight-blue.

To my surprise, the miners were only working on the left side of the chamber. Curious, I headed over to the right. No lanterns were strung up on this side, so I couldn't tell how far away the opposite wall was, although strangely enough, I could have sworn that a breeze was gusting across my face. I took another cautious step forward, but my foot didn't meet solid ground, only empty air—

Penelope grabbed my arm and jerked me back. "Careful! That chasm just opened up a few weeks ago."

I glanced down. The lanterns' glow made the tearstone shift colors, and the swirls of gray and blue spread out like a rainbow, creating an optical illusion on this side of the chamber. A very dangerous illusion, since I hadn't noticed that I was about to step off the edge of a chasm. Penelope was right. I needed to be more careful. Mind magier or not, the mountain could kill me as easily as it could anyone else.

I flashed her a grateful smile. "Thanks."

She nodded and released my arm.

A thought occurred to me. "Wait. Is this how that woman died? You said that one of the forewomen accidentally stepped into a chasm. Her name was Clarissa, right?"

Penelope shivered, even though the chamber wasn't all that cold. "Yeah. The mountain shifted, maybe because of miners digging in a nearby shaft, and Clarissa was in the wrong place at the wrong time. The chasm opened up right under her feet. It took us two days to recover her body."

She didn't trip over the words, and her voice remained smooth and even, but I could still tell that she was lying.

Most people's lies were small things, more to soothe others' feelings than to do any true harm. *Of course that gown looks lovely on you. I absolutely adore the song you've composed for me. No, I don't know what happened to the last piece of cranberry-apple pie.*

Those sorts of lies always felt like tiny stings, like a rambunctious puppy had scratched my hand, but Penelope's lies were much sharper, as though that puppy had morphed into a greywolf that had just sunk its teeth deep into my arm. Her guilt and fear also punched into my stomach as hard as a gladiator gutting a hated rival in an arena.

I could understand Penelope's fear. No one wanted to die down here. But why would she feel so guilty about Clarissa's death? Especially when she had just said it was an accident?

Penelope shivered again. Before I could question her further, one of the other miners called out to her, and she went over to him.

I stayed behind, though, staring down into the black abyss and wondering what other murderous secrets the mountain contained.

CHAPTER THREE

Penelope finished her conversation with the other miner, and we grabbed some pickaxes and headed over to the back of the chamber.

Thick seams of tearstone ran from the top of the rock wall all the way down to the bottom, and the miners would be working in here for months to pry out every last shard. The larger, more common light gray chunks would probably be shaped into swords, daggers, and shields, while the smaller, rarer midnight-blue pieces would most likely be used to add sparkle, flash, and beauty glamours to rings, necklaces, and bracelets.

I dug my axe into the surrounding rock, then chipped away at it so that I could get to the embedded tearstone. A few minutes later, I pried a dark blue, fist-size chunk out of the wall.

This wasn't the first time I had dug tearstone. Even pampered princesses were required to learn about their kingdom's industries, and a good portion of my royal education had focused on mining, since it was such a large part of Andvarian life, as well as how my ancestors had made their fortunes. Plus, I had served as Alvis's informal apprentice for years. The metalstone master had taught me everything he knew about shaping precious metals and gems into beautiful jewelry, just as he had taught Everleigh Blair before me.

"Gemma?" Penelope asked. "Are you okay? Why did you stop working?"

"Sorry. I was just admiring the stone."

Penelope eyed me like I'd grown a second head, so I dropped the tearstone into the bucket at my feet and went back to work.

Rock by rock, bit by bit, piece by piece, Penelope and I chipped, chiseled, and cracked chunks of tearstone out of the cavern wall and placed them in the buckets. The other miners did the same. Every hour on the hour, the mine steward would stroll by and mark our progress on his clipboard. Two men trailed along behind the steward, grabbing the full buckets and setting out empty ones.

While we worked, I studied the other miners, who were a mix of ages, shapes, sizes, and abilities. Several were mutts, a common, if somewhat derogatory, term for those with relatively simple, straightforward powers, like enhanced speed or strength. Like the man who was chipping tearstone out of the wall twice as fast as anyone else. Or the woman who was hauling around boulder-size rocks as though they were as light as loaves of bread.

Some of the other miners were masters, those who could control a specific object or element. Like the metalstone master who was moving his hand back and forth, using his magic instead of a tool to dig into the wall.

There were also a few morphs, those who could shape-shift into larger, stronger creatures. Like Reiko, the woman standing next to me.

Reiko was a couple inches shorter than me, and much more slender, with high cheekbones, emerald-green eyes, golden skin, and long black hair pulled back into a fishtail braid. Unlike the other miners, Reiko wasn't wearing gloves, and a dragon face with emerald-green scales and black eyes adorned her right hand, indicating the creature she could shift into.

Reiko didn't so much as glance in my direction, but the tattoo-like dragon on her hand must have sensed my curious stare because it winked at me. Reiko had partially shifted and was using the long black talons that had sprouted on her fingertips to pry pieces of tearstone out of the wall.

I was the only magier in the chamber, though. Having someone who could conjure fire, lightning, or some other raw power was extremely risky in a mine, since you never knew when you might hit a pocket of gas that the smallest spark—magical or otherwise—could ignite.

As the morning wore on, the miners shared the latest gossip to break up the monotony of filling bucket after bucket. I listened to everything they said and used my magic to skim their thoughts, but I didn't hear anything suspicious. Some people's inner musings were easier to sense than others, but if anyone here was involved in Clarissa's death, then they were hiding it well, and their malevolence was buried deep in their minds.

When the day's gossip had been exhausted, some folks started singing Andvarian songs about love, loss, and, of course, mining. Reiko, the dragon morph, had a particularly lovely singing voice, and soon the other miners were swinging their axes and tapping their hammers into the wall in time to her songs.

"Do you know 'The Bluest Crown'?" someone asked during a water break.

"Doesn't everyone in Andvari know that song?" Reiko replied, a mocking tone in her voice.

Everyone laughed, except for me.

Reiko must have noticed my lack of merriment because her gaze locked with mine. I started to skim her thoughts, but her steady stare, along with that of the dragon on her hand, made me stop. Morph musings were often difficult to hear, perhaps because there were two beings in every morph's body, and the person's thoughts often mixed with those of the creature hidden inside them.

Either way, I didn't want Reiko to suspect that I was anything more than a miner, so I calmly stared back at her, as though her song choice didn't matter to me.

Amusement flickered across Reiko's face, and the green dragon on her hand opened its mouth in a wide, silent chuckle, as though it were laughing at some joke at my expense. Suspicion filled me.

"'The Bluest Crown' it is," Reiko announced.

She launched into the song. All the other miners joined in, including Penelope, and their cheery chorus rang throughout the chamber, punctuated by the *tink-tink-tinks* of the tools digging into the rocks. I swung my pickaxe even harder at the wall. I might be a mind magier, but even I couldn't block out that bloody catchy melody.

Despite the torturous song, and the two boisterous encores that followed, the morning passed by quickly. There were no clocks, and the lanterns' steady, unwavering glow made it difficult to determine the time. If the mine steward and his men hadn't come by to collect the buckets every hour, I would have thought we had been down here for only a few minutes.

Eventually, a small silver bell tied to a bright blue string at the front of the chamber started jingling. Each chamber featured a similar bell, and they were all threaded together, like an elaborate underground spiderweb. Soon, other bells joined in, until they were clanging throughout the entire mine, and the sounds rippled through the thick walls and echoed back on themselves in light, pealing waves.

Lunchtime.

We set our tools down, trudged out of the chamber, and climbed back into the cart at the front of the shaft. This time, instead of depending on the driver to steer us down into the dark, everyone grabbed hold of a thick rope that was part of a pulley system attached to the wall. Together, we hauled ourselves and the cart back up the steep incline. The mutts with strength magic did most of the work, along with Reiko.

Many morphs were strong, but Reiko seemed to have more power than most, despite her short, slender frame. Even though I couldn't see her in the blackness, I could still sense her magic. The dragon morph was sitting in front of me, and my fingertips tingled every time she yanked on the rope.

As soon as we reached the top of the shaft, the miners relaxed, and their collective relief swept over me like a cool, refreshing breeze. Penelope and I grabbed our lunch boxes from our lockers, walked back through Basecamp, and headed outside into the plaza.

The other miners flocked to the merchants' carts, purchasing kebabs of grilled beef, chicken, and spicy vegetables, bread bowls brimming with hot broccoli-cheese soup, and thick slices of cranberry-apple pie, my favorite. Penelope and I bought mugs of pear lemonade, then sat down on a bench close to the low wall that separated the plaza from the mine. In the distance, the fountain bubbled merrily, as though the stone gargoyle were playfully splashing around in the water-filled basin.

Penelope opened her lunch box and pulled out a roast-beef sandwich, along with a bloodcrisp apple and sweet-and-sour carrot sticks. I opened up my own lunch box, which also contained a bloodcrisp apple, along with a paper bag filled with fried sweet-potato chips sprinkled with cinnamon. I grabbed the sandwich I had made this morning—hearty sourdough bread stuffed with thick slices of gruyère cheese and slathered with apricot jam.

I sank my teeth into the sandwich and sighed with happiness. The tangy bread and the creamy, salty cheese combined perfectly with the apricots' bright flavor. The sandwich would have been even better hot and toasted, with the bread crispy, the cheese melting, and the jam oozing out the sides, like the ones the kitchen staff made for me at Glitnir. Of course Miner Gemma didn't have such luxuries, but I didn't care. Even cold, the sandwich was still delicious.

Penelope and I polished off our food and sat on the bench, sipping our tart lemonade with its sweet pear syrup. Penelope chattered all through lunch, sharing tidbits and funny stories about the other miners. I studied each person she mentioned, but everyone seemed content to enjoy their food and the lovely fall day, and no one was acting suspiciously.

"Does anything interesting ever happen around here?" I asked.

Penelope frowned. "What do you mean?"

"You know that I'm from a small town and that this is my first time working in such a large mine," I lied. "I was just wondering if anything exciting ever happens, especially since we're so close to the Mortan border."

Penelope shrugged. "Not really. Lots of Mortans visit Blauberg to shop, trade, and the like, but they don't usually come to the mine unless they're placing or picking up an order. But even that's rare. We mostly mine tearstone, and the Ripley royal family prefers to sell it to the Bellonans or Ungers, rather than to the Mortans."

I already knew all that, but it was still good to have confirmation.

Penelope turned the conversation to other things, and her cheery chatter washed over me again. The whole time she talked, I kept dreaming up ways I could find out more about the missing tearstone. Perhaps after my shift ended, I could slip away from Penelope and hide in the mine or the refinery and see if anything untoward happened overnight. I hadn't made as much progress as I'd hoped, and my time in Blauberg was running out. Princess Gemma needed to be back in Glitnir next week to attend to some courtly duties.

Penelope was still talking, and I was still plotting when Conley strode out of the mine, along with six big, burly men. Four of the men were clutching pickaxes, while the other two were each pushing a wheelbarrow. Black canvas tarps covered the wheelbarrows, although the containers obviously held raw ore, given the uneven lumps jutting up against the tops of the tarps.

My eyes narrowed. Perhaps I wouldn't have to sneak around the mine tonight. Perhaps my prime suspect was going to incriminate himself right here and now, although rolling wheelbarrows full of tearstone out of the mine in broad daylight was incredibly brazen. Then again, Conley didn't strike me as being particularly subtle.

Several miners around the plaza were also staring at the group—or rather, *not* staring at them. Those miners dropped their heads and focused on their food, as if pretending that the carts weren't rolling by meant that it wasn't actually happening. Tension clouded the air, and the miners went quiet and still, as though they were frozen in place just like the gargoyle in the fountain.

I didn't bother skimming people's thoughts. Conley was obviously up to no good, and he must have a much tighter grip on the miners than I'd realized for people to turn such blind eyes to his actions.

The foreman swaggered across the plaza while the wheelbarrows clattered ominously across the cobblestones. I glanced around, wondering how I could slip away from Penelope and follow Conley—

"Oh, no," Penelope whispered.

"What's wrong?" I asked. "Who are those men?"

"Conley's crew," she replied. "You know how the enforcer in a gladiator troupe handles disputes between the fighters? Well, Conley uses those men to take care of squabbles between the miners. And for . . . other things."

In other words, the men were Conley's personal gang. "What are they doing with those wheelbarrows?"

Penelope fell silent, but guilt rippled off her.

To my surprise, Conley veered in this direction and stopped in front of us. His shadow engulfed us both as he looked down his nose first at Penelope, then me. "You two. With me."

Penelope stared at him with wide eyes, and her worry throbbed in my mind right alongside my own concern. What did Conley want?

I reached out with my magic, but Conley's thoughts were scattered and turbulent, like fall leaves swirling on a gusty breeze. All I could really tell was that he was extremely agitated.

"Now," he growled.

Penelope slammed her lunch box shut, set it aside, and surged to her feet. I also set my lunch box aside and stood up.

"Follow me," Conley growled again.

He strode past us. The two men pushing the wheelbarrows walked by as well, but the other four miners stood there, clutching their pickaxes.

Penelope shot me a regretful look, then headed after Conley. The four miners hefted their tools—weapons—their message crystal clear. Come along, or else.

All around the plaza, the other miners kept their heads down, and another, stronger cloud of tension drifted through the air. No one was going to question Conley, much less try to stop him and his enforcers from doing whatever they wanted with the wheelbarrows—and me.

Despite the obvious danger, curiosity surged through me, along with more than a little eagerness. After weeks of running around the countryside chasing rumors, I finally had a chance to discover what was really going on. So I fell in step beside Penelope, with the four miners closing ranks behind me. Together, we all followed Conley away from the mine.

Conley swaggered through the plaza and along the main thoroughfare beyond as though he owned it. He called out greetings to several merchants, although they too ducked their heads and focused on their goods, lest they attract too much of his attention. I wondered if Conley had frightened or bribed them to look the other way. Perhaps both. Well, his grip on the mine was rapidly coming to an end.

Penelope and I trailed Conley and his men about a quarter mile down the street. The crowd was much thinner here, and Conley paused and glanced around before ducking into an alley. The merchants and miners were still averting their eyes, and Penelope and I had no choice but to follow the foreman.

As we walked along, I skimmed the minds of the six men.

Someone needs to grease the wheel on this thing . . .

Why couldn't we do this after lunch?

Going to drink my fill at the tavern tonight with my cut of the money . . .

That last thought all but confirmed my suspicions that the wheelbarrows were full of tearstone.

I reached out with my magic again, this time searching for Topacia and trying to locate her warm presence, but she must have been deeper in the city, because I didn't sense her. Even if

I did call out to her, there was no guarantee she would hear me. Usually only mind magiers, or those with strong, special bonds like Grimley and me, could mentally communicate with each other with any regularity over great distances. Although, sometimes if I was close enough, I could whisper thoughts to Topacia, given our long-standing friendship.

I reached out yet again, this time searching for Grimley. I easily sensed his cool, solid presence, like he was the stone masthead attached to my internal ship, but our connection was weak, indicating that he was miles away. He must have gone hunting with the other gargoyles in the countryside.

I was on my own.

Beside me, tension and guilt radiated off Penelope, the emotions strong enough to cause my gargoyle pendant to grow warm against my skin. Her worry increased my own, but unlike Penelope, I wasn't concerned about Conley, his men, or where we were going.

No, mine was an old, familiar, insidious fear—that I would lose control of my magic, of *myself*, and drown in the sea of thoughts and storm of emotions swirling around me. That I would become frozen, paralyzed, useless. That people would get hurt—that people would *die*—because I was too fucking weak to save them.

Just like Uncle Frederich, Lord Hans, and the other Andvarians had died during the Seven Spire massacre.

Phantom screams ripped through my mind, causing my heart to pound and sweat to gather on the back of my neck. I raised a shaking hand to my chest. I couldn't touch the gargoyle pendant, since it was still tucked underneath my clothes, so I settled for pressing it against my heart. The silver base dug into my skin like a hot coal, but the discomfort helped me to shove away the horrible memories. My fear, guilt, and shame lingered, though. I had never been able to get rid of them.

Cowardice tended to stain one's heart for all time.

"Gemma?" Penelope whispered. "Are you okay? You look sick."

Her worry churned in my stomach again, but this time, I blocked it out, along with my own fear. The pendant cooled against my skin, and I dropped my hand from my chest.

"I'm fine," I whispered back.

Penelope gave me a disbelieving look, but we had no choice but to keep following Conley.

The foreman led us through several alleys. None of the men said a word. Penelope and I didn't speak again either, and the only sounds were the muffled *tink-tink-tinks* of the chunks of ore rattling around inside the wheelbarrows.

Conley ducked into yet another alley, and I slowed down, glancing around. Dented metal bins overflowing with spoiled food and other garbage, broken glass littering the ground, a wide crack zigzagging through one of the walls. An eerie, un-welcome sense of déjà vu filled me. This was the same alley I had come through this morning, and I had a sneaking suspicion I knew exactly where we were going—and even worse, whom we were meeting.

Conley marched out the far end of the alley, through the trees, and into the clearing beyond. He stopped near the center of the open space, and the two men set down their wheelbarrows. The other four miners spread out, still holding their pickaxes, while Penelope grabbed my arm and jerked me to the side.

"I'm sorry," she whispered. "I didn't mean to get you in-volved in this."

Surprise filled me. Had she done this before? Was she *part* of Conley's crew?

Before I could ask Penelope any questions, half a dozen men stepped out of the trees on the opposite side of the clearing.

No crests adorned their black tunics, leggings, and boots, but they were all wearing purple cloaks that clearly marked them as Mortans. People in Blauberg didn't wear that color because they didn't want to be mistaken as being from the other kingdom. The men were clutching swords with the ease and familiarity of seasoned soldiers, and they all oozed cool confidence, unlike Conley, Penelope, and the other miners, who were radiating rigid tension.

The Mortans parted, and a seventh man strode into the clearing. He was more than six feet tall, with short black hair, hazel eyes, bronze skin, and a body that was all thick, solid muscle. Heavy stubble darkened his square jaw, and he would have been handsome, if not for the cruel twist of his lips.

He too was wearing a purple cloak, and a fancy cursive *M* surrounded by a ring of strix feathers was done in gold thread on his black tunic, over his heart. The Morricone royal crest marked him as a captain, although instead of a sword, he was holding something much more unusual—the end of a long coldiron chain.

The captain stopped and yanked on the chain, as though it were attached to some poor dog that he wanted to drag forward and whip to within an inch of its life.

"Come on," he growled. "Don't make this any harder on yourself."

He gave the chain another yank. The captain must have had some strength magic, because another man stumbled into the clearing. This man's hands were bound in front of him with coldiron shackles that were attached to the chain, and a coldiron collar glinted around his neck.

The captain stuck his foot out, tripping the other man, who landed in an undignified heap. Pain spiked through my own skull, making me wince. That fall had definitely hurt, although the injured man didn't make the smallest sound of discomfort.

The captain sneered down at his prisoner, while the six guards stepped forward and kicked the other man, driving their boots into his ribs, hips, and legs. The prisoner huddled on the ground, his head tucked down, his back toward me, and his arms wrapped around his sides, trying to protect himself.

More pain spiked through my skull, and sympathy pricked my heart like a red-hot needle. Thanks to the Seven Spire massacre, I knew *exactly* how awful it was to be down on the ground, alone and helpless, and surrounded by enemies. How fearful it was to never know when or where the next blow was coming from, or how much it would hurt, or if the next attack would be the one that finally killed you—

"Enough!" the captain bellowed. "You've had your fun."

The guards stopped their assault and stepped back. Silence dropped over the clearing. The prisoner rolled over onto his stomach, then pushed himself up to his hands and knees and leaned back on his heels.

The injured man raised his head. Black hair, dark amethyst eyes, tan skin. Shock knifed through me, even sharper and harder than his pain had.

The prisoner was Prince Leonidas Morricone.

CHAPTER FOUR

I sucked in a loud, surprised breath, and Leonidas glanced over at me.

Our gazes locked. Even though I had seen him earlier, this was the first time I had looked him in the eyes since we were children. For once, phantom screams didn't ring in my ears. No, all I could hear was the sudden, painful hammering of my heart, picking up force and speed with every passing second.

I held my breath, waiting for recognition to erupt in his eyes, and anger to stain his cheeks as he realized exactly who I was, but his features remained blank and impassive, except for the tiny frown that quirked his lips, as though he wasn't sure what to make of me.

"Get up," the captain growled.

He yanked on the chain again, almost jerking the prince back down to the ground, but Leonidas stiffly climbed to his feet. He glared at the captain, his amethyst eyes as dark as storm clouds. The cold fury in his features made me shiver. Even shackled, he was still extremely dangerous.

Leonidas's gaze darted over to me again. Magic flared in his eyes, although it was a dull, dim flash, like a match trying to sputter to life in a monsoon, given the coldiron collar and shackles that were dampening his abilities. Still, his power brushed up against me, as light as a feather tickling my skin, but with a hot, electric undercurrent that made my stomach clench with anger, worry, and something else that was far more troublesome.

The faint, weak sensation was as soft and polite as a servant's knock on a door, but I immediately swatted his magic away with my own power, as hard and fast as Grimley knocking a vase off a table with his tail.

The feathery, electric feel of his magic vanished, but Leonidas's eyes narrowed, and he studied me even more closely. I cursed my own foolishness. I shouldn't have reacted to his power, much less batted it away with my own. Now he knew I was more than what I appeared to be.

"See something you like, princeling?" the captain mocked. "I had no idea you were so fascinated by miners. Why, I thought you were too good to tumble with the palace servants."

"Just marking the faces of my enemies," Leonidas replied in an icy tone. "I will kill you for this, Wexel, along with everyone else here."

He looked at first one guard, then the next with cold calculation, as though he was figuring out how best to murder them all, despite his shackles. Some of his captors shifted on their feet, while a couple sidled back a few steps.

Wexel was the only one who didn't shrink away from the prince's glare. "I don't take orders from you. Never have, never will. You should have stayed in Morta. Not stuck your nose in where it doesn't belong."

"Forget him," Conley snapped. "Let's get down to business."

Wexel's gaze swung over to the foreman. To his credit, Conley didn't wilt under the captain's hot, steady glower, which made him both brave and foolish.

The captain strode forward, still clutching the coldiron chain, which *clank-clank-clanked*. The harsh, ominous sound made me wince. Beside me, Penelope stood rooted in place, her breath escaping in shallow gasps. The other miners hefted their pickaxes a little higher, and even Conley swallowed, betraying his nerves.

Wexel stopped in front of the foreman and smiled, his white teeth flashing like sharp, pointed pearls. "What were you saying?"

"I—I—I brought what you wanted," Conley stammered.

"Then quit wasting time and show it to me," Wexel growled.

The foreman flapped his hand at the two men with the wheelbarrows, who rolled the containers forward and set them down. Conley ripped the black tarps off first one wheelbarrow, then the other.

Jagged chunks of tearstone glinted in the sun, their colors shifting from light gray to dark blue and back again.

Wexel grabbed a chunk of tearstone and hefted the ore in his hand, as if testing its weight. He nodded, apparently satisfied, then tossed the piece over to one of his men, who caught it. "Load it up."

Four guards strode forward and transferred the tearstone from the wheelbarrows into several large black leather satchels. Those men must all have had strength magic, because carrying the bulging bags didn't seem to bother them.

Leonidas eyed the satchels. "What are you going to do with the tearstone?"

A low, ugly laugh rumbled out of Wexel's mouth. "Wouldn't you like to know?"

He sneered at the prince, then looked at Conley. I tensed

again, thinking that Wexel might order his guards to murder the foreman, along with the rest of us. Conley must have been considering the same thing, because he wet his lips and took a step back, as though he was ready to run for his life.

Several seconds ticked by in utter silence. Worry blasted off Conley, Penelope, and the other miners and squeezed around me like a python strangling its prey.

Wexel jerked his head, and a guard stepped forward and threw another, different satchel down onto the ground in front of Conley. Several *clink-clink-clinks* rang out, and a few gold crowns spilled out of the bag. Instead of a Ripley gargoyle, the gold was stamped with a woman's face, with two tiny coins forming her eyes and a third coin forming her mouth.

The coined woman was the crest of the DiLucris, the powerful, wealthy family behind the Fortuna Mint, a bank that dealt with all sorts of unsavory characters and engaged in its own dark deeds. Smart of Wexel to pay Conley with DiLucri gold so that the stolen tearstone couldn't be traced directly back to the Mortans.

Greed surged off Conley, the hungry, gnawing emotion even stronger than his worry, and he dropped to his knees, scooped the errant coins back into the satchel, and hoisted it onto his shoulder. Conley climbed back to his feet, staggering a little under the satchel's heavy weight, but more greed surged off him, and he steadied himself.

Conley started creeping backward, but Wexel held up a hand, and the foreman froze.

"I need you to take care of something else," Wexel said.

Conley frowned. "I've told you before. I need at least a week to stockpile this much tearstone, as per our usual schedule."

"The usual delivery schedule is fine. I have a more pressing problem." The captain stabbed his finger at Leonidas.

Conley frowned again, still confused. "What do you mean?"

A cruel, thin smile split Wexel's face. "He needs to disappear—permanently."

My gaze snapped over to the prince. Leonidas's face was calm and blank, but his anger and frustration punched into my heart like a red-hot poker.

Who was Wexel working for? I couldn't imagine the arrogant captain obeying anyone other than the Morricone royals, and the highest-ranking royal was . . .

Queen Maeven.

Shock slammed into my stomach. Would Maeven be so heartless as to order her own son's execution?

"Well?" Wexel demanded. "Can you handle this?"

Conley wet his lips again. "Of—of course."

"Excellent. I'm glad we understand each other."

The captain jerked his head. Two of the guards reached for Leonidas, but he struck first, head-butting one of the men, who grunted and staggered away. Leonidas drove his elbow into the gut of the second guard, who also grunted and staggered away. His attacks created an opening in the ring of men, but instead of bolting into the woods and trying to escape, the prince charged at Wexel, his hands stretching out toward the captain's throat.

Wexel jerked back in surprise. He was still clutching the chain, and the inadvertent motion sent Leonidas tumbling down to the ground. He growled, surged back up onto his feet, and charged at the captain again.

An instant before he would have reached Wexel, the two guards he'd attacked latched onto the prince's arms. Leonidas struggled, but given the guards' strength magic, he couldn't break their grips, and the coldiron shackles around his wrists, as well as the collar circling his neck, kept him from unleashing his mind magier power.

Even with the restraints, all the guards shot him wary looks, as if they realized that Leonidas Morricone was still capable of killing every single one of them with his bare hands.

Wexel dropped the chain and drew the sword on his belt. The metal made an evil *hiss* as it slid free from the scabbard. The captain twirled the sword around in his hand.

"Any last words, Your Highness?" Wexel mocked.

Leonidas gave him another icy, murderous glare. "You won't get away with this—"

Wexel lunged, his sword racing toward the prince's heart.

NO!

I didn't know if I was hearing Leonidas's silent scream, or if the thought was my own, but I flinched in pain and surprise. More of that treacherous sympathy pricked my heart, and I did something I never, ever thought that I would do again.

I tried to save Leonidas Morricone.

I grabbed the invisible thread of energy attached to Wexel's sword and flicked my fingers, using my magic to force the weapon off course. Instead of sinking into the prince's heart, the blade stabbed into his upper chest, close to his shoulder.

Leonidas screamed and jerked back, but the two guards held him in place.

Wexel grinned and twisted his sword, trying to shove it even deeper into Leonidas's chest. But once again, I reached out with my magic, this time curling my fingers into a tight fist, and stopped the blade.

The captain growled in frustration, wrapped both hands around the sword's hilt, and surged forward. Wexel put his considerable mutt strength behind the blow, and his power battered against my own, threatening to break my invisible grip on his sword. If that happened, the blade would punch all the way through Leonidas's chest, killing him instantly.

Anger spiked through me. If anyone here was going to murder Leonidas Morricone, then it was going to be *me*.

But Wexel was exceptionally strong, and I couldn't hold his sword back forever, not without tipping him off that someone was using magic against him, so I aimed my power lower, yanking on his right ankle. His boot slipped on the grass, making him stagger to the side, although he managed to keep one hand on his sword.

Wexel growled again, but he must have thought that he'd mortally wounded Leonidas because he yanked his sword out of the prince's chest, making him scream again. The guards released Leonidas, who swayed back and forth like a tree about to topple under a woodcutter's axe.

More pinpricks of sympathy stabbed into my heart. I didn't know why I'd helped him. *Because you're still a fool, all these years later*, my own snide little voice whispered in my mind.

Leonidas's gaze darted over to me, and his pain-glazed eyes locked with mine, as if he'd heard my silent admonishment. I froze, my breath trapped in my throat and my heart hammering against my ribs again. He opened his mouth, but no words escaped his lips. Then his eyes rolled up in the back of his head, and he collapsed.

Silence dropped over the clearing. Wexel loomed over Leonidas, but no one else moved or spoke. I reached out with my magic again. Leonidas's mind was as blank as an empty chalkboard, but his heart was still *thump-thump-thumping*, although the sound was growing slower and weaker. He was still alive, but he wouldn't stay that way for long without help.

I was no bone master, so I couldn't heal Leonidas, but I could at least slow his blood loss. Once again, I curled my fingers into a fist. Only this time, instead of stopping Wexel's sword, I imagined balling up Leonidas's tunic in my hand and then shoving the fabric into his wound.

Ball up, and shove down. Ball and shove. Ball and shove . . .

I did that over and over again, until I had packed as much fabric into the wound as I could. Lucky for me, and him too, the prince was still wearing his black cloak and riding coat, and no one seemed to notice his tunic moving and rippling underneath the other garments.

I released my magic and listened again. *Thump-thump-thump.* Leonidas's heart was still beating, the sound steady, if a bit slow. Maybe I had saved him. Maybe not, but I'd done all that I could for him.

Wexel must have seen my hand move out of the corner of his eye, because his gaze snapped over to me. I stood absolutely still and kept my face schooled into a neutral expression, as if watching the attempted murder of a prince was an everyday occurrence and no more noteworthy than the cool breeze gusting through the clearing.

The captain faced Conley again. "Dump his body someplace it will never be found."

"Of—of course," Conley stammered.

Wexel opened his mouth as if to say something else, but instead he grimaced and looked up, as though expecting to see something other than clouds in the sky. An unexpected emotion surged off him and zinged up against my skin—fear.

I frowned. Wexel had just tried to murder his own prince. What could possibly worry him after doing something so brutal and treacherous?

The captain dropped his gaze from the sky, whirled around, and strode off toward the woods on the opposite side of the clearing. Instead of relaxing, now that his foul deed was done, he clutched his sword and continued to glance upward, as though he was expecting a lightning bolt or something else equally dangerous to strike him down.

"Let's go!" Wexel ordered.

The guards hefted their bags of tearstone a little higher in their arms, then followed him. The Mortans disappeared into the trees, leaving Leonidas lying in the clearing.

Conley, Penelope, and the other miners all visibly relaxed, and tension rushed out of them like air leaking from a child's balloon.

The foreman stared down at the fallen prince "This is *not* part of our arrangement. Wexel should have given me an extra bag of gold for cleaning up his mess."

Conley huffed in aggravation, then stabbed his finger at Penelope and me. The motion made the coins *tink-tink-tink* together inside the satchel still hanging off his shoulder. "You two. Load the body into one of the wheelbarrows, and get rid of it. Then bring both wheelbarrows back to the mine. And be quick about it."

Penelope bobbed her head. "Yes, sir."

Conley eyed Penelope, but he must have heard the tremble in her voice and seen how badly her hands were shaking, because he fixed his gaze on me. I bobbed my head as well, as though I were as frightened as she was.

He jerked his head at the other men. "Fun's over. Back to work. You can all pick up your cut of the gold at the end of your shifts."

Conley walked across the clearing, waddling under the weight of his gold-laden satchel, and vanished into the trees. The other miners followed him, leaving Penelope and me behind. The second Conley and his men were gone, I whirled around to her.

"What have you gotten me into?" I hissed. "I thought we were just helping the foreman. I didn't know about any of *this*!"

I gestured at Leonidas, still unconscious on the ground.

Penelope blanched. "I'm sorry, Gemma. So sorry! I didn't know the Mortans were going to kill somebody. I swear! I thought the exchange would take place just like usual."

Her words snuffed out my faint hope that Conley had picked us out at random to help with his scheme. *"Like usual?"*

"Yeah. I thought Conley would give the tearstone to some Mortan guards. I didn't know a Mortan *captain* was going to be here. Conley must have been worried about getting double-crossed. That's probably why he brought us along, as a show of strength."

"Oh, please," I snapped. "Conley would have shoved us into the guards' swords while he ran away. We were nothing more than human shields."

Penelope winced. "Well, it all worked out okay. Right?"

Anger exploded in my chest, and I struggled to keep my voice calm. "How long has this been going on?"

"I don't know how long Conley has been siphoning tearstone from the mine, but I've been helping him for the last three weeks."

"Why?"

Penelope sighed. "Because my daughter fell out of a tree while she was playing and broke her leg. It was a really bad break, and she was in a lot of pain. I got her as much medicine as I could, but I didn't have enough money to get her leg properly set by a bone master, so I asked Conley if I could work some extra shifts. He said that if I helped him with a special project that he would give me more than enough money to heal my daughter."

Understanding trickled through me, cooling some of my anger. I might have done the same if someone I loved had been hurt.

I reached out with my magic, checking on Leonidas.

Thump-thump-thump. His heart was still beating at that slow, steady pace, and he didn't seem to be getting any weaker.

I needed to get him out of here, so I could try to heal him, but I also needed more information about Conley's treachery. I wavered, torn between helping Leonidas and furthering my own mission. But protecting my people from the Mortans was more important than the life of one man, especially *this* man, so I focused on Penelope again.

"What did you do for Conley? Before today?"

"At first, he asked me to smuggle tearstone out of the shaft. Just what I could fit into my pockets. I would hide the pieces in my locker, and he would collect them at night, after everyone else had left." Penelope shrugged. "I didn't think it was a big deal. What's a couple of missing rocks here and there?"

More anger spiked through me. It wasn't just a couple of missing rocks. Conley's entire crew was probably stealing tearstone. All those chunks of ore had added up to those two wheelbarrows today, and there was no telling how much more Conley had already sold to the Mortans.

"So you stole tearstone for a while, then Conley started bringing you along to deliver it—to *Mortan* guards."

Penelope flinched at my harsh accusation, but then she crossed her arms over her chest. "Yes, *Mortan* guards. They work for the Morricones just like I work for the Ripleys. What does it matter who gets the tearstone? Morricones, Ripleys, Rubins, Blairs. They're all the same. Sure, they let us work in their mines and fight in their gladiator arenas, but the royals don't care anything about *us*, about common folk like you and me."

I blinked, shocked by the heat and especially the venom in her voice. "That's not true. Heinrich is a good king. He cares about his people and tries to do what's best for them."

"Maybe he does, but Heinrich is still sitting in his palace while you and I are down in the dirt in the dark," Penelope said, her tone even more bitter and caustic than before. "And do you really think Princess Glitzma concerns herself with what's best for us common folk?"

A loud, derisive snort erupted out of her mouth. "Not a chance. All Glitzma cares about is draping herself in pretty gowns and sparkling jewels—jewels that *we* pry out of the mountains for her."

This time, I was the one who flinched. A few years ago, a noble lady had snidely called me Glitzma during a royal ball, saying that the glittering diamonds on my gown nearly blinded her. The nickname had stuck and spread through Andvari and all the other kingdoms even faster than the cursed "Bluest Crown" song.

At first, the nickname had amused me, and I had thoroughly embraced it, using it to further cultivate my pampered princess persona and create an even better cover for my spy missions. But lately, *Glitzma* had started to bother me. Oh, some people used the term to mock and belittle me, especially in their own minds, where they thought I couldn't hear, but even when folks said it with kindness and affection, the nickname still grated on my heart.

It seemed as though I had done my job far too well, and no one thought I was anything more than a lovely doll to admire. Or perhaps I just wanted someone to peer beneath the pretty gowns and sparkling jewels and see the *real* me—and accept me despite all my worries, quirks, and especially my fears that I wasn't good enough, strong enough, to be queen of Andvari.

That no matter how much information I gathered, and how many missions I went on, and how many schemes I thwarted, that I would *never* be able to atone for my shameful inaction during the Seven Spire massacre. That I truly was a coward at heart, with magic that I couldn't fully control, who would only let people down, who would only let them *die*, just as I had during the massacre.

Penelope sighed again, and some of the anger leaked out of her body. "Forget about the Ripleys. They're not here, so they don't matter. The simple truth is this—if I hadn't done what Conley wanted, then he would have just found someone else to help him. And then he would have made things even worse for me at the mine."

Her regret clamped around my heart like a vise. She truly was sorry about everything she'd done. Perhaps she'd also been scared, especially after what had happened to Clarissa. Either way, I'd gotten some information out of Penelope, and now I needed to focus on the person who might be able to give me even more—Leonidas Morricone.

I stalked over and dropped to my knees beside the prince, who hadn't so much as twitched this whole time.

"Stealing tearstone is one thing." I gestured at Leonidas. "But what about *this*? Did you know this was going to happen?"

Penelope reared back as though I had punched her. "Of course not! I never would have come along if I'd known that someone was going to get hurt." She wet her lips. "Is he . . . *dead*?"

I pressed my fingers up against his neck. *Thump-thump-thump*. His pulse drummed along steadily, although an alarming amount of blood had soaked into his clothes, despite my shoving his tunic into the wound. But I still had a chance to save him—or I could let him bleed out.

Memories of my childhood encounters with Leonidas Morricone bubbled up in my mind like hot lava, burning away my weak, treacherous sympathy for him. All I had to do was walk away, and he would die where he lay. The cold, cruel, petty part of me *longed* to do that, to let him suffer at the hands of his own countrymen, just as he'd let me suffer at the hands of those turncoat guards all those years ago. Even better, letting him die would finally destroy whatever lingering shred of kinship I foolishly felt for him.

I dropped my hand from his neck and started to rise, but my gaze snagged on a splash of purple a few feet away from Leonidas's shackled hands—an ice violet, just like the one he'd given to that girl this morning. He could have easily killed the girl, but instead, he'd let her go, even though she could have run away screaming and revealed his position.

I wavered a moment longer, then sighed and pushed my hurt and anger back into the past, where they belonged. Like it or not, Leonidas had spared an innocent Andvarian life, and I had a duty to save his in return. Not because I was a princess and he was a prince, and not even to find out more about the stolen tearstone. No, this was just me, just *Gemma*, trying to help another person simply because it was the right thing to do.

Besides, if I didn't at least *try* to save him, then I would be no better than Maeven, who had watched while men, women, and children were slaughtered during the Seven Spire massacre. And if there was one thing I would never, ever be, it was anything like Queen Maeven Morricone.

"Is he dead?" Penelope asked again.

"Yes," I lied. "He's dead. Help me get him into one of the wheelbarrows."

She blanched at my cold, clipped tone, but she took hold of his legs, while I grabbed his shoulders. Together, we hoisted him up off the ground and into one of the now-empty wheelbarrows. Leonidas didn't make a sound, and his face was ashen enough to make it seem as though he truly was dead. He would be soon enough, if I didn't find a way to help him.

But first, I had to get rid of Penelope. She might not have wanted anyone to get hurt, but I couldn't trust her not to run straight to Conley with the news that Leonidas was still alive. So I reached out with my magic and twisted my fingers, as though I were turning an invisible door knob. Penelope made a small, choked sound and clutched her stomach, as though she suddenly felt nauseous.

Normally, I only used my power to move objects and skim

people's thoughts. Unlike some mind magiers, I didn't whisper commands to people, or make them see things that weren't really there, or hurt them with my magic. Not unless I had no other choice. But this was a life-or-death situation, and Leonidas was running out of time.

"I don't . . . feel so good," Penelope rasped, her hands still on her stomach.

"I can handle this. Just tell me where to dump him."

"Are you sure? I dragged you into this. I should be the one to . . . take care of things."

"I'm sure," I replied in a firm voice. "Roll the other wheelbarrow back to the mine. Maybe you'll feel better once you're away from here. Just tell me where I can get rid of his body."

Penelope bit her lip, still hesitating, so I twisted my hand again. Her eyes widened, her stomach gurgled ominously, and it took her a few seconds to swallow down this second, stronger round of nausea.

"There's a ravine on the far side of the woods, about half a mile away," she said. "Rock slides happen all the time there, so his body should get covered up in a day or two."

"Okay. You go back to the mine and tell Conley that I'll return soon."

Penelope nodded, and her relief washed over me, even stronger than the nausea I'd inflicted on her. She grabbed the handles of the second wheelbarrow; gave me a brief, wobbly smile; and then pushed it into the trees.

When I was sure she was gone, I stared down at Leonidas.

He lay sprawled in the wheelbarrow like a sack of potatoes. His arms and legs hung off the sides at awkward angles, while his face was even paler than before. For a moment, I thought he truly was dead, but then his chest fluttered up and eased back down with a shallow breath.

"Doing the right thing is a lot bloody harder than it should be," I muttered. "Especially when it comes to *you*."

Of course he didn't answer me, and if I didn't act now, he wouldn't be talking ever again. So I sighed, grabbed the wheelbarrow, and rolled my mortal enemy out of the clearing.

CHAPTER FIVE

Pushing a wheelbarrow full of a mostly dead prince through the woods wasn't as easy as I'd thought it would be.

Given the rocky, hilly terrain, I couldn't have managed it without my magic. But one good thing about being a mind magier was that I could move much larger objects with my magic than I ever could with my own mortal strength; although, the heavier the object, the more magic, willpower, and concentration were required. So I pushed the wheelbarrow along with my arms and legs, and used my magic to shove it past, around, and over the rocks, dead logs, and other detritus that littered the forest floor.

Leonidas didn't stir, no matter how bumpy the ride got or how viciously I cursed. Those coldiron shackles were still wrapped around his wrists, and they *clank-clank-clanked* together as loudly as a bell ringing around a cow's neck. Between the clanking shackles, the attached rattling chain, and the wheelbarrow's squeaky wheel, I was making far too much noise, but speed was more important than stealth.

I made it back to the clearing in front of the cottage without running into anyone. Just a little bit farther, and I could stop pushing, roll Leonidas out of the wheelbarrow, and see how badly he was injured—

A presence brushed up against my mind, as soft as a feather tickling my skin, and a shadow fell over me, blotting out the sun. I jerked to a stop, and my sudden, awkward motion almost tipped over the wheelbarrow.

A harsh warning cry rang out. My head snapped up, and I realized why Captain Wexel had kept glancing up at the sky after he had stabbed Leonidas.

Lyra was hovering above me. The strix was pumping her wings hard and fast, and the resulting blasts of wind blew my miner's helmet clear off my head. With another harsh cry, the strix streaked downward, her talons aimed at my chest, ready to tear me to pieces.

I dropped the wheelbarrow handles, lifted my hands, and reached for my magic. But before I could shove the strix off course, a dark gray blur streaked through the air and slammed into her.

Grimley was here.

Lyra and Grimley both went down hard and tumbled wings over tails across the clearing, their talons raking over the ground and throwing up grass, dirt, and rocks in their chaotic wake. They slammed into the broad trunk of a maple hard enough to make a shower of scarlet leaves cascade down and comically cover their bodies, as though they were children who had deliberately jumped into a pile of raked leaves.

Lyra hopped up and whipped around to face Grimley, who shook off the leaves, leaped up, and pawed at the ground. Strixes and gargoyles were natural competitors for food, and Lyra and Grimley both looked like they wanted to rip each other to shreds. Lyra's beak, talons, and onyx-tipped wings were some of the few things hard, strong, and sharp enough to penetrate

Grimley's stone skin, while his horns, teeth, talons, and arrow-tipped tail could be used to equally brutal effect on her. It was a fight that could end only one way—with the two of them killing each other.

Even though it was stupid and dangerous, I leaped in between the two creatures just as they started to charge at each other. Grimley immediately halted, and to my surprise, Lyra jerked to the side to keep from running into me, although she whipped right back around.

"Stop!" I hissed, looking first at the gargoyle and then the strix. "Do you two want everyone in Blauberg to know we're here?"

Grimley shuffled back, chastised by my harsh tone. Lyra bobbed her head, as though she was also sorry, then hopped over to Leonidas, who was still lying in the wheelbarrow.

She bent down and nudged him with her beak, but he didn't stir. "Leo's hurt." She faced me again, her eyes narrowing to slits. "Did *you* hurt him?"

I held my hands out to my sides, trying to look as nonthreatening as possible. "No. It was a Mortan captain named Wexel."

Lyra let out an odd, low cry that sounded very similar to one of Grimley's growls, then raked her talons through the grass, leaving long gouges behind. "Kill him for this. *Finally.*"

Finally? How long had the strix wanted to kill the captain? And why?

I pushed my questions aside and pointed at Leonidas. "I have some medicine inside that might heal his wound. It's the only chance he has."

Lyra quirked her head from side to side, still studying me with narrowed eyes, and I could feel her distrust raking across my heart, the sensation as sharp as her talons tearing through the grass.

"Look at it this way. If you kill me now, then Leonidas will definitely die. But if you let me live, then he might live too." I paused, an idea popping into my mind. "Besides, you can always kill me later."

Topacia would have groaned at my pointing out that fact. She was always saying that I needed to be far less flippant and cheerful about things like my own death. She was probably right.

Grimley stepped up beside me. "*Try* to kill you later," he snarled. "She won't succeed."

Lyra fluffed out her purple feathers in indignation. "Arrogant gargoyle. I smash little rocks like you all the time."

Grimley grinned, showing off his teeth. "And I gobble down little chicks like you all the time."

The two creatures glared at each other again.

"We're wasting time," I snapped.

A few seconds ticked by in tense silence. Then Lyra's feathers smoothed down. "Help my Leo," she chirped, her voice far softer than before. "Please."

Gemma, Grimley's voice sounded in my mind. *You can't trust this strix. She'll try to peck your eyes out the first chance she gets.*

No, she won't. She just wants to save her human, even if that means letting me live. Wouldn't you do the same if I had been hurt?

You know I would.

Then it's settled.

Lyra's head quirked to the side, almost as if she could sense my silent conversation with Grimley. Maybe she could, given her own bond with Leonidas.

I went over, grabbed the wheelbarrow handles, and pushed the container to the front door, which I unlocked and shoved open with my magic. Luckily, the door was wide enough for me to roll the wheelbarrow inside the cottage.

Grimley started to follow me, but I jerked my head at Lyra. He gave me a sour look, but he stayed outside with the strix. I would just have to hope that the two creatures wouldn't kill each other—and that their scuffle hadn't already killed Leonidas.

I kicked the door shut behind me, then rolled the wheelbarrow into the living room and set it down. Next, I used my magic to grab hold of Leonidas, lift him out of the wheelbarrow, and float him down to the rug in front of the fireplace. He still didn't stir.

I grabbed some supplies, then dropped to my knees beside the prince. His face was still deathly pale, and a sheen of sweat coated his forehead, but his chest rose and fell in that slow, steady rhythm—

Tap.

Tap-tap.

Tap-tap-tap.

Startled, I turned around. Lyra was standing by a window, pecking her beak against the glass in a quick, annoyed rhythm, clearly telling me to hurry up. Grimley was lurking behind her, his tail lashing from side to side, ready to pounce if the strix did anything stupid, like break through the window to try to kill me.

Don't worry. He'll be okay. I sent the thought to the strix, being careful to merely whisper the words, since I had never mentally communicated with her before.

Lyra stopped her incessant pecking, her head jerking back in surprise. Then she leaned closer to the window again.

He'd better be, her voice sounded in my mind, her singsong tone somehow high and menacing at the same time.

I grimaced and turned back to Leonidas.

The first thing I did was remove the shackles from his wrists and the collar from his neck. The coldiron gleamed a dull, flat black, and the metal felt cool and strangely sticky, as though I were holding solid rings of leeches that were eager to feed on my magic.

"Nasty things," I muttered, tossing the collar, shackles, and attached chain aside.

Next, I unhooked the pin on the front of Leonidas's cloak—a silver strix with glittering amethyst eyes that looked like Lyra—and tugged the fabric out from under his body. I also wrestled off his riding coat, leaving the prince in his black tunic, leggings, and boots.

Wexel had been aiming for Leonidas's heart, but thanks to my magic, the captain's sword had instead punched into the prince's chest, close to his shoulder. Despite the bumpy wheelbarrow ride, my magic had held the tunic in place, and the black fabric was still balled up around and stuffed down into the wound. Blood had soaked into the fabric, but the makeshift bandage had stopped him from bleeding out.

I grabbed a pair of scissors and cut the tunic off him, leaving only the wad of fabric around the wound. Part of me hoped that Leonidas would be hideous beneath his clothing, covered with hairy green warts, fat red boils, and dry scaly skin like a cursed prince out of some old fairy tale, but of course he was gorgeous. Muscles rippled across his chest and stomach, while a light sprinkling of black hair arrowed down below his leggings. Even the bruises that covered his body from the guards' attacks didn't detract from his appeal.

My pulse quickened, and my fingertips itched with the sudden urge to stroke his skin and see if his muscles were as hard and glorious as they looked—

Tap.

Tap-tap.

Tap-tap-tap.

Lyra pecked on the window again, jarring me out of my reverie.

I kept my face averted from the strix, so she wouldn't see the blush scalding my cheeks. Then I took hold of the blood-soaked fabric and gently pulled it out of the wound.

Wexel might not have hit Leonidas's heart, but he had still

done plenty of damage. Blood welled up out of the deep, jagged gash and trickled down Leonidas's ribs, each drop shimmering like a liquid ruby streaking down his skin. The coppery stench of his blood also punched into my nose, making those familiar screams wail in my mind again.

Back in Glitnir, I could go days, weeks, sometimes even months without hearing those screams, but ever since I'd come to Blauberg, they had been bubbling up in my mind like hungry krakens rising to the surface of the sea, eager to wrap their tentacles around my internal ship and drag it—and me—down under the choppy waves.

The sight and stench of Leonidas's blood made it more difficult than usual, but I managed to shove those krakens back down into the murky deep of my mind.

First, I used a soft cloth and some warm water to thoroughly clean the wound. Then I opened a bottle of witch hazel and poured it into the gash to help lower the risk of infection. While I waited for the witch hazel to dry, I grabbed a jar filled with cucumber-ginger ointment made by Helene Blume, a family friend and powerful plant magier.

Helene was best known for the luxe beauty creams, lotions, and perfumes she sold to wealthy nobles, but she also crafted healing salves, balms, and ointments. Before I had left Glitnir, Helene had given me her latest experimental formula. I just hoped it worked as well as she claimed.

I opened the jar and dipped my fingers into the sticky ointment. A bright tang of ginger flooded my nose, along with softer, more soothing notes of cool cucumber. Just sniffing it made me feel better, and the strong scent also cleansed the coppery stench of blood from the air.

I slathered the ointment all over Leonidas's wounds. My rubbing activated Helene's magic, and my fingers started tingling as the hidden power sparked to life. The thick coating seeped into Leonidas's skin, and the ointment quickly changed colors, going from a pale, almost translucent green to a darker, more vibrant forest-green. The bruises faded away, and the jagged edges of his wound slowly closed, as though the ointment were full of tiny vines that were stitching his torn flesh back together the way it should be.

A minute later, the last of the ointment vanished into Leonidas's skin, and Helene's magic faded away. The wound had closed, although a large, raised, ugly pink stain remained on his chest. He wasn't completely healed, but he wouldn't bleed to death now.

Tap.

Tap-tap.

Tap-tap-tap.

Lyra pecked on the glass again, so I went over and opened the window. The strix stuck her head inside, and I had to jerk back to keep from getting stabbed by her razor-sharp beak. Behind her, Grimley let out a low, warning growl, but I shook my head, telling him to stand down. Lyra hadn't been trying to hurt me. She was just worried.

"Will Leo be okay?" she chirped.

"The ointment closed his wound. We'll just have to wait and see how he feels when he wakes up."

If he wakes up. I didn't voice my thought, though. I didn't want to further upset the strix, especially not when her beak was still dangerously close to my heart.

In the distance, lightning flashed, and thunder rolled, like an ominous trumpet heralding the purple-gray storm clouds drifting in this direction. I'd told Penelope that I would bring the wheelbarrow back to the mine, but I wouldn't be able to beat the storm there. My absence would probably make Conley suspicious, but I'd rather face his wrath than the unpredictable mountain weather.

My gaze flicked back over to the prince. Besides, I couldn't leave him alone. I knew better than to trust Leonidas Morricone, even when he was unconscious.

I looked at Lyra again. "You need to find a place to hide. The gargoyles will return to the city because of the storm, and they won't like you being here."

Lyra fluffed out her feathers. "No. I will stay with Leo."

Concern surged off her, but I shook my head. "You can't do anything to help him, and the cottage isn't big enough for you and Grimley to both be inside at once. It's barely large enough for Grimley, and he's always knocking something over with his tail."

Lyra trilled out a laugh, while Grimley glowered at me.

"Besides," I continued, "you're no good to Leonidas if the gargoyles kill you."

Lyra stabbed one of her wings at Grimley. "You stopped him. You could stop the others."

She was wrong. The other gargoyles might roost on the city rooftops, but they were still wild creatures with minds and wills of their own. Some of my ancestors, like Queen Armina Ripley, had been able to communicate with legions of gargoyles, but I wasn't that strong or skilled in my magic. Oh, I could mentally talk to two or three gargoyles at once, but I certainly couldn't command a whole city of them, much less order them *not* to attack a strix in their midst.

"Grimley is my friend," I replied. "That's why he stopped for me, but I'm not friends with all the gargoyles. Leonidas will be safe here. I'll put some more ointment on his wound, and maybe he'll wake up by morning. But you need to find a place to hunker down before the storm arrives. Grimley will help you find a spot."

"No," he growled. "I will stay here with you."

I shook my head again. "You need to stay with Lyra and make sure the other gargoyles don't attack her. They might not listen to me, but they will definitely listen to you."

Grimley might not be the biggest gargoyle, but he was certainly one of the fiercest. If anyone could keep Lyra safe, then it was him.

Please. I sent the thought to him. *Wouldn't you want some creature to do the same for you if you were in a strange land and I was hurt?*

Grimley gave me another sour look, but he jerked his head at Lyra. "Come."

The strix bristled at his commanding tone.

Grimley snorted. "Fine. Be stupid and stubborn. But don't blame me if the other gargoyles pluck off all your pretty purple feathers and eat you."

Lyra's eyes narrowed. "No one is eating *me*, least of all *you*."

Grimley snorted again. "Why would I want to eat you? You're nothing but fluff and bones. Hardly tasty at all."

"The two of you squabbling doesn't do anyone any good," I said. "Now go. If Leonidas takes a turn for the worse, then I'll summon Grimley."

Lyra glanced back and forth between me and the gargoyle, and her amethyst eyes brightened with understanding. "Ah, she's your human. That's why you're so protective of her."

"Of course she's my human." Grimley's chin lifted with pride. "And I will defend her to my death."

"Just as I would my Leo," Lyra chirped back.

The two creatures glared at each other again. Grimley's tail lashed from side to side, while Lyra raked her talons across the ground. Several long, tense seconds slid by.

Grimley's tail dropped, and he jerked his head. "Come. I know of a nearby cave where you will be safe and dry." He paused. "There are lots of rabbits there too, if you are hungry."

Lyra's feathers ruffled again, but she seemed more intrigued than offended. "Oh, I love Andvarian rabbits! They're so much more tender than the scrawny jackalopes we have in Morta . . ."

The strix kept extolling the virtues of plump, succulent Andvarian wildlife as she hopped into the woods with Grimley. Perhaps they wouldn't kill each other after all.

I shut the window, then glanced over at Leonidas. Some color had returned to his face, and his breathing seemed much easier than before. Relief fluttered through my stomach, but I swatted it away. Any sympathy I felt for him was the same as I would feel for anyone who had been betrayed, attacked, and injured. Nothing more, nothing less.

Besides, he was of no use to me dead.

My mind started whirring with possibilities. Perhaps Leonidas could tell me whom Captain Wexel was working for and why that person wanted so much tearstone. Perhaps he could even tell me where Wexel had taken the tearstone. Oh, yes. Leonidas Morricone could be a potential fount of information, and I was going to wring every last drop out of him. As for what I would do with him after that . . . Well, I would cross that mountain when I came to it.

As I stood there, plotting over the prince, a strange thought filled my mind—Xenia would be so proud of me for setting aside my emotions and history with Leonidas and doing what needed to be done. So would Everleigh. They had both taught me well.

Now it was time to use their lessons to get to the bottom of things—and thwart whatever plot was brewing against my kingdom.

CHAPTER SIX

Leonidas might not have been bleeding anymore, but he was still a long way from being fully healed, much less alert enough to be questioned, so I rubbed more ointment onto his wound and found some white cloth to use as a bandage.

I draped one end of the cloth over his chest, then grabbed his shoulder and turned him onto his side, so that I could wrap the cloth around his back. I rolled the prince a little more to the side, exposing even more of his back, and revealing . . .

Scars—so many scars.

Long, thin white lines slashed across Leonidas's back, starting at the tops of his shoulders and marching down his spine before disappearing below the waistband of his leggings. Small round scars puckered up here and there, along with larger, jagged marks that resembled uneven lines of thick white thread that had been stitched into his skin.

Sick shock punched into my stomach, pummeling the air from my lungs. I had endured my fair share of painful injuries, and I had inflicted horrible, fatal wounds on others in return, but I had never seen anything like *this*.

Leonidas Morricone had been tortured.

No, not merely tortured. He had been *brutalized*—often and repeatedly, over the course of several months, if not years.

Shock kept crashing over me in nauseating waves, but I drew in a shaky breath, leaned down, and took a closer look at his scars. The long lines had probably been made with some sort of whip, while the round spots seemed more like burn marks, caused by a hot fireplace poker or something similar. As for the zigzag, threadlike scars . . . well, I didn't even want to *imagine* what had made those.

I shuddered, but I forced myself to check for recent injuries, anything that Helene's ointment might be able to heal. But he didn't have any new wounds, just layers and layers of scars. Given how old and faded they were, the wounds must have been inflicted quite some time ago, probably when Leonidas was a boy.

Horror and revulsion twisted and twisted my stomach, as though it were a wet dishrag that was being wrung out, even as sorrow and sympathy flared in my heart, like warm, bright fluorestones lighting up a cold, dark room.

"Who did this to you?" I whispered.

Leonidas didn't respond, but his muscles clenched under my fingertips, almost as if his unconscious mind could hear my shocked tone and didn't like my staring at all the pain and trauma he had suffered. I shuddered again, then wrapped the bandage around his back and tied the two ends together—

A knock sounded on the front door.

I shot to my feet, whirled around, and reached out with my magic, wondering if Conley and the other miners were lurking outside. Or worse, Captain Wexel and the Mortan guards. Instead, a calm, familiar presence filled my mind, so I went over and flung open the door.

Topacia stepped inside, then frowned. "Gemma? Are you okay?"

"I'm fine."

Her hazel gaze flicked over me, but I smiled as though nothing was wrong and I didn't have a half-dead prince laid out on the floor.

"Did you find out anything?" I asked.

Her lips pressed into a thin, worried line. "Yes, and none of it's good. Several Mortan guards flew into town on strixes and rented rooms last night, along with their captain, someone named Wexel."

"I saw Wexel and his men earlier."

I told Topacia about Conley's meeting with Wexel. The longer I talked, the darker Topacia's face became. Soon, she looked as livid as the storm clouds still looming in the distance.

"That bloody *traitor!*" she hissed. "Selling tearstone to the Mortans. We should go over to the mine, drag Conley outside, and gut him in the plaza for everyone to see."

Her hand curled around the sword on her belt. Topacia was loyal to the core, and she was always happy to cut down any threat against me, my family, or Andvari.

"I wasn't the only unexpected guest at Conley and Wexel's meeting." I stepped into the living room and gestured at Leonidas, who was still unconscious. "Meet Leonidas Morricone."

Topacia stopped short. "As in *Prince* Leonidas Morricone?"

"One and the same."

Her fingers curled even tighter around her sword, as if she expected him to leap up and attack us. "Why is he stretched out on the floor like a throw rug?"

I told her about Wexel stabbing Leonidas, and then Conley ordering Penelope and me to dispose of him.

"But why would you ever help a Mortan?" Topacia asked. "Especially a Morricone? He'll probably try to kill you the second he wakes up."

"*Or* he might be persuaded to tell me everything he knows

about the tearstone. Leonidas was snooping around for some reason. I want to know what he was doing in Blauberg, and healing him seemed like the best way to convince him to cooperate."

Topacia shook her head. "You've been reading too many storybooks about Armina Ripley and Everleigh Blair. This sounds like something they would do—cold and calculated."

"And *smart*," I replied. "Armina founded our kingdom, and no one has protected their people more fiercely than Aunt Evie has against the Morricones, the DiLucris, and all our other common enemies. Dozens of Andvarians are already dead. I don't want that number to climb any higher. So if there's even the smallest chance I can get some information that will unravel this latest Mortan scheme, then I need to take it."

"And what if you can't get any information out of him?" she countered.

"I could call in the royal guards to imprison him, but he wasn't the one buying tearstone, so he hasn't really done anything wrong. Nothing that would justify holding him and further increasing tensions with Queen Maeven." I shrugged. "So I suppose that I'll cut him loose and let him fly his strix back to Morta."

"He came here on a *strix*?" Topacia clutched her sword again. "Where is it?"

"Her name is Lyra. She's in the woods."

"You brought a Morricone *and* a strix here?" Topacia shook her head again. "I don't know whether to admire your audacity or throttle you for putting yourself in so much danger."

I grinned. "Audacity should *always* be admired."

She huffed and crossed her arms over her chest.

"Of course I know how dangerous it is, but it's worth the risk. Besides, Grimley is watching Lyra. The strix won't be a problem."

"Unless the prince dies," Topacia pointed out. "Then she'll probably crash through the windows and peck your eyes out—before she stabs her beak into your heart."

My guard started pacing back and forth. "It's no wonder I have so much gray hair," she muttered. "Perhaps I should start drinking. That might help pass the time and dull the pain before King Heinrich and Prince Dominic have me executed for this."

I stepped in front of her, cutting off her quick, worried strides. "No one is going to execute you. Everything is fine. Lyra was friendly enough, and Grimley will watch over her. As for the prince, well, he'll be lucky if he can get out of bed in a week. He's no threat to me."

My heart twinged with doubt. He might not be a physical threat right now, but even unconscious, I found Leonidas Morricone far more appealing than was wise.

Topacia sighed, and some of the worry leaked out of her body. "What do you want me to do?"

"Go back into the city, and see if you can find out where Wexel is staying."

"And what are you going to do?"

I gestured at Leonidas again. "Stay here and see if he wakes up. Maybe he'll be willing to talk once I get some food and water in him."

Topacia nudged the prince with her boot, but he still didn't stir. She stabbed her finger at me. "Be careful. And if you need anything—*anything*—then you call for Grimley. And me too, if you can."

"I'll be fine. I can take care of myself. You and Rhea made sure of that."

"I suppose so," she grumbled. "And as much as I hate to admit it, you're right. If you can get him to talk, then perhaps we can thwart this latest Mortan plot before anyone else is killed."

I hugged her. "Thank you for trusting me."

"I always trust *you*, Gemma. It's everyone else I'm suspicious of."

Topacia hugged me back, then left the cottage. I stood on the threshold and watched while she disappeared into the woods.

Wind whistled around the cottage, and thunder rumbled through the air again. Those purple-gray clouds had picked up speed, and sheets of rain spattered down in the distance, sweeping this way. Worry filled me, but Topacia should be able to get back to the city before the storm hit.

I shut and locked the door, then flipped a switch on the wall, making the fluorestone lamps flare to life. Even though it was only midafternoon, the approaching storm had cast the cottage in a murky gray gloom.

Another, louder rumble of thunder roared, and the first wave of rain *tap-tap-tapped* against the roof. I peered out a window, watching the wind tangle the tree branches. Part of me longed to make some hot chocolate, curl up in a chair, and watch the storm. Maybe I would do that, after I hauled Leonidas off the floor and onto the bed. I moved away from the window and went to check on my wounded enemy—

I jerked to a stop beside the blue settee that divided the kitchen from the living room. The area in front of the fireplace was empty.

The prince had vanished.

I hurried over to the rug where Leonidas had been lying. My gaze darted around the living room, but he was nowhere in sight. Where had he gone?

A light, feathery, electric presence brushed up against

my mind, and I whirled around. Leonidas erupted out of the shadows from behind a nearby door and shoved me up against the wall next to the fireplace hard enough to rattle my teeth. I started to push him away, but he whipped up his right hand, brandishing a sword. I froze. He had grabbed my sword off the table where I'd left it this morning.

"Who are you?" he demanded. "Where am I?"

His amethyst eyes were wild, confused, and glazed with pain, and he was sweating again, probably from the effort of hauling himself upright. He tottered back and forth on his feet, and his arm bobbed, dipped, and weaved from the strain of holding up the sword, even though the tearstone blade was much lighter than a normal weapon.

"I'm the person who saved your life." I held my arms out to my sides, staying calm in the face of his confused, disheveled anger. "You're in my cottage on the outskirts of Blauberg."

His arm dipped, but he managed to brandish the sword at me again. "Who do you work for? Wexel?"

"I work for myself. Now, why don't you put that sword down before I take it away from you?"

Leonidas laughed, although it was a low, weak rasp. "I might be wounded, but I can still cut your throat faster than you can wrest this sword away—"

I reached out with my magic, grabbed the invisible strings wrapped around the sword, and yanked the blade out of his hand. The weapon flew across the room and *thunked* into an ebony dressing screen in the corner.

Leonidas turned in that direction, tracking the sword. I surged forward and shoved him away. He staggered back and almost tripped over the low table in front of the settee before he managed to right himself.

I held my position by the fireplace, my hands clenched into

fists, ready to toss him back with my magic if he attacked me again. Leonidas stood in front of me, his own hands clenched into fists. Sweat was now dripping down his face, neck, and chest, but his gaze was sharper and clearer than before.

"You're a mind magier," he accused.

"Just like you are. Now, are you going to make me hurt you, or are you going to sit down and be reasonable?"

I gestured at the settee. Leonidas eyed me with suspicion, but he shuffled around the table and plummeted down onto the cushions, as though the strength in his legs had suddenly deserted him.

He glanced around the cottage, staring out first one window, then another. "Where's Lyra?"

"In a cave in the woods."

Magic flared in his eyes, making them burn a bright purple, and that faint feathery presence tickled my mind again.

Lyra, I heard him whisper, although I didn't hear what reply she made. Still, their communication soothed the prince, and some of the tension eased out of his shoulders.

His eyes dimmed, and the feel of his magic vanished. He slumped back against the cushions, and his head dropped, as though he was about to pass out. Several seconds ticked by. Then Leonidas lifted his head and stared at me, his gaze locking with mine.

He sank back a little deeper into the cushions, even as his gaze traced down my body, going from my short, messy, dyed black hair to my grime-covered face to my equally grimy coveralls. He wasn't leering at me, not like Conley had this morning, but his intense scrutiny still made me uncomfortable.

"You're . . . a miner," he said, although his faint hesitation gave me the impression that he'd had some other word in mind. Perhaps *miner* was the nicest thing he could think to say.

His black eyebrows also drew together in confusion, as though something about me greatly puzzled him.

For a horrific, heart-stopping moment, I thought that he had recognized me, not only as Princess Gemma Ripley, but also as that frightened, frantic girl he had encountered in the Spire Mountains so long ago.

The one who had tried to kill him.

Equal parts worry and anticipation gnawed at my heart. Countless times, I had imagined what I would say—what I would *do*—if I ever came face-to-face with Leonidas Morricone again. But now that the moment was here, all my plans, schemes, and dreams of revenge floated away, leaving me adrift in my own churning sea of emotion.

Several more seconds ticked by, each one more painfully silent than the last. I reached out with my magic, trying to skim his thoughts, but Leonidas immediately put up a wall between his mind and mine, as hard, fast, and abrupt as a door slamming in my face. Then he reached out with his own magic, trying to hear my thoughts, but I quickly erected my own defenses, as though I were using a gladiator shield to block his power.

He glowered at me, and I glared right back at him. It wasn't surprising that we had both tried—and failed—to hear the other's silent musings. Mind magiers and their respective powers had a tendency to cancel each other out, like magnets of the same strength and size constantly attracting and repelling one another in equal measure.

Since I couldn't read his thoughts, I watched him closely, but his expression didn't change, and no sharp, obvious emotion surged off him. Leonidas didn't seem to recognize me. I wasn't quite sure why I was so disappointed by that, but I shoved that sensation away, along with all the other messy, conflicting feelings he inspired.

"You're a miner," he repeated.

"Well, aren't you observant? And you're a Mortan. Isn't that right, Prince Leonidas?"

He didn't bat an eye at my using his name and title, although he kept staring at me, still wary and suspicious. "You were in the woods with the other miners. You were there when Wexel tried to kill me." Understanding filled his face. "*You* used your magic to save me, to force Wexel's sword away from my heart."

"Yes."

"Why?"

That was the question of the hour, the day, the century—and one I couldn't quite answer, not even for myself. So I shrugged. "It didn't seem fair. All those guards, and you wrapped up in chains like a yuletide present someone had forgotten to open."

Leonidas's hand crept up to his throat, as if he could still feel the coldiron collar biting into his skin. "So you decided to save me out of the sheer goodness of your heart?"

A razor-thin smile curved my lips. "I'm not that good."

He snorted, although the sound was tinged with more amusement than derision. Leonidas fell silent, as did I, although we kept studying each other.

"What should I . . . call you?" he asked.

Once again, that faint hesitation marred his tone, filling me with unease, but I saw no reason not to answer.

"You can call me Armina." Whenever I needed an alias, I always used my middle name, since it was familiar enough for me to answer to when called upon.

Something flickered across his face. Strangely enough, it looked like disappointment, but the emotion vanished, and he arched an eyebrow. "Not going to tell me your real name?"

"I have lots of names."

That much was true. Princess Gemma Armina Merilde Ripley was a whole mouthful of grand, fanciful names, and at least two more than any person needed.

"Fine, *Armina*." Leonidas emphasized my obviously fake name. "What do you want for saving me? A reward?"

"Why would you think that?"

"Because people *always* want something from princes." His face hardened. "So what's your price?"

He was right. People did *always* want something from royals. More pesky pinpricks of sympathy and familiarity stabbed into my heart.

"Well, some gold crowns would certainly be nice."

His eyes narrowed. "But?"

"But I want to know about the tearstone—where it's going, who bought it, and especially what they're planning to do with it."

Cold calculation filled his face. No doubt the same icy expression frosted my own features, as each of us tried to get more than we were forced to give.

"Why do you care so much about a couple of wheelbarrows full of tearstone?" he asked. "Unless you aren't the simple miner you appear to be."

It was far more than just a couple of wheelbarrows of tearstone. By my calculations, several thousand pounds had gone missing all together over the past few months, which was more than enough to make all sorts of deadly things.

I might need to keep my real identity hidden from Leonidas at all costs, but I saw no reason to lie about what I was doing in Blauberg. Besides, Xenia always said that the best lies were mostly truth.

"I'm a spy."

His eyebrows shot up in surprise. "For whom?"

"People who *do* care about those wheelbarrows full of tearstone. Given how eager Wexel was to kill you, I thought you might be able to help me with that."

"Ah," he drawled. "So you're after information."

"As a spy? Always." As a princess too, although I could never tell him that.

A bitter laugh tumbled out of his lips. "Sorry to disappoint, but I don't have any information."

"What do you mean?"

Leonidas shook his head. "I don't know anything about the tearstone. I heard some . . . troubling rumors, so I came to Blauberg to investigate. But all I got for my troubles was a sword in the chest." He glanced down at the bandage that covered the wound.

A miserable truth echoed in his words. So he had been spying on his own people, and he'd almost died as a result. More sympathy surged through me, although a wave of frustration quickly drowned it out. I'd hauled him over to the cottage, faced off against Lyra, and healed him, and now I was getting a fat lot of nothing in return for *my* troubles.

A humorless smile curved Leonidas's lips. "I bet you wish that you had let me bleed out in the clearing. Or dumped my body down a ravine and let the gargoyles fight over my bones."

"Well, I was hoping for something a bit more useful than *I don't know anything*, but I don't regret saving you."

The words popped out before I could stop them, and they had the same miserable ring of truth as Leonidas's confession. My cheeks burned with embarrassment. Once upon a time, I'd tried to kill Leonidas Morricone, and now here I was, doing my best to reassure him. What was bloody *wrong* with me?

Cold calculation filled Leonidas's face again, as if he was choosing his next words very carefully. "I would think that you would dearly regret saving me."

Once again, something about his words nagged at me, but he continued before I could figure out what it was. "After all, I'm a Morricone."

He stared at me, wary again, wanting an explanation. I couldn't tell him what I didn't understand myself, so I opted for a slightly different version of the truth.

"I saw you in the clearing this morning. When you first landed. When that little girl came skipping out of the woods."

"So?"

"So she could have run off, screaming and telling everyone about you. Killing her would have been the smartest, safest thing to do. But yet, you didn't. Instead, you gave her a flower and told her to move along. That was quite an unexpected kindness."

"She was a *kid*," he snapped. "I would *never* hurt a child, no matter how much danger she might have put me in."

If he had been anyone else, I might have believed him, especially given his earlier actions today, but our childhood encounters made me doubt his sincerity. Although, to be fair, I had tried to murder him back then, so I supposed I couldn't throw stones.

Still, Leonidas's familiar features, especially his dark amethyst eyes, made me think of another place, another time, another Morricone.

I'm going to enjoy this.

Those words whispered through my mind, as soft and smug as a cat's purr. That was what Maeven had been thinking as she'd watched everyone gather on the Seven Spire lawn before the massacre. She had repeated the phrase to herself over and over again, almost like a chant.

I should have realized then that something was wrong, but hers was the first thought I had ever heard in my own mind, and I was so shocked by it that I had run away. Instead of telling Uncle Frederich what I'd sensed, I'd gone to get a piece of cranberry-apple pie.

So many people had died because of my cowardice.

"I would never harm a child," Leonidas repeated, breaking into my dark thoughts.

"Your mother had no such compunctions during the Seven Spire massacre." Once again, the words slipped out before I could stop them.

My harsh truth crackled through the air, but it vanished just as quickly, and an ugly silence sprang up between us. Leonidas's face remained blank, although a muscle ticced in his jaw, and his whole body tensed.

"Despite what you and everyone else might think, I am *not* my mother," he replied in a cold, clipped tone. "I don't agree with many of the things she has done. Especially not the Seven Spire massacre."

His regret stabbed into my mind, sharper than a gladiator's sword, while his anger cracked against my body like a red-hot whip peeling the flesh from my bones. He didn't like being compared to Maeven. I could understand that, although the knowledge didn't drown out the phantom screams echoing in my ears.

I waited until the worst of the screams had faded away before I spoke again. "Point taken. Think of it this way. You spared that girl's life, so I decided to spare yours in return."

"How benevolent of you."

I ignored his snide tone. "Will anyone besides Lyra come looking for you?"

"Planning to kill me now that you realize I'm of no use?" he asked, his tone snider than before.

"Not unless you give me a reason to. Unlike your charming mother, I don't go around murdering people for sport."

"How very reassuring," he drawled. "Although, for the record, my mother never does anything for mere *sport*."

"I just want to know if Wexel might descend on the cottage with more guards."

Leonidas shook his head. "No. Wexel's too arrogant to realize that he didn't kill me. He won't send anyone to check and make sure that I'm dead. What about you? Where are your . . . associates?"

Yet again, I got the impression that he meant an entirely different word, although I couldn't imagine what it might be. "I have a friend in the city, trying to track down Wexel."

"I doubt your friend will have much luck," Leonidas replied. "From the rumors I've heard, as soon as Wexel has the tearstone, he and his men fly their strixes back to Morta."

More frustration surged through me. Maybe Topacia could at least find out where the Mortans had been staying. Maybe if Wexel picked up another load of tearstone, he would return to the same place, and the Andvarian guards could capture him then.

"Who does Wexel work for?" I asked. "Queen Maeven?"

"Don't worry about Wexel. I plan on killing him just as soon as I get the chance." Deadly intent rippled through the prince's voice.

"You didn't answer my question."

"What does it matter who Wexel works for? You've obviously made up your mind that all Morricones, all Mortans, are evil. That we are all cruel, heartless monsters and nothing more." He sighed. "I can't blame you for your distrust."

"But?"

Leonidas shrugged. "But if I tell you that Wexel works for my mother, then I'll just be confirming your worst suspicions about her. If I claim that he works for someone else, then you probably won't believe me. So what's the point of saying anything at all?"

His words stung, because they were all too true. I *did* see the Morricones, especially Maeven, as monsters, and it was far easier to view Leonidas that way too. Otherwise, I would have to admit that he was a person with flaws, foibles, and feelings, and a man that I found far too interesting for my own good.

I thought about demanding some answers, but I doubted

there was anything I could threaten him with that would be worse than what he'd already endured, given the scars on his back.

"So what now?" Leonidas asked, a tired note creeping into his voice.

By this point, he was slumped back against the settee cushions, and his body sagged with pain and exhaustion. Like it or not, he still needed my help, and I wasn't going to toss him out on his ass just because he hadn't revealed the information I'd wanted. That would have been petty and cruel, even for a spy like me.

"Now I check your wound."

And we try not to kill each other in the meantime. I didn't voice my thought, but Leonidas's eyes narrowed again, as though he was thinking something similar.

I held back a sigh. It was going to be a long, long night.

chapter seven

I offered to help Leonidas into the bathroom, but he growled that he was fine on his own. The prince heaved himself up and off the settee and took a step forward. One of his knees came dangerously close to buckling, but he managed to catch himself. Still, by the time he slowly righted his body, he was sweating again, and his face was gray with pain.

"Your stubbornness is going to be the death of you someday," I drawled.

Leonidas glowered at me, but he staggered into the bathroom and shut the door. An audible *click* sounded, but him throwing the lock didn't concern me. There was only a small window in the bathroom, but I doubted he had the strength to break the glass, much less climb out of the frame.

Squeak. A faucet turned, and water started running in the sink. Since he seemed to be behaving, I moved around the cottage, disposing of his ruined tunic, the bloody bowl of water, and the other used supplies. I also rolled the wheelbarrow back outside.

Fifteen minutes later, the bathroom door opened, and

Leonidas stepped back out into the living room, his stride a little steadier than before. He was still wearing his black leggings, along with his boots, and he had slung a damp towel around his neck. Water glistened like silver rain in his onyx-black hair, while a few drops clung to his bare muscled chest. Mesmerized, I watched one rivulet glide down the center of his breastbone, going lower . . . and lower . . . and lower . . .

"See something that interests you?" Leonidas asked, a mocking note in his voice.

My gaze snapped up to his. An unwanted blush scalded my cheeks, and I had to clear the dryness out of my throat. "Nothing particularly impressive."

Amusement danced in his eyes, and his lips curved up into a smug smirk, melting some of his icy reserve. Leonidas Morricone knew *exactly* how attractive he was. No doubt everyone from palace servants to merchants' bored wives to noble ladies searching for a suitably rich husband had thrown themselves at him.

Leonidas stepped closer, looming over me, and his gaze raked down my body. I held my ground and let him look his fill.

"See something that interests you?" I tossed his own words back at him.

"Very much so."

His admission surprised me, as did the heat suddenly glimmering in his eyes, and his deep voice curled around me like an invisible string of energy, even though neither one of us was using our magic.

If he had been anyone else, I might have moved forward, tangled my fingers in his hair, pressed my lips to his, and seen what happened next. I took all the proper herbs and precautions, and I'd had a few discreet affairs while undercover on missions. But I'd never found someone so strangely, hypnotically appealing as Leonidas.

Still, despite our seemingly mutual attraction, I couldn't trust him not to betray me the second he climbed out of my bed—if not sooner. Even if he hadn't been my childhood enemy, Leonidas was still a Mortan. There was charmingly star-crossed, and then there was bloody *impossible*, and any sort of Ripley-Morricone dalliance fell squarely into that latter category.

"Well, I suppose we'll both just have to be disappointed," I drawled.

"Pity," he murmured, although he kept staring at me as though I were a sweet cake he wanted to gobble up.

I dropped my gaze to his shoulder, which was the only part of him I should be examining. He'd removed the bandage, and the ugly, angry pink stain of the stab wound had faded considerably. I made a mental note to thank Helene the next time I saw her. The cucumber-ginger healing ointment had worked even better than promised, and it had saved the prince's life.

I grabbed the jar of ointment from a nearby table and approached Leonidas. "Let me put some more of this on your wound."

He plucked the jar from my hand. "I can do it."

Then he did a most curious thing. Instead of turning around and heading into the bathroom face-first like a normal person, he eased backward, keeping his gaze on me.

I rolled my eyes. "Don't be an idiot. I went to far too much trouble to save you just to kill you now."

Instead of answering my taunt with one of his own, he grimaced and quickened his pace, still backing into the bathroom. What was he doing?

Before he could close the door, I moved forward, crossed my arms over my chest, and leaned my shoulder against the doorjamb. Leonidas shot me a sour look, but he didn't demand that I leave. Instead, still facing me, he grabbed the towel from around his neck and draped it on the sink. Then he reached for his shoulder. He stopped halfway, a loud hiss of pain escaping through his clenched teeth.

I arched an eyebrow. He tried again, with the same hiss of pain. My eyebrow rose a little higher.

He started to try a third time, but he must have thought better of it because he stopped. "Maybe you should do it after all," he grumbled.

I stepped into the bathroom, dipped my fingers into the ointment, and reached for him. Leonidas jerked back, as skittish as a long-tailed gargoyle in a room full of rocking chairs. My eyebrow crept up even higher, and he finally stilled.

The water had dried on his chest, although a few drops still glimmered in his hair, and I had the oddest urge to run my fingers through his longish, wavy locks and flick the drops away. He smelled faintly of honeysuckle, the scent completely masculine and strangely intoxicating. The only thing that ruined his good looks was the mass of scars on his back, which I could clearly see in the mirror. The scars made Leonidas seem like a coin with two distinct sides—handsome, arrogant prince and wary, weary survivor. I found both halves far more appealing than I should have.

Leonidas tracked my gaze and stiffened. A sharp dagger of pain sliced through my mind, while anger, shame, and embarrassment throbbed like red-hot nails that had been driven into my chest. He might not care if I ogled his bare chest, but he didn't like me studying his scars. That must have been why he'd so awkwardly backed into the bathroom.

Once again, that treacherous sympathy pricked my heart, and I suddenly longed to tell him that the marks were nothing to be ashamed of and that I had my own deep, painful scars, only mine were on the inside, where no one could see them. But I didn't want to answer questions about my emotional scars any more than he wanted to talk about his physical ones, so I kept quiet as I eased closer to him, as slowly and carefully as I would approach a wounded animal.

Leonidas sighed, then gingerly lifted his left arm out to the side.

"This might sting," I murmured.

"Don't worry," he muttered. "I've had worse."

Yes, he had, given those horrific scars, although I didn't voice the obvious thought. Instead, I smeared the ointment onto his wound. The cucumber-ginger scent tickled my nose, and that warm tingling spread through my fingertips again.

It's just the ointment, I told myself in a stern voice. Just the ointment, and nothing to do with the man—enemy—before me.

Leonidas's smooth, hard muscles involuntarily bunched and flexed at my touch, although the prince himself remained perfectly still, as though he were a strix about to swoop down from a high perch and attack its prey. His body might be locked in place, but his presence, his magic, brushed up against my own, like a warm, feathery cloak wrapping around me from head to toe. The light sensation was surprisingly heady, made even more so by the obvious strength and power lurking underneath his cold, quiet veneer.

Oh, yes, Leonidas Morricone was most definitely a strix at heart—a beautiful creature that was capable of great violence at any moment.

Despite everything that had happened between us, both today and years ago, I found the Morricone prince highly intriguing in a way that the rich nobles, merchants, and all my other potential suitors at Glitnir were not. Of course we were already bound together by our respective families' long-standing animosity. And our royal backgrounds, as well as our deep connections to Lyra and Grimley, were quite similar. But perhaps the thing I found most appealing about Leonidas Morricone was that he seemed to feel the same sort of hidden pain and simmering rage that relentlessly stormed in my own heart.

I used the last of the ointment and wrapped another bandage

around his torso, careful not to touch the scars on his back. The second I had tied off the bandage, Leonidas shifted away, putting some distance between us. It must be difficult to let anyone get close, even to heal you, when you had suffered so much agony at someone else's hands.

More sympathy flared in my heart, burning as brightly as a fluorestone, but I squashed the feeling. Leonidas might be wounded and vulnerable, but he was still a Morricone, still Maeven's son, which made him extremely dangerous. I needed to remember how he had hurt me before, not how appealing I found him now.

"Thank you," he rasped.

"You're welcome."

Our gazes met and held. Tension gathered around us, but it wasn't the uneasy feeling of mistrust. No, this tension was deeper, stronger, and hot enough to warm my cheeks, along with other, more intimate parts of my body.

Leonidas's gaze traced over my face, and a frown creased his lips. My gaze darted to my own reflection in the mirror. Tangled hair, grimy skin, dirty coveralls. Not exactly an attractive image, despite his earlier assertion.

"I should get cleaned up. There are clothes in the armoire, and food in the kitchen, if you're hungry."

He skirted past me, and I pressed myself up against the wall so that he wouldn't have to touch me. He hesitated at the door, as though he was thinking about backing away from me again. But he must have realized that it was too late to hide his scars, because he stepped out of the bathroom and shuffled over to the armoire, giving me a clear look at the marks.

I shut and locked the door behind him, my hands shaking as I leaned up against the sink. I clutched the cold porcelain until my emotions were under control again.

I also listened, wondering if Leonidas might use this opportunity to slip out of the cottage, but I only heard the soft *thud* of the armoire door closing, along with the *creak-creak* of the kitchen cabinets opening. He seemed content to stay here—for now.

I shook off my whirling thoughts, then twisted the knob to run a bath in the claw-foot tub. If only I could wash my troubles away as easily as water swirled down a drain.

But no one could do that, not even a princess like me.

I took a quick hot bath and donned a fresh gray tunic, along with some black leggings that were hanging on a hook on the bathroom door. I stuffed my feet back into my dirty boots and slid my tearstone dagger into the scabbard on my black leather belt. Then I opened the door and stepped out into the living room.

Leonidas had also donned a gray tunic. He was sitting at the kitchen table with several dishes arranged in front of him, although he hadn't eaten a single bite yet. Even more surprising was the empty plate he'd set out across from his own.

"I thought you might be hungry too," he said.

His thoughtfulness surprised me, and I took the chair across from him. "Thank you."

He nodded, then started piling meats, cheeses, and dried fruit onto his plate. I made a cold gruyère and apricot jam sandwich, just like the one I'd had for lunch. Leonidas watched me wolf it down, an amused smile cracking through his icy expression.

"What's so funny?" I mumbled.

"I've never seen anyone eat a cheese-and-jam sandwich before."

"Well, it's delicious. My very own secret, delectable recipe. I could tell you how to make it, but then I'd have to kill you."

He laughed at the old, familiar joke, and the soft, low sound sent an unwanted shiver skittering down my spine. Still, his laughter broke the tension, and we ate the rest of our meal in quiet, companionable silence. When we finished, I dumped the dirty dishes in the sink, while he returned the leftover food to the cabinets and the metal chiller in the corner.

It had stopped storming, although the rain continued, drumming on the roof. The sun had set only a few minutes ago, but the landscape was already dark, so I closed all the curtains.

I reached out with my magic, and Grimley's warm, drowsy presence filled my mind. The gargoyle must still be in that cave with Lyra. I reached out again, this time searching for Topacia. I only got a flicker of feeling off her, but she too seemed warm and safe.

Even though it was barely after six o'clock, I was exhausted. Dark circles ringed Leonidas's eyes, and he wobbled on his feet again.

"Go to bed." I gestured toward the open door that led to the bedroom in the back of the cottage. "I'll build a fire and sleep out here on the settee."

He stiffened, as though I had slapped him across the face and offended his honor. "You take the bed. I can sleep out here."

"You're the one who got hurt, so *you* take the bed. I've slept on far worse things than a lumpy settee."

Something flickered across his face, but it vanished in an instant. Leonidas opened his mouth as if to keep arguing, but I stabbed a finger at him.

"Don't be an idiot. You need rest far more than I do. Especially since you look like you're about to pass out again."

He grumbled something under his breath, but this was a battle he would never win. Miner, princess, or spy, Gemma Ripley was nothing if not a good hostess, even to her mortal enemy.

Leonidas shuffled toward the bedroom. He stopped at the

door and looked at me. "Thank you. For saving me. I would be dead right now if it wasn't for you." His lips twisted a little, as if the sentiment left a sour taste in his mouth.

I shrugged off his thanks. "Just promise me one thing."

"What?"

"That you'll keep giving Andvarian girls flowers instead of trying to kill them." The words came out harsher and crueler than I intended, perhaps because of our shared past.

Leonidas flinched, but he tilted his head. "As my lady wishes."

He lifted his right arm out to his side and crossed his left one over his waist, dipping into a traditional Mortan bow, although the motion was stiff and shallow. The prince straightened. He gazed at me a moment longer, then vanished into the bedroom and shut the door.

I waited a few seconds, but the lock didn't *click* home. Perhaps he finally believed that I wasn't going to murder him. Not tonight, anyway. Soft footsteps sounded, then the faint *creak* of bedsprings whispered through the walls.

I yanked my sword out of the dressing screen and grabbed my shield. I set the weapons within easy reach on the table beside the settee, then built a fire.

The heat warmed my face, but the continued *crack-crack-cracks* of the wood reverberated through my mind, just as those phantom screams had been doing all day long. I didn't always have to be around other people in order for my magic to overwhelm me. Sometimes, a smell was enough to upset my power. A particular color. Or, in this case, a sound.

I grimaced, got to my feet, and spun away from the fireplace, trying to ignore the storm, the magic, rising up inside me.

Too late.

I took a step toward the settee, but from one moment to the

next, the living room dropped away, and I found myself standing in the middle of a forest . . .

Crack.

*A twig snapped under someone's foot, and I whirled
around. Three people were trudging through the woods.*

*The first was a short, sixty-something man. Wrinkles
grooved into his ebony skin, and a generous amount of silver
glinted in his short black hair, but his hazel eyes were warm
and kind. Alvis, the Seven Spire royal jeweler.*

*The second was a woman, also in her sixties, with
wavy coppery red hair, golden amber eyes, and bronze skin.
A snarling ogre face with the same red hair and amber eyes
that the woman herself had was visible on her neck. Lady
Xenia Rubin, a famed spymaster.*

*The third person was a twelve-year-old girl with long,
tangled dark brown hair and pale skin. Her dress was tattered and torn, and purple circles of exhaustion ringed her
blue eyes. Me. Gemma Ripley. Or Gems, as I'd thought of
myself back then.*

*The three of them approached me, but I didn't bother
hiding. They couldn't see me, since this wasn't really* happening. *At least, it wasn't happening* right now. *No, this
trek had taken place in the Spire Mountains about two weeks
after the Seven Spire massacre.*

*My mother, Merilde Ripley, had been a time magier who
had often seen the future. I had inherited a bit of her magic,
but more often than not, I got dragged back into the past, as
if I were a spectator watching previous events that had been
recorded by a memory stone. Yet another frustrating way in
which my power controlled me, rather than me controlling it.
Because if I could have managed my magic, I never would
have thought about the massacre or its aftermath ever again.*

*My mother and Alvis had both called this cursed abil-
ity ghosting. I could see and hear everything, even remember everything I had thought, felt, and experienced. I just
couldn't change the outcome—or ignore the pain that was
sure to pummel my heart yet again.*

*I grabbed my gargoyle pendant and squeezed it tight.
Sometimes, the sensation of the tearstone shards pricking
my palm was enough to snap me back to the present and
stave off the unwanted memory. I waited, but nothing happened, no matter how tightly I squeezed or how deeply the
shards sank into my skin. Damn it.*

*Eventually, my magic would settle back down, and I
would return to the real world, but for now, I sighed, released
my pendant, and fell in step beside the younger version of
myself, knowing that there was nothing I could do but see
this unfortunate incident through to the end.*

*While we walked, I studied Gems. The girl grimaced
with every step she took, and memories surged off her.
Glasses shattering. Tables flipping over. Chairs splintering to
pieces. Screams.*

*The phantom noises flitting through her mind matched
the ones that had been ringing in my ears all day long. She
was thinking about the Seven Spire massacre. Of course she
was. Neither one of us could ever escape it, no matter how
hard we tried.*

*After all, the massacre was when her, my, our mind
magier magic had first manifested itself.*

*More sounds and images filled my mind. The shock
and disbelief on Uncle Frederich's face. The strangled gasps
of Lord Hans and the other Andvarians. And perhaps worst
of all, Uncle Frederich's pain burning like a wildfire in my
chest, as though Vasilia had plunged her dagger into my
heart instead of his.*

I shuddered, not sure if the thoughts were Gems's or my own memories. At times like these, I thought that my magic was slowly driving me mad. Or perhaps I was already mad and just didn't realize it yet. Hysterical laughter bubbled up in my chest, although I swallowed it before it could escape.

Alvis stepped into a clearing and turned to Xenia. "What do you think? Can we stop for a few hours?"

"Yes, we can stop and rest," Xenia replied.

Alvis used some rocks to make a fire pit, while Xenia and Gems collected dead branches and pine cones. Eventually, the three of them sat down around a crackling fire.

"Here, Gems. Try this." Alvis handed the girl two toasted pieces of bread. "It's a sandwich with cheese and apricot jam. I'm afraid it's our only option as far as food goes."

Xenia's nostrils flared with disgust, but she too took a toasted sandwich from Alvis.

Gems blew on the sandwich to cool it down, then took a bite. The tasty combination of crunchy, toasted bread; warm, melted cheese; and sweet, tangy jam filled my own mouth, as though I had taken a bite of the sandwich too. A ghost of a smile tugged at my lips.

"This is really good!" Gems beamed at Alvis.

He grinned at her, gave Xenia a smug look, and ate his own sandwich. Xenia rolled her eyes, but she too wolfed down her sandwich, and her inner ogre smacked its lips together in silent appreciation.

After the three of them finished eating, Alvis and Xenia started talking in low voices. They didn't want Gems to hear what they were saying, but of course their thoughts crowded into her mind anyway.

Not much water left . . .

Not sure we lost that last group of guards . . .

We're still miles away from the Andvarian border . . .

Even worse than their thoughts was their worry, which stung her—my—heart over and over again, like dozens of bees.

"Gems?" Alvis asked. "Is something wrong?"

She stopped rubbing her chest. "Of course not."

His eyes narrowed with suspicion. I had been such a terrible liar back then.

Gems jumped to her feet. "I need to go . . . you know." She flapped her hand at the trees. "I'll be back soon."

Ten feet, twenty, fifty . . . I followed my younger self into the woods until Alvis's and Xenia's whispered thoughts faded away, along with their stinging worry. Gems stopped, leaned up against a tree, and closed her eyes.

Even though this was just a memory, I could still feel the uneven bark digging into my shoulders, and exhaustion, fear, and worry swept through my body just as vividly as they had back then.

"What is bloody wrong with me?" Gems whispered to herself. "Why can't I control these thoughts and feelings? Why can't I just block them out? Along with the massacre?"

Unfortunately, those were questions I still couldn't answer to this day—

Crack.

Gems jerked away from the tree, her eyes wide, *and my own heart leaped up into my throat, even though I knew what was coming next.*

Crack.

Crack-crack.

Crack-crack-crack.

The sounds came again, morphing into distinct footsteps, and flashes of movement appeared through the trees, along with bright silver glints. Gems squinted in that direction.

"I see footprints."

"This looks like a path."

"They must be right up ahead. Quiet, men. Quiet!"

Several turncoat guards came into view, all of them clutching swords.

Gems's chest heaved, and she struggled to suck down air. My own chest squeezed tight.

"Run, Gems," I whispered, even though this was just a memory. "Go warn your friends. Don't be a coward like you were during the massacre."

Even though she couldn't hear me, even though this had all happened long ago, Gems sucked down another breath, then started running back to camp to warn Alvis and Xenia . . .

Another piece of wood snapped in the fireplace, the *crack* loud enough to break the unwanted spell of my magic and jog me out of the past. In an instant, the forest vanished, and I was back in the cottage, back in the present where I belonged.

I staggered over and plopped down on the settee. Then I raised a shaking hand and wiped the cold sweat off my forehead. It took me a few minutes and several deep breaths to stop trembling, but I managed it. Eventually. My magic kept roiling inside me, though, ready to lash out and drag me back into the past again.

Desperate for something else to focus on, I stared at the closed bedroom door, straining to hear what Leonidas was doing, but no noises sounded. He must be asleep. A relieved breath tumbled out of my lips. Good. The last thing I needed was for him to witness one of my ghosting episodes—or worse, grab my sword and stab me in the back when I was lost in the past.

When I was sure my magic wasn't going to flare up again, I grabbed a blanket and a pillow from the armoire and made myself a cozy nest on the settee. Even though it had been a long day, and I was exhausted, I didn't think I would sleep. Too many things were rattling around in my mind. But eventually, the warmth of the fire lulled me to sleep . . .

Sometime later, a soft *click* intruded on the quiet. For a moment, I thought my magic had gone haywire and tossed me back into the past again. Then a second *click* sounded, and I realized that this sound was happening in the here and now.

I jerked upright on the settee, my hand dragging my dagger out from under my pillow. The fire had burned down to ash and embers, and the first twinges of the pale purple dawn were slipping in through the white lace curtains.

My gaze snagged on the bedroom door, which was standing wide open. Inside, the bed was empty, and the blankets had been neatly smoothed back into place.

Leonidas Morricone was gone.

Still clutching my dagger, I scrambled to my feet and looked down at the table in front of the settee, but my sword and shield were sitting where I'd left them last night. I didn't sense the prince in the cottage, but I still quietly crept around, peering into the adjoining rooms. They were all empty.

Where was he?

Finally, I reached the kitchen, and I realized what had made those telltale *clicks*—someone opening and then closing the front door. I hurried over to one of the windows and shoved the curtains aside.

I wasn't quite sure what I was expecting to see. Perhaps Captain Wexel and his men, getting ready to storm inside the cottage, but the yard was empty except for a lone figure.

Leonidas.

He was once again wearing his long black cloak over his riding coat and other clothes. He was moving stiffly, but he must be feeling better if he was leaving. Or perhaps he didn't trust me any more than I trusted him and wanted to escape as soon as possible.

A shiver swept over me. I had been so soundly asleep that I hadn't heard him get out of bed and creep through the cottage. He could have easily killed me. So why hadn't he?

Leonidas stopped, as if he could feel my gaze and hear my thoughts. Maybe he could with his own mind magier power. He slowly faced me.

His amethyst eyes locked with mine, and a jolt shot through my chest and zinged out through the rest of my body. In an instant, my fingertips were tingling, my toes were curling, and my heart was hammering. I recognized the sensation.

Anticipation—although of what, I couldn't say.

The seconds ticked by, softly counted out by the cuckoo clock on the wall, but neither one of us looked away. Then Leonidas bowed, still keeping his eyes on mine.

Thank you, his voice whispered in my mind.

Before I could send a thought back, Prince Leonidas Morricone straightened up, turned around, and vanished into the woods.

My mortal enemy was gone.

CHAPTER EIGHT

I stood at the window, clutching my dagger and scanning the area, but no one appeared. Leonidas had left, and Captain Wexel hadn't tracked him here.

Welcome developments, but disappointment still filled me. I told myself it was because I hadn't gotten any information out of Leonidas about the tearstone, and not because he had been going to leave without saying goodbye. Yes, the lack of progress in my spy mission was the reason for my sudden deflation, and not my curiosity about the Morricone prince.

A rueful snort escaped my lips. I hadn't been a very good liar as a child, and I wasn't particularly good at it as an adult either, at least when it came to deceiving myself.

Still, Leonidas was gone, and I had to be at work soon, so I donned a fresh set of coveralls, then made hot oatmeal topped with dried figs and toasted slivered almonds and dusted with cinnamon and chocolate flakes. I was eating my breakfast when a knock sounded on the door and a familiar presence filled my mind.

I waved my hand and unlocked the door. "It's open!"

Topacia came inside. Her hand curled around her sword, and her hazel gaze darted around the kitchen before scanning the living room beyond. "Where's your patient?"

"Gone. He snuck out early this morning."

She relaxed. "Good. He didn't give you any trouble?"

"Nope. He was actually rather . . . pleasant."

That was the most benign word I could think of to describe Leonidas. I certainly couldn't admit that he was intriguing. Infuriating. Intelligent. Cold. Powerful. Muscled. Handsome. My face heated at the unwanted thoughts, and I shoved another bite of oatmeal into my mouth.

"*Pleasant* for a Mortan means that they'll stab you face-to-face instead of burying their sword in your back," Topacia muttered.

There was no point arguing with her. Leonidas might have accused me of thinking that all Mortans were as evil as evil could be, especially the Morricones, but Topacia firmly believed it.

Given the myriad schemes Queen Maeven had hatched against my family over the years, I couldn't disagree with my friend, although Leonidas seemed to be the exception to the rule, despite how he had hurt me when we were children. Either way, he was gone, and I would probably never see him again. Regret pinched my heart, but I pushed the feeling aside. The sensation was probably just gas.

I fixed Topacia some oatmeal. While she ate, I reached out with my magic, scanning the woods again, but I still didn't sense anyone nearby. I stretched out a little farther with my power, but Lyra's faint, feathery presence had also vanished. Of course it had. Leonidas would never leave his beloved strix behind, and he certainly wasn't going to walk back to Morta.

Lyra's presence might be gone, but another one filled my mind, like a rock rolling steadily in this direction. A few seconds later, another knock sounded on the door, although this sound was more of a sharp *thwack*, like an arrow banging off the wood. I grinned, went over, and opened the door.

Grimley was sitting on the stoop, perched on his front paws like a cat, with his long tail lashing from side to side. I scratched the top of his head, right in between his curved horns.

"Thank you for knocking this time."

"Stupid doors," he grumbled. "They're only fun to crash through."

I laughed. Grimley had barreled through his fair share of doors, much to the consternation of the wood, glass, and metal-stone masters at Glitnir, who kept having to replace the ones the gargoyle demolished, along with windows, flagstones, and entire sections of the palace walls.

Grimley sauntered inside. I had stoked the fire before breakfast, and within seconds, he was stretched out on the rug, soaking up the heat from the flames.

I shut the door, then sat down across from Topacia at the kitchen table. "Did you find out anything about Wexel?"

"Not really," she replied. "I was holed up in a tavern waiting for the storm to pass. Someone told me where the Mortans were staying, but by the time I got to that inn, they had already left. I staked out the inn all night, but they never returned."

She ate a bite of oatmeal before continuing. "I nosed around this morning and even bribed a few chambermaids, but Wexel and his men were pretty tight-lipped about what they were doing here. As far as anyone at the inn knew, they were merchants conducting business, although they never mentioned what that business was. The chambermaids said this was the first time they had seen the Mortans. Wexel must use a different inn every time he comes to Blauberg. I'm sorry, Gemma, but it's a dead end."

Frustration filled me. "It's okay. Wexel doesn't strike me as the kind to be reckless. If nothing else, at least we know how careful he is and that he's able to keep his men in line."

Topacia nodded and returned to her food. I ate a few more bites of my own oatmeal, but I wasn't enjoying it anymore, so I pushed my bowl aside.

Despite everything that had happened, we were still no closer to learning *why* the Mortans suddenly wanted so much tearstone, and especially what they were planning to *do* with it. All Topacia and I had done the past few weeks was chase whispers that had led us nowhere.

More frustration coursed through me, turning the oatmeal in my stomach into hard lumps, as though I'd just eaten a bowl full of opals, like Grimley was so fond of doing.

Spy the storm brewing, and you won't get struck by lightning. Ignore the clouds, and you'll get burned to a crisp, Xenia's voice whispered through my mind.

The ogre morph and spymaster had said that to me more than once over the years, including when we had been fleeing from Bellona after the Seven Spire massacre. Well, I could clearly hear the rumblings, and I could definitely sense the danger, but I still couldn't quite see the shape, size, and scope of the storm rushing toward us.

But chasing whispers until they congealed into louder, more distinct murmurs and then hard, concrete evidence was a spy's job. I might not know what the Mortans were up to, but I had seen Conley's treason. Perhaps the foreman would cough up some answers when he was arrested and interrogated by the royal guards—and Princess Gemma.

Topacia waved her spoon at my coveralls. "Going back down into the mine today?"

"Yes. I should maintain my cover for as long as possible, and I want to find out exactly how many people are stealing from the mine. So far, it's Conley, his six men, and Penelope. I want to make sure we nab everyone at once. Otherwise, someone might start up Conley's scheme again after we leave."

While Topacia finished her food, my thoughts turned back to the tearstone. Two wheelbarrows of tearstone was enough to make at least a dozen swords, or twice that many daggers, but those were drops in the proverbial bucket given the thousands of pounds that had already been stolen from other places. Or perhaps the Mortans were planning to do something else with the ore—something worse.

Worry and uncertainty filled me, lumping with the frustration and the oatmeal in my stomach. Despite everything I'd learned, I still felt like my time had run out and that it was already too late to stop whatever horrible thing the Mortans were plotting.

I cleaned up the kitchen, petted Grimley again, and left the cottage. I also grabbed the wheelbarrow and rolled it back toward the city. Conley was sure to be suspicious about my not returning to the mine yesterday afternoon as ordered, but I would just have to endure whatever punishment he might dole out.

Topacia and I went to the same alley we had stopped in yesterday. Miners trudging to work, merchants hawking their wares, the gargoyle fountain bubbling in the plaza. Everything looked the same as before, but the longer I glanced around, the more uneasy I became.

I reached out with my magic, skimming people's thoughts, but no one was thinking anything suspicious, and I couldn't put my finger on what was bothering me. Perhaps it was simply my own guilt at having to work with Penelope today. Now that I knew she was part of Conley's scheme, I would have to tell the royal guards, and she would be arrested, along with the other miners involved. At least her motive hadn't been pure greed. Perhaps Grandfather Heinrich would pass down a lighter judgment once I explained how badly injured Penelope's daughter had been.

"Go back into the city, and see if you can find any more inns where Wexel and his men have stayed," I told Topacia. "Maybe someone will remember something useful about them. And be careful. Wexel might have left a guard behind to deal with anyone asking too many questions."

"I'll find out everything I can," Topacia promised. "Meet you back here at lunch to compare notes?"

I agreed, and we went our separate ways.

I pushed the wheelbarrow out of the alley and fell in step behind the miners. No one gave me a second glance, despite the steady *squeak-squeak-squeak* of the wheel.

I started to roll the container by the gargoyle fountain, but that uneasy feeling swept over me again. Some good luck certainly couldn't hurt, so I stopped, dug a penny out of my pocket, and tossed it into the gurgling water. I had two more pennies so I threw them into the fountain as well. If one penny brought good luck, then three should give me a plethora of grand fortune. Either way, the superstition eased some of my nagging worry.

I left the wheelbarrow with a group of them outside the mine, then hurried through the entrance into Basecamp. I didn't see Penelope in the cavern, so I got in line with the other miners.

Instead of Conley, a lower-ranking foreman was sitting at the checkpoint table. He glanced at me, marked something off on his list, and handed over my map and shaft assignment. He didn't say a word to me, but nervousness surged off him, as clear and loud as cymbals clanging together in my mind.

"Next!" he bellowed.

Several miners were in line behind me, and I had no choice but to move forward. I stowed away my lunch box, pulled on my gloves, and shut my locker. The other miners were doing the same, and nothing seemed amiss, but I couldn't quite shake my worry.

"Have you seen Penelope?" I asked one of the other miners.

He jerked his thumb over his shoulder. "Yeah. She already went down for the morning. Shaft 4, I think."

The miner walked on, but his words made even more worry trickle through me. Penelope had lagged behind every morning, either in Basecamp or here by the lockers, so that we could go down into the shaft together. Perhaps she didn't want to face me, given what had happened yesterday.

I dawdled by my locker, pretending to tighten my bootlaces, while the other miners streamed past me. Soon, I was the only one left, along with Reiko. The dragon morph had partially shifted and was sitting on a bench, using a file to add an extra sharp edge to her black talons. Her head was bowed, and she was focused on her filing, but the green dragon on her right hand swiveled around on her skin and stared up at me.

I nodded respectfully at the dragon, which rolled its black eyes and peered up at Reiko again. The morph kept right on sharpening her talons, still not looking at me.

I finished my pretend inspection of my bootlaces, then straightened up and reached out with my magic. *Grimley. Come to the mine, please.*

He answered me a few seconds later. *Is something wrong?*

I'm not sure. There's no sign of Penelope or Conley.

On my way. I'll find a spot on one of the rooftops and keep watch over the plaza.

I didn't know how he could help me, but knowing he was going to be nearby eased some of my worry. Reiko was still filing her talons, so I turned my back to her, grabbed the chain around my neck, and fished my gargoyle pendant out from underneath my clothes.

The silver pendant was warm from where it had been resting against my skin, although the sensation quickly vanished in the cool air. I rubbed my thumb over the pieces of black jet and the blue tearstone shards that made up Grimley's snarling face. The weight of the pendant in my palm and the pricks of the jewels against my skin steadied me. I rubbed Grimley's midnight-blue eyes, my own version of a good-luck charm, then tucked the pendant back underneath my clothes and left the locker area.

A couple of miners were waiting to take a cart down into the shaft. Footsteps scuffed behind me, and Reiko joined the group. She leaned a shoulder against the wall and crossed her arms over her chest.

An empty cart arrived, and we all climbed inside it. Reiko ended up sitting next to me. She kept her gaze fixed straight ahead, although the dragon on her hand kept sneaking glances at me, its face creased into a frown, as if it felt the same unease in the air that I did.

The driver released the brake, and the cart rolled forward and dropped down into the shaft. Nobody spoke, but this time, I found the darkness suffocating instead of soothing.

Eventually, the cart slowed, and we coasted into the shaft at the bottom of the mine, the same one I had worked in yesterday. The other miners headed into their assigned sections, but Reiko lingered by the cart, frowning down at her map as though she didn't like what it showed—

"It's about time!" a loud voice barked out.

I glanced to my left to find Conley striding toward me. What was he doing down here?

Conley stopped and looked me up and down, leering at me the same way he had Penelope yesterday morning. His lust punched into my gut, making me nauseous. Then his dark brown gaze moved past me, and his eyebrows drew together in anger.

"Why are you lollygagging around?" He stabbed his finger

at Reiko, who was still lingering by the cart. "Get to your assignment. Now."

Reiko's face remained blank, but her talons punched through the paper map, betraying her anger. Her gaze darted over to mine for a moment, then she whirled around and stalked into another chamber, disappearing from view.

Conley gestured for me to follow him. As we moved through the shaft, I reached out with my magic, but all I sensed was his smugness. Sometimes, when people's emotions were particularly strong, it blocked out their actual thoughts, and Conley was extremely pleased with himself right now.

We ended up in the cavern at the very back of the shaft. Fluorestone lanterns hanging on the wall, miners digging their tools into the rocks, half-full buckets of tearstone sitting at their feet. Everything looked the same as yesterday, but tension filled the air, squeezing my chest like a vise. Perhaps the miners were nervous because Conley was here.

An open spot along the wall caught my eye, and I finally realized who was missing—Penelope. My gaze flicked over the miners, but they were all men. Strange. Had Penelope been assigned to another chamber?

More unease filled me, but Conley jerked his head, and we stepped off to the side, away from the other miners, who kept *tink-tink-tinking* their tools into the rocks.

Conley got close to the chasm, but I stopped in front of him, making sure my back was facing the wall so that I wouldn't accidentally step off the edge.

"What did you think of my meeting yesterday?" Conley asked.

"It's not my job to think about things like that."

He nodded, as if my answer pleased him. "Good girl."

I bristled at him calling me *girl* again, but he didn't seem to notice. Instead, he stepped forward, so close that I could smell the eggs, garlic, and onions he'd had for breakfast.

"What did you do with the body?" he asked.

I didn't know what Penelope had told Conley, so I shrugged and gave a vague answer. "Dumped it in a ravine where no one will ever find it."

He stared at me, but I kept my eyes on his. Conley must have thought I was telling the truth, because he relaxed. "Good. Now it's time for your cut."

"Great. I could use it."

An amused chuckle rumbled out of Conley's lips, echoing through the cavern and bouncing back to me like a child's ball.

"What's so funny?"

A sly light filled his eyes. "It's hard to use money when you're dead."

His snide words echoed as loudly as his laughter had. Suddenly, the *tink-tink-tink* of the miners digging into the wall stopped, and malevolence filled the cavern, surging around me like an icy whirlpool.

I backed away from Conley and spun around. Two of the miners were standing in front of me, and they lunged forward and latched onto my arms.

"What are you doing?" I asked, struggling to break free of their tight grips.

"Getting rid of my last loose end."

Conley jerked his head at the men, who used their mutt strength to pick me up off my feet and carry me forward—toward the chasm.

The mountain shifted . . . and Clarissa was in the wrong place at the wrong time. The chasm opened up right under her feet.

Penelope's voice whispered in my mind. That's what she claimed had happened to Clarissa, the forewoman who had first reported the missing tearstone. Now Conley wanted me to have a similar *accident*. Greedy, murdering bastard.

Anger and determination roared through me, and I grabbed

hold of my magic and used the invisible force of it to punch one of the miners in the throat. That man choked, dropped my arm, and stumbled away. The instant my feet touched the ground, I spun around and slammed my physical fist into the throat of the second miner, who was clutching my other arm. He too choked and stumbled away.

"Get her!" Conley hissed.

The other four miners advanced on me, all of them clutching a pickaxe. These were all Conley's men, the same miners who'd been in the clearing yesterday, just like the first two who'd grabbed me.

She won't get past me . . .

Hope she screams before we kill her . . .

This is going to be fun . . .

Their horrible thoughts crashed over me, each one as hard and vicious as a slap across the face. Suddenly, I was rooted in place, although my paralysis didn't stop their malice from blasting over me like winds howling off a tornado.

With every step the miners took, the gargoyle pendant grew warmer and warmer against my chest, as the pieces of jet strained to block out the men's deadly intentions. I seized on to that sensation and let it scorch away the horrid thoughts crowding into my mind and paralyzing my body. Then I focused on my own anger, which was burning even hotter than my pendant was.

One of the miners charged forward and swung his pickaxe at my head. I ducked his blow and curled my hand into a tight fist, grabbing hold of the invisible strings of energy attached to his weapon. A flick of my fingers yanked the pickaxe out of his hand. Another flick sent him staggering back into the rock wall.

The other three miners yelled and rushed toward me, along with the first two that I'd sucker-punched.

In the dim gray glow of the fluorestones, I battled them all, using both my physical fighting skills and strength, along with my magic, to dodge their weapons and shove them away.

I'd just thrown a fourth miner across the chamber and was reaching for the dagger in my boot when a fifth man, a mutt with enhanced speed, slipped past my defenses and punched me in the face. Pain exploded in my jaw, radiating up into my skull, and white stars exploded in my eyes. My head spun, throwing me off balance and making me stumble around. Given the dim light and the stars still erupting in my eyes, I couldn't see where I was going, and I didn't realize how close I was to the chasm until my boot slipped off the edge.

Somehow, I managed to jerk my foot back and stagger away from the chasm. I blinked some of the stars out of my eyes and whirled around—

Conley was standing right in front of me. I had been so busy battling the six other men that I'd lost track of him.

He gave me an evil grin. "If you want something done right."

Conley surged forward and shoved me into the chasm.

CHAPTER NINE

For a split second, I had the sensation of being utterly weightless, like a butterfly floating along on a breeze.

Then, in the next instant, I plummeted down.

My arms and legs flailed wildly through the air. Desperate, I reached for my magic, hoping to find some thread of energy to grab on to, or some way to use my power to propel myself closer to the rock wall so that I might have a chance to latch onto something—*anything*—that would keep me from falling to my death. But my mind kept spinning and spinning, and my magic just wouldn't work—

The left side of my body slammed into solid rock, and several audible *crack-crack-cracks* sounded as the bones in my left arm and leg shattered one after another. White-hot agony blazed through me, burning brighter than a magier's lightning, although the force of the fall punched the air from my lungs, leaving me unable to scream and release any of the torment rushing through me.

Seconds passed. A minute. Two. Maybe ten. I couldn't tell. All I could see, hear, and especially feel was that white-hot agony blazing through my body, pushed along with every frantic beat of my heart. Slowly, the agony receded enough for me to notice other things, although I still felt like a porcelain doll that had been dropped on the floor and shattered into a hundred pieces.

Rock scraped beneath my twitching fingers, and I blinked and blinked, trying to focus in the dim, murky light. I was sprawled across a small ledge that jutted out from the chasm wall, with open air only a foot past my face. Despite the overwhelming pain, I was lucky I had landed on the ledge instead of tumbling down to the bottom of the abyss . . . however deep that was.

Pain spiraled out through my left arm and leg, but the right side of my body had landed on something that wasn't hard, solid rock, something that seemed soft, wet, and sort of . . . *squishy*. I slowly turned my head to the right, trying to figure out what else might be down here—

Penelope's sightless blue eyes stared back at me.

If I'd had the breath and strength for it, I would have shrieked and jerked back in surprise, which would have sent me tumbling off the ledge to my death. But all I could do was lie there and stare at Penelope.

Conley must have shoved her into the chasm too. Only Penelope had landed solely on the hard, unyielding ledge, and the fall had killed her outright.

"I didn't hear her hit the bottom." Conley's voice drifted down to me. "Give me a lantern. I want to make sure she's dead."

Several harsh scrapes sounded, and I shut my eyes an instant before a light fell on my face. I kept my eyes closed and willed myself not to move, twitch, or especially moan with pain.

Several seconds ticked by. I stayed frozen in place, although tears leaked out the corners of my eyes.

"She's as dead as the other one is." Conley's voice drifted down to me again. "Problems solved. Now get back to work."

The other miners grumbled, and the light on my face vanished.

I opened my eyes and peered upward, but all I could see were the faint gray glows of the flourestone lanterns casting twisted shadows on the cavern ceiling high, high above.

The steady *tink* of pickaxes digging into the wall rang out again. Penelope's murder and my impending death weren't enough to disrupt the mine's busy schedule. After all, Conley had more tearstone to steal and deliver to the Mortans.

Tink-tink-tink. Tink-tink-tink. Tink-tink-tink.

Perhaps the severity of my injuries was dulling my senses, but the harsh sounds of the miners' tools seemed as soft and soothing as a lullaby coaxing me to sleep. My eyes slid shut, and I drowned in the darkness.

One moment, I was lying on the ledge, willing myself not to scream with pain. The next, I was sitting at the top of the chasm, strangely pain-free, with my legs dangling off the side and my boots scraping against the rock wall below.

I glanced around, but the cavern was empty. The lanterns had been turned down low, although oddly enough, I could see much better now than before, when Conley had shoved me into the chasm.

I looked down. Thirty feet below, I could see my own body lying on the ledge, still partially sprawled across Penelope's corpse. My eyes were shut, and my chest was rising and falling in a slow, steady rhythm.

I sighed. I wasn't awake. Not really. Sometimes, when I was asleep, or in this case unconscious, I sort of . . . hovered outside my physical self, as though my mind and body were two separate entities. This sort of ghosting usually only happened when

I was extremely troubled about something—or when I had been severely injured. Alvis had said it was a defense mechanism, that my magic was letting my mind wander free while my body struggled to repair itself.

I sighed again, but I leaned forward and peered down at, well, *myself*. It was a bit like looking in a carnival mirror, although far more unnerving. A shiver rippled through my ghostly form, as well as my physical body below, but I studied the cliff face, which looked as slick as glass. Even if my arm and leg hadn't been broken, I still wouldn't have been able to climb to safety. I might have used my magic to glue myself to and then push my body up the rocks, but I was far too weak for that now.

The truth slammed into me as hard as I had hit the ledge earlier. I was going to die down here, alone in the dark—

"What are you doing?" a deep, familiar voice asked.

Startled, my ghostly form jerked back, and my head snapped up. A moment ago, I had been all alone in this fever dream, or whatever it truly was. Now Leonidas was standing in the chamber.

The prince looked much better than when I had last seen him in the clearing outside my cottage. The color had returned to his face, and his body no longer seemed stiff with pain. He was also wearing a new black riding coat with glittering amethyst buttons, which added to his tall, strong, imposing presence.

My heart lifted like a gargoyle shooting up into the sky, but it plummeted back down just as quickly. Leonidas Morricone wasn't *here*. Not really. He had just wandered into my fever dream.

"What are you doing?" he asked again.

I sighed for the third time. "Dying."

Leonidas's eyebrows shot up in surprise, but he walked forward and peered down into the chasm. A frown creased his face when he spotted my body lying on the ledge.

Several seconds ticked by in silence. I expected him to return to his own dream—or mind—but instead, he lowered himself to the ground and sat on the edge of the chasm next to me, the sleeve of his coat close enough to brush my elbow, if either one of us had been in our real bodies.

"What happened?" he asked.

"Something I should have expected. Conley, the mine foreman, shoved Penelope into the chasm and killed her. Then he did the same thing to me. He didn't want to share his blood money with us. Greedy bastard. My only regret is that I didn't find some way to drag him down with me."

A small smile quirked Leonidas's lips. "I didn't realize you were so murderous."

I thought of how I had frozen when the miners first attacked me. Over the years, I had worked so bloody *hard* with Alvis and had trained so bloody *much* with Rhea to keep from being overwhelmed by other people's thoughts and feelings, to keep from being paralyzed like I had been during the Seven Spire massacre, but it had happened again anyway.

That was the problem with my mind magier magic—it made me feel *too much*. Most people only had to handle their own fear, anger, or terror, but I got assaulted by everyone else's emotions too. Or perhaps the problem wasn't my magic. Perhaps the problem was *me*, and my inability to handle all those messy feelings, especially my own, no matter how deep down I tried to shove them.

Either way, it was finally going to cost me my life. Although I supposed that was fitting, since I had cost so many people their lives during the massacre. Poetic justice was finally being served to Coward Gemma.

Leonidas kept staring at me, so I shrugged, as though I weren't silently cursing my own bloody weakness.

"Perhaps if I had been more murderous, I wouldn't be in this situation." I changed the subject. "What are you doing here?"

"I was going about my business when I heard you cry out in my mind. Even worse, I felt your pain. I knew that you were in trouble, so I sort of . . . cast my mind about and followed the cry and the pain back here to you."

It sounded like he was talking about seeking, an ability that let some mind magiers step outside their own bodies and view whatever person or place they wished. If he could do that, then he was even more powerful and dangerous than I'd realized.

"I also heard another cry, but it didn't sound like you," Leonidas continued. "It was lower, rougher, almost like . . . rocks crunching together."

He had to be talking about Grimley. The gargoyle must have felt my injury through our mental bond, the same way that I could sense whenever he had been hurt. I had been in so much pain before that I hadn't even tried to communicate with him.

Grims? I sent the thought out. *Are you there?*

Gemma! he replied, although his voice was the faintest whisper in my mind.

Grims! Grims!

I called out to him again and again, but an eerie, buzzing silence filled my head, along with a gaping emptiness in my heart where his strong, solid, comforting presence should have been. His absence made me want to weep, but I didn't have the strength for that either, not even in this ghostly form.

Thanks to my injuries, my magic was rapidly weakening, right along with my body. Strangely enough, the thought didn't fill me with as much fear as I'd expected, just a cold, growing numbness. I'd joked to Leonidas about dying, but the truth was that I was already dead—my mind and body just didn't quite know it yet.

"Don't do that," Leonidas snapped, intruding on my morbid musings. "Don't give up."

"I'm not giving up. I'm facing the inevitable." I gestured

down at my physical body. "My left arm and leg are both badly broken, and I probably have other internal injuries. I'm trapped deep in a mine on a ledge that could give way under my weight at any time. *I'm dead.* The only thing that's left to ponder is if I'll wake up—truly wake up—before the end."

Leonidas's jaw clenched, and determination flared in his eyes. "You're not going to die. I'm going to save you."

I barked out a harsh, bitter laugh. "How are you going to do that? Unless I miss my guess, you're already back in Morta. Even if you could return to Blauberg in time, there's no way you could get past Conley and the other miners, much less make it down into this chamber."

He stared at me, his jaw still clenched tight, and the determination burning in his eyes never wavered or dimmed, not even for an instant. He truly thought he could rescue me. He was an even bigger fool than I'd realized.

Leonidas leaned over and nudged me with his elbow. The motion was careful, gentle, controlled, as if he was concerned that he would send my ghostly form tumbling down into the chasm just like my physical body had. To my surprise, I actually *felt* the sensation, as though he had touched me in real life, and I had to hold back a shiver.

"My friends call me Leo."

"Do you have a lot of friends?" I asked. "Back home in Morta?"

Perhaps it was a trick of the gloomy lantern light, but I could have sworn that sadness flickered across his face. "There's Lyra, of course. My sister, Delmira." He paused. "And my mother. But I suppose she has to be my friend."

Maeven's smiling face filled my mind. I remembered the smug glee that had rolled off her as the turncoat guards had cut people down during the Seven Spire massacre, along with her silent words. *I'm going to enjoy this.*

I shuddered. "No, I don't think your mother has to be your friend."

"No, I suppose not," Leonidas replied.

We sat there in silence, each of us lost in our own dark thoughts. I didn't have the strength to sit upright anymore, not even in this ghostly form, so I pulled my legs up over the lip of the chasm and scooted back. Then I lay down on the cavern floor, using my right arm as a pillow to cushion my head.

"Goodbye, Leo," I said, my words slurring a bit. "Enjoy the rest of your princely life. Oh, and pet Lyra for me. I always wanted to pet a strix, but I never got the chance."

I must truly be dying to sputter nonsense like that. The thought made me laugh, at least in my own mind, but no sound came out of my lips.

Leonidas leaned over me, concern creasing his face. He shook my shoulder. "Hey! Stay awake! Don't go back to sleep!"

But the sharp motion didn't rouse me, and I was already asleep. This was just a dream, after all. Still, for some reason, I could have sworn that I felt the hot shock of his hand cupping my cheek before I tumbled back down the cliff into the blackness waiting in my body.

CHAPTER TEN

The blackness wrapped around me like the softest cloak, blotting out everything else.

I wasn't sure how long I lay on the ledge. Minutes, hours, days . . . Penelope's body quickly grew cold and stiff against my own, and I couldn't tell where the ledge ended and she began. But it didn't really matter since I would soon be as cold, stiff, and dead as she was.

Gemma! Gemma!

Every once in a while, Grimley's worried voice would pierce the blackness, like a low, gravelly bell tolling in the night. But I didn't have the strength to respond, and I tumbled back down into the darkness again.

Eventually, that darkness grew brighter, sharper, until it morphed into a river of dreams carrying me along and showing me all sorts of images.

Grimley crouching on a rooftop, snarling and staring at the mine entrance. Topacia standing in a barracks, speaking to a stern-looking captain of the royal guard. Conley sitting at a desk, letting coins trickle down through his fingers and spatter onto an even larger pile of gold.

No, these weren't dreams. For once, my ghosting magic was showing me things that were happening right now, out in the real world. My friends were trying to save me, and Conley was counting his blood money. Greedy bastard.

I got glimpses of other things too, of places I had never been before. Lyra perching on a tower of a small, crumbling mountaintop castle, her purple feathers ruffling as she squawked at the other strixes gathered around her. Leonidas shoving food and other supplies into a satchel. Then Leonidas climbing onto Lyra's back, and the two of them sailing up, up, up into the brilliant blue autumn sky . . .

Those images faded away, and that cloak of blackness wrapped around me again. But the cloak was just an illusion, and my body soon grew as cold as the rocks around me. I didn't mind the chill, though. It helped douse some of the hot pain throbbing through my broken bones—

Thump.

Thump-thump.

Thump-thump-thump-thump.

Noises rang out, interrupting my slow spiral down toward death. I couldn't tell if I was actually awake or just dreaming again, although some small part of me struggled to figure out what was happening. The noises almost sounded like . . .

Footsteps.

Several sets, all headed this way.

My heart lifted, but it tumbled back down just as fast, like a baby strix trying—and failing—to fly for the first time. No one was coming to rescue me. The miners were probably just returning from lunch, or whatever time it was now. Even if someone did enter the cavern, I didn't have the strength to lift my head, much less call out for help. That cold, numb lethargy swept over me again, pulling me back down, down, down into the darkness—

A light fell on my face, snapping me fully awake. My eyes popped open, but I had to shut them against the harsh glare.

"Over here!" A familiar feminine voice assaulted my ears, further startling me. "I see her!"

Other voices rose up, although I couldn't decipher any of the excited chatter. More lights blazed to life, illuminating my face, arms, and legs. After being in the murky gray gloom for so long, the bright white glow brought tears to my eyes. I squinted, trying to figure out what was happening, but all I could see were the lights bobbing up and down like fireflies.

"She's blinking! She's still alive!" the feminine voice sounded again.

"Stand back!" This time, a deep, masculine voice rose up above the others.

I frowned. That almost sounded like . . . like . . . I tried to concentrate, but the answer wouldn't come to me.

Several seconds passed by in silence, although the lights remained bright and steady on my body. Then my fingertips started tingling, the way they always did in the presence of powerful magic. An instant later, this . . . *pressure* wrapped all around me, as though two giant hands were scooping up my body and slowly hoisting it—*me*—off the ledge.

Gentle though it was, that first, slightly jerky lift made the pain of my injuries explode in my body again, like stitches that had been ripped open with a dagger. This time, I couldn't stop myself from screaming, although it was a weak, hoarse sound, like the keening of a wounded animal.

Those invisible hands holding me flinched, as though I had startled them. I screamed again, and again, but those hands slowly, relentlessly, ruthlessly hoisted my body higher and higher into the air.

"She's in pain." That feminine voice intruded on my cries. "Perhaps you should set her back down."

"No," the masculine voice replied. "I know she's hurting, but this is the quickest, easiest way to get her out of there."

Those invisible hands lifted me higher . . . and higher . . . and higher still . . .

I must have passed out because the next thing I knew, I was lying on the cavern floor, with people gathered around me.

How long has she been down here . . .

She's a broken mess . . .

Can't believe she survived that fall . . .

Their thoughts crashed over me, along with their curiosity, sympathy, and horror, but for once, the sensations didn't overwhelm me. Right now, they were as insignificant as spiders skittering across my skin compared to the pain of my injuries.

My gaze flicked from one face to another. I didn't recognize any of the people, but their helmets and coveralls marked them as miners. Panic filled me. I studied them all again, but none of them were Conley's men, and no one seemed to want to kick me back down into the chasm.

Someone pushed through the ring of miners and dropped to a knee beside me. The figure took off their helmet and lifted their head, revealing black hair, green eyes, and pretty features.

Reiko, the dragon morph, leaned down closer to me. "Don't worry," she said, her voice surprisingly gentle. "You're going to be okay."

"Heal her." That masculine voice called out again. *"Now."*

The icy command boomed through the cavern, and a man scuttled forward, crouched down beside me, and removed his helmet. This man looked to be in his sixties, with brown eyes and gray hair that was pulled back into a low ponytail. Deep wrinkles grooved into his bronze skin, although his face and hands were curiously free of the dust that coated the other miners.

"Hello. My name is Javier. I'm one of the mine's bone masters."

Javier studied me with a sharp, critical gaze, magic flaring like matches in his eyes as he took stock of my injuries. "I'm sorry," he murmured in an apologetic voice. "But this is going to hurt."

Before I could croak out a response, he placed one hand on my left arm and the other on my left leg. More magic flared in his eyes, making them gleam a bright topaz. Then his power slammed into my body.

Javier was probably trying to be gentle, but the bones in my left arm and leg writhed around like coral vipers as they wriggled into place and then fused back together. Then those vipers invaded the rest of my body, relentlessly pulling, yanking, and tugging everything back the way it was supposed to be.

In some ways, the pain was even worse than when I had first hit the ledge, and the continued, prolonged, white-hot agony was so intense that I couldn't even scream, although tears and sweat poured down my face, stinging my eyes and adding to my misery.

Slowly, much too slowly, the writhing vipers stilled, and the white-hot agony dulled to warm daggers stabbing into my body. Eventually, the daggers shrank to pinpricks, which faded away to nothingness. I lay on the ground, still crying and sweating, although my breath came much easier, and my mind was clear now.

Javier dropped his hands, released his magic, and sat back on his heels. "I took care of the worst of her injuries, but she needs several more rounds of healing, as well as food and water and good, old-fashioned rest."

"Can she be moved?"

Javier nodded. "Yes. She is stable enough to be taken out of the mine."

He stood up, and another man strode forward and knelt down beside me.

Instead of a miner's grimy gray coveralls, this man was wearing a black cloak over a black riding coat, along with matching gloves, leggings, and boots. A light gray tearstone sword and matching dagger dangled from his black leather belt.

The fluorestones gilded his black hair in a silvery sheen that also accentuated his sharp cheekbones and straight nose. His eyes seemed more black than purple, and he looked like a shadow knight, a dark, unstoppable force that had stepped out of a nightmare and into the real world to wreak havoc and destruction on anyone who dared to get in his way.

"Leonidas?" I rasped, my tongue heavy in my dry, dusty mouth. "What are you doing here?"

"Saving you." He bent down and put his mouth close to my ear. "And it's Leo, remember?"

His warm breath tickled my skin, and an involuntary shiver swept through my body.

Only to your friends, I murmured in my mind.

Amusement filled his face. *Aren't we friends? After all, we've saved each other's lives.*

If I'd had the strength for it, I would have shaken my head. *I don't know what we are.*

Certainly not *friends*. Like it or not, he was still a Morricone, and I was still a Ripley. We might have saved each other's lives now, but we had both tried to kill each other as children, something that I clearly remembered, even if he did not.

Reiko was still kneeling beside me. "My lord, what do you want us to do with . . ." Her voice trailed off, as though she didn't know my name.

"Lady Armina." Leonidas supplied my alias. "We need to get her aboveground at once. Give me some room."

Reiko tipped her head. "Of course, my lord."

She got to her feet and shooed Javier and the miners back.

Leonidas bent forward. He carefully hooked one arm under my knees and slid the other under my shoulders. Then he stood, easily climbing to his feet. His muscles tightened as he cradled me in his arms, and the heat of his body soaked into my own, despite his thick coat. I drew in a breath, and his honeysuckle scent washed over me, soft, masculine, and intoxicating all at once.

I lolled my head to the side, too tired to do anything other than stare up at him.

"Don't worry," Leonidas murmured. "You'll always be safe with me."

His words were soft, but each syllable rang with a fierce promise that made my weak, treacherous heart quicken. His gaze locked with mine. Then he turned and strode away from the edge of the chasm, still cradling me in his arms.

Leonidas carried me to the front of the shaft. He gently set me down inside the cart before climbing in next to me. "Take us back to the surface."

His icy command left no room for argument, only obedience.

Reiko gestured at the other miners. "You heard him. Let's move."

She, Javier, and the miners pulled on the rope attached to the wall, and the cart quickly rose to the top of the shaft.

Once again, Leonidas scooped me up into his arms and carried me out into Basecamp. After being down in the dark, the bright golden rays filtering in through the mine entrance made me hiss with pain. Still, I didn't shut my eyes against the warm, harsh glare.

I was far too grateful to be seeing sunlight again.

Slowly, my eyes adjusted to the light. I couldn't tell exactly what time it was, although I got the sense it was in the afternoon, which meant I had been in the chasm for several hours.

Someone's boot scraped against the ground, catching my attention. Off to the right, a dozen miners clutching pickaxes surrounded another, smaller group of men who were huddled on their knees. What was going on?

Leonidas stopped in front of the miners. Suspicion surged off those folks, and they backed away from him. The miners might be holding sharp tools and greatly outnumber him, but the stone-cold look on Leonidas's face clearly indicated he would kill anyone who tried to stop him.

"Move," he commanded.

The miners stepped back a little more, revealing the seven men huddled on the ground—Conley and his crew.

Conley's eyes bulged, and his shock stabbed into my gut like a dagger.

I glanced around at the rest of the miners, most of whom looked wary, worried, and confused—except for Reiko. The dragon morph grabbed a nearby chair, brought it over, and set it down in front of Conley. She nodded at Leonidas, then stepped back, although her gaze kept flicking from me to the prince and back again.

Leonidas carefully swung me down and into the chair. I wobbled, so I grabbed the sides of the seat to steady myself.

"Can you sit up?" he asked.

"Yes," I rasped.

"Good." He turned his head to the side. "Get her some water."

Javier scurried away, then returned with a glass of water, which he pressed into my hand. "Slowly. Just take a few sips at a time."

Even though it was just plain, lukewarm water, I wanted to cry as the wetness coated my tongue and washed the dirt, dust, and grime out of my mouth. Water was something else I never thought I would experience again.

Leonidas studied the men kneeling on the ground. Conley ducked his head, but the prince pointed him out, and a couple of the other miners grabbed the foreman's arms and hauled him upright.

"Let me go!" Conley shouted, but the other miners forced him to stand along one of the walls.

Leonidas studied Conley with an icy expression, as though the foreman were a slug he was thinking of squishing beneath his boot. A chill rippled down my spine. In this moment, Leonidas looked eerily like Maeven had during the Seven Spire massacre.

A couple of miners moved forward, carrying something between them—Penelope. Leonidas must have raised her off the ledge too.

The miners set Penelope's body down in the open space between Conley and me. Someone had closed her eyes, but her face was still twisted in shock and pain. The water I'd drunk roiled in my stomach. That could have been me—that *would* have been me, if not for Leonidas.

The prince stabbed his finger at Conley. "Is this the man who threw you and that other woman down into the chasm?"

His accusation boomed through the cavern like thunder. Shocked murmurs rippled through the miners' ranks, and they all glanced back and forth between Conley and me.

I stared at the foreman. Despite my weakened condition and the lethargy creeping through my body, I could still clearly hear the silent pleas running through his mind.

Please say no, please say no, please, please, please . . .

I wondered if Penelope had begged for her life before he'd tossed her into the chasm. Or Clarissa, the forewoman he'd killed. Anger stormed through me, drowning out his silent cries for mercy.

"Yes. Conley lured me down into the shaft. Then he and those other six men attacked me. Conley shoved me off the edge of the chasm and left me for dead."

More shocked gasps sounded, although they were quickly swallowed up by low, angry mutters. Working in the mine was dangerous enough without people sabotaging each other.

All the miners seemed truly stunned—except for Reiko. The dragon morph looked more thoughtful than surprised.

"You bitch!" Conley hissed, his hands clenching into fists. "Why couldn't you just die along with the other one?"

More anger roared through me. "Her name was Penelope, you greedy bastard."

Conley opened his mouth, probably to curse me some more, but Reiko stepped up and plowed her fist into his gut. The foreman's face turned tomato-red, and he sagged back against the wall, gasping for breath.

Leonidas turned back to me. "Why did Conley push you into the chasm?"

"Because he was stealing tearstone from the mine."

More low, angry mutters rang out, growing in strength and number, and the miners hefted the pickaxes in their hands. The six men dropped their heads and hunkered down on their knees, trying to make themselves as small as possible, but Conley remained standing, his face growing even redder with rage.

"Conley also killed Clarissa, another mine forewoman, a few weeks ago," I said. "She must have found out about the stolen tearstone and tried to report it."

She *had* reported it, but the miners didn't need to know that.

Leonidas drew the sword from the scabbard on his belt. The soft *rasp* of the weapon sliding free cut through the mutters, and a tense, expectant hush fell over the cavern. No one moved or spoke, and the only sound was Leonidas's soft footsteps as he stalked over to Conley.

The foreman gave the prince a petulant look. He opened his mouth, probably to deny my accusations, but Leonidas snapped up his sword and surged forward. My breath caught in my throat. He was going to run Conley through with the blade—

Leonidas stopped just short, although the tip of his sword nicked the foreman's neck, drawing a bit of blood.

Conley's eyes bulged even wider than before, and his silent, frantic cries filled my mind again. *Please don't, please don't, please, please, please . . .*

More anger sizzled through me. The bastard didn't deserve any sympathy, and he certainly hadn't earned the mercy of a quick death.

Leonidas glanced over at me, as if sensing my anger with his magic. He studied me for a moment, that cold, unreadable expression still on his face, then looked at Conley again.

"If we were in Morta, I would gut you like the spineless coward you are." Leonidas lowered his sword. "But lucky for you, we are not in Morta. I will let the Andvarian royal guards deal with you and your men." He glanced around at the other miners. "If that is agreeable?"

Leonidas might be tacitly asking for their approval, but he was still clearly in control. The miners' mouths were gaping in shock, but they all bobbed their heads. Even Reiko joined in with the gesture, although she still looked more thoughtful than surprised.

The prince stepped back and sheathed his sword.

Conley sucked down a breath, wet his lips, and sidled forward. "Let me go, my lord. I can give you more tearstone. Gold, jewels, anything you want from the mine. Just let me go—"

Leonidas flicked his fingers. He could pull on those invisible strings of energy just like I could, and a wave of magic picked up Conley and slammed him back into the wall. The foreman dropped to the ground without a sound, knocked unconscious.

Snap-snap-snap-snap-snap-snap.

In quick succession, Leonidas used his magic to lift the other six men up off their feet, toss them back into the wall, and render them all unconscious as well. The other miners froze again, shocked by the violent display, but Leonidas ignored them and dropped to one knee in front of me.

I stared into his dark amethyst eyes, and he gazed right back at me, his face still ice-cold. I expected him to make some pithy remark about how we were even now, but instead, he took the empty water glass from my hand and passed it over to Javier. Then he leaned forward, pulled me out of the chair and over into his arms, and stood up.

I sagged against his body, as weak and boneless as a sleeping gargoyle. "What are you doing?"

"Getting you out of here."

Leonidas carried me out of the mine, with Reiko and Javier following along behind us. My gaze locked with Reiko's, and she smirked at me, as if she knew some grand joke that I didn't.

Leonidas stepped out of the cavern. Sunlight stabbed into my eyes, even brighter than before, and it took me a few seconds to focus on my surroundings. Once again, my breath caught in my throat.

Strixes lined the plaza.

Roughly a dozen of the enormous purple birds were lined up in front of the mine entrance, keeping watch like feathered soldiers. Merchants and shoppers had gathered in the plaza beyond, whispering and staring at the creatures. Strixes were not an uncommon sight in Blauberg, but none of these birds were wearing saddles, indicating they were wild creatures. I thought of the ghosting vision I'd had of Lyra squawking orders at the other strixes. She must have brought them here to protect Leonidas while he went into the mine.

The prince strode forward, still carrying me. Every step he took jostled my body and made more pain bloom deep inside me, and I had to grit my teeth to keep from hissing. Javier was right. I still needed more healing, but I pushed the pain away and looked out over the crowd.

Topacia was standing on the rim of the gargoyle fountain, head and shoulders above everyone else. Her worried gaze met mine. Her body sagged, and her relief washed over me like a cool, soothing balm. Then she realized who was carrying me. Topacia's hand curled around her sword, and her mouth flattened out into a thin line.

No. I sent the thought to her. *Don't interfere. It's too dangerous.*

Topacia jerked back. For once, she'd heard me. She didn't like it, but she dropped her hand from her sword. Once I was sure she wasn't going to leap off the fountain rim, charge forward, and get herself killed, I lifted my gaze higher, to the buildings that surrounded the plaza.

Grimley was perched on the rooftop closest to the mine.

The gargoyle's eyes burned with sapphire fire, his long tail zipped from side to side, and his broad, powerful wings twitched as though he was about to dive off the roof, fly across the plaza, and hurl himself at the strixes.

No. I sent the thought to him. *It's too dangerous. The strixes will kill you.*

Grimley didn't move forward, although his wings kept twitching and his expression remained fierce. *But they're our enemies, just like the Mortans are.*

I know. But Leonidas isn't going to hurt me. He went to too much trouble to save me.

Grimley frowned. *Why would he do that?*

I have no idea.

And I truly didn't. I didn't know why Leonidas had come here and risked so much to help me. Sure, I had saved his life first, but only because he had spared that little girl. Saving him might have been the right thing to do, but my motives had been far from pure, and I had also been hoping to gather more infor-mation about the missing tearstone. A calculated gamble, rather than any true benevolence on my part.

Besides, it hadn't cost me anything to help Leonidas, but this could cost him a great deal if—or rather *when*—our respec-tive families discovered what had happened.

This was the kind of thing that started wars.

"Put me down," I rasped. "The people in the plaza can help me."

Leonidas's arms tightened around me. "I can't do that."

"Why not?"

"Because you need much more healing than what these peo-ple can provide. I didn't go down into that mine just to let some inexperienced fool botch making you better." He stared down at me. "And because I need you."

Another chill slithered down my spine. "For what?"

A humorless smile lifted his lips, and his eyes were as cold as chips of amethyst ice. "To see the true heart of the Morricones."

His mysterious words filled me with even more dread. What *true heart*?

One of the strixes hopped forward and lowered itself down to the ground. Lyra. Her beak opened in what seemed like a grin, and she winked at me.

Leonidas stopped in front of the strix. His eyes flashed a bright purple, and another wave of magic rolled off him. This time, he used his power to lift himself—and me—up off the ground.

Surprised gasps and awed murmurs rippled through the Andvarians gathered in the plaza, even as the twin swords of Topacia's and Grimley's worry sliced into my mind.

Leonidas used his magic to float us up and onto Lyra's back. He settled himself on the strix, then positioned me in front of him and hooked a strong, muscled arm around my waist, as though I were a child about to ride a pony, and he wanted to make sure I didn't fall off.

Once we were securely seated, Lyra raised her head and let out a loud, wild *caw!* The other strixes hopped forward and flexed their wings.

For the first time, I realized exactly what was happening and just how much danger I was in—much more danger than what I had faced in the mine.

"It's okay," Leonidas murmured. "Don't be afraid. I made you a promise in the mine, and I intend to keep it. You will always be safe with me."

Suddenly, it was too much—it was all too bloody *much*.

Hitting the ledge. Being fished out of the chasm and then halfway healed. Facing down Conley. And now perching atop a strix as though I was going for an afternoon pleasure ride. Fear, worry, and dread crashed through my body in cold, choppy waves, along with larger, stronger storms of pain and exhaustion. I was seconds away from passing out again, but I still lolled my head to the side and looked up at Leonidas.

"Where . . . are you . . . taking me?" I rasped.

All sorts of deadly scenarios flashed through my mind, and the last thing I heard before going under was him confirming my worst fear.

"Home," he replied in a soft voice. "To Morta."

PART TWO

SPY

CHAPTER ELEVEN

I had the strangest feeling of safety.

Of being nestled in strong arms. Of warmth soaking into my body. Of someone murmuring soothing words into my ear, and another, higher voice answering with musical, singsong notes. The trilling melody lulled me back down into the darkness again . . .

Other things filled my mind. The wind tangling my hair. The bunch and flex of powerful wings. The faint scent of honeysuckle tickling my nose. But through it all, those strong arms held me, and I wasn't afraid . . .

Until I woke up.

The first thing I saw was the enormous strix carved into the ceiling above my head. Amethysts glittered as the strix's eyes, while bits of polished onyx tipped its gray stone wings and tail, giving the creature a strange, shadowy sheen.

I gasped and jerked back. Well, as much as I could jerk back, since I was lying in a bed. Was I walking through someone else's dream? No strixes were carved into the ceilings, walls, or anything else at Glitnir. And especially not in my chambers, where the ceiling featured an amazing image of Queen Armina Ripley riding Arton, her gargoyle, and leading her gargoyle army into battle against the Mortans . . .

The word *Mortans* chimed in my ears like a bell waking up my mind, and everything came rushing back. Leonidas carrying me out of the mine. Topacia's and Grimley's tense, worried faces. Lyra flying the prince and me away . . .

More memories sputtered in my mind, like fluorestones flaring to life. Leonidas carrying me through a hallway covered with black vines. Pain rushing through my body as several bone masters healed my remaining injuries. Hands and fingers fluttering around, giving me a bath, combing my hair, dressing me in a nightgown . . .

I scrambled up to sitting, my hands clenching into fists, and my head snapping back and forth as I searched for enemies.

The four-poster ebony bed stood in the back of the chambers, which also featured an armoire, writing desk, and vanity table. A door off to the left opened up into a bathroom done in gray tile. To the right, three glass doors lined part of the wall. Another wall featured a fireplace.

I was alone—except for the strixes.

Images of the creature filled the chambers—gold-framed paintings hanging on the walls, silver statues perching on the writing desk, bronze bookends squatting on a shelf. Most of the figurines featured amethyst eyes, all of which seemed to be glaring at me, the interloper in their midst.

I shivered. Still, the strixes made me remember who I was missing.

Grimley? I sent the thought out as far and wide as I could. *Are you here?*

I waited, but there was no answer, just a buzzing silence in my mind and an empty, aching spot in my heart where the gargoyle's presence should have been. Panic welled up in my chest, but I forced it down, closed my eyes, and pictured Grimley—his bright sapphire eyes, his arrow-tipped tail, the warm, slightly rough feel of his stone skin.

Something flickered in the very back of my mind, like a match sputtering to life in a cold, dark cave. *Gemma*, Grimley's voice whispered, but the sound was faint and far away.

Grimley? Grimley!

He didn't respond, but at least I felt his presence now, even though it was as light and thin as a strand in a spider's web. The gargoyle wasn't here, but he wasn't all the way back in Blauberg either. Otherwise, I probably wouldn't have been able to hear or sense him at all. Grimley was probably flying in this direction, trying to find me. My stomach twisted with worry. A dangerous journey, but if anyone could make it, then it was my Grims.

Thinking about the gargoyle reminded me of something else I might be missing. My fingers crept up to my neck, but nothing was there. I patted the front of my chest, my fingers flopping around in my haste. Where was it? Where *was* it?

A glimmer of blue caught my eye, and my head snapped to the right. My gargoyle pendant was lying on the nightstand beside the bed, along with my dagger. I lurched over, snatched the silver chain, and dropped it down over my head.

The pendant thumped against my chest and settled into its usual spot. My breath hissed out in relief at the slight, familiar weight nestled close to my heart. With a shaking hand, I held the pendant up to the light, looking for any signs of damage, but the black jet and blue tearstone shards were all intact. Still, a worrisome thought bloomed in my mind, wilting my relief.

I hadn't taken off the pendant. I would *never* do that, not even in my most injured, addled, delirious state. Someone else had removed the chain from around my neck, as well as the dagger from my boot, and placed them on the nightstand.

Leonidas.

Sick realization flooded my stomach. If he had examined the pendant and the dagger—and how could he not have?—then he had to know who I really was.

I had to get out of here.

I grabbed my dagger off the nightstand, then threw back the blankets, surged up out of bed, stepped forward—

And almost fell flat on my face.

My legs buckled, and I had to grab one of the bedposts for support. My head spun around, and a dull lethargy swept through my body, even though I'd just spent hours—days?—sleeping.

Despite the healing I'd received, I hadn't fully recovered my strength yet. So I hung on to the bedpost until the room stopped spinning, then took a smaller, slower, more careful step forward. This time, my legs didn't buckle.

Instead of lurching forward in a blind panic again, I reached out with my magic. I was alone in these chambers, and I didn't sense any guards posted outside the closed doors at the opposite end of the room. Maybe I could leave before Leonidas returned. He obviously wanted *something* from me, and I didn't want to be here when he started asking for it.

So I staggered over and opened the armoire. Tunics, camisoles, leggings, undergarments, and socks were folded on the shelves, while several pairs of boots lined the bottom. Most of the clothes were varying shades of purple—Mortan purple.

My lips curled in disgust, but I stripped off my nightgown (also purple) and dressed in a pale lavender tunic, along with black leggings, socks, and boots. I also shoved my dagger into the side of my right boot.

Next, I staggered over to the vanity table, dropped into the chair, and peered at my reflection in the mirror. My hair was horribly tangled, exhaustion dimmed my blue eyes, and my face was paler than usual.

Seeing my own frightened—and frightful—reflection dulled

the sharpest edges of my jumbled emotions. I fisted my hand around my gargoyle pendant and forced myself to draw in slow, deep breaths, just like Alvis had taught me to do whenever I was working on a tricky, intricate jewelry design and needed to steady my hands.

The last of my worry, panic, and confusion dissipated, and I started thinking clearly again. Leonidas hadn't imprisoned me, which meant I still had a chance to escape—*if* I was smart. Rushing across the room, throwing the doors open, and running out into whatever corridor lay beyond was *not* smart. No, if I wanted to escape, then I needed to be cold, calm, and logical.

Given my haggard appearance, people would take one look at me and realize that I didn't belong here, so I yanked a comb through my snarled locks, then examined the color. My shoulder-length hair was still a flat black with no hint of its usual dark brown. Good. Between that and the lavender tunic, I looked even less like Princess Gemma than usual.

I dabbed some light purple berry balm onto my lips and dusted my face with lilac-scented powder, trying to hide the dark circles under my eyes. I wasn't very successful, but the makeup made me seem less like someone who had barely escaped death.

I opened the rest of the vanity-table drawers, searching for valuables. There was no money inside, although I found several hairpins studded with amethysts, which I stuck into my pockets. Perhaps I could trade them for safe passage away from here.

I didn't see anything else in the chambers that would aid my escape, so I went over to the closed double doors, which were locked. I could have opened them with my magic, but someone might sense my power and come to investigate. Perhaps there was an easier way out of here.

So I headed over to the glass doors set into the wall. They were unlocked, and I cautiously opened one and peered outside. The doors led to a large balcony—one without any stairs.

I muttered a curse, but I walked over to the railing and focused on the ground some five stories below. If I had been at full strength, I would have tried to climb and float down, but given how weak I still was, I wouldn't be able to hold on to the slick stones, not even with my magic. A frustrated growl tumbled from my lips, but I raised my gaze, trying to find another way to escape.

A gleam of gold caught my eye, and I glanced to my right. In the distance, the sun was rising over a river that curved through the landscape. Several ships bobbed along the water, heading toward a large port, and homes and shops flanked both sides of the river, stretching out for miles. Nothing unusual there, except for the buildings—tall, wide structures with clusters of diamond-shaped windows and steep, pointed roofs topped with black spikes that looked like arrows streaking up to pierce the morning sky.

My heart plummeted. Diamond-shaped windows and spike-lined roofs were a common style in Mortan architecture. Combine that with the water, which had to be the Meander River, and there was only one place I could be.

Majesta, the Mortan capital.

I dragged my gaze away from the homes, shops, and riverfront and studied the grounds immediately around me.

My balcony overlooked a courtyard made of dark gray stone. To my left, another balcony jutted out over the same area. Down below, a gray stone fountain shaped like a strix bubbled in the center of the open space, which also featured purple flowers planted in zigzagging rows.

The flowers were nothing special, but thick black vines covered with black thorns bigger and longer than my fingers twined through the blossoms before snaking across the flagstones and curling around the fountain. Helene Blume had once shown me a similar cutting in her greenhouse workshop at Glitnir, so

I knew what the tendrils were—liladorn, an incredibly tough vine with thorns that blossomed into spikes of fragrant lilac.

There was only one place I had heard of where you would find this much liladorn. Things were even worse than I'd feared. I wasn't just in the capital.

I was in Myrkvior—the Morricone royal palace, the very heart of Morta, and the most dangerous place on the Buchovian continent for the crown princess of Andvari to be.

Shock slithered through my body in icy tendrils, just like the liladorn had curled through the courtyard, and worry scraped against my heart like thorns dragging across my skin. Leonidas could have taken me anywhere in Morta, but he had brought me *here*, to Myrkvior, the royal palace. Why? Had he figured out who I really was?

Dread simmered in my stomach as I left the balcony, hurried back inside, and headed over to the double doors at the far end of the chambers. I reached out with my magic again, but no one was standing outside, so I waved my hand. The lock softly *clicked*, and one of the doors swung outward.

I left the chambers and slipped out into a gray stone hallway lined with fluorestone lamps. I quickly moved from that hallway to another one, then another one.

The corridors were sparsely furnished, with only a few paintings and tapestries adorning the walls, and the only sound was my boots scuffing along the flagstones. This section of the palace was also quite chilly, as though not enough people lived here to bother with heating it. I shivered, wishing I'd grabbed a cloak from the armoire before I'd bolted from the chambers.

Various presences started tickling my mind, like white dandelion puffs drifting along on a summer breeze, but I kept moving forward. It was better than going back to those chambers and waiting for death to come find me.

I eased down several flights of stairs and stepped into another hallway. No one else was on this level, so I tiptoed over to the stone railing. My eyes widened, and my body froze, stunned by the sight before me.

This second-floor hallway formed part of a diamond-shaped balcony that ringed an enormous seven-story rotunda topped by a glass dome. Seams of silver ran through the glass, forming pretty patterns, while a massive arrow-shaped silver chandelier dangled from a chain in the center of the dome. White fluorestones dripped down the silver like hot wax, throwing out sprays of dazzling light and giving the rotunda a pleasing warmth.

Down below, a stunning mosaic of a strix with its wings stretched out wide was embedded in the gray stone floor, the massive creation running for more than two hundred feet. The strix was made of polished purple marble so dark that it almost looked black, and every slice of sunlight made the marble shimmer, as though the strix was beating its wings and flying through the floor. Two giant amethysts bigger than my head glinted as the strix's eyes, while slabs of onyx tipped its wings. More slabs of onyx made up the creature's beak and talons.

The amethysts and the onyx in the mosaic actually jutted up out of the floor, although dozens of people moved around the gemstones with practiced ease, not even glancing down to see where they were putting their feet. Servants mostly, dressed in pale purple tunics, although palace stewards, merchants, and nobles also flowed across the floor.

My gaze skipped past them all and landed on the guards, who were wearing dark purple tunics with swords dangling from their belts. The guards were stationed all around the rotunda, although they didn't appear to be searching for someone, for *me*. Still, I reached out with my magic, skimming everyone's thoughts.

I hate working the morning shift . . .

Must get this breakfast tray to Lady Arrington before she pitches a fit . . .

Can't believe Lord Dickson thought no one would notice the berry balm stains on his collar. Lecherous old fool . . .

The thoughts cascaded over me one after another, all completely ordinary and oddly comforting. But listening to the Mortans wasn't furthering my escape, so I found another set of stairs and crept down to the first floor.

This level featured several archways, and I ducked behind a diamond-shaped column and watched the people moving through the openings. The servants scurried toward an archway to my left, probably heading toward the palace kitchen, while the merchants and nobles streamed through a different opening, most likely heading toward libraries and other meeting rooms.

I eyed several more archways, but a variety of people were moving through them, and I couldn't tell where they might lead. A nearby guard kept glancing at me, clearly wondering what I was doing, so I picked an archway and walked toward it.

I was halfway across the rotunda when this . . . *presence* brushed up against my mind, stronger and sharper than all the others. The sensation was faint at first, like a light breeze tickling my face and warning of an approaching storm. Then my fingertips began violently tingling, as though I were trying to clutch a lightning bolt in my hands.

Someone very powerful was coming this way.

The last thing I needed to do was run into a magier, so I jerked back, but I wasn't watching where I was going, and my boot scraped against one of the amethyst eyes jutting up out of the strix mosaic. I stumbled, although I managed to catch myself before I hit the floor.

As soon as I regained my balance, I turned to head back in the direction I'd come, but it was too late. All around the rotunda, the guards, servants, merchants, and nobles stopped what they were doing, and their collective unease rippled through the air like a heat wave. These people might not be able to sense the magier's power like I could, but they instinctively knew that someone dangerous was approaching. All conversation ceased, although another sound rose up—the loud, steady *snap-snap-snap-snap* of heels striking the flagstones.

A woman appeared in one of the archways. Everyone froze, as though they had suddenly become mired in quicksand, and I had no choice but to freeze as well. The woman kept striding forward, the *snap-snap-snap-snap* of her heels growing louder and closer, like thunder rumbling in my direction.

The woman finally stopped near the center of the rotunda, right next to the amethyst eye that had tripped me. She was quite striking, with golden hair sleeked up into a high bun, although several streaks of silver glinted at her temples. Her face was thinner than I remembered, and wrinkles had grooved into her pale skin, especially around her dark amethyst eyes. Deeper wrinkles fanned out around her mouth, as though she had spent most of her fifty-something years perpetually pursing her lips in a displeased pucker.

She was wearing a beautiful gown of midnight-purple velvet, and the Morricone royal crest—that fancy cursive *M* surrounded by a ring of strix feathers—stretched across her chest in glittering silver thread. A silver choker studded with amethysts sparkled around her throat, while matching cuffs and rings glimmered on her wrists and fingers. All the gems practically dripped with magic, as did the woman herself.

Queen Maeven Aella Toril Morricone.

CHAPTER TWELVE

Part of me couldn't believe what I was seeing. That this was actually *happening*. Being trapped in the Morricone royal palace was bad enough, but I'd never dreamed that I'd come face-to-face with *her*.

But here I was, a few scant feet away from Queen Maeven. The woman who had orchestrated the murders of Uncle Frederich, Lord Hans, and so many others during the Seven Spire massacre. The woman who had wanted me to die right alongside them. The woman who had caused so much pain, misery, and suffering in my life, as well as in the lives of countless Andvarians and Bellonans, including Uncle Lucas and Aunt Evie.

I'm going to enjoy this. Maeven's voice whispered through my mind just as it had before the massacre.

Rage erupted inside me with all the force of a Vacunan volcano, filling my heart with boiling venom and murderous hate that seared through my shock and charred my worry to ash. Forget about escaping. Killing Maeven was the only thing that mattered.

First, I would grab the dagger out of my boot and hurl it at the bitch. If that didn't kill her, then I would reach out with my magic, force my way past her own lightning magier power, and grab hold of the energy surrounding Maeven, grab hold of *her*. Then I would give a vicious yank, toss her into the nearest column, and snap her bloody spine.

Maeven would be dead before she even hit the floor.

The gargoyle pendant hidden under my tunic grew ice-cold against my skin, almost in warning. The pieces of black jet heated up when they blocked others' thoughts, but the blue tearstone shards chilled as they soaked up my power—and strained to contain it.

The pendant grew colder—and colder still—against my heart, and the bitter chill finally iced over some of my rage. Despite my burning desire for revenge, I couldn't murder Maeven. The guards would draw their swords and rush forward the instant they realized their queen was under attack, and I wouldn't be able to kill them all before they overwhelmed and cut me down. No, escaping with my life was much more important than any revenge I could take on Maeven.

I let out a tense, ragged breath, and my pendant lost some of its bitter chill, as if it could sense that I was back in control of my emotions and my magic.

Maeven looked around the rotunda, then waved her hand. At the signal, the guards shifted on their feet, and the servants, merchants, and nobles ducked their heads and scurried away, returning to their chores and conversations, albeit much more quietly than before.

I hesitated, still not sure which way to go. Maeven must have noticed my lack of movement because she glanced in my direction. I whirled around to stride away—

"You there. Wait."

I gritted my teeth, but running from the queen wasn't an option, and I had no choice but to turn around.

Maeven strolled over and stopped in front of me, her sharp gaze locking onto my face. I stood rooted in place, not sure what to do or say.

A small flutter of movement caught my eye, and a woman stepped up beside the queen. She was a couple years younger than me, twenty-five or so, and quite lovely, with long, wavy onyx-black hair, pale skin, and dark amethyst eyes.

A short dark purple velvet cape trimmed with purple feathers covered her shoulders, while a lilac-colored gown floated around her body. A silver choker ringed her neck, and the design in the delicate filigree reminded me of the liladorn I had seen earlier. Glittering onyx vines adorned the choker, along with tiny amethysts shaped like thorns.

I had seen portraits and other likenesses of the woman, so I knew exactly who she was—Princess Delmira Myrina Cahira Morricone, Maeven's only daughter.

Delmira smiled at me and tilted her head, not in greeting, but as though she was trying to tell me something important—

My eyes widened in understanding, and I dropped down into a deep curtsy. "Your Majesty," I murmured, striving for a humble tone. "Please forgive my lack of etiquette. Your presence . . . overwhelmed me."

Silence.

The servants, merchants, and nobles kept moving through the rotunda, their whispered footsteps and murmured conversations droning through the air like bees, but a dangerous silence reigned in the bubble of space around the queen, the princess, and me.

I stayed frozen in my curtsy, even though my arms and legs trembled from the effort, and sweat gathered on the back of my neck. My body was about as firm, steady, and strong as a scoop of apricot sherbet melting in the summer sun, but I gritted my teeth and held the pose.

Even worse than the continued silence and my own exhaustion was Maeven's magic, which sizzled over me in hot, electric waves, as though I were swimming in a sea of lightning. The Mortan queen was one of the most powerful magiers on the Buchovian continent, and the tingling in my fingertips intensified to an almost painful level, while more sweat pricked the back of my neck.

"Rise," Maeven finally commanded.

I shot to my feet and clasped my hands together, trying to strike an attentive but submissive pose. I also plastered a smile on my face, as though I were absolutely *thrilled* to be the subject of the queen's attention, and not worried she was going to order the guards to murder me.

Maeven's gaze roamed over my clothes before settling on my face again. Not a flicker of emotion crossed her features, and I couldn't tell what she thought of me.

"Who are you?" she asked, a demanding note in her low, silky voice.

An excellent question. I drew in a breath, trying to think of a lie that would please the mercurial queen—

"Lady Armina!" a familiar voice called out. "There you are!"

Leonidas strode across the rotunda and stopped by my side. He was once again bundled up from head to toe in a long black cloak over an equally long black coat, while gloves covered his hands.

Relief coursed through me, along with an equal amount of wariness. He wasn't summoning the guards to have me thrown in the dungeon—or executed—but I was far from safe.

"Leonidas," Maeven said, her voice much warmer than before. "I didn't expect you to return from Ravensrock so soon."

Her words were perfectly pleasant, but a faint, chiding tone rippled through them, as if he'd somehow displeased her.

Leonidas dipped his head in apology. "Of course I returned. I would never miss your birthday."

He smiled, stepped forward, and kissed his mother's cheeks. Maeven stood there and accepted his affections, her face still poised in that blank mask.

Leonidas turned to Delmira, who surged forward and kissed his cheeks. Then she reached out and clasped his hands in hers, smiling wide.

"It's so wonderful to have you home!" she said, her voice as light and pleasant as wind chimes tinkling together.

The warmth of her love for him gusted over me, but it didn't melt any of my own icy unease.

Leonidas returned Delmira's smile with a genuine one of his own. "It's good to be back."

Delmira dropped his hands and focused on me. "And who is this?"

Leonidas stepped to the side, putting himself in between me and Maeven. "This is Lady Armina, a jeweler and metalstone master from Ravensrock. Lady Armina was being waylaid by bandits who were trying to steal the precious gems she had bought in Majesta and was taking home to Ravensrock. I dispatched the bandits, with Lyra's help, but Lady Armina was injured in the fight, so I brought her to the palace to be healed."

The smooth lies spewed from his lips one after another, and he put just the right amount of sympathy into his voice. If I hadn't known better, even I would have believed him. I hadn't been waylaid by bandits, though. Just a very charming, clever, duplicitous prince.

"Oh! How awful!" Delmira clasped her hands to her heart. "Lady Armina, I hope you're all right now."

I dipped into another curtsy, although this one was much shallower than the one I'd given to Maeven. "Thank you. I am feeling much better, Your Highness."

Delmira waved her hand. "I've never cared much for formalities. Please. Call me Delmira. Everyone does."

I doubted that, but she was the princess here, not me, and I had to cede to her request. "As you wish . . . Delmira."

Maeven stepped forward, staring at me again. "Lady Armina, you must stay at the palace until you're fully recovered," she purred. "I insist on it."

Stay at the palace? That was the very *last* thing I wanted to do, but Lady Armina could hardly argue with her supposed queen, so I bowed my head. "Thank you, Your Majesty. I would be honored."

"And, of course, you must attend all the festivities," Maeven continued.

Festivities? Then I remembered what Leonidas had said. "I'm sure the events surrounding your birthday will be a wonderful treat."

"Mmm. Yes. A treat." Her benign words didn't match her dry tone. "While you're here, you will have to make something for my daughter and me. It's been quite a while since we've commissioned pieces from an unknown jeweler."

Maeven kept staring at me, an expectant look on her face, and I forced myself to smile wide, as though I were absolutely *delighted* at the command. Getting a commission from a queen could boost a jeweler's business to incredible new heights.

"Of course!" I made my voice as light and happy as I could. "Thank you for such a wonderful opportunity!"

Maeven's lips quirked into a small, amused smile, but she waved her hand, as though her benevolence was nothing of importance. Then she focused on Leonidas again. "You must join Delmira and me for dinner tonight. Your brother and his betrothed will also be there." Once again, her benign words didn't match her dry, caustic tone.

A few months ago, an engagement had been announced between Crown Prince Milo Morricone and Lady Corvina Dumond, and the news had set tongues a-wagging in the Glitnir court. The Mortans might be our enemies, but a royal wedding was always a source of rampant speculation, gossip, and envy, before, during, and after the festivities.

Leonidas dipped his head. "Of course."

Maeven waved her hand again, dismissing his words just as she had mine. Then her gaze zoomed back over to me, much more intense and critical than before, as though she were silently cataloguing, critiquing, and calculating my worth.

I stood absolutely still, scarcely daring to breathe. Leonidas and Delmira might not have recognized me, but there was a very real chance Maeven would. After all, she utterly despised my family, so I imagined that she was as familiar with me as I was with her.

"Lady Armina," Maeven purred again, as though the most marvelous thought had just occurred to her. "You must also come to dinner tonight. As my special guest. I'm sure we can find a seat for you at my table."

Worry spiked through me. Running into the queen in the palace was one thing, but actually sitting across from her at a dining table for hours on end was another.

I dipped into yet another curtsy, giving myself a few seconds to think, before slowly rising. "Forgive me, Your Majesty, but I was not expecting such a high honor. I'm afraid that all my garments were ruined in the bandit attack, and I wouldn't want to disgrace your table by wearing something less than worthy." I put a high, nervous stammer into my voice, as though I were both disappointed that I couldn't attend the event and terrified of contradicting the queen.

If I couldn't escape from the palace before dinner, then I needed some reason not to attend. The less that Maeven saw of me, the better.

Yet again, Maeven waved her hand, dismissing my weak excuses. "Oh, I'm sure Delmira can find you something to wear.

We so rarely get visitors from Ravensrock that I would be remiss if I didn't offer you a seat at my table." A thin smile curved her lips. "Besides, I insist."

And just like that, I was trapped. I couldn't refuse now, not without making her even more suspicious, so I dipped into yet another curtsy. "Thank you, Your Majesty. I will be honored to dine at your table."

"Until tonight, Lady Armina." Maeven eyed me a second longer, then swept past me.

CHAPTER THIRTEEN

Maeven strode across the rotunda and vanished through an archway. Her heels *snap-snap-snap-snapped* against the floor again, although the sound quickly faded away. So did the feel of her magic, and my fingertips finally stopped tingling.

The storm had blown right on by me, and I hadn't been struck by its lightning—yet.

The guards, servants, merchants, and nobles all visibly relaxed, and everyone moved and spoke at a more normal pace and volume again. Leonidas, Delmira, and I remained in the center of the rotunda.

Delmira gave me another sunny smile. "Mother's right. I can find something for you to wear to dinner. Let me speak to my thread master, and I'll have some things sent to my chambers. You can visit me there this afternoon, after you've had a chance to eat and rest. I'll send a servant to fetch you."

I planned to be long gone by then, but I couldn't refuse her offer any more than I'd been able to refuse Maeven's order. "Thank you, Your Highness—"

She shot me a warning look.

"Thank you, Delmira."

The princess smiled at me again, then glided off, the gauzy layers of her lilac dress seeming as thin and fragile as butterfly wings trailing along behind her. That left me alone with Leonidas.

"Lady Armina." He offered me his arm. "You must be famished after your ordeal. Please allow me to escort you to breakfast."

"Of course, Your Highness." I threaded my arm through his, trying not to notice the coiled strength in his muscles.

Leonidas steered me through one of the archways and down a hallway. As we walked along, he played the part of the perfect host, pointing out the paintings and tapestries decorating the walls, along with the historic sculptures, books, and weapons tucked away in various nooks and alcoves.

Our journey did not go unnoticed. Several nobles and merchants were moving through the same hallway, and they all nodded respectfully as Leonidas led me past them. None of them said anything, but I could still hear their thoughts.

Who's that with the prince . . .

She's not even wearing a proper gown . . .

Why is she wasting her time on him? He'll never be king. Leonidas will be lucky if he makes it to yuletide without being murdered by Milo . . .

Leonidas grimaced, as if he too had heard that last snide thought.

I eyed the prince, wondering why Milo, his own brother, wanted to murder him. Still, the news didn't surprise me. The Morricones weren't known to be a particularly loving family, and I'd heard more than one rumor that Milo was even more ruthless than Queen Maeven.

Leonidas led me up the stairs and back into the wing where I'd first woken up. More people roamed through the halls than before, servants mostly, going about their chores, but this part of the palace still seemed largely, strangely empty.

We reached a pair of double doors. Leonidas waved his hand, and the doors unlocked and opened. He led me inside. "This is my personal library."

The library was housed in a square tower that rose up three stories. To my right, several dark purple velvet settees and chairs flanked an enormous fireplace that took up the entire wall. Flames crackled merrily behind the iron grate, driving away some of the chill that permeated this wing of the palace.

To my left, ebony bookcases stretched up to the ceiling. Books filled the shelves, along with maps, statues, and other odds and ends. An ebony writing desk covered with more books, stacks of papers, black feather pens, and pots of purple ink squatted in the back of the room. Behind the desk, glass doors were set into the wall, showing a glimpse of a courtyard below—the same courtyard that my chambers overlooked.

"Your library is lovely," I said, and meant it. "Warm and cozy and perfectly cluttered."

A rare, genuine smile creased Leonidas's face, softening his angular features and making him look far more relaxed—and much more handsome—than usual. I resisted the urge to return his smile. Instead, I untangled my arm from his and went over to the fireplace, putting some distance between us.

I scanned the mantel, but no swords adorned it, so I dropped my gaze, looking for a poker or something else I might use as a weapon, along with the dagger in my boot, should the need arise. Sadly, I didn't see anything like that, although the fireplace itself was quite unusual.

At first glance, it seemed to be made of gleaming onyx, but then I realized that vines of liladorn had punched through the gray stone and curled around the fireplace, like fingers stretching out in search of warmth. The way the vines and their long black thorns curved made it seem as though the liladorn was supporting the wall, instead of the other way around.

I trailed my fingers over one of the vines, which was as smooth and slick as glass, yet rock-hard and strangely flexible at the same time, just like Grimley's skin. Curious. I would have to ask Helene what she knew about liladorn when I returned to Glitnir.

If I returned to Glitnir.

Footsteps scuffed, and servants streamed into the library, carrying everything from linens to silverware to crystal carafes filled with fruit juices. The servants bustled over to a table close to the fireplace and deposited their items with quick, practiced efficiency. They retreated, and another wave of servants entered, carrying platters of food. In less than two minutes, the servants had laid out a feast fit for a prince.

"Lady Armina, given your ordeal over the past few days, I thought you might enjoy a quiet breakfast," Leonidas said.

"Exactly how long have I been convalescing in Myrkvior?" I asked. "Everything is a bit of a blur."

"I came across you on the afternoon of the twenty-third. We arrived at the palace late last night, and it is now the morning of the twenty-fifth."

So I had been down in the mine for roughly half a day before he had rescued me, and I had been unconscious for more than an entire day after that. Topacia would have immediately alerted my father and grandfather that Leonidas had spirited me away from Blauberg. They all had to be worried sick, but I couldn't do anything about that right now.

"You must be hungry," Leonidas continued. "So I had the servants prepare extras of everything."

He seemed determined to maintain his lies about who I was and what I was doing here, so I decided to play along. Since he had referred to me by my fake name and title, I dipped into a shallow curtsy before rising and addressing him.

"How thoughtful. Thank you, Your Highness."

Leonidas smirked at my snide tone, as though my petulance amused him. "Oh, Lady Armina. There's no need to stand on formality. Please call me Leonidas." He gestured at the table. "Let us eat."

Once again, I had no choice but to do as commanded. Leonidas pulled out a chair, and I dropped into it, grateful to sit down, since I was still tired. He moved around the table and took the seat across from mine.

Leonidas nodded at the servants. "Thank you. That will be all."

The servants left the library. One of them pulled the doors shut behind her, leaving me alone with the prince. Leonidas tilted his head to the side, and his eyes narrowed, as though he was using his magic to make sure that the servants had really retreated.

"I hope you like blackberry pancakes," he said, shaking his head in warning. "They are one of my favorites."

His voice wasn't any louder than normal, although he was clearly putting on a show for whoever was lurking out in the hallway.

"Of course," I replied, matching his fake politeness. "I'm quite famished after my long journey from *Ravensrock* and especially my *ordeal* with those horrible *bandits*."

Leonidas arched an eyebrow at my sarcastic emphasis, but he gestured at the platters of food. "Then please eat."

My mouth watered, and my stomach rumbled even more loudly than Grimley's did whenever he waxed poetic about plump wild turkeys. I piled a plate high with the aforementioned blackberry pancakes, along with smoked sausages, fried potatoes, fresh fruit, and cheeses. My stomach kept rumbling, demanding food, but I waited until Leonidas had taken a bite of everything to make sure that the dishes weren't poisoned. When he didn't keel over, I started eating.

Light, airy pancakes stuffed with tart blackberries. Hearty sausages seasoned with sage. Golden brown potatoes sprinkled with dill. I quickly polished off that plate of food and ate another one, and gulped down three glasses of a sweet cranberry-apple punch with a refreshing zing of lemon.

Leonidas stopped eating after just one plate, but I kept chewing, working on my third serving of everything. While I ate, he talked about inane things. The food, the weather, the Mortan gladiator troupes and their popular fighters. All the usual things one would chitchat about over breakfast. I made the appropriate grunts when called upon, but I mostly concentrated on shoveling food into my mouth. My body needed fuel to finish recovering from the injuries I'd sustained in the mine, and I didn't know when I might get another chance to eat.

I was wondering if I could stuff another pancake into my stomach when Leonidas pushed back from the table. My hand tightened around my fork, but he merely went over and grabbed a long purple riding coat from a rack in the corner. He returned and held the garment out to me.

"May I?" he murmured.

I eyed him with suspicion, but he didn't seem to be up to anything nefarious, and I didn't sense any magic or poison emanating from the garment, so I released my fork, stood up, and reluctantly turned my back to him. Leonidas slipped the coat onto my arms. His warm breath brushed up against my cheek, and a ribbon of heat unspooled in my stomach.

I stepped away from him and buttoned up the coat, which was similar to his black one, although it was obviously made for a woman. I wondered why it was in his library—and who might have worn it before me.

"You looked a bit chilled," Leonidas murmured. "That should keep you warm."

He was right. Even with the fire, the library was still cool and drafty, and the coat was surprisingly warm, soft, and lightweight. I drew in a breath. The garment also smelled like honeysuckle, like *him*, which both pleased and annoyed me.

"Thank you," I muttered.

"Let's take a walk. There is so much more of the palace for you to see." His voice wasn't particularly loud, but I once again got the impression he was saying the words for someone else's benefit, instead of mine.

Leonidas held his arm out to me again. I stared at it—at *him*—still trying to determine his motives. Just because he hadn't killed me yet didn't mean that he didn't have some awful death in mind for me later. But I wasn't going to get any answers by standing here, so I threaded my arm through his again.

He opened the library doors with a wave of his hand, and we stepped back out into the hallway. A servant was standing a few feet away, ostensibly dusting a table, although she kept sneaking glances at us. Leonidas walked right on by the old woman as if he didn't even see her, much less realize that she was spying on him.

The prince led me through several corridors. The servant trailed after us, but Leonidas finally lost her by climbing up some steps, quickly walking along a hallway to a different set of steps, going down them, and doubling back the way we'd just come.

We didn't pass any more servants, spies, or anyone else. These corridors were sparsely furnished, with only a few tables and chairs, and it was still quite chilly in this section of the palace, despite the fires burning in the libraries and other common rooms. I shivered, grateful for the warmth of the borrowed coat.

"Are you sure we're actually in Myrkvior?" I sniped as we stepped into yet another deserted corridor. "Or did the queen banish you to the wing that was the farthest away from hers?"

"Something like that," he replied. "I learned at a very young age that it was safer for me, as a bastard prince, to be as far away from the legitimate Morricone royals as possible."

"But surely that changed after—" I bit back the rest of my words.

"After my mother killed King Maximus, her own brother, and took the throne for herself? And my uncle Nox killed Mercer, the legitimate crown prince?" Leonidas laughed, although the sound was brimming with bitterness. "Oh, yes. Things did change after that. But not for the better. Not for everyone."

Not for me.

He didn't say the words aloud, or even think them in his mind, but they still resonated in the air between us. A tiny needle of sympathy pricked my heart. Being a royal was never easy, not even for Princess Gemma with her pampered Glitzma persona and supposedly charmed, carefree life. I'd seen the toll being a bastard prince had taken on my uncle, Lucas Sullivan, and I could imagine how much worse it would have been for Leonidas—and Maeven too.

After she had murdered Maximus during the Regalia Games roughly sixteen years ago, several of the legitimate Morricone royals had tried to take the throne from the bastard queen. Maeven had killed everyone who had openly challenged her, but the ones who were smart enough to submit to her rule supposedly *despised* the queen. So did many of the wealthier nobles who'd wanted the crown for themselves, and I'd heard more than one rumor about assassination attempts, both against Maeven and her children.

More needles of sympathy pricked my heart. Leonidas's daily life at Myrkvior was probably more fraught with danger than mine had ever been on any of my spy missions. Except for this one, of course.

"I'm sorry," I said. "That things have been . . . difficult for you."

He nodded, accepting my condolences, although he didn't look at me.

We walked in silence, moving through the hallways before stepping through some glass doors and emerging onto a third-floor balcony. Leonidas led me over to the shadows that were pooled around a column, and I peered over the railing. Instead of some interior section of the palace, this balcony overlooked an enormous open-air courtyard with an archway that led out into the city of Majesta beyond.

"And this," Leonidas said, sweeping his hand out wide, "is the true heart of the Morricones."

In the courtyard below, butchers, bakers, and other merchants manned wooden carts and stalls, hawking everything from cuts of meat to loaves of bread to bolts of cloth, while shoppers meandered along, admiring all the goods. Servants, guards, nobles, commoners. Men, women, children. People of all shapes, sizes, and stations moved through the busy marketplace, and a hundred conversations buzzed in my ears. My gargoyle pendant grew warm against my chest, but we were high enough above the crowd that people's thoughts were soft whispers that didn't overwhelm me.

The pendant heating up against my skin reminded me that Leonidas had to have seen it, along with the gargoyle crest embedded in the dagger still hidden in my right boot. And yet, he hadn't said anything about either one of them. His lack of interest made me even more suspicious about what he truly wanted from me.

"What do you think of Myrkvior?" Leonidas asked, pride rippling through his voice.

"It's wonderful," I said, and meant it.

He glanced around, as if making sure we were still alone and hidden in the shadows. Then he turned to me, his face serious. "I know that Mortans don't have the best reputation, especially in Andvari and Bellona, but we really are just people who are trying to do our jobs and support our families and live our lives in peace."

Peace was most definitely not the word that came to my mind when thinking about Mortans. As a child, I had often pictured the Morricone royals holed up in creepy candlelit chambers, gleefully cackling as they plotted the destruction of my family, along with their other enemies.

But Leonidas was right—the people below were going about the business of running their kingdom just like Andvarians, Bellonans, and everyone else did. I wasn't sure how I felt about that. About seeing the Mortans as actual *people* instead of name-less, faceless enemies who wanted me and my family dead. It was a bit disconcerting, to say the least.

"I wanted you to see this," Leonidas continued. "Before you go."

My eyebrows shot up in surprise. "Go where? To the palace dungeon?"

Leonidas's face crinkled with confusion. "Home, of course. I would never throw you in the dungeon. Especially not after you saved my life."

He seemed sincere, but he had also seemed sincere in the woods when we were children, right before he had handed me over to a turncoat guard.

"Rescuing me from the mine was one thing. You owed me for saving you from Wexel. But why bring me here?"

He shrugged. "The best healers in Morta are in Myrkvior, and you were still more dead than alive, even after getting par-tially healed in the mine."

"So you brought me, an Andvarian spy, to the Mortan royal

palace, and now you're going to let me go? Just like that?" I didn't bother to keep the suspicion out of my voice.

"Just like that."

"Well, I suppose I should take you up on your offer—before your brother murders you."

Leonidas's face remained smooth, although his body tensed, just a bit. "I don't know what you're talking about."

I snorted. "Oh, please. You overheard the same thought that I did when we were walking through the palace earlier. Is Milo really plotting to kill you?"

He didn't respond, but his lips pressed into a tight, unhappy line.

"Well, if you won't answer my questions, then I'll just have to assume that the rumors are true."

"What rumors?" Leonidas asked in a guarded tone.

"Crown Prince Milo Morricone is *quite* the legend in Andvari," I drawled. "Not only is he rumored to be an extremely powerful lightning magier, but he is also said to be exceedingly smart, cruel, and ruthless. Many Mortan nobles and merchants who have visited Glitnir whisper that *everyone* at Myrkvior is afraid of Milo, including Queen Maeven and the other Morricone royals. Which would include *you*."

This time, Leonidas snorted. "I am *not* afraid of Milo."

"But your brother *is* dangerous, and he *does* want to kill you."

A humorless smile curved his lips. "Milo wouldn't be a Morricone otherwise."

My mind whirred, trying to make sense of this new information. Suddenly, I saw everything that had happened in Blauberg in a new light. "Your brother has *already* tried to kill you, through Wexel. The captain works for Milo, doesn't he?"

Leonidas didn't confirm my suspicion, but I didn't need him to. Delmira had been thrilled to see him in the rotunda earlier, and Maeven had seemed fond enough of her second son. Neither one of them appeared to have any murderous intentions toward Leonidas, which left Milo as the most likely suspect.

Leonidas's lips puckered, as though he had bitten into something sour. "My brother has always been . . . ambitious."

Ambitious? That was a polite way of saying that Milo was just as greedy, vicious, and ruthless as the Morricone kings and queens who had come before him.

Milo had long objected to the tenuous peace and trade treaties that Queen Maeven had struck and maintained with the other kingdoms, but the crown prince seemed to have a special hatred for Andvari. I wasn't sure why he despised my kingdom so much, other than all the old prejudices that Mortans and Andvarians had against each other. The two kingdoms and their respective peoples had never gotten along, much like strixes and gargoyles were more apt to fight whenever they saw each other, instead of simply letting each other be.

"Given the articles he's published in the penny papers, everyone knows that Milo wants to restore Morta to what he views as its glory days," I said. "Back when King Maximus almost succeeded in getting Andvari and Bellona to go to war against each other."

Back when your mother orchestrated my uncle's murder. The thought whispered through my mind, but I shoved it down, lest he overhear it with his magic.

Leonidas shook his head. "Milo is much more aggressive and volatile than Maximus ever was. He doesn't want to sit back and watch a war between two other kingdoms. Milo wants to be the one who *starts* the war."

I reared back in surprise. There had long been rumors that Milo wanted to attack the other kingdoms, but I hadn't thought him bold—or stupid—enough to actually do it. Not given how Grandfather Heinrich, Father, and Rhea had bolstered the Andvarian army and our other defenses over the last sixteen years, and the treaties that guaranteed Bellona, Unger, and the other kingdoms would come to our aid if Morta ever did attack Andvari.

And there was one other large, glaring problem with Milo wanting to start a war—he was still just the crown prince. Maeven was the queen, which meant that *she* commanded the Mortan army and its legions of soldiers. Not Milo.

Not until Maeven was no longer queen.

Understanding punched into my stomach. "You think your brother is going to try to depose your mother."

Leonidas's lips puckered again. "Mother is one of the few things holding Milo back from his . . . ambitions."

Ambitions? What he really meant was *rage and slaughter*, and we both knew it.

Leonidas leaned a shoulder against the column, as if suddenly weary. A liladorn vine had twined around the stone, and he idly rubbed his thumb over it. The vine undulated beneath his finger, like a cat arching into a welcome back scratch, although he didn't seem to notice the motion.

He dropped his hand from the vine and looked at me again. "Yes, I do think Milo has . . . plans for my mother."

A sea of emotions roiled through me. Worry, concern, disgust—and more than a little malicious glee. As a child, I had often dreamed of killing Maeven, of stabbing a dagger straight into her heart, just as Vasilia Blair had done to Uncle Frederich during the Seven Spire massacre. I still fantasized about it sometimes, especially when I snapped out of one of my ghosting visions, shaking and sweating from all the horrible memories my magic had dredged up.

"But my mother can take care of herself," Leonidas continued. "My main concern right now is the tearstone that's been stolen from your mine."

My mind kept whirring, putting the rest of the puzzle pieces together. "So *Milo* is the one stealing and stockpiling Andvarian tearstone. Why? What is he planning to do with it?"

"I don't know."

I huffed in disbelief and crossed my arms over my chest.

Leonidas shook his head. "Doubt me if you want, but I don't know my brother's exact plans. I wasn't even sure that he was the one buying the tearstone. Not until Wexel tried to kill me in Blauberg. That's when I knew the rumors were true."

"What rumors?" This time, I had to ask the question.

He stared out over the marketplace, but his eyes dimmed, as though he was peering at something in his own mind instead of at the people shopping below. "That Milo is having the tearstone brought to his personal workshop. That he's been experimenting, trying to turn it into some sort of weapon." He paused, and his voice dropped even lower. "One that he wants to use against Andvari and the other kingdoms."

So my suspicion about the tearstone being turned into weapons was correct, although I'd mistakenly thought it was Maeven's scheme, instead of Milo's plot. Still, Leonidas's revelations increased my worry and dread.

The Morricones were famed tinkerers who experimented with magic, blood, creatures, and more. Years ago, King Maximus had created a powder of crushed tearstone and amethyst-eye poison that helped him absorb magic by drinking strix blood. If what Leonidas said was true and Milo was even worse than his uncle . . . Well, I didn't even want to *imagine* what sorts of horrors the crown prince had created in his workshop.

"Milo knows that I don't agree with his ambitions," Leonidas continued. "But he has a lot of support among the nobles and others in the palace."

Once again, he was hinting at the truth without actually delivering the full, heavy weight of it.

"You mean that your brother has people watching your every move and reporting back to him, like that old woman who followed us earlier. And that he'll see you coming if you try to thwart him."

"Yes. Milo has spies everywhere, and he is well protected."

"So that's why you were in Blauberg," I said. "You couldn't find out what Milo was up to here at Myrkvior, so you decided to attack the problem from the other end. To track down where the tearstone was coming from and see if you could pick up any clues there."

"Yes. But instead of clues, I found you."

His low, deep voice rasped against my skin, and something flared in his eyes, making them burn bright and hot. The emotion vanished before I could put a proper name to it, but his intense expression made my stomach clench. My arms were still crossed over my chest, and my fingers dug into my elbows, as if that would shield me from whatever he was thinking, as well as from my own treacherous attraction to him.

"But my feud with my brother is none of your concern," Leonidas said. "It will end the way such things always do between Morricones."

"And how is that?"

"With one of us killing the other."

His cold, matter-of-fact tone sent a shiver down my spine. We might both be mind magiers, might both be royals, but in some ways, we were as different as night and day, especially when it came to our families. I would die to protect Father, Grandfather Heinrich, Rhea, Grimley, Topacia, Alvis, Xenia, Uncle Lucas, and Aunt Evie. Leonidas would probably have to murder his own brother just to make it to the end of the year.

He dug into his coat pocket, pulled out a purple velvet pouch, and tossed it over to me. I caught it, and the *tink-tink-tink* of coins filled the air.

"There's more than enough money in there for you to travel

back to Blauberg." Leonidas gestured at the courtyard below. "All you have to do is slip out of the marketplace. No one will stop you."

I hefted the bag in my hand, even as I weighed options in my mind. He was right. I could go down to the marketplace, walk out through the open gates, and disappear into the city. From there, I could take a train back to the Mortan-Andvarian border, then call out to Grimley and have him fly me back over the Spire Mountains to Blauberg.

Or I could stay here and spy on the Morricones.

Despite everything I'd learned, I still had no idea what Milo planned to do with the thousands of pounds of tearstone that he'd stolen. If he was making a new weapon, like Leonidas had suggested, then I needed to find out as much about it as possible. Milo had already orchestrated the deaths of dozens of Andvarians. What kind of future queen would I be if I didn't do everything in my power to keep him from murdering even more of my people?

Back in Blauberg, I'd joked to Topacia and Grimley that this mission was an adventure. But it was turning out to be a *necessity*, one that just might make the difference between Andvari falling to Morta or emerging intact from this growing conflict.

And then there was the not-so-simple matter of my own pride. I hadn't saved myself in Blauberg, which rankled me as badly as a burr under a horse's saddle. I hadn't been clever enough to figure out that Conley was planning to kill me, and I hadn't been strong enough, either physically or in my magic, to keep him and his men from getting the better of me. As much as I hated to admit it, the only reason I was still alive was because Leonidas had rescued me.

Well, now I had a chance to potentially save everyone in Andvari, and I wasn't going to let my people, my family, or myself down. I was *not* going to be a bloody failure. Not again. Not like I'd been in the mine, and especially not like I'd been during the Seven Spire massacre.

"Where, exactly, is Ravensrock?"

"It's a small city in northern Morta." Confusion filled Leonidas's face. "Why do you ask?"

"Lady Armina should know where her hometown is."

His eyebrows shot up. "You can't possibly want to stay here."

"Why not? I'm an Andvarian spy, and you've paved the way for me to skulk around Myrkvior to my heart's content. I would be remiss if I didn't take advantage of such a golden opportunity."

He shook his head again. "We both know it's not safe for you to stay here. I saw your gargoyle pendant and the matching crest in your dagger. I know that you . . . work for the Ripleys."

Leonidas stumbled over the last few words, as though my family's name was difficult for him to say. Perhaps it was, given all the misery that Maeven and the Bastard Brigade had inflicted on my family. I wondered if Leonidas remembered how much pain *he* had inflicted on me when we had met as children. Probably not.

I shoved away my petty feelings about the past and focused on what was important right now. "Who else saw my pendant and dagger? Who else have you told about me?"

"No one," he replied. "I took off your pendant and removed your dagger before I let the bone masters heal you, and I only put them back in your chambers when I was sure no one would disturb you. No one here has any reason to think you are anyone other than Lady Armina from Ravensrock."

I eyed him, but he once again seemed sincere. "Good. Then I can pretend to be Lady Armina, nose around, and see what I can find out about Milo and the missing tearstone. You said it yourself that your brother has people watching you. Perhaps they won't pay as much attention to me."

"Your idea is madness—*utter madness*," Leonidas snapped. "If Milo finds out who you are, he will torture and kill you. *Immediately*. And if my mother finds out . . ." His voice trailed off. "Well, it will be worse than anything Milo can dream up."

Memories of the massacre flickered through my mind. He was probably right about that.

"Just . . . go home, Armina."

His calling me Armina instead of my real name grated like sandpaper on my already raw nerves. He was ordering me about, and he didn't even have the bloody courtesy to recognize or remember me. I knew it was a ridiculous sentiment, and that I was far safer this way, but it still angered and frustrated me, especially since I'd *never* been able to forget him, no matter how hard I had tried.

And I had fucking tried—for *years*.

"I am not yours to command," I replied in an icy tone.

"Please." Leonidas ground out the word, as though saying it pained him even more than uttering the Ripley name. "Please go home. Before it's too late."

"No. You can either help me or stay out of my way. Your choice."

His eyes narrowed. "I am not yours to command either."

"At last, something we both agree on."

Leonidas glared at me, then dropped his head and leaned a little more heavily against the liladorn vine that had twined around the column, as though he needed the support of both the sturdy plant and the stone underneath. A weary sigh escaped his lips, but he lifted his head and raised his gaze to mine again.

"I've been trying to uncover Milo's plot for weeks. All my spies mysteriously vanished for several days before their bodies turned up in various parts of Majesta. They all had one thing in common—they had been tortured before they died." He kept staring at me. "I don't want the same thing to happen to you."

Once again, his concern seemed genuine, but I pushed it aside.

"I can easily pass for a noble, if that's what you're worried about. After all, nobles rarely do any real work, and their main occupations are complaining, scheming, and making other people's lives difficult."

"You are certainly making mine difficult," Leonidas grumbled.

I ignored his complaint and considered the rest of my Lady Armina persona. "Being a jeweler is no big stretch for me either, and metalstone magic is easy to fake, especially for a mind magier. All I'll have to do is wave my hand and move some rocks around."

I was already quite familiar with such a charade. Throughout Andvari and the other kingdoms, Princess Gemma Ripley was known as a metalstone master with a moderate amount of magic. Only my family and a few trusted friends knew that I was really a mind magier.

And Leonidas, of course. He had seen how dangerous I was, even if he didn't seem to bloody remember it.

"You've thought of everything, haven't you?" he muttered.

I grinned. "I do try."

He rolled his eyes. "Well, you might be pleased with your scheme, but Milo is sure to be suspicious of anyone I come into contact with, especially a mysterious noble lady no one has ever heard of before that I supposedly rescued from bandits. I've read fairy tales that weren't so ridiculously dramatic."

I arched an eyebrow. "And yet, that's the story *you* conjured. Does Prince Leonidas have a deep-seated wish to play the part of the dashing hero?"

He barked out a bitter laugh. "I am no one's bloody *hero*. But I wouldn't have had to come up with such a ridiculous story if you had just stayed in your room. I was going to smuggle you out of the palace without anyone important realizing you had even been here."

Yet again, he seemed sincere. Leonidas had gone to a lot of trouble to save me from the mine, bring me here, and have me healed. Those gestures warmed my heart, but I couldn't forget how he had betrayed me in the past—and could do so again at any moment.

"Well, since I've already ruined your plans, then you might as well go along with mine," I said in a cheery tone. "We both want the same thing, and we have a far better chance of finding out what Milo is plotting by working together, rather than trampling over each other like we've been doing so far."

"What, exactly, are you proposing?" he asked, his voice wary.

"A partnership," I replied. "Milo might be suspicious of me, but he will still focus his attention on *you*. So you keep your brother and his spies occupied, and I will roam around the palace, pick up gossip, and find out what Milo plans to do with the stolen tearstone."

If I was anywhere else but Myrkvior, I would have taken my chances spying on my own. But this was Leonidas's home, not mine, and it would be far better to align myself with the prince, especially since he could blow my Lady Armina cover at any moment. Also, if I kept him close, then perhaps I could anticipate any moves he might make against me—and escape another dangerous betrayal.

"And then what?" Leonidas asked.

"And then I'll leave."

His eyes narrowed. "You'll leave Myrkvior once you uncover Milo's plot? Just like that?"

"Just like that."

"And what about . . . the Ripleys?" Once again, he stumbled over my family's name.

I shrugged. "The Ripleys wanted me to find out who was

stealing their tearstone. I already did that, and Conley should be rotting in jail even as we speak. But the Ripleys probably think I ran off, instead of being waylaid by you. Returning with information about what Milo is plotting will help smooth things over with the Ripleys."

I might be twisting the truth around to suit my own purposes, but I wasn't lying about everything. Learning about Milo's plans for the tearstone *would* go a long way toward appeasing my father and grandfather, who were sure to be livid about the danger I was putting myself in.

Thinking about my family prompted me to toss the bag of coins back at Leonidas. "Keep your money. Give me a Cardea mirror instead. A small handheld one will do."

His eyes narrowed again. "Why do you want a Cardea mirror?"

"So I can contact my employers and tell them what I'm doing. That way, if my body does show up in some alley, then they'll at least know why I was killed."

Once again, my words weren't all lies. I did want to let my family know what had happened to me—and especially that Milo was targeting Andvari.

Leonidas hesitated. Uncertainty creased his face, along with a faint flicker of worry.

"No mirror, no deal," I said.

His features iced over, and he stepped forward, looming over me. In an instant, he had morphed back into the same dark, deadly shadow knight he'd been in the mine. A prince that you either obeyed or suffered his wrath. "I don't have to agree to your demands *or* your deal. I can summon some guards to have you forcibly removed from the palace right now."

Worry snaked through my stomach, but I gave him a nonchalant shrug. "Then I'll just find some way to slip back into the palace."

Frustration filled his face. "You are going to get yourself killed."

He was probably right about that, although I would never admit it.

"I am *not* yours to command," I repeated, my voice even colder than before. "My life is my own, and this is the gamble that *I* choose to make with it."

Leonidas glared at me, fury sparking in his eyes. I glared right back at him. The prince's fingers twitched, as though he wanted to throttle me, just as I wanted to throttle him right now.

"You want to be partners? Very well," he snapped. "If I give you a Cardea mirror and help you skulk about the palace, then you will leave Myrkvior the moment we figure out what Milo is planning to do with the tearstone. That is *my* demand."

I hesitated. Despite all my tough talk, I still had serious misgivings about this scheme. Being in Blauberg had been dangerous enough, but now I was in the Mortan capital, in the heart of the royal palace, literally surrounded by enemies on all sides. If anyone were to even *suspect* that I was Gemma Ripley, then I would be imprisoned and tortured—at the very *least*. As much as I despised the Morricones, I had to admit they were exceedingly sly and clever. All it would take to doom myself was one wrong look, one false word, one small slip of the tongue.

Still, I would never have a better opportunity to prove myself as a spy—and as a future queen. Everleigh Blair and Zariza Rubin had defended their kingdoms from the Morricones, and I wanted to do the same, just as my father, grandfather, Armina Ripley, and all my other ancestors had done before me. People might think I was Glitzma, a ditzy, dumb, pampered princess, but I wanted to show everyone I was *more* than that, that I was strong enough to protect them. This would be my chance to prove that to everyone.

Perhaps this would also convince my father and grandfather

that I could take care of myself and that I wasn't the scared, battered, broken girl who'd returned from the Seven Spire massacre and hadn't been able to leave her room for days at a time.

Perhaps it would finally convince me of that too.

Either way, it was simply too good an opportunity to pass up. If Milo Morricone was stockpiling tearstone for an attack on Andvari, then I needed to know exactly what he was plotting. Plus, skulking around the palace would also give me a chance to spy on the Mortan nobles, as well as the queen. Maybe I could also gather enough intelligence to thwart whatever schemes Maeven might be hatching.

Leonidas held his hand out to me. "Are we agreed?"

I was already behind enemy lines. I might as well make the most of it. So I stepped forward and took his hand. "Agreed."

I started to let go, but his fingers tightened around mine, and something flared in his eyes, something even hotter and more intense than his previous fury, although I couldn't quite put a name to it. Anticipation, maybe. Or maybe an expectation, although of what, I couldn't imagine. Either way, his steady gaze made another ribbon of heat unspool in my stomach.

Leonidas released my hand. "Very well. But don't say I didn't warn you."

He spun around and stalked away, his black cloak swirling around his body. I let out the breath I hadn't even realized I'd been holding and followed him, wondering just how big of a mistake I was truly making.

CHAPTER FOURTEEN

Now that our deal had been struck, Leonidas led me off the balcony and back to his library. He rummaged around in his desk for a minute, then straightened up and slipped something into his pocket.

He gestured at me, and I followed him out of the library and back to the chambers I had woken up in this morning. Servants had made the bed and set out trays of sweet cakes, fresh fruit, and other treats, along with chilled carafes of water, juices, and teas. A fire had also been lit, adding some cozy warmth to the area.

Leonidas tilted his head to the side, as if reaching out with his magic and making sure no one was hiding nearby. When he was satisfied, he dug into his pocket, drew out a small silver compact, and held it out to me. Liladorn vines and thorns were embossed in the metal, and the compact looked like it might contain almond powder to take the shine off a noble's nose.

"What's this?" I asked, taking the compact.

"A Cardea mirror."

Surprise shot through me. "You just *happened* to have a Cardea mirror tucked away in your desk?"

"If you don't want it . . ."

My fingers curled around the compact, and I pulled it back out of his reach. Another one of those smug, infuriating smirks stretched across his face. My fingers tightened around the disk, and I had the childish urge to throw it back at him. But that would have been foolish, so I dropped my hand to my side instead.

Leonidas's smirk widened, as if he knew exactly what I was thinking. "The compact contains a mirror, along with a compass. You can use the mirror two ways. Just open the cover and speak a name, and the mirror will show you that person, no matter where they are, although you won't be able to talk to them."

"And the second way?"

He gestured over at the vanity-table mirror. "Open the compact and set it against the base of any mirror, and it will turn that larger glass into a true Cardea mirror, one that will let you see and speak to other people through their own Cardea mirrors."

My fingers curled a little tighter around the compact. A very useful tool.

"I would contact your people now. Delmira will summon you to her chambers soon, and she will probably have racks of dresses for you to try on." His tone was dry, and I couldn't tell if he was pleased by his sister's impending generosity or warning me about it. Perhaps both.

"And what will you be doing?"

His features hardened into that cold, familiar mask. "Trying to figure out what Milo has been up to while I've been gone."

Once again, I was struck by just how much Leonidas resembled Maeven, and I had to hold back a shudder.

"Delmira will escort you to the dinner," Leonidas continued. "It begins with a social hour. If you are still determined to go through with your scheme, perhaps you can nose around then and see if you can pick up any gossip about Milo. Even the smallest whisper could be useful in figuring out where he's hiding the tearstone."

Picking up gossip was something I excelled at, both as a princess and as a spy. "Very well. Until tonight."

"Until tonight."

His eyes locked with mine, and more of that unwanted heat spiraled through my stomach. I shifted on my feet, suddenly uncomfortable, and a faint *swish* of fabric caught my ear. I was still wearing the purple riding coat, the one that smelled of his heady honeysuckle scent.

"Here. You should take this back."

I started to unbutton the coat, but Leonidas shook his head. "Keep it. The palace can be quite chilly."

We stared at each other for a heartbeat longer, then Leonidas gave me a deep, formal bow, as though I truly were a noble lady that he fancied, and not the unwanted spy that he'd foolishly brought into his palace. He straightened up, spun around, and left the chambers. He waved his hand, and the doors closed behind him.

I waited, expecting to hear the telltale *click* of the lock sliding home, but it never sounded. I reached out with my magic, but Leonidas's presence grew dim and faint, then vanished. He had gone to another part of the palace.

I was surprised he hadn't locked me in the chambers. Then again, I supposed there was no point, since I had escaped earlier. Or perhaps it was a more subtle ploy, and he thought that leaving the doors open would make me trust him. Or perhaps he knew the same hard truth I did—that a couple of locked doors weren't nearly enough to protect me from the danger waiting around every corner here.

As much as it pained me, I took Leonidas's advice, sat down at the vanity table, and opened the compact. A compass was nestled in one side of the silver, with a mirror embedded in the other side. The compass was just a compass, but magic poured off the mirror in steady waves. It truly was a Cardea mirror.

Some of the tight knots of tension in my stomach loosened. I still didn't—*couldn't*—trust Leonidas, but he had kept his word. About this, at least.

I reached out with my magic, but I didn't sense anyone loitering outside my chambers. Since there were no spies around, I placed the compact on the table, making sure the side with the mirror touched the bottom of the much larger vanity-table mirror. Many Cardea mirrors were one large sheet of glass that was enchanted, and then split in two, so that the person with one half of the mirror could talk to the person with the other half. But Leonidas had said the compact would let me talk to anyone with a Cardea mirror.

Time to find out.

I closed my eyes and pictured Topacia in my mind. Her dark brown hair, the freckles dotting her nose, her cheery smile. Then I opened my eyes, leaned forward, and spoke to the compact. "Show me Topacia."

As soon as I said her name, the compact started glowing with a bright silvery light, and waves of magic rippled out of the small round mirror and traveled up into the larger rectangular one atop the vanity table. The glass there rocked violently, as though my command was a stone that had been dropped into the mirror and upset its naturally smooth surface.

A few seconds later, the intense light in the compact mirror faded to a softer glow, the ripples of magic stopped, and the surface of the vanity-table mirror grew still again. Now, instead of my own reflection, I was staring into the cottage in Blauberg.

Topacia always insisted that we travel with a Cardea mirror

so that we could contact my father if needed, and she had set up the freestanding mirror in the corner of the living room. It was the same mirror I had used to check my miner's disguise the day this whole adventure had started.

"Topacia?" I called out. "Are you there?"

Silence. Several seconds ticked by. She must not be in the cottage—

"Gemma? Gemma! Is that you?" Footsteps pounded in the distance, the sound a bit muffled and distorted through the mirror, and Topacia lunged into view.

Several more tight knots of tension in my stomach loosened. "Yes, it's me."

Tears gleamed in her eyes, and Topacia put her hand over her mouth, as if to stifle a sob. Then she cleared her throat and drew back.

"Where are you? What happened? Are you injured?" Her eyebrows creased together. "And why are you wearing Mortan purple?"

I told her everything, from Conley shoving me into the chasm, to Leonidas rescuing me, to him bringing me to Myrkvior, to our bargain to get to the bottom of Milo's plot together. By the time I finished, Topacia's eyes were as big and round as coins.

"Are you out of your mind?" she hissed. "You can't stay at the Mortan palace! You have to escape! As soon as possible!"

"No, I have to stay. I have to at least *try* to find out what Milo Morricone is planning."

Topacia rubbed her temples, as if her head was suddenly aching. "Prince Dominic will have me executed for this."

"No, he won't," I chirped in a cheery voice. "My father will be far too busy throwing me into the Glitnir dungeon where he can keep an eye on me to even think about punishing you."

Topacia gave me a sour look and dropped her hands from her temples. "At least tell me that Grimley found you."

I frowned. "What do you mean?"

"After Leonidas Morricone flew you away on his strix, the other creatures stayed behind in the plaza for a few minutes. Once those strixes finally left, Grimley took off flying and never looked back. I assumed that he was following you."

My heart swelled with love. Of course Grimley would have followed me, just as I would have followed him anywhere. Plus, I'd thought the gargoyle had been headed in this direction when I'd reached out to him earlier.

Worry washed over me, snuffing out my happiness. It was just as dangerous for Grimley here as it was for me. Strixes were as common in Morta as gargoyles were in Andvari, and the birds wouldn't take kindly to a strange creature flying through their city. Not to mention the Mortan guards who might spot the gargoyle and try to capture or kill him.

Grimley? I sent the thought out as far and wide as I could. *Are you here? In Majesta?*

That eerie, buzzing silence filled my mind again. More worry crashed through me. Maybe he was hurt. Maybe he'd been captured. Maybe the worst had happened, and he was dead—

Yes, the gargoyle's gravelly voice whispered in my mind, a bit louder and stronger than before. *Getting closer. Tired. Must rest now.*

My breath escaped in a relieved rush. Once again, equal parts love and worry flowed through me, but I couldn't stop him from coming here any more than Topacia could stop me from staying.

Be careful. I love you, bruiser. I sent the thought to Grimley.

I will. Love you too, runt.

"Well?" Topacia asked. "Is Grimley there?"

"He's on his way," I replied. "So what happened while I was in the mine?"

"When you didn't come out for lunch like we had planned, I got worried, so I went to see the captain of the royal guard. I told him that you were inside the mine, but he didn't believe me. Arrogant fool," she grumbled. "Anyway, one of the guards said that several strixes had gathered in the plaza, so I rushed over there. The captain and his men followed me, and after the strixes left, we all went inside the mine."

"What did you find?" I asked.

"The other miners had tied up Conley and his crew, and they told us how Conley had thrown you and that other woman into a chasm to hide the fact that he was stealing tearstone. Conley sang like a canary and confessed to everything. He's currently in the Blauberg city prison, awaiting trial, along with his men."

"Good. I hope you thanked Javier, the bone master who healed me. And Reiko, the dragon morph who helped rescue me."

Topacia nodded. "I did thank Javier, but I don't remember seeing a dragon morph."

I frowned. Strange. Reiko was definitely memorable. I wondered what had happened to her, but I had other things to worry about. "How did my father and grandfather take the news?"

Topacia snorted. "Not well. After the yelling subsided, Prince Dominic and Captain Rhea dispatched some of the Glitnir palace guards to Blauberg. They should be here soon. Now that I know where you are, we can come and get you."

"No. You know how tenuous the peace is between the two kingdoms. Sending Andvarian guards into Morta could start a war, especially if you all were captured or killed."

Topacia threw up her hands in frustration. "Well, what would you have me do? I can't just leave you there."

"Stay put and wait for the Glitnir guards to arrive. In the meantime, keep nosing around Blauberg, and see if you can find out anything else about Wexel and his men. Leonidas thinks that the tearstone is here at Myrkvior, but Wexel could have taken it somewhere else. The captain might even be planning another attack along the border. As soon as I discover what Milo is plotting, I'll slip out of the palace, find Grimley, and fly back to Blauberg."

Topacia threw up her hands again and paced back and forth in front of the mirror, muttering to herself. After several seconds, her steps slowed, and she faced the glass again.

"All right," she grumbled. "I'll stay here, but only because I can't come get you without making things worse."

"Thank you, Topacia."

She stabbed a finger at me. "But promise me that you will contact your father as soon as we're done."

"I promise. And don't worry. Everything is going to be fine."

Topacia tried to smile, but it was a grim, lopsided expression. "Please be careful, Gemma."

"Aren't I always?" I drawled.

My friend barked out a laugh. "Never."

She was right about that, but my joke made some of the worry trickle out of her face. I nodded at her, then pulled the compact away from the mirror, breaking our connection. Topacia's image flickered and faded away.

I sighed, but I had made her a promise, so I pressed the compact up to the vanity-table mirror again and asked to see my father's study, since that was the most likely place for him to be this time of day. Magic flared, and a few seconds later, the room came into view.

My gaze traced over the ebony writing desk, bookcases, and other familiar furnishings. Like most royals, Father had his own Cardea mirror so that he could talk to the leaders of the other kingdoms, as well as nobles, merchants, guilders, and anyone else that he needed to in order to help Grandfather Heinrich rule Andvari.

"Father?" I called out. "Are you there?"

I'd barely finished speaking when footsteps sounded, and a man rushed into view. He was in his fifties with tan skin and the same blue eyes and dark brown hair that I had, although his locks were sprinkled with silver. He was wearing a dark gray jacket, and the Ripley royal crest—a snarling gargoyle face—gleamed in shiny black thread over his heart. He wasn't sporting a crown, but he didn't need to. Everyone in Andvari knew the face of Crown Prince Dominic Ripley.

"Gemma!" My father's relief rippled through the mirror, even stronger than the waves of magic.

"Father."

I kept my voice steady, but I had to blink back the tears stinging my eyes. Now was *not* the time to show any emotion, no matter how happy I was to see him. My father wouldn't agree to my scheme if he thought I had any doubts.

Father leaned forward, peering at me. "Where are you?" He frowned. "And why are you wearing Mortan purple?"

I told him everything, from Conley shoving me into the chasm, to Leonidas saving me, to the deal I'd struck with the Morricone prince.

By the time I finished, Father was shaking his head *no, no, no*, a familiar, frustrating motion he always did whenever I wanted to do something he didn't approve of, like my spy missions.

"You can't be serious," he said. "You can't actually think staying at Myrkvior and spying on Milo Morricone is a good idea."

I bristled at his chiding tone. "It's an *excellent* idea. We'll never get a better chance to learn about Milo's plans. Besides, you've often wished you could plant an Andvarian spy in the Mortan court."

Father grimaced. He and Grandfather Heinrich had had several conversations to that effect, and he didn't like me using his own words against him.

"You need to find Grimley and come home at once, Gemma," Father said in a deep, stern voice. "Majesta is perilous enough, and Myrkvior even more so. If anyone at the palace were to realize your true identity . . ." His voice trailed off. "Well, we both know how much the Morricones love torturing their enemies."

This time, I was the one who grimaced. Yes, I did, thanks to the Seven Spire massacre.

"At this point, my best chance to find out what Milo is plotting and to return home safely is to work with Leonidas."

Father harrumphed. "Trusting a Morricone is like trying to grab a lightning bolt. Even if you manage to latch onto it, you're still going to get burned."

He was probably right about that, especially given how Leonidas and I had tried to murder each other as children.

"Well, like it or not, I'm stuck with him. On the bright side, Leonidas doesn't seem quite as cruel as the other Morricones. Besides, we both know that he has helped Aunt Evie in the past, including at the Regalia Games all those years ago."

Father's lips puckered with displeasure much the same way Maeven's had earlier. He didn't like me pointing out that fact either. "Yes, but that doesn't mean he will help you *now*. Leonidas Morricone was a desperate boy when he aided Everleigh during the Regalia Games. He is all grown up and far more powerful and dangerous than he ever was back then."

Leonidas was certainly strong in his magic, but I was equally formidable, at least when my power worked, something my father always seemed to forget, much to my frustration.

"Yes, Leonidas is powerful, but I am too. You and Rhea made sure of that, as did Alvis, Xenia, Uncle Lucas, and Aunt Evie."

Father's lips puckered again. He didn't like those facts either. "No. Forget about the tearstone. Uncovering Milo's scheme isn't worth your life, Gemma."

But he was wrong—it *was* worth my life. I hadn't warned

Uncle Frederich and the other Andvarians, and they had been slaughtered during the Seven Spire massacre. This was my chance to protect my people, to save lives, and to finally make up for my cowardice, for my weakness. Why couldn't he understand that?

Father drew himself up to his full height and peered down his nose, giving me an official Crown Prince Dominic Ripley glower, the kind that made most people quake in their boots. "You *will* slip out of the palace, find Grimley, and head toward the Andvarian border immediately."

This time, I shook my head *no, no, no.* "I can't do that. I *won't.*"

He peered down his nose at me again. "You forget that I am not just your father. I am also your crown prince, and I outrank you."

I ground my teeth. We engaged in this same argument every time I went on one of my missions. True, this venture was by far the most dangerous I had ever attempted, but the potential reward was also so much greater, the kind of thing that could change our kingdom—for the better.

"And what about what is best for *Andvari*?" I snapped, my voice just as harsh as his. "For our *people*? Or would you prefer that I just stand idly by while Milo Morricone dreams up new and terrible ways to kill us all?"

Equal parts guilt and anger darkened his face, but I kept talking, trying to convince him.

"You and Grandfather Heinrich have been far more worried about the simmering tensions with Morta than you've let on."

Father opened his mouth, probably to refute my claim, but I tapped my index finger on my heart. "I have *felt* how worried the two of you have been, and I've heard more than one stray thought from both you and Grandfather Heinrich wondering what the Morricones are plotting. Well, this is our chance to find out."

"You are *not* a spy, Gemma," he snapped. "No matter how

much you would like to be one. You are a *princess*, the crown princess of Andvari. You are the future leader of our people, and you need to start acting like it!"

Anger surged through my body, sizzling like lightning trapped in my veins. "I *am* acting like it. Finding out what Milo is plotting is the best, most important thing I can do for our kingdom right now, and perhaps in my entire lifetime. Do you want to be blindsided when Milo finally decides to strike out at us? Do you want to explain to the families of the people he slaughters why we didn't act sooner? Why we didn't do everything in our power to thwart him? I thought our bloody *duty* as royals, as leaders, was to stop tragedies—not enable them."

I had never spoken so harshly to my father, and he jerked back as though I had slapped him. He blinked at me in surprise, as though he had never seen me before.

"No, I don't want that." Some of the anger leaked out of his eyes. "But I love you, Gemma, and I don't want to lose you the same way we lost Frederich at Seven Spire."

His worry slipped through the mirror and stabbed me in the gut. Shame and regret bloomed in my heart like poisonous vines, throttling my own anger.

"I know, and I love you too," I said in a softer, calmer voice. "But I'm not one of the Ripley royal crowns. You can't keep me in a velvet box under lock and key and only bring me out to admire on special occasions."

Father winced, but he didn't disagree. If he and Grandfather Heinrich had had their way, I would have never set one foot outside of Glitnir after the massacre.

"I might be your daughter, but you said it yourself—I am also a princess. I want to do my duty and protect our people from the Morricones, no matter how dangerous it is. You and Grandfather Heinrich have always said nothing is more noble than doing one's duty and sacrificing one's happiness for the good of others. So let me do that. Let me live up to your example, to Grandfather's example. *Please*."

I sucked in a breath to keep arguing, but Father dropped his head and held up his hand, asking for quiet. So I perched on the edge of my seat and waited.

Several long, tense seconds passed before he raised his gaze to mine again. "Very well. Stay at Myrkvior, wait for Grimley, and spy on the Morricones in the meantime."

Happiness flooded my heart. "Thank you, Father."

He leaned forward and stabbed a finger at me. "But the second you find out what Milo Morricone is plotting, you slip out of the palace and start making your way home to Andvari. And if you think someone knows who you really are, then you forget about the tearstone and leave the palace *immediately*. That is a direct order from your crown prince. Understood?"

I didn't like it, but he'd given me far more leeway than I'd expected. "Understood. I'll be careful. I promise."

"You'd better be," he growled. Then his face softened again. "Please be safe, Gemma. I love you."

"I will. And I love you too. I'll contact you again as soon as I have any news."

My father gave me a single, sharp nod, tears gleaming in his eyes. Similar tears stung my own eyes, but once again I blinked them back.

Father kept his gaze locked on my face as I leaned forward and moved the compact away from the mirror, breaking our connection. The glass rippled, and his face vanished, although the throbbing sting of his worry lingered in my heart.

CHAPTER FIFTEEN

It wasn't even noon yet, but it had already been a long day, and I was physically and mentally exhausted. So I stuffed the silver compact into the pocket of my borrowed coat, then stumbled over to the bed, curled up on it, and went to sleep.

Sometime later, a knock sounded, startling me awake. One of the doors creaked open, and a servant girl dressed in a light purple tunic, along with black leggings and boots, poked her head inside the room. She looked to be about thirteen, maybe fourteen, with gray eyes and rosy skin. Her black hair had been twisted up on top of her head, although a couple of long tendrils had escaped to frame her round face, which hadn't yet lost its last bit of childish softness.

"Pardon me, my lady, but I am Anaka. Princess Delmira asked me to escort you to her chambers so you can dress for dinner."

"Yes, of course," I mumbled, my head still spinning with sleep as I got to my feet. "Lead the way."

Anaka took me back to the strix rotunda and then into another wing of the palace. We stepped through an archway, and I felt as though we had entered another realm. Unlike the chilly, deserted hallways around Leonidas's library, an army of servants flitted about here, polishing the vases and statues tucked away in various nooks, straightening the paintings and tapestries on the walls, and stoking the fires in the common rooms until the flames added the perfect amount of cheery, crackling warmth to the air.

Scores of palace stewards, nobles, merchants, and guilders also hustled through the corridors, and dozens of conversations trilled through the air. The gargoyle pendant hidden under my tunic grew warm against my skin, but I ignored the sensation and ducked my head, avoiding the curious stares that came my way.

I also kept an eye on the guards, but the men chatted to each other and ogled the pretty servants who raced by, just like the guards at Glitnir did. To everyone else, this was a normal day, but tension twisted my stomach into knots, and the space between my shoulder blades continually itched, as if in anticipation of someone plunging a blade into my back.

Anaka walked past some open doors. Music drifted out of the chambers, accompanied by the dulcet tones of someone singing a sweet melody.

My steps slowed. The song was a common one, but that beautiful voice sounded strangely familiar, as though I had heard the person sing before. Perhaps it was a minstrel or a music master who had visited Glitnir. Despite the simmering hostilities between Andvari and Morta, artisans often traveled between the two courts, as well as to courts in other kingdoms, seeking commissions from rich benefactors.

I craned my neck, peering into the room. A recital was taking place to amuse the nobles, but the angle was wrong, and I couldn't see who was singing.

Anaka hurried on, and I followed her.

The girl glanced at me over her shoulder. "The princess's chambers are up ahead—"

She rounded a corner and plowed into a guard heading in the opposite direction. Anaka hit the man's chest, bounced off, and stumbled back. She opened her mouth, as if to upbraid the guard for almost knocking her over, but then her eyes widened in recognition.

Short black hair, hazel eyes, bronze skin, a heavily stubbled square jaw that jutted out over the rest of his thick, muscled body. Not just a mere guard, but Captain Wexel.

Even though Leonidas and I had talked about Wexel earlier, I hadn't given much thought as to where the captain might be. But of course he would be at the palace, and of course I would run into him.

I froze, right alongside Anaka. If there was one person at Myrkvior who might immediately recognize me, then it was Wexel. Not as Princess Gemma, but rather as Miner Gemma, who'd watched him try to murder his own prince.

"Watch where you're going," Wexel growled.

Anaka shrank down like a tortoise pulling itself back into its protective shell to keep its head from being bitten off. "Sir! I'm so sorry!"

Wexel opened his mouth to growl at her again, but then he noticed me. "Who are you?"

Despite the danger, I lifted my chin, playing the part of an arrogant noble. "Lady Armina from Ravensrock. Who are *you*?"

"Captain Wexel," he boasted, his voice dripping with pride and arrogance. "I'm in charge of the royal guards, along with Crown Prince Milo's personal security."

He dropped his hand to the sword dangling from his belt, puffed up his chest, and preened, as if his words should make me cower like Anaka was still doing.

Part of me wanted to duck my head and slink away to avoid further scrutiny, but Lady Armina wouldn't let Wexel just walk all over her, no matter whom he worked for. Still, I didn't know the exact pecking order here, or how much power Wexel truly had, and I needed to err on the side of caution. So instead of dressing him down, I let out an indignant little sniff, as though I was unimpressed with his title.

Wexel's eyes narrowed, and his hand slid off his sword and clenched into a fist, as though he wanted to punch me. I didn't think he would dare to strike a noble lady. At least, not with a servant standing here as a witness. But I still needed to tread carefully, so I schooled my features into a blank mask.

Several seconds dragged by in tense silence. Wexel's fist slowly relaxed, although anger kept glimmering in his eyes. He jerked his head at Anaka, giving her permission to leave.

"This—this way, my lady," she stammered.

She started to sidle past Wexel, but he held out his hand, blocking her path, although he never took his suspicious gaze off me.

"Have I seen you before?" he demanded.

A cold finger of worry slid down my back, increasing that uncomfortable itch between my shoulder blades, but I shrugged. "Not unless you've been to Ravensrock. And I doubt you have, what with all your important duties here at the palace."

My words were innocent enough, but I didn't bother to mask my venomous disdain. An angry red flush zipped up Wexel's neck and stained his cheeks. Beside me, Anaka sucked in a breath and scrunched down, once again trying to make herself as small as possible.

I should have kept my mouth shut, or at least made my tone more civil, but Princess Gemma had gotten the better of Spy Gemma, as she so often did when confronted with a cruel, arrogant bully. Still, I couldn't back down now. Wexel would pounce on any sign of weakness, and the captain thinking me weak was far more dangerous than him simply hating me. You could still be wary of people that you despised. Wexel would abuse, torture, and kill anyone he considered weaker than himself.

I kept staring at Wexel with that same blank expression. When he realized that I wasn't going to give in, he focused on Anaka again, since she was the easier target.

"Watch where you're fucking going," he snarled, then pushed past her, knocking the girl back into the wall.

He pushed past me as well, but I tensed my legs, not giving him the satisfaction of moving. Wexel glared at me again, then strode down the hallway, rounded the corner, and vanished.

I waited until his heavy, angry footsteps had faded away before I turned to Anaka. "Are you all right?"

She eased away from the wall. "Yes, thank you."

The girl glanced around as if to make sure we were still alone before looking at me again. "I know that you're new here, Lady Armina, but you don't want to make an enemy out of Captain Wexel," she said, her voice a low, warning whisper. "He controls many of the guards, and he only answers to Queen Maeven and Prince Milo. Wexel can make things . . . difficult for you."

"Difficult how?"

Anaka shivered and hugged her arms around her chest. "You don't want to know."

She shivered again, then beckoned me to follow her. I thought about skimming her thoughts, but she was right. I didn't want to know. I could well imagine all the petty ways Wexel would torture those he considered beneath him. And if he remembered that he had seen me in Blauberg . . .

Well, the captain would come for me, and he wouldn't be so kind as to give me a quick, merciful death.

A few minutes later, Anaka stopped in front of some double doors. Instead of wood or glass, these doors were made entirely of liladorn vines that had twisted together into a thick, solid mass.

"Princess Delmira is waiting inside." Anaka bobbed her head and scuttled off.

I rapped my knuckles on one of the vines, careful not to scratch my skin on the long black thorns. The vines quivered at my touch, almost as though they were unlocking themselves, and one of the doors creaked open. I stepped through to the other side.

Unlike Leonidas's cozy tower library, these chambers were far larger and all on one wide level, and the furnishings were much finer and far more feminine. Off to my right, a set of doors opened up into a room with a four-poster bed draped with panels of lilac silk and covered with mounds of pillows. Beyond the bed, more doors led to a bathroom patterned with lilac tile.

Here in the first, main part of the chambers, cushioned settees clustered around a fireplace, while floor-to-ceiling shelves cluttered with books, maps, and jeweled figurines shaped like flowers, strixes, and caladriuses hugged the walls. An ebony writing desk was perched in one corner, and a window seat ran along the back wall, which was made of glass.

But the most interesting thing was the long, wide ebony table situated in front of the window seat. An odd jumble of items covered the surface—swords, daggers, iron nails, potted herbs, glittering spheres of glass, a flute, a violin, sticks of colored chalks, even a few half-finished paintings.

The objects were those that a magier would use to determine what, if any, magic a person had. Curious. Why would Delmira have a testing table in her chambers? She was in her mid-twenties. Her magic, whatever it was, should have revealed itself years ago.

Besides the testing table, the other most eye-catching thing was the liladorn. The black vines adorned many of the palace's corridors, but they were practically *everywhere* in here—snaking along the floor, twining in between the furniture, crawling up the walls, and even clinging to the ceiling like oddly shaped bats.

Except for the odd abundance of liladorn, these chambers reminded me of my own rooms at Glitnir. Everything a princess could ever want was in here, and you could while away the hours without ever venturing out into the rest of the palace.

After the Seven Spire massacre, I had spent days at a time in my rooms, curled up in bed, reading storybooks and trying to forget all the horrible things that had happened. I wondered how much time Delmira spent in here, and if she preferred to stay in her chambers rather than deal with her duplicitous family and the poisonous palace politics. If so, the Morricone princess and I were far more alike than I'd realized.

"Lady Armina! There you are!" Delmira's light, lilting voice floated over to me, and she strode through another pair of doors that led into an enormous dressing room.

She rushed over and clasped my hands, smiling as though we were the best of friends and not strangers who had just met this morning. I reached out, trying to skim her thoughts, but I couldn't hear them. Not a single one. I also couldn't feel her emotions, not even the faintest flicker of happiness, annoyance, or jealousy.

Everything about the princess seemed . . . *muffled*, as though she were cocooned in soft, invisible armor from head to toe. Perhaps Delmira Morricone was more well protected—and powerful—than I'd suspected.

Delmira frowned and dropped my hands. "Is something wrong?"

"Not at all," I lied. "I was just admiring your chambers. The books, the maps, the figurines. You seem to be quite the collector."

She let out a very unprincesslike snort. "That's a nice way of saying that I love odd, broken things."

Just like me.

This time, I did hear a whisper of her thoughts, although the words quickly vanished into the muffled silence that cloaked her.

Another smile split her face. "Come! Let me give you a tour."

Delmira led me around the main room, sharing tidbits about all the items on display, except for those on the testing table. She avoided that area completely, and she didn't so much as glance at those objects. Still, I managed to get close enough to eye the papers on the table, many of which featured dates, times, and numbers. Delmira seemed to be conducting experiments with the items, although none of them were going very well, given all the dark purple *X*s that marred the papers.

I thought back, trying to remember everything I had ever heard about Delmira Morricone. She was rumored to be a lightning magier, although I didn't sense any magic rolling off her. Maeven's power had been strong enough to make my fingertips tingle, but I didn't get any sense of that from Delmira. Perhaps she was weak in her magic. A very dangerous thing to be, especially for a Morricone royal. Perhaps that was why she seemed to spend so much time in her chambers.

Delmira headed over to a glass door in the back wall, and I followed her outside into a courtyard. No other doors or windows overlooked this courtyard, and I didn't see another exit, just high stone walls topped with parapets and a few neighboring towers with steep, sloped roofs.

And then there was the liladorn.

Even more vines were clustered out here than in the princess's chambers, and the tendrils had woven themselves through the flagstones and walls and even climbed the towers, winding all the way up to the tops of the black spikes and hanging there like thorn-crusted flags.

I poked one of the vines with my finger. It sprang right back into place, even though the vine itself was as hard and solid as stone. Even stranger was the *feeling* I got from it, as though a presence was hidden somewhere among the many vines, and each thorn was a sharp black eye, silently watching and judging me.

"Do you have liladorn in Ravensrock?" Delmira asked, noting my interest in the vines.

I had no idea, so I gave her a vague answer. "Not nearly as much as you have here. It must be so beautiful when it blooms. I've heard the thorns transform into spikes of fragrant lilac."

"I've been told that as well, although I've never seen it. None of the liladorn in Myrkvior has bloomed in years. Not since I was a baby, according to my mother. Of course, the vines are beautiful all by themselves, but I would dearly love to see it bloom, just once," she said, a wistful note in her voice.

Delmira walked along one of the paths, carelessly trailing her fingers along the vines without scratching herself on the numerous thorns. At first, I thought she was using magic to push the thorns aside, but no power was rippling off her, and I realized that the vines were moving *themselves*. The tendrils were twisting, bending, and turning ever so slightly so that Delmira could slide her hand along their shiny black surfaces without getting injured, although she didn't seem to notice the vines' protective motions.

"Most of the noble ladies don't like my courtyard. They think it's too dull and gloomy without any flowers, but it's one of my favorite places," Delmira said. "I like to come out here to think."

She sat down on the rim of a gray stone fountain in the middle of the courtyard. Liladorn ringed the rim, and the vines had snaked through the gurgling water, crawled up to and wrapped around the figure in the center—a woman with a caladrius perched on her shoulder and her head bowed over a book.

I perched stiffly on the fountain rim beside Delmira. I eyed the liladorn vines that ran past my boots, but they remained still.

A smile played across the princess's lips. "Leonidas has never brought a woman home before."

The sudden change in topic startled me, and it took me a few seconds to pick up on what she was implying.

I shook my head. "No. It's not like that. Leonidas came to my rescue when those . . . bandits attacked and was kind enough to bring me here to recuperate. There's nothing more between us."

"Mmm. Whatever you say." Delmira's smile widened, and her eyes sparkled with merriment.

She obviously thought I was lying, but I didn't correct her. Better for her to think I was besotted with Leonidas than spying on Milo.

"Well, however you got here, I'm so glad you've come to Myrkvior. Leonidas spends far too much time alone, holed up in his dusty, cluttered library." Her nose crinkled with comical distaste.

I could have pointed out that her chambers were just as cluttered as her brother's, and that she seemed to spend just as much time alone as he did, but I changed the topic instead. "What about your other brother, Milo? I hear he is engaged."

The more I learned about Milo, the better I could navigate the treacherous palace politics, and the sooner I could figure out what he was planning to do with the tearstone.

Delmira's smile vanished. "Yes, Milo has been engaged to Lady Corvina for a few months. She comes from a very old, powerful, wealthy noble family. The Dumonds. I'm sure you've heard of them."

"Of course."

In addition to the Morricones, my father and grandfather also paid close attention to other influential Mortan families, especially the Dumonds, who had almost as much magic, money, land, and men as the Morricones did. Over the years, various Dumonds had tried to wrest the throne away from Maeven, although none had been successful. Marrying Milo to a Du-mond must be Maeven's way of trying to appease the noble family while still making sure the throne stayed firmly in Mor-ricone hands.

"Does Milo spend much time at Myrkvior?" I asked. "Surely he has his own chambers here."

Delmira shrugged. "He has his own private workshop, of course, although he rarely lets anyone inside it. Milo used to spend far more time traveling, especially to some of the eastern kingdoms, but this year, he's spent most of his time at Myrkvior."

A private workshop? That sounded promising, and it matched up with what Leonidas had told me earlier. I didn't think Leonidas would lie about where Milo might be hiding the tearstone, but it didn't hurt to confirm his claims.

I opened my mouth to ask Delmira another question when a shadow fell over us, and a loud, harsh *caw!* rang out. Wings flapped, and a strix streaked down from the sky and landed in the courtyard.

I tensed, thinking the strix might be here to attack me, but then I recognized the creature. Lyra. I relaxed a bit. She prob-ably wouldn't hurt me. Probably.

Delmira laughed and held out her hand, and Lyra rubbed up against the princess's fingers like an oversize house cat. Leoni-das might be Lyra's favorite human, but Delmira seemed to be a close second. Then the strix turned to me, quirking her head from side to side.

"Go on," Delmira encouraged. "Hold out your hand. Lyra won't hurt you. She is Leonidas's strix, and the two of you met before. During the bandit attack, right?"

Something about the way she said that made me think Delmira didn't believe her brother's lies about me, but I had no real reason to doubt her, other than my own paranoia.

"Of course," I murmured.

Delmira was the princess here, not me, so I did as she asked. Lyra hopped over and rubbed her head against my outstretched hand. Laughter bubbled up out of my lips too, and I scratched her head right in between her eyes, the same spot where Grimley always liked to be petted—

An idea popped into my mind, and I leaned closer to the strix and stared into her bright, shiny amethyst eyes. *Lyra.* I gently sent the thought to her. *Will you help me? Please?*

The strix squawked and hopped back, clearly startled. I kept staring at her, and she eased closer to me again.

What do you want? Her singsong voice filled my mind.

Grimley, my gargoyle, is coming to Myrkvior. Can you find him and make sure he gets to the palace safely? I don't want the other strixes to hurt him.

Lyra let out a sound that was somewhere between a huff and a snort. *Stupid rocks-for-brains gargoyle coming to my city. He's going to get himself killed. The others will attack him the moment they see him.*

That was exactly what I was afraid of. *I know you don't like him, but please find Grimley and help him. I couldn't bear it if anything happened to him because of me.*

The strix bobbed her head in what seemed like agreement. Lyra cawed again, then spread her wings and shot up into the sky. I watched until she vanished from sight, then turned back to Delmira, who was staring at me with a thoughtful expression.

"Strixes are such beautiful creatures," I said, trying to explain my seeming fascination with Lyra.

"Yes, they are. I have often wished for one of my own."

"But don't you ride strixes when you visit other cities in Morta?"

Delmira shrugged. "Of course. But I've never bonded with any of the strixes the way Leo has with Lyra. I've always been a bit jealous of their connection, of their friendship."

Sadness rippled through her voice, and she reached out and idly rubbed her hand over the closest liladorn vine. Once again, the thorns drew back so that she wouldn't nick her fingers.

Delmira dropped her hand from the vine and got to her feet. "Come. We should start getting ready for dinner. I think it will be a night to remember."

Her words were innocent enough, and I managed to hide the grimace twisting my face until she moved away. She was far closer to the truth than she realized.

If I lived through the dinner, then I would consider it one of the crowning achievements of my life thus far.

CHAPTER SIXTEEN

I spent the rest of the afternoon in Delmira's chambers. The princess summoned her personal thread master, and the three of us went to her dressing room, along with Anaka and several other servants carrying platters of sweet cakes and other treats.

Long metal racks set at varying heights adorned two of the walls, while floor-to-ceiling shelves lined the other two walls. Day dresses, ball gowns, tunics, leggings, and capes hung on the racks, while heels, boots, and slippers filled the shelves. A freestanding ebony island in the center of the room was studded with purple-velvet-lined drawers filled with jewelry, ribbons, brushes, hairpins, and berry balms.

I was used to such finery at Glitnir, but my dressing room was a small, pale imitation of this opulence, and Delmira's collection was truly dazzling. The Morricone princess seemed to love pretty things just as much as I did.

"Now," Delmira said, rubbing her hands together in anticipation. "Let's see what Edna has created for us."

Edna, the thread master, snapped her fingers, and more

servants streamed into the room, pushing several racks of dresses in front of them.

To my surprise, I found myself relaxing and having fun. Delmira's pleasantry wasn't an act, and I genuinely liked the princess, who was firm without being cruel, and strong without being overbearing. She knew every servant's name, and she inquired about their families while still maintaining control of the room. It was a difficult tightrope to walk, but Delmira did it beautifully.

In another place and time, we could have been friends. But we were stuck in this place and time, and I had a part to play—Lady Armina, the noble from a small, distant town who was absolutely awed by the sights, sounds, and fashions of the royal palace. So I *oohed* and *aahed* over the truly fine dresses, as well as admired the beautiful jewelry and shoes.

Delmira seemed pleased by my company, grinning and laughing at my jokes. More than once, I tried to skim her thoughts, but I still couldn't slip past whatever magic was protecting her, so I settled for eavesdropping on the servants' musings, but they were all calm, happy, and devoted to their princess. Even better, none of them were spies for Milo or anyone else.

Two hours later, Delmira pronounced that we were finally ready for dinner. After trying on more than a dozen dresses, and making me do the same, she had decided on a strapless, lilac-colored gown patterned with black velvet vines and thorns, along with spikes of liladorn made of pale, almost translucent amethysts. Matching black velvet heels with amethyst-crusted toes glittered on her feet, and a short midnight-purple cape covered her shoulders. Her black hair had been braided into an elaborate crown that arched over her head, while dark plum berry balm stained her lips.

I had donned a gown made of a dark silk that wasn't quite purple but wasn't quite blue either. I had picked it out because of the high neckline and the silver feathers fluttering down the front, both of which hid my gargoyle pendant. I'd also managed to smuggle my dagger and Leonidas's silver compact into my dress pockets. Black velvet heels adorned my feet, and the servants had put loose, gentle waves into my hair and painted my lips a light violet.

Edna wished us both a good night, then left the dressing room, along with Anaka and the other servants.

"Are you sure you wouldn't like a necklace or some other jewelry?" Delmira gestured at the ebony island. "I have plenty to choose from."

"No, thank you." I reached up and patted my chest, making sure my pendant was in its usual place.

Her eyes sharpened. Too late, I realized what I was doing. I dropped my hand, but she had already caught the motion.

"What's that?" she asked.

"I . . . have my own necklace. It's the only thing those awful bandits didn't steal," I lied.

Delmira perked up. "I didn't notice your necklace earlier. May I see it?"

I bit my lip, silently cursing my foolishness, but I had no choice but to fish the silver chain out from under my gown and show her the pendant.

"How pretty!" she exclaimed, bending down to get a closer look at it. "I adore the mix of black jet and blue tearstone. Was this made by Alvis, the famed Andvarian jeweler?"

I blinked, surprised she knew his name. "Yes. How can you tell?"

Delmira straightened. "The shards design, of course. It's his trademark. I've long admired his pieces. I actually sent him a letter once, when I was a little girl, begging him to make something for me, but of course he never responded. Then again, why would he? Even as a child, I should have known better than to ask an Andvarian metalstone master for such a boon."

She let out a small, trilling laugh, playing her words off as a joke, but hurt rippled through the sound. And why had she called it a *boon*? I got the sense that Delmira had wanted more than just a pretty piece of jewelry, although I couldn't imagine what she had hoped to gain by writing to Alvis.

Delmira gave my pendant a wistful look. Then her eyes narrowed, and she seemed to see the design for the very first time. Her lips puckered in thought, making her look eerily like Maeven. "Although the gargoyle shape is quite unusual. I've never seen anyone wear that particular symbol before. At least, not in Myrkvior."

I grimaced. Of course she hadn't. Gargoyles were an Andvarian creature and tradition, not a Mortan one. I scrambled to offer a reasonable explanation before she remembered that gargoyles were also the symbol for the Ripley royal family.

"The pendant was a gift from a man who is like a second father to me, and I wear it as a way to keep him in my thoughts."

My voice sounded weak, even to my own ears, but Delmira nodded, as if my half-truths made perfect sense.

"Come," she said. "Dinner will begin soon."

She gave my necklace another longing glance and left the dressing room. I exhaled, then tucked the pendant back under my gown and followed her.

Throngs of people dressed in gowns and formal jackets were strolling through the hallways, and everyone stopped and bowed their heads as Delmira passed them. She returned the gestures with smiles and nods of her own, while I trailed along in her wake. My gargoyle pendant grew warm against my chest as the thoughts of everyone we encountered rumbled through my mind.

Delmira looks particularly lovely tonight . . .

I wonder how Milo will treat Delmira at dinner . . .

Such a sweet girl. Such a shame her magic is so weak . . .

Delmira's magic was weak? What kind of power did she even have? I latched onto that whisper and tried to probe deeper, but we swept past the person it belonged to, and the thought drowned in the waves of all the others slapping up against my mind.

But the princess's appearance wasn't the only one that caused a commotion. More than a few thoughts focused on me.

Who is that with Delmira?

I've been trying to get the princess's attention for months! And that nobody waltzes in here and becomes her new best friend in one day. It's not fair! Not fair!

She's strolling along as though she's someone important, instead of a poor country bumpkin from backwater Ravensrock who didn't even have the common sense not to get robbed . . .

My pendant grew even hotter against my skin, but I gritted my teeth, plastered a smile on my face, and ignored the cruel, snide thoughts.

Eventually, we reached a set of double doors that stretched from the floor all the way up to the ceiling some two hundred feet overhead. Delmira stopped to chat with some nobles, so I peered through the opening.

The doors led to an enormous throne room. A rectangular table with enough chairs for at least a hundred people ran down the center. Several smaller tables were arranged around it, and even more tables lined the second-floor balcony.

A raised dais made of dark gray stone stood in the back of the room. No throne perched on the platform, although several thick strands of liladorn wrapped around the base and snaked up the steps. A midnight-purple banner featuring the Morricone royal crest done in gleaming silver thread adorned the wall behind the dais.

Scores of nobles, merchants, guilders, and courtiers were already inside, drinking wine and other spirits and nibbling on fresh fruits, cheeses, and crackers provided by the scurrying servants. Guards dressed in purple tunics with swords belted to their waists were stationed around the room, as well as on the second-floor balcony.

A crush of nobles came up behind me, sweeping me away from Delmira and carrying me into the throne room. Even more people were in here than out in the corridors, and my gargoyle pendant grew uncomfortably hot against my heart, but I didn't dare reach for it. That would attract even more unwanted attention than I was already getting, as well as leave my mind completely defenseless.

Delmira must have lent that lady one of her gowns . . .

She's not nearly as pretty as I expected . . .

Surely, she hasn't caught the eye of Prince Leonidas . . .

Maeven would never let her son marry anyone less than a princess . . .

Once again, several cruel, snide thoughts whipped against my mind, and I slipped through the crowd until I was standing in the shadows beside one of the diamond-shaped columns that supported the second-floor balcony. At least here, I was mostly out of people's lines of sight and, thus, their thoughts. I sighed with relief as the harsh buzz faded from my mind, and the pendant cooled against my skin.

I had no desire to sit through a long, tedious dinner surrounded by people who would judge me all night long. Besides, if everyone was in here, then no one would see me skulk through the palace while I searched for Milo's workshop.

I was contemplating how I could slip out of the throne room without being seen when heels clattered on the flagstones and a shadow eased up on the floor next to mine. I kept my gaze fixed on the open doors in the distance. Perhaps if I ignored the person, they would wander away.

The shadow crept a little closer, and a woman holding a crystal goblet stepped into view. I tensed, bracing myself for a snide comment about my borrowed dress, unfortunately small, unimportant hometown, or something else equally petty.

"I've always wanted to visit Myrkvior," the woman drawled. "Although I can't imagine you feel the same way."

The soft words and familiar tone made me turn toward the woman, who was dressed in a long, tight emerald-green gown with a scalloped neckline and cap sleeves that showed off her muscled arms. A gold pendant shaped like a flying dragon hung from a gold chain around her neck. Emeralds glittered as the dragon's eyes, and jet and ruby shards erupted out of its mouth, as if it were spewing smoke and fire. The pendant was eerily similar to the morph mark on the woman's right hand—a green dragon with black eyes that was peering up at me with a smug expression.

My gaze snapped up to the woman's face. Bright green eyes, high cheekbones, long black hair. Reiko, the miner from Blauberg, the dragon morph who'd had such a lovely singing voice—the same voice I'd heard floating through the palace during that recital earlier.

Shock spiked through me, and I was too stunned to try to hide it. "What are *you* doing here?"

Reiko smirked at me. "I could ask the same thing of you . . . Gemma Ripley."

The loud, noisy chatter filling the throne room faded away, and all I could hear were her words echoing in my mind, growing louder and louder with every repetition, like thunder rolling in my direction.

Gemma Ripley, Gemma Ripley, Gemma Ripley . . .

I gritted my teeth, shoved the echoes away, and glanced around. Reiko and I were standing in the shadows, and no one else had heard her words. I studied the other woman, forcing myself to think. Reiko could have easily screamed out my true identity at the top of her lungs, but instead, she had quietly sidled up to me.

"What do you want?" I asked.

She shrugged. "The same thing you do—to find the tearstone the Mortans stole from your mine."

More shock knifed through me, and I thought back to when Reiko had helped Leonidas rescue me in the mine. Everyone else had been wary of the prince, but she had seemed more thoughtful than anything else, as if she was carefully weighing everything that was happening and how it would impact future events. I had seen that same sort of calculation on Xenia's face more than once, and I cursed myself for not realizing what Reiko was before now.

"You're a spy."

Reiko tipped her head, confirming my suspicion. "Just like you are." She arched an eyebrow. "Although *I* wasn't careless enough to get tossed into a chasm, rescued by a Morricone prince, and taken to Myrkvior. I'm surprised you haven't been exposed and executed yet."

Annoyance surged through me at her dry, mocking tone. "Perhaps I'm better at being a spy than you give me credit for."

"Gemma Ripley? Also known as Glitzma? The most pampered of all the pampered princesses? Are you kidding me?" Reiko let out a merry little laugh, and her inner dragon joined in with its own silent chuckles.

I ignored their mirth and studied her even more carefully. The name *Reiko* tickled the back of my brain, and I mentally flipped through the pages and pages of family trees that my tutors had forced me to memorize as a child. "You're Reiko Yamato, cousin to Ruri Yamato, the Ryusaman queen."

Reiko and her inner dragon quit laughing, and surprise flickered across both their faces. "How do you know that?"

"I make a point of knowing *all* the royals and their families, down to the very last, most distant cousin."

I also reviewed the information twice a year and memorized the names of the children who had been born and the royals who had died. During my ambassador travels, I often ran into distant royal cousins, many of whom were eager to share tidbits about their more important relatives twice removed.

"Why is Ryusama suddenly so interested in Andvarian tearstone?"

Reiko took a sip of her punch, then peered at me over the rim of her goblet. "I'll answer your question if you answer mine."

"Which is?"

"Why would a Ripley princess save a Morricone prince from certain death?"

More surprise shot through me. Reiko must have followed Conley out of the mine and been lurking around the clearing that day. She must have seen me help Leonidas, but instead of interfering, she had watched and waited and let things play out. Then, after Leonidas had flown me away from Blauberg, she had come to Myrkvior, most likely to watch and wait some more. Why would she go to all that trouble? Unless . . .

"Your queen is worried about the tearstone. Ruri Yamato thinks the Mortans are going to use it against her, against Ryusama."

Reiko blinked in surprise again, as did her inner dragon. Apparently, neither of them thought very highly of me, and it seemed as though I was just Glitzma to them, the same way I was to so many other folks. People underestimated me at their own peril. Just because I was pampered didn't mean that I was stupid. Far from it.

I followed my thought to its logical conclusion. "The only reason Queen Ruri would be worried about Andvarian tearstone was if she—or you, her spy—had heard rumblings that Milo Morricone was stockpiling it."

My eyes narrowed. "What do you know about Milo?"

Reiko took another sip of her punch. "I have no idea what you're talking about."

I snorted. We both knew she was lying. Then again, I could hardly point fingers, given all the lies I was currently juggling like a magier tossing balls of fire into the air before a gladiator bout. Still, perhaps Reiko being here was a good thing. If something terrible did happen to me, perhaps she would at least be kind enough to report it to my family. Andvari and Ryusama had never been particularly close allies, given Ryusama's distance across the Blue Glass Sea, but the two kingdoms had become much friendlier in recent years, trading resources and even visiting each other's courts on occasion.

Like it or not, Reiko Yamato was the closest thing I had to an ally in Myrkvior.

"Instead of trading insults, we could do the smart thing and agree to work together," I suggested.

Reiko let out another merry laugh that sounded like bells pealing. Or talons scraping across stone. I couldn't quite decide which.

"Why would *I* want to work with *you*? I already made my way inside the palace, and I didn't have to get hoodwinked by a common thief, severely injured, and kidnapped by a prince to do it." Her chin lifted with pride. "I am an *excellent* spy, the best in all of Ryusama. Why, I'm just as good as Lady Xenia Rubin. Maybe even better."

Well, Reiko certainly was confident, although comparing herself to Xenia was a bit much. If Xenia were here, the ogre morph would have whacked the younger woman with her cane for her impertinence. Still, Reiko's boast gave me an idea.

"Yes, do tell, who are you masquerading as? I would *hate* to blow your cover by calling you by the wrong name."

Reiko crossed her arms over her chest, and her inner dragon glared at me. They didn't like my pointing out that they were just as dependent on my keeping Reiko's identity a secret as I was on her protecting mine.

She sighed. "Reiko Morita, a Ryusaman metalstone master who is offering her jewelry designs to wealthy nobles so they can bedeck themselves in stunning style for the queen's birthday ball tomorrow night."

"You obviously don't have any metalstone magic. Do you even know how to make jewelry?"

She lifted her chin again. "I know enough."

No, in other words, although she would probably never admit that.

"Well, if you need any help . . ."

"I won't." Reiko eyed me. "What name are *you* using?"

"Lady Armina, a Mortan noble from Ravensrock who was waylaid by bandits and rescued by Prince Leonidas."

"He even had to save you in your cover story. How sad."

My teeth ground together, and my hands fisted in my skirt. With those sorts of catty comments, she should have been a panther morph instead of a bloody dragon.

"I wonder what Prince Leo would say if he realized exactly who he had brought to Myrkvior." Reiko frowned. "Why *did* he bring you here? I can understand saving your life in the mine. Unlike some of his other relatives, Leonidas actually seems to have a modicum of honor and common decency. But why not leave you in Blauberg? Why haul you all the way to the palace?"

I still didn't know. Oh, I could have said that Leonidas had brought me to the palace to be properly, fully healed, but that didn't feel like a satisfactory answer to my own suspicious mind.

Reiko was right. Leonidas had risked a lot to save me from the mine, and he had gambled even more by bringing me to Myrkvior. Perhaps he had only saved me to use me for his own ends. Perhaps he was playing some Bellonan long game that I hadn't picked up on yet. The idea hurt my wary heart far more than I cared to admit.

I focused on the dragon morph again. "My offer remains the same. We should work together. That's the best way for us to get to the bottom of things—and not get executed. I adore being a pampered princess, and I plan to return to it after this is over."

Reiko and her inner dragon both studied me. I reached out, trying to skim their thoughts, but their whispers were as silent as smoke curling through the air, and I couldn't hear any of their musings. Not surprising, given their combined morph magic.

Her gaze flicked past me, and she dropped into a curtsy.

Delmira stepped up beside me. "Lady Reiko! I'm so glad you were able to come to dinner."

Reiko straightened. "It was an honor to be invited, Your Highness."

Delmira beamed at the other woman, then glanced at me. "Lady Reiko recently arrived at the palace. In addition to being a metalstone master, she also has an exquisite singing voice. She was kind enough to give me a private recital this morning, as well as entertain the nobles this afternoon."

"Did she now," I murmured, staring at the spy.

Reiko stared right back at me. Delmira kept smiling, not seeming to pick up on the tension between the two of us.

A series of bells chimed, signaling that the dinner was about to begin.

Delmira touched my arm. "Come, Armina. I've made arrangements for you to sit at the main table with me and Leo." She gave me a conspiratorial wink.

I bit back a groan at her obvious matchmaking attempt. I

would much rather sit at a remote table with some lesser nobles and merchants, but Delmira had other ideas.

"Of course. Thank you, Your Highness."

Delmira winked at me again. "You're welcome." She looked over at Reiko. "I tried to secure a seat for you as well, but there was only one extra chair at the table."

Surprise flashed across Reiko's face. She might have performed for Delmira, but apparently she hadn't realized that the princess had paid that much attention to her. But I was starting to think Delmira Morricone was far more than just a pretty face. She would have to be, in order to survive in Myrkvior, and especially among the rest of the Morricones, for any length of time.

"You and Armina must join me for breakfast tomorrow," Delmira continued. "I haven't had a chance to see either one of your jewelry designs yet."

Reiko bowed her head. "Thank you, Your Highness. I would be honored."

The princess waved her hand. "Please. I've told you both to call me Delmira."

"Yes, Delmira," Reiko and I said in unison.

She beamed at both of us again. "Excellent! Reiko, I'll see you at breakfast. Armina, follow me, please."

She headed toward the center table.

"Enjoy the spotlight, Lady Armina," Reiko murmured. "But don't be surprised if the bright glare burns you alive."

She smirked at me, as did her inner dragon, then glided away.

I grimaced, hoping her words weren't a terrible omen and that I could find some way to track down the tearstone and escape from the palace before all my secrets were exposed.

chapter seventeen

Delmira waved at me, and I had no choice but to join her at the main, center table. I was hoping she might be seated in the middle, among the less important people, but no such luck. She was at the head of the table, right next to where the queen would be. Delmira slipped into her seat, then gestured at the one next to her. I reluctantly stepped forward, but before I could grab the chair, a hand took hold of the seat and pulled it out.

"Allow me," a low voice murmured.

My head snapped up, and a delicious chill swept down my spine.

Leonidas was here.

The prince had dressed for dinner in a short, formal lilac-colored jacket trimmed with silver buttons stamped with flying strixes. The Morricone crest was done in silver thread on his jacket, and the symbol was situated right over his heart, like a bull's-eye telling an archer where to aim. His black hair gleamed, the wavy locks looking almost like onyx-tipped feathers, and he once again smelled faintly of honeysuckle, probably from the soap he used. The intoxicating scent made my head spin and my stomach clench.

This morning, when he had been wearing his black cloak and riding coat, Leonidas had looked like a knight out of some old fairy tale—strong, dark, fierce, powerful. But tonight, he was every inch the handsome, charming, polished, debonair prince. Both versions were far more appealing than I had expected.

"Lady Armina," Leonidas said, his voice as smooth as velvet sliding across my skin. "Please, allow me."

Delmira was watching us with great interest, as were the other people at the table, so I smiled, stepped forward, and dropped into the seat, as though I were absolutely *thrilled* to be the focus of the prince's attention.

Leonidas drew his hands away from the chair, although his fingertips trailed along my back as he stepped to the side and took the seat next to mine. He wasn't wearing his usual gloves, and the heat of his skin scorched through my dress. I didn't know if it was accidental or not, but the light touch made another chill sweep down my spine.

Leonidas looked at me. "Have you enjoyed your time in the palace today?"

"Oh, it's been lovely, Your Highness," I replied in an equally smooth voice, aware of the other people still watching us.

No thanks to you, I silently grumbled. *Delmira made me try on more than a dozen dresses before she let me pick one to wear.*

His eyes sparkled with mischief, and his lips quirked up into a small smile, both of which I found ridiculously attractive. *Oh, I knew that you could handle yourself, even when faced with my sister's rampant love of fashion.*

I would have kept silently grumbling to him, but a flutter of movement caught my eye, and I spotted Reiko at a table about thirty feet away. She had chosen a seat directly in my line of sight. The dragon morph toasted me with her goblet, then started talking to the man next to her.

A trumpet blared out a series of loud, boisterous notes, drowning out the chatter. The trumpet trailed off, and everyone fell deathly quiet. In the distance, a man cleared his throat.

"Announcing Her Royal Majesty, Queen Maeven Aella Toril Morricone!" the man's voice boomed out, each word louder than a thunderclap.

Everyone pushed back from their tables and shot to their feet. I did the same, as did Delmira and Leonidas on either side of me.

Delmira leaned past me and looked at her brother. "Where is Milo?"

My gaze flicked to the two conspicuously empty chairs across the table from Delmira and me. The crown prince should have arrived before the queen, as protocol dictated, but he was nowhere in sight.

"Where *is* he?" Delmira managed to hiss the words while still keeping a smile fixed on her face. An impressive feat, even for a princess.

Leonidas shrugged, as if he didn't know, but worry filled his face. Delmira leaned back, her smile even tighter than before, as though she were grinding her teeth to hold it in place.

The last echoes of the man's voice faded away, and silence descended over the throne room again. No one moved or spoke, and a faint noise rang out—the same *snap-snap-snap-snap* of heels striking the floor I'd heard in the rotunda this morning. The steady rhythm filled me with dread, but there was no escape.

Not from the queen.

Maeven strode into view, her head held high, and her gaze fixed straight ahead. The white light from the fluorestone chandeliers brought out the sharp, angular planes of her face while softening the fine lines around her eyes and the deeper wrinkles around her mouth. Maeven had shed her simpler day clothes for a stunning silk gown that was such a dark purple it almost looked black. The same shade of berry balm stained her lips.

The streaks of silver in her hair had been braided, like marks of honor, and then sleeked back into the rest of her golden bun. A modest amethyst-and-diamond crown was perched on her head, while silver bracelets studded with amethysts were stacked up on her wrists. Matching rings glittered on her fingers, and a large, square amethyst almost as big as my palm hung from a silver chain around her neck.

The jewels were filled with Maeven's lightning magic, and the collective treasure trove of power made my fingertips tingle even more violently than they had this morning, as though I were continuously getting static-shocked. Curious that Maeven would wear so many gems filled with so much magic to a formal dinner.

Maeven strode to the head of the table, and a servant pulled out her chair. Instead of sitting down, the queen looked out over the sea of people. She glanced at Delmira first, then Leonidas, and nodded to them. Her gaze skittered across the table to the two empty seats, but she quickly moved on, as though the spaces were of no importance, even though it was a glaring oversight and a highly insulting bit of protocol.

Then Maeven focused on me. Her sharp, critical gaze trailed down my dress before drifting back up to my face. The queen studied me for several seconds, but I stood tall and straight and stared right back at her. I would have *loved* to have known what she was thinking, but I didn't dare try to skim her thoughts, lest she sense my magic.

Maeven swept her skirt out to the side and sat down. Everyone waited until she was settled, then took their own seats again.

The queen opened her mouth, probably to welcome everyone to her birthday dinner—

In the distance, a door *banged* open, as though it had been forcibly slammed into the wall behind it. The sound boomed through the throne room, although it was quickly replaced by the loud *slap-slap-slap-slap* of footsteps. Several whispers of surprise surged through the crowd.

I couldn't see what was going on without craning my neck, so I studied Reiko. Sometime over the past few minutes, her morph mark had migrated from her hand up to her neck. Reiko's eyes narrowed, and smoke boiled out of the dragon's mouth, the black plume streaking across her skin before fading away. Whatever Reiko was looking at angered both her and her inner dragon—

Someone stepped in front of me, cutting off my view of Reiko and creating a long shadow that engulfed me. I looked up. A man was standing on the opposite side of the table. He was tall and muscled, with tan skin, dark amethyst eyes, and wavy hair that gleamed like liquid gold. No hint of stubble dared to darken his sharp, pointed chin, and he had the same angular nose and cheekbones as Maeven.

A short, formal midnight-purple jacket draped perfectly off his broad shoulders. Gold buttons marched down the front of the jacket, while the Morricone crest done in gold thread stretched all the way across his chest. Bold of him to wear such a large crest. That sort of thing was usually reserved for the ruling royal, especially at a formal dinner.

Then again, I doubted that Milo Maximus Moreland Morricone cared much for the niceties of protocol.

I had seen his likeness more than once, so I knew exactly who he was. Even worse, the crown prince's power blasted over me, and my fingertips started violently tingling again. He seemed to be just as strong in his lightning magic as Maeven was in hers, although her plethora of amethyst jewelry gave her a clear edge. Still, Milo was easily one of the most powerful magiers I had ever encountered.

Milo didn't bother greeting the queen or his siblings. Instead, his cold gaze flicked over me, the new person at the table. He must have thought I was one of Delmira's friends because he turned away, dismissing me as unimportant. He gestured with his hand, and a woman stepped into view.

She was stunningly beautiful, with pale gray eyes and rosy skin. Her red velvet gown brought out the matching highlights in her long auburn hair, and a gorgeous gold-and-ruby choker ringed her neck. That must be Corvina Dumond, Milo's fiancée.

My fingertips tingled yet again, and they also grew cold and wet, as though I had dipped them in a bucket of ice water. Corvina was rumored to be a powerful weather magier, as were most of the Dumonds.

"Sorry we're late," Milo said, although there was no true apology in his deep voice.

"Oh, yes, Mother Maeven. Please forgive us," Corvina chimed in.

Mother Maeven? Blech. Corvina was laying it on a bit thick, but I didn't envy her position. Having Maeven as a mother-in-law was a terrifying prospect. I would have been bowing and scraping and doing everything I could to earn her favor, lest she decide to kill me and marry her son to someone else.

The queen stared at the younger, twenty-something woman, and Corvina's smile quickly cracked and slipped off her face. No doubt many a noble had wilted under that icy, inscrutable glare.

"I do not know how things are done in other families," Maeven said, her voice deceptively light and pleasant. "But in *my* family, one is not late for a formal engagement."

Milo rolled his eyes, but Maeven ignored her son and kept

staring at Corvina, as though she blamed solely the younger woman for the couple's tardiness.

Corvina dropped into a deep curtsy. "My apologies, Mother Maeven. We were busy with the wedding planning."

"I am your *queen*, not your mother," Maeven said in that same deceptively pleasant voice. "Surely simple familial lineage is not beyond your grasp."

Several amused chuckles rang out. Courtiers enjoyed few things more than seeing someone cut down with cruel words.

Corvina snapped upright. An angry flush stained her cheeks, and she opened her mouth, but the queen kept giving her that same icy stare, and Corvina had the good sense to pinch her lips together and bite back whatever insult she'd been about to hurl at Maeven.

"Come," Milo said, breaking the tense silence. "Let us sit."

He pulled out the chair across from mine, and Corvina dropped down into it. She made a big show of arranging her skirt, but rage glittered in her eyes, making them gleam like gray stars.

Arrogant old bitch. I didn't even have to reach out with my magic. Corvina's vicious thought pounded into my mind with the same red-hot rage that was hammering in her heart.

Calm, calm, calm, Corvina muttered in her mind. *Must stay calm*.

Then another, softer thought whispered in my mind. *This farce will be over soon enough*.

Now *that* was interesting. Corvina could be thinking about the dinner, but her words sounded snide and sinister, as if she was talking about something much more important than the meal. Could Corvina be plotting against Maeven?

Milo sat down in his own chair. He was on the queen's left, while Delmira was on her mother's right. I was next to Delmira, with Corvina across from me. Leonidas was on my right, with a noblewoman across from him. More nobles filled out the rest of the table.

Another series of bells rang, servants streamed into the throne room, and the queen's birthday dinner officially began.

I had never been to a Mortan dinner before, but it was as fine, grand, and extravagant as any formal occasion I had ever attended in Andvari, Bellona, or Unger.

Dish after dish was placed before me. Cold vegetable soups brimming with spices. Hot fruit soups adorned with crispy, caramelized sugar chips. Stacks of fried green tomatoes served with cilantro sour cream. Peaches, pears, and raspberries tossed in a tangy ginger-lime vinaigrette. Soft yeast rolls dripping with savory dill butter. Hard, crusty baguettes drizzled with sourwood honey. Most of the dishes were small, no more than three bites, but each one was exquisite.

The more generous main course was sweet-and-sour meatballs served with fat raviolis stuffed with parmesan and ricotta cheeses and dusted with toasted sourdough breadcrumbs seasoned with sage. For dessert, there were dried fruits paired with a variety of cheeses, along with sweet nuts and spiced chocolates.

I washed everything down with a light, refreshing cherry lemonade, sighed with happiness, and placed my napkin on the table. If this was my last meal, then it had been a most excellent one.

Once the dessert dishes had been cleared away, the servants brought out trays of after-dinner drinks. I chose a flavored ice sweetened with mangoes, strawberries, limes, and a splash of mango liqueur. The cold, fruity concoction was so delicious that I sipped it slowly, trying to make it last as long as possible.

There hadn't been much conversation during dinner, although one noble after another had gotten up at the start of each new course to wish Maeven a happy early birthday, since the grand occasion wasn't until tomorrow. Hearing the nobles sing their queen's praises made me grind my teeth, but I had concentrated on my food and managed to ignore most of their flowery platitudes, along with the snide whispers they were truly thinking about their not-so-beloved queen.

Now that the food was gone, I didn't know what would happen. I glanced at the double doors in the distance, but they remained closed. No escape yet.

The woman across from Leonidas leaned forward, looking past Corvina and Milo and focusing on Maeven. "Let me also wish you a happy early birthday, my queen," she said in a sultry voice.

"Thank you, Lady Dumond," Maeven replied in her deceptively pleasant tone, although she gave the other woman an icy glare, just like she had Corvina earlier.

Lady Dumond? I studied the other woman. She had the same auburn hair, rosy skin, and gray eyes that Corvina did, although she was at least twenty-five years older, in her late fifties, like Maeven was. She had to be Lady Emperia, Corvina's mother and the current head of the Dumond family.

I shifted in my chair, even more uneasy. The Dumonds were known to be just as cruel as the Morricones, and I couldn't afford to draw their attention either.

"Tell me, Delmira, who is your guest?" Emperia turned her attention to me.

I silently cursed myself. Sometimes I thought that my magic enjoyed playing tricks on me. More often than not, every time I thought about someone, that person immediately zoomed in on me, like a gargoyle streaking toward its prey.

Everyone stared at me. Maeven, Milo, Corvina, Emperia, Delmira, Leonidas. I was swimming in a sticky soup of enemies. I just hoped I didn't end up boiled alive like a lobster before the end of the evening.

"This is Lady Armina from Ravensrock," Delmira said.

"She was attacked by bandits, but Leonidas was nearby and rescued her."

Emperia's gaze sharpened. "How very lucky."

"More like incredibly romantic," Delmira pronounced, giving me a sly look. "Just like something out of a storybook."

Perhaps if that storybook involved stolen tearstone, dozens of murders, numerous betrayals, and the attempted and almost successful assassinations of both Leonidas and myself. Not to mention my being kidnapped and taken to a foreign palace where I was surrounded by enemies, all of whom would dearly love to see me dead. Including my aforementioned rescuer, the prince, my childhood nemesis, who had grown up into a strangely fascinating, delectably handsome man.

I didn't know of any storybooks like that, though. Perhaps Delmira had one in her chambers that I could borrow to pass the time—after I was exposed and thrown in the dungeon.

"So you're Leonidas's newest stray pet," Milo sneered at me.

Anger spurted through me at being called a bloody *pet*, but Crown Prince Milo outranked Lady Armina, so I kept a bland smile fixed on my face.

Milo leaned forward, as though he was imparting some great secret to me. "Leonidas likes to invite people to the palace. Commoners, mostly. People with little magic and dubious talents that they peddle as high art. Paint masters, sculptors, minstrels, even a few so-called *poets*." He shuddered, as though the last word was the most horrific thing he had ever encountered.

Milo leaned back and waved his hand in an airy, dismissive motion. "People with small, trite skills that Leonidas thinks are more important and valuable than they truly are. They all tend to leave the palace rather quickly." A cruel light glinted in his eyes. "Especially the women. I suppose my brother isn't particularly *talented* in certain areas himself."

Beside me, Leonidas stiffened, and his anger spiked through

my mind. "I invite artisans to the palace so that the nobles, merchants, and everyone else can see the best of what Morta has to
offer. Those paint masters, sculptors, minstrels, and so-called
poets are our kingdom's future, and they should be treated and
nurtured as such."

Milo sneered at his brother the same way he had at me.
"People making cheap trinkets and composing ridiculous songs
isn't going to help Morta's standing among the other kingdoms."

"What do *you* think will help Morta's standing?"

The question popped out of my mouth before I could stop it,
although the second the words came out, I cursed my own foolishness. *Stupid, stupid, Gemma!* My tongue and my temper had
gotten the better of me, the way they so often did.

Milo's eyes narrowed, and he studied me more closely.
My heart quickened with dread. If he recognized me, then I
wouldn't leave this table alive.

And he wasn't the only one staring. Corvina and Emperia
were both peering at me, while Delmira was looking at me with
wide eyes. Even Maeven was studying me, her lips puckered in
thought.

Milo shrugged. "Building up our army and navy. Breeding
larger and more aggressive and vicious strixes. Coming up with
new ways to defend our borders, expand our holdings, and as-
sert ourselves."

And my new weapon. Once again, I didn't have to reach out
with my magic. His thought slammed into my mind like a tidal
wave, along with smaller ripples of smug satisfaction that made
my stomach churn.

A weapon? Oh, I knew Milo hadn't stolen all that tearstone
just to make jewelry with it, but his unrelenting smugness gave
me the sense he was thinking about something far more dangerous than typical swords, daggers, and shields. What new
horror had he created?

"Well, I agree with Leonidas." Delmira waded into the dangerous conversational waters. "Inviting artisans to Myrkvior is a wonderful idea."

Milo snorted and gave another dismissive hand wave. "What would you know about art or anything else? You barely have enough magic to fill a teacup."

Delmira's eyes narrowed, and she sucked in a breath as if to deliver some insult. Milo arched an eyebrow and stared at his sister, clearly daring her to say something. Delmira's gaze flicked to Corvina and Emperia, who were now sneering at her instead of me.

The princess just . . . *wilted*, much the same way Corvina had earlier under Maeven's icy glower. Delmira's face twisted into a defeated, miserable expression, her shoulders sagged, and she dropped her head, although not before I saw the sheen of tears in her eyes.

Why do I have to be so bloody weak? *So* broken? *Why can't I be strong like Mother always is?*

Her thoughts whispered in my mind, and I thought of the testing table in her chambers. It seemed as though the princess was still trying to find her magic, as well as her place in the palace.

Sympathy flooded my heart, washing away the nauseating feel of Milo's cruel smugness. Below the table, out of sight of the others, I reached over and squeezed her hand. Delmira didn't lift her head, but she curled her fingers into mine.

Milo turned his attention back to me. "And what magic or skills do *you* have, Lady Armina?"

"I make jewelry."

"What kind of jewelry?" Corvina's eyes brightened with interest. "Are you a metalstone master?"

"I have a small bit of metalstone magic. It helps me shape the pieces, although I'm not strong enough to actually infuse my magic into the gems."

It was the same general story Leonidas had told about me earlier, but I put my own touches on it, polishing it into a better version the same way I would polish a necklace in Alvis's workshop. I really could make jewelry, although my pieces were serviceable at best, since I didn't have any metalstone magic.

The interest vanished from Corvina's face. "Not even strong enough to put beauty glamours into your designs? Well, that makes them—and you—rather inferior."

She probably thought her insult was so devastating that it would leave me in tears, perhaps even send me running from the table, but a low, mocking laugh erupted from my lips instead. Scores of people had called me far worse things than *inferior*. Corvina needed to up her viciousness if she wanted to wound me.

Corvina glared at me. Magic crackled in her eyes, reminding me that I needed to be just as careful of her as I did of Milo.

"Yes, well, I suppose that I am rather inferior when it comes to my magic," I said in a diplomatic voice, trying to smooth things over. "Although I've never cared much about what other people think of me, as long as they buy my jewelry designs."

"Then you're a fool," Emperia said. "Reputation can make—or break—you in an instant."

"Oh, I doubt that Lady Armina is a fool," Maeven murmured, finally joining the conversation. "She seems like the sort who has very surprising, unexpected depths."

My heart froze, suddenly as cold as the mango-flavored ice I had eaten earlier. Had Maeven guessed my secret? Did she know who I really was?

I stared at the queen, who looked right back at me, an unreadable expression on her face. Somehow, I managed to keep my own features calm, even as the ice cracked off my heart, which started galloping around like a runaway Floresian stallion in my chest.

"Several jewelers have invaded Myrkvior in recent days, but none with such an interesting story as you, Lady Armina," Maeven continued. "My earlier offer stands. You must make a piece for Delmira. I could also use a new trinket. After all, it is my birthday tomorrow."

I bowed my head, staring at my crumpled napkin and desperately trying to gather my thoughts. "Of course, Your Majesty. I would be honored to make pieces for you and your daughter."

I lifted my head and attempted to smile at Maeven, but my face must have betrayed my wariness, because Emperia and Corvina both snickered. They enjoyed watching the queen put me on the spot, because they knew what an extremely perilous place it was to be.

Maeven ignored their laughter, tossed her own napkin onto the table, and stood up.

Delmira shot to her feet, as did Leonidas. I followed suit, as did everyone else seated at this table and all the others around the room. Milo hesitated, as did Corvina and Emperia, but the three of them also rose, albeit far more slowly than everyone else.

"I have some work to attend to." Maeven's voice didn't seem overly loud, but it still boomed through the throne room. "Thank you all for your kind sentiments and such a lovely birthday dinner. Please, stay and enjoy yourselves."

Once again, her gaze locked with mine, and her lips puckered, as though she didn't particularly like what she saw. Maeven stared at me a moment longer, then strode away.

The queen might be leaving, but strangely enough, I felt as though I were in more danger than ever before.

CHAPTER EIGHTEEN

As soon as Maeven left, everyone in the throne room relaxed. The servants passed out more wine, and the nobles, merchants, and other guests started drinking, gossiping, and laughing. Everyone was taking the queen's order to enjoy themselves to heart.

Milo didn't even glance at his siblings. Instead, he and Corvina drifted away, talking to Emperia, who gestured for some other nobles to join them. Delmira and Leonidas both eyed the group, concern creasing their faces.

"I should go check on Mother." Delmira paused, then her face brightened, as though the most wonderful idea had just occurred to her. "Leo, why don't you escort Armina back to her chambers?"

She made the suggestion in a neutral tone, but her lips curved up into a sly smile. I bit back a groan at her trying to play matchmaker again. The last thing I needed to do was spend more time with Leonidas. He was my enemy just as much as Maeven was, something I desperately needed to remember, especially since he could do far more damage to me. The queen could only kill me once, but the prince . . . Well, I didn't want to even think about the much deeper wounds he could inflict on my mind and especially on my heart.

"I would be delighted to escort Lady Armina." Leonidas offered me his arm. "If I may?"

"Of course, Your Highness." I threaded my arm through his, trying not to notice how his muscles bunched and flexed under my light touch.

Delmira winked at me, and I rolled my eyes, telling her that I knew exactly what she was doing. "Don't forget that you and Lady Reiko promised to have breakfast with me tomorrow."

"I'm sure Lady Reiko is looking forward to it just as much as I am."

Reiko was chatting with a noble a few feet away, but her gaze flicked in my direction, as if she'd heard me say her name. I tipped my head to the dragon morph, who ignored me in return. And that was the last I saw of her before Leonidas led me out of the throne room.

Several people had drifted outside the chamber and were clustered in small groups, drinking, laughing, and gossiping. Leonidas nodded to a few folks, but he led me past them without stopping. Soon, we were in a hallway by ourselves. The second we were alone, I untangled my arm from his and stepped back.

"What's wrong? You don't like being escorted by me?" he asked in a dry, sardonic tone.

I shot him an angry glare. "I don't like sitting within arm's reach of your mother. Not to mention your brother. It's difficult to spy on someone after he's seen your face."

Leonidas shrugged. "Milo thinks you're a jeweler with a negligible amount of metalstone magic. He'll have forgotten your name by the time he downs his next drink."

He was probably right, given how Milo had sneered at me, but I couldn't help but think of how Maeven had stared at me during dinner. Unless I was gravely mistaken, the queen hadn't believed my lies, and she knew that I didn't belong here. The sooner I found the tearstone, the sooner I could leave, and the safer I would be from *all* the Morricones, including Leonidas.

Especially Leonidas.

A thought occurred to me. "How long will Milo stay in the throne room?"

Leonidas shrugged again. "Probably until the bitter end. Milo fancies himself a great politician. He doesn't realize that the nobles tolerate him simply because they know he's going to be their king someday."

This farce will be over soon enough. Corvina's earlier thought drifted through my mind. Perhaps Corvina and her fiancé wanted that someday to get here sooner rather than later. Milo seemed to have no love for either Leonidas or Delmira, and I doubted the crown prince would let his mother stand in his way either.

A shiver swept through my body. I had no desire to be trapped in Myrkvior should such a coup take place. Oh, yes. The sooner I found the tearstone, the more likely my head stayed attached to my shoulders.

"Where is Milo's workshop?" I asked.

Understanding filled Leonidas's face. "You want to search his workshop right now, while he's still at the dinner."

"Well, I certainly can't search it while he's in there. Don't you want to see what your brother is hiding?"

His eyes glittered with a cold, calculating light. "Absolutely."

Leonidas took my arm again, and we ambled through the palace as though we were out for a simple after-dinner stroll. We passed dozens of couples doing the same thing, as well as a few in shadowy alcoves who were engaged in far more . . . *vigorous* activities. The grunts, moans, and gasps of pleasure made me even more aware of my arm tangled up with Leonidas's, his muscles flexing under my fingertips and our bodies swaying together as we walked along.

Leonidas cleared his throat, as though he were as uncomfortable as I was. "Come, Lady Armina," he said, opening a door. "Let me show you the rookery."

A few people nearby eyed us, and one man openly snickered as though *showing me the rookery* was code for *fucking me senseless*. I ignored the laughing noble, and Leonidas steered me outside and shut the door behind us.

We stepped into a courtyard covered with thick strands of liladorn, and Leonidas led me toward a fountain bubbling in the center. Once we had rounded it, he glanced back over his shoulder. The light and noise from the palace had faded away, leaving the two of us standing in the silent, silvery moonlight.

Leonidas turned toward me. Startled, I lurched back, and my heel hit one of the vines that had snaked across the flagstones. I stumbled sideways and would have fallen if Leonidas hadn't grabbed me around the waist and yanked me back toward him. I instinctively reached out, fisting my hands in the front of his jacket.

We both froze, staring into each other's eyes. His hands curled around my waist, the heat of his palms scorching my skin even through the thick fabric of my dress. My fingertips tingled in response, not from any magic, but simply from his strong, muscled body so close to my own, his warm breath caressing my cheeks, and his honeysuckle scent sinking deeper and deeper into my lungs with every ragged breath I took.

Leonidas stared down at me with an unreadable expression, his face cold and calm, although his eyes betrayed him. Emotions flashed like lightning strikes in his amethyst gaze— hunger, desire, and a raw, aching need that made every part of me clench with anticipation.

His gaze dropped to my lips, and his hands tightened. The motion was almost imperceptible, and he didn't draw me any closer, but I felt as though I were standing in a high, high tower, about to step off the side and fall into . . . Well, I wasn't quite sure what.

My destruction, most likely.

A bit of self-preservation rose up inside me, breaking the strange spell his eyes and the moonlight had cast, and I yanked myself out of his arms. This time, I avoided the vines and stepped back without tripping. I started to take another step back, but my heel brushed up against another liladorn vine—one that hadn't been there a moment ago.

I froze again, staring down at the vine. It seemed to be moving ever so slightly, as though it was trying to nudge me back toward Leonidas.

What are you doing? I sent the thought out to the vine, wondering if it could actually hear me, if it was actually aware enough to understand my words.

Helping, a soft voice rasped back to me.

Helping? How? By playing matchmaker like Delmira had earlier? No, that was ridiculous. Why would the vines care about my love life? Unless . . . they were somehow mirroring Delmira's thoughts and desires, or doing what they thought she wanted them to. No, that idea seemed even more ridiculous. It was far more likely that being in Myrkvior was slowly but surely driving me mad.

Madness might be preferable to the desire still surging through my body.

The vine slithered toward me again. I jerked my foot away from it and moved over to an open space in the courtyard, as far away from the liladorn as I could get.

Leonidas frowned. "Is something wrong?"

I shook my head, not wanting to admit that the vines had spoken to me. "No."

Disbelief flickered across his face, but he jerked his head. "The rookery is this way."

I eyed the vines again, making sure they were going to leave me alone, then followed him.

Leonidas led me out the far side of the courtyard and through several more. He didn't speak, and neither did I, and the only sounds were our footsteps scuffing across the flagstones. At one point, we passed the throne room. Leonidas paused and stared in through the windows. I peered inside too.

Milo, Corvina, and Emperia were still drinking and talking to some nobles, and it didn't seem as though they were in any hurry to leave. I scanned the rest of the room, but I didn't spot Reiko anywhere. I wondered if the dragon morph had also taken this opportunity to skulk around the palace. Probably.

"Let's go," Leonidas said.

We hurried through that courtyard and a couple more beyond it. Eventually, we reached two double doors made of liladorn, similar to the ones outside Delmira's chambers. The doors soared more than seven stories into the air, making them impossibly heavy. Leonidas waved his hand, and they easily swung open, although I thought that had more to do with the liladorn obeying the prince's command than the strength of his magic. I shivered. Either way, it was unnerving.

Leonidas strode through to the other side, and I trailed along behind him.

"And this," he said, pride and joy filling his voice, "is the rookery."

I looked up and let out a startled gasp. We were in an enormous open-air tower dimly lit by strings of soft white fluorestones. Liladorn vines twined through the gray stone walls, which featured dozens and dozens of hollowed-out spaces. At first, the spaces appeared to be empty, but then two eyes appeared, glowing like purple matches in the shadows. Then two more eyes in another space, then two more, and two more, until dozens and dozens of pairs of eyes were peering at me.

My breath caught in my throat. Slowly, the eyes crept forward, and the shadows morphed into strixes. The hollowed-out spaces were their nests, starting at the ground level and climbing to the tops of the tower walls. Some of the strixes were larger than Floresian stallions, while others were babies, no bigger than kittens, with lilac-colored feathers, instead of the darker amethyst ones that marked the older creatures.

At the sight of the prince, the strixes fluffed out their feathers and chirped out high, happy, singsong greetings. Soon, the notes *Leo! Leo! Leo!* pealed through the air like bells ringing. Longing pierced my heart. The gargoyles often greeted me with similar, albeit lower and more grumbling, cries whenever I visited them on the Glitnir rooftops.

One of the strixes flew down from a high perch, landed in front of Leonidas, and nuzzled up against him. Lyra, of course.

Leonidas laughed and stroked one of her wings. "Sorry I haven't been around much today. Maybe we can go for a ride tomorrow."

"Hold you to it," Lyra chirped, then fixed her bright eyes on me. "Maybe she can come with us. The gargoyle is almost here."

Leonidas frowned. "Gargoyle?"

Lyra opened her beak, but I cut her off before she could answer him.

"As much as I'm enjoying seeing the rookery, I thought we were going to break into Milo's workshop. We need to do that before he leaves the dinner."

Leonidas eyed me. He knew I was changing the subject, but he didn't call me on it. He stroked Lyra's wing again, then gestured at me. "This way."

He rounded a fountain and headed deeper into the rookery. Lyra hopped along behind us, her talons scraping against the flagstones, while the rest of the strixes watched silently from their nests.

Leonidas walked to the very back of the rookery and stopped in front of one of the walls.

"What are you doing?" I asked. "We're wasting time. Milo could decide to leave the throne room at any second."

"We're taking a shortcut."

A mischievous grin creased his face, softening his features and brightening his eyes, and I was suddenly reminded of the boy he had been—the one who had seemed so genuinely concerned about me. My heart twinged, but I ignored the tug on its strings.

Leonidas pulled down on a particularly large thorn on one of the liladorn vines. A soft *click* sounded, and part of the wall slid back, revealing a narrow corridor with a low ceiling. "This way."

He stepped into the corridor. Lyra looked at me, as did the other strixes. I wondered if the creatures would eat me if I didn't do as their prince wanted. Probably. Either way, I doubted I could leave the rookery without getting torn to pieces, so I stepped into the chamber.

Lyra stayed behind in the courtyard. She pushed that same thorn back up with her beak. The wall closed behind me, casting the chamber in total darkness.

A hand grabbed mine, and I had to swallow down a surprised shriek.

"This way," Leonidas said. "You can trust me. Promise."

I couldn't see his face, but his voice floated through the darkness and wrapped around me as surely as his hand clutched mine.

"Lead the way," I whispered back.

His fingers slowly curled into mine, and he carefully drew me along behind him.

I didn't know how long we were in the passageway. It could have been a minute, or two, or ten. But sometime later, Leonidas abruptly stopped, and I slammed into his side. We stood there, pressed up against each other. I tried to ignore how warm and strong his body was, how good he smelled, and especially how this innocent contact made me think of other, far more pleasurable and wicked things we could do in the dark together.

Leonidas dropped my hand and stepped away. I started to reach for him but clenched my fingers into a fist instead, grateful the shadows hid the traitorous motion.

He must have pulled on a handle, because another soft *click* sounded, and I heard something slide back.

"This way," he whispered. "And be quiet. A guard or two is usually posted outside."

Leonidas took my hand and led me forward again. The longer we walked, the more light that appeared, and I blinked against the growing glare. A few seconds later, we stepped out of the passageway and into a large chamber.

Unlike the rest of the palace, no paintings or tapestries adorned the walls. A few purple rugs featuring the Morricone royal crest done in gold thread were strewn across the floor, but they were the only bits of softness in here. Shelves filled with books, maps, and more hugged the walls, while large stone tables covered with glass tubes, jars, and beakers marched down the center of the room. Tools also littered many of the tables, along with swords, daggers, and shields. The air smelled sharp and clean, like orangey soap, although a faint coppery stench lingered under the other, stronger aroma, like rust hiding on the back of a shield.

To the left, an open archway led to a smaller area with a bed and several settees, and a door beyond that opened up into a bathroom done in black tile. Milo seemed to spend as much time in his workshop as Leonidas and Delmira did in their respective chambers.

I drifted forward, staring at the table closest to me, which was empty—except for the dried blood.

Dull brown stains covered much of the tabletop, and the surface was nicked and scratched, as though more than one sharp blade had scraped across it—or had been driven through someone's body to pin them to the stone underneath.

A cold finger of dread slid down my spine. "This is Milo's workshop?" I whispered.

Disgust filled Leonidas's face. "Unfortunately."

I didn't know what I'd been expecting, but it certainly wasn't this—whatever *this* truly was, other than horrifying. "Have you been in here before?"

"Yes, although not for a few weeks," Leonidas replied in a low, soft voice. "I've never found any tearstone in here, but I keep hoping that Milo will slip up and leave a clue behind about his plans. Let's see what we can find."

He went over to a table filled with tools. I started at one end of another table and walked down the length of it, scanning the contents.

At first glance, most of the items were ordinary, if a bit strange. A bronze sword with a bent, dented blade. A gold spear with a shattered tip. A silver shield that had been cleaved cleanly in two.

But the closer I got to the back of the workshop, the odder and more grotesque the items became. A jar filled with purple strix feathers spattered with what I assumed was strix blood. A lilac-colored strix egg that had been smashed to bits and left to rot inside another jar. Gray, brittle, withered liladorn vines with chopped off thorns that were curled up on a tray like a nest of dead coral vipers.

Milo seemed to enjoy experimenting on—*torturing*—creatures.

I wondered if his experiments also included people. I shivered again. Part of me didn't want to know.

But perhaps the most curious things were the rocks littering one of the tables. Chunks of limestone, slabs of granite, even a few diamonds, sapphires, and other gemstones. Some of the rocks were whole, smooth, and intact, while others had been cracked and dented, and a few had been shattered to shards.

Next to the rocks were open journals with worn, tattered purple covers, although the handwriting on the faded, yellowed pages was so tiny and cramped that I couldn't make sense of the scribbled words and rows of numbers. The only thing I could see clearly was the large, bold signature at the bottoms of the pages—*King Maximus*.

Another shiver zipped down my spine. These were Maximus's journals, although Milo seemed to be using the information to help with his own experiments. No matter how disturbing I found the notion, I could understand Milo tinkering with creatures and trying to take as much of their blood and magic as possible, just like his uncle had done. But what was he doing with the rocks? And how did his experiments tie in with the tearstone?

"Find anything?" Leonidas asked.

"Just your uncle's journals and your brother's experiments. You?"

"Nothing important. Just the tools Milo uses to inflict pain on others."

I gestured at the jar with the smashed, rotten egg. "Does he only experiment on strixes? Or does he use other creatures too?"

Grief lined Leonidas's face, and pain rippled off him. "Strixes, mostly. Some coral vipers too. No gargoyles or caladriuses, as far as I know, but not for lack of trying. Milo is *always* looking for new creatures to experiment on. We've had quite a few fights about it."

"Let me guess. You care about the strixes, and Milo doesn't."

Anger flared in his eyes. "I am fucking sick and tired of people slaughtering strixes. They're magnificent creatures and the bloody *symbol* of Morta, of the Morricones. We should be protecting strixes, nurturing them. Not burning them up like candles and then tossing them aside when their blood and magic are gone and they're of no further use." He spat out the words as though they left a bad taste in his mouth.

More disgust crinkled Leonidas's face, and he spun back around to the table, angrily sorting through the tools there, his fingers curling around the pliers, saws, and more as though he longed to use the tools on his brother the same way Milo had used them on the strixes.

I moved on to another table covered with books, papers, and maps. I eyed the books, which all had to do with various creatures. Strixes mostly, although several volumes focused on gargoyles and caladriuses. Leonidas was right. Milo wanted to experiment on other creatures, not just the strixes he had easy access to.

"Can Milo absorb magic from strix blood?" I asked. "Like King Maximus could?"

Leonidas jerked upright as though I had just shoved a sword into his back. An answering heat exploded in my gargoyle pendant, making it burn against my chest, but it couldn't hold back all of his emotion, and his rage slammed into my heart like a red-hot hammer, leaving me breathless.

"No," he growled. "Milo can't absorb power from strix or any other kind of blood. He didn't inherit that bit of Morricone mutt magic, thank the gods."

He paused, as if struggling to find the right words. More of his rage slammed into my heart, although waves of cold bitterness and roiling anguish quickly washed it away. "Milo is always searching for more magic and better, easier, quicker ways to kill his enemies. But he mostly experiments on the strixes because

he knows how much it hurts me. My brother might kill the creatures, but they die because of *me*."

Leonidas dropped his head, and his fingers clenched the
edge of the table as though he wanted to rip it apart with his bare
hands.

Sympathy filled me, and I had the strangest desire to walk
over, wrap my arms around his waist, lay my head on his back,
and tell him that it wasn't his fault. That *nothing* in this sick,
twisted workshop was his fault.

The urge to comfort him was so strong that I actually took a
step in his direction, before I thought better of it and stopped.

Leonidas raised his head, released the table, and returned
to his search. He didn't speak, but his rage, bitterness, and anguish kept cascading over me, making me sway from side to side
as I turned back to my own table. He had knocked my internal
ship off course, in more ways than one.

His confession also made me even more puzzled. If Milo
couldn't absorb magic, then why was he so eager to experiment
on creatures? He might be cruel, but the piles of books and
pages of notes indicated that he had *some* goal in mind, something more important and sinister than simply torturing his
younger brother.

I sorted through the books again, glancing at the titles, and
scanning the sections Milo had marked. Most of the passages
were dry, technical treatises speculating how strix, gargoyle,
and caladrius magic was different than the power that human
magiers, morphs, masters, and mutts wielded. Milo had also
marked several sections theorizing about how magic could be
used, absorbed, created, transmitted, and destroyed. Strange,
and a bit frightening, but the books and notes still didn't tell me
what he was plotting.

I picked up another book, and a bright gray gleam caught
my eye. Curious, I set the book down, snagged the item with my

fingertips, and pulled it out from underneath a stack of papers to reveal . . .

An arrow.

Disappointment surged through me, along with relief that it wasn't a dead coral viper, or something else equally disturbing. I started to shove the arrow back underneath the papers, but its bright gray gleam caught my eye again, and I held it up to the light for a better look.

The arrow was quite a bit shorter than normal, only stretching from my wrist up to my fingertips. The pointed tip was razor-sharp, but the arrowhead itself was unusually large and lined with hooked barbs that reminded me of fishing lures. I wasn't a weapons expert like my stepmother, Captain Rhea, but this arrow was clearly designed to do as much damage as possible. Even if you survived the initial impact, removing the arrowhead would be extremely painful, since its hooked barbs would tear out even more of a person's flesh.

"Find something?" Leonidas asked, glancing over at me.

"An arrow."

He nodded and continued with his own search, distracted by something on his table, but I kept staring at the arrow. Suspicion bloomed in my mind, and I twirled the weapon back and forth in my fingers. The arrow was a bright light gray, although it turned a dark midnight-blue when I moved it away from the light . . .

The arrow was made of tearstone.

Surprise shot through me. I'd heard Milo silently bragging to himself about his weapon at dinner, and I was certain this was it, although I was puzzled as to why he would think this arrow was something special. The small, compact design was wicked, to be sure, but it was still just a common weapon. It wasn't even the first tearstone arrow I had seen. Alvis crafted them for Rhea from time to time.

So why was Milo so impressed with himself for creating *this* arrow? What could it do that a regular one couldn't—

Across the workshop, a soft *click* sounded. I froze, recognizing the sound of a key turning in a lock.

Milo was here.

CHAPTER NINETEEN

*C*lick.

A key turned ominously in a second lock.

Leonidas whirled around to face me. "We have to get out of here!" he hissed. "Now!"

He sprinted over to the secret door, which was still standing open, and stopped inside the entrance, waiting for me.

I hesitated, wanting to put the arrow back where I'd found it, but there was no time to slide it under the stack of papers, so I shoved it into my pocket instead. Then I rounded the table and hurried toward Leonidas, keeping an eye on the closed doors at the front of the workshop—

My dress snagged on the corner of the table, jerking me to a stop. I grunted and tried to pull free, but neither my dress nor the table would budge. I couldn't move forward, so I backed up, reached down, and yanked the fabric free.

Click.

A key turned in a third lock, and one of the double doors cracked opened. My gaze snapped over to Leonidas, who was still standing in the secret passageway.

"Hide!" he hissed again.

I whirled around, searching for a settee, a desk, or some other piece of furniture large enough to crouch behind, but there was nothing like that in here. No doors led out of these chambers, and there were no windows. Desperate, I spun around and around, trying to find someplace to go—

A gleam of glass caught my eye, and my head snapped up. There *was* a window in the workshop, but it was fifty feet up on the wall. Normally, I could have used my magic to float myself up to the glass, but if I tried it now, Milo would probably sense my power, storm into the workshop, and fry me with his lightning.

Still, it was the only chance I had, so I rushed over to that wall, the only place in the entire workshop where there was any liladorn. The vines looked weak and brittle, as if they were starved of sunlight, but I took hold of them anyway and started climbing. The vines were as hard and slick as ebony glass, and the long thorns scratched my hands and ripped into my dress, but I kept going.

Ten feet, twenty, thirty . . . I scrambled up the vines, climbing as high as I could, but the liladorn stopped about five feet short of the window. I stood on my tiptoes, stretching out and up, but I couldn't reach the windowsill.

Move! Leonidas's voice sounded in my mind. *Before it's too late!*

I glanced down. One of the workshop doors was now standing wide open, but Milo wasn't striding inside. Instead, a faint giggle sounded, along with the rustle of clothing.

I looked over my shoulder at Leonidas, whose mouth was set into a hard, grim line. He knew that I couldn't reach the window. No doubt he would vanish into the passageway and save himself. After all, I was just an Andvarian spy he had foolishly brought to the palace. Totally expendable.

I didn't know if he heard my snide thoughts, but Leonidas

squared his shoulders and stepped forward, as though he was going to come and help me, and damn the consequences—

Several liladorn vines shot out of the secret passageway and wrapped around the prince's arms, stopping him.

What are you doing? Leonidas's voice filled my mind, even though he was talking to the vines. *Stop! Stop!*

The liladorn didn't listen. Instead, the vines dragged him back into the passageway. A moment later, the door slid shut, cutting off Leonidas from the workshop.

Armina! His voice sounded in my mind again. *Get out of there!*

His voice quickly grew fainter, as though the liladorn was pulling him away from the workshop and back through the secret passageway toward the rookery. Still, Leonidas's abrupt departure gave me an idea.

I curled my hands around the vines and focused on the tangle of thorns in front of my face. *Help me.* I sent the thought to the liladorn. *Please.*

Nothing happened. No vines twitched, no thorns quivered, no voices sounded in my mind. Apparently, the liladorn only concerned itself with the Morricones.

Down below, the door opened a little wider, and footsteps shuffled forward. I closed my eyes and banged my head on the vines in frustration. This was it. This was the end. Milo would discover me in his workshop and sound the alarm. If I was lucky, he would blast me off the wall with his lightning, and the fall would kill me outright—

A vine snaked around my ankle.

I choked down a surprised shriek, but I jerked back without thinking, and my heels slipped off the vine that I was standing on. I started to fall—

The liladorn caught me.

Another, larger vine shot out and curled around my waist, and I hung in midair, like a puppet suspended over a stage. Then the liladorn hoisted me up next to the window. I reached out, intending to open the window and crawl outside onto the roof, but once again, the liladorn had other ideas. The vines whipped me around, then plastered me up against the wall. My head snapped back against the stone, causing a dull ache to bloom in my skull.

Another vine crept toward me, then another one, then another one. In seconds, the liladorn had covered my entire body, except for my face. I felt like a fly stuck in a spider's web. A very hard, thorny spider's web.

Did liladorn vines drink human blood? I shuddered. Oh, I hoped not.

I tried to move, to escape, to reach the window that was so tantalizingly close, but the vines were as hard as stone, and I couldn't budge them. A thorn whipped out and dragged along my right cheek, not quite deep enough to break my skin, but more than enough to get my attention.

Stop struggling, a stern voice sounded in my mind. *Helping*.

Helping? I didn't know about that, but I quit moving. I didn't have another choice.

Down below, Milo finally strode through the open door. "You're right. It is past time that I showed you my workshop."

He held out his hand. Another giggle sounded, and a woman stepped into the room.

Emperia Dumond.

My eyes bulged with shock. I had expected Milo's paramour to be Corvina, his fiancée, not her mother. What was Emperia doing here?

She wasn't . . . They weren't actually . . .

Milo drew the older woman into his arms and crushed his lips to hers, while Emperia swooned into his embrace. Waves of lust rolled off both of them, making me even more uncomfortable than the vines still wrapped around my body. If I had to stay up here and watch them . . . Well, that would be almost as bad as being caught. Almost.

Emperia broke off the heated kiss and trailed her hands up and down Milo's chest. He started to yank her toward him again, but she put a finger up against his lips, stopping him.

"Business first," she murmured. "Pleasure later."

Milo leered down at her. "Isn't it all one and the same?"

"When destroying our enemies? Absolutely," she purred.

Milo reached around and pinched her ass, making Emperia gasp with surprise. Then he turned to the side and held out his arm, playing the part of the polite prince. Emperia threaded her arm through his, and he led her through the workshop, pointing out various tables and objects.

I listened closely to everything he said, but Milo did an excellent job of talking about his experiments in vague terms, using phrases like *unusual properties* and *shows great promise*, without revealing what he actually hoped to accomplish with his tinkerings. Smart of him to employ such a tactic. He was far more cunning than I'd realized.

Emperia smiled, nodded, and murmured the appropriate responses, although annoyance kept pinching her face, as though she too was frustrated with his obtuse talk.

Finally, Milo reached the table with the piles of books. He moved several of them aside, clearly searching for something. My hand fisted in my skirt. I knew what he was looking for—the arrow in my pocket.

"You promised to show me an example of your new weapon," Emperia cooed. "I'm most eager to see it."

Irritation filled Milo's face, although his back was to Emperia, so she didn't see it. "I thought I had left one in here. I must have put it in the old armory with the others."

He shrugged, as if the arrow's location was of little importance, but I latched onto his words. Old armory? Was that where he was keeping the tearstone? And just how many arrows had he crafted out of it?

"Perhaps we can go there tomorrow morning, and you can show it to me then," Emperia said. "I should be able to sneak away from Corvina."

Milo nodded. "Very well."

Emperia eyed him, a calculating look on her face. "Maeven will not approve of any of this. Not your new weapon, and especially not *us*. If she were to find out what we're planning, well, death would be a blessing, rather than the prolonged torture she would inflict on us."

Milo huffed. "I am well aware of what my mother is capable of, but I can handle her. I'm almost as strong in my magic as she is."

"*Almost* isn't good enough," Emperia replied in a sharp tone. "Not where Maeven is concerned."

For the first time tonight, I agreed with her. Maeven was an extremely powerful lightning magier, which made her a dangerous enemy, but even more impressive was the fact that she had held on to her throne for the last sixteen years, despite all the potential usurpers in Myrkvior. No, as much as I despised the Mortan queen, Maeven was most definitely not to be taken lightly, or worse, underestimated.

Milo rolled his eyes. "My mother is getting older and weaker every single day. You saw her tonight. She left her own birthday dinner early, rather than stay and shore up her support with the nobles. She *never* would have made such a glaring mistake in years past."

"Leaving a dinner early doesn't mean anything," Emperia replied, her voice even sharper than before.

Milo finally noticed her tone, and he peered down his nose at her. "I told you before—*I* will handle my mother when the time comes. If you're having second thoughts, then perhaps I should find another ally. Someone who isn't so interested in questioning my judgment."

Emperia's lips pressed together, as though she didn't appreciate him making light of her concerns. She was right to be worried. I would have been worried too, if I were plotting against Maeven.

"Besides, my mother won't be queen for much longer," Milo continued. "We'll put our plan into action as scheduled. First, we'll take the palace. Then, when all my weapons are ready, we'll turn our sights toward our true enemies."

So Milo was planning to wrest the throne away from Maeven. No surprise there, but I wondered who he considered his *true enemies*. Andvari? Bellona? Ryusama? He could be targeting any one of them. Or perhaps he was as ambitious as King Maximus had been and wanted to conquer *all* the kingdoms.

Emperia's concern melted into a sly, seductive smile, and she stepped forward and started toying with the gold buttons on Milo's jacket. "I do have one request regarding your mother."

"What?"

Her smile took on a toothy edge. "I want to be there when you finally give that arrogant bitch what she so richly deserves."

"Of course," Milo replied. "You've been so helpful supplying the men and the funds I needed to secure the tearstone and smuggle it out of Andvari. I promise that you'll be right by my side when I finally tear my mother down off her throne."

My eyes narrowed. So Emperia was financing Milo's scheme. Smart of the prince to get the noble to pay for his border raids. Still, the information only increased my worry. Dealing with the Morricones was bad enough, but the Dumonds were equally dangerous. An alliance between the two families could spell disaster for Andvari.

"And what will you do with Maeven afterward?" Emperia's

voice sounded casual, but her long red nails dug into Milo's jacket, indicating how important his answer was to her.

Milo shrugged again. "I'll have to kill her. She's too stupid to realize that she's already lost, and she'll fight for the throne until the bitter end."

Even though Leonidas had said that his brother was plotting against Maeven, more shock still spiked through me. Milo was talking about *assassinating* the queen, his own mother. No, not just talking about it—actively *planning* it with a noble rich and powerful enough to help him pull it off.

I shouldn't have been surprised, though. If the Seven Spire massacre had taught me nothing else, it was that assassinations, even of queens, were easy enough to arrange.

Emperia nodded, as if satisfied with Milo's answer. "What about your brother and sister? They won't take your mother's death very well."

Milo shrugged yet again. "Leonidas and I have never seen eye to eye. He's always been soft and weak. Always wanting to broker peace with the other kingdoms rather than bringing them to heel under Mortan rule like they should be. I'll kill him too. That way he can't cause us any trouble."

Worry churned in my stomach, and twin spikes of fear and dread skewered my heart. I still wasn't sure how I felt about Leonidas, but he had saved me from the mine, and I didn't want him to be killed, especially not so Milo could seize power.

Emperia nodded again. "And Delmira?"

"If she makes too much of a fuss, then yes, I will kill her too," Milo replied in a flat, emotionless voice. "But I doubt that she'll do anything more strenuous than cry. Delmira doesn't have enough magic to threaten me, so I'll marry her off to some lord in search of a young, pretty wife. Someone rich and loyal, who shares my vision for Morta."

Emperia nodded for a third time, apparently pleased by his plotting. Then another seductive smile spread across her face. "I must return to my chambers soon, before Corvina wonders where I've been. But before I go, perhaps we can finish what we started in the hallway." She tilted her head toward the open archway. "That looks like a perfectly serviceable bed."

Milo grinned. "I do so love experiments. Let's test out your theory."

He leaned forward and kissed her neck, even as his hands slid down her back and he pinched her ass again. Emperia let out another girlish giggle and wrapped her arms around his neck, a triumphant smirk filling her face. Milo might think he was in charge, but the noble lady definitely had her own agenda. She was probably just using him to kill Maeven, and then she would turn around and kill him, clearing her own path to the throne.

Milo started walking Emperia backward toward the archway. She giggled again, then took his hand and tugged him into the other room. A few seconds later, springs *squeak-squeak-squeaked* as they dropped down onto the bed. After that, well, I tried to block out their passionate sounds, although I wasn't entirely successful.

Once I was sure that Milo and Emperia were fully . . . *engaged*, I reached out with my magic, speaking to the liladorn again.

Let me go now. Please.

The vines quivered, then slowly loosened their grip and retreated. I turned around, plastered my chest up against the wall, and tiptoed over to the window.

I tried to open the window, but the frame was stuck. Frustration filled me, but I forced myself to stop and listen. Milo and Emperia were still engaged with each other, so I sent out a tiny trickle of magic, just enough to loosen the frame.

It *screeched* as I lifted it, but no shouts rang out, so I pushed the frame up as high as it would go, then hooked my leg over the sill and crawled out of Milo Morricone's workshop of horrors.

The window opened up onto a steep, sloping roof that was cold and slick with frost. As soon as I was outside, I used my magic to shut the frame behind me. Hopefully, Milo and Emperia would be too distracted to sense my small bursts of power.

My relief didn't last long, though. I might have escaped the workshop, but I was still stuck on a roof, some five stories above the ground. I started to get to my feet, but one of my heels slipped, so I took off the shoes and shoved them into my pockets. The frost burned my hands and feet, but my skin sticking to the stone made for much better traction. I sat on my ass and slowly wiggled down the roof, making sure not to go too fast lest I slide off and plummet to the courtyard far, far below. Nothing would save me from a fall that high.

I reached the bottom of the roof, where a stone gutter cordoned it off from the open air. I glanced around, trying to figure out how to get off this roof and onto the one below, and I spotted a drainpipe at the corner that ran down vertically to the next level of the palace. The drainpipe was also slick with frost, but I gripped the stone with my toes and used my magic to anchor my hands around it. Then I lowered myself down the drainpipe an inch at a time.

It was difficult, but I managed to climb down one story. A balcony jutted out from this level, and I stepped over onto the railing. Perhaps I could slip back inside this way—

A door opened, and Corvina Dumond strolled out onto the balcony.

I froze, with one arm still hooked around the drainpipe and my feet on the narrow railing. Then my mind kicked into gear, and I plastered myself up against the palace wall, hiding as best I could in the shadows. My heart pounded, and sweat dripped down the back of my neck as I waited for the inevitable shouts of surprise and discovery.

But they never came.

Instead, an arm snaked around Corvina's waist, and a man stepped forward and kissed the side of her neck, making her giggle just like her mother had. I grimaced at the eerily familiar sound. Corvina moved into a patch of light, revealing the man behind her.

Captain Wexel.

I almost fell off the balcony railing. First Milo and Emperia. Now Corvina and Wexel. Was no one here fucking whom they were supposed to be fucking? Myrkvior was an even more duplicitous place than I'd realized.

Corvina whirled around to face Wexel. She looped her arms around his neck and gave him a pretty pout. "I thought you had to work. That's what you said earlier when I asked you to meet me here."

Wexel pulled her closer. "I managed to get out of guarding Milo's chambers. I'd much rather plunder yours."

Corvina giggled again and batted her lashes at the captain. "Did you stay long enough to see my mother sneak into Milo's workshop?"

Once again, I almost fell off the railing. Corvina *knew* about her mother's affair with her fiancé?

"You were right," Wexel said. "Emperia seems to have Milo wrapped around her little finger. He was quite eager to get her alone in his workshop."

Corvina nodded, as if she had expected the information.

The captain frowned. "Doesn't it bother you? Your mother and Milo? He is *your* fiancé."

She shrugged. "Milo is just a means to an end. The only reason we got engaged is because Maeven wants to broker a lasting peace between the Morricones and the Dumonds. She thinks once Milo and I are married that my family will finally bow down and accept her rule. But that will *never* happen, not as long as one Dumond lives. She's killed far too many of us over the years, including my grandmother."

Corvina's face hardened, anger sparked in her eyes, and a few small gray hailstones flew out of her fingertips. I'd thought no one could hate Maeven more than me, but I was starting to think I was wrong about that—and a great many other things.

"So I'll go along with the engagement and smile and pretend that everything is fine. Let my mother fuck Milo all she wants in the meantime. It will save me the trouble of climbing into his bed." Corvina's red lips curled with disgust.

Wexel's eyes narrowed. "What are you planning?"

"I'm not planning anything. Even better, I don't have to actually *do* anything. That's the beauty of this whole situation. Emperia thinks she's being clever, manipulating Milo, and he thinks he's doing the same to her. Let them plot and scheme to kill Maeven. If they succeed, then I will heartily applaud them."

"And then?" he asked.

Corvina smiled, but it was a cold, cruel expression. "And then, when the time is right, I will get rid of Milo *and* my mother, and *I* will be the one sitting on the Mortan throne. With my loyal captain by my side, of course."

She stood on her tiptoes and pressed her lips to his. Wexel growled and yanked her even closer. Their loud, smacking kiss went on for quite some time before they broke apart.

Wexel brushed a stray lock of Corvina's hair back over her shoulder. "What if Milo and Emperia fail? What if the queen is the one who comes out on top?"

Corvina shrugged again. "Then Maeven will most likely kill my mother, and Milo too. I'll claim that I had no idea what my mother was scheming, and Maeven will have no choice but to believe me. She still needs my family and our magic, money, and connections too badly to get rid of me as well. Then, after an appropriate amount of tears and groveling, I'll suggest to Maeven that I get engaged to Leonidas to heal this ugly rift between our families. I'll handle Leonidas the same way I have Milo, with soft words and sweet promises I never keep."

She grinned. "Then, when the time is right, I'll stick a dagger in Leonidas's back and slit Maeven's throat. It might take longer than I want, but make no mistake. One way or another, I *will* be queen of Morta."

"Well, then, allow me the honor of being the first to pledge allegiance, my queen." Wexel lowered his lips to hers.

The two of them started kissing again, although Corvina quickly broke it off and tilted her head toward the open door. "Let's go inside. Someone might see us out here."

Wexel grinned. "I thought the risk of getting caught was part of the appeal."

Corvina returned his grin with a wicked one of her own. "Definitely. But it's too cold to fuck out here. I want a warm bed tonight—with you in it."

She grabbed the front of his jacket and tugged him inside. The door banged shut behind them, and Corvina's soft laughter drifted out through the glass. I remained frozen in place on the balcony railing, still clutching the drainpipe.

Milo was fucking Emperia, his fiancée's mother, while Corvina, his fiancée, was fucking Captain Wexel, Milo's personal guard. Talk about tangled webs—and deadly ones as well. Everyone had their eyes on the Mortan crown, and they would scheme, fuck, kill, and do whatever else it took in order to snag that ultimate prize.

If Maeven found out about any of this, especially Milo's plot to depose her, then she would probably kill every last one of them, including her own son. Milo, Emperia, Corvina, and Wexel thought that Maeven was a fool, but they underestimated the queen at their own peril.

Maeven might be older now, but she was no doubt wiser, given how many of her own schemes against Everleigh Blair and Grandfather Heinrich had failed over the years. I was willing to bet the queen had her own plans in place to counter any move that Milo, the Dumonds, or anyone else made against her.

My head was spinning with information, but I still needed to get down to the ground. Corvina and Wexel might come back out onto the balcony, and it was too risky to stay here. So I wrapped my hands around the drainpipe again and stepped off the railing, but my feet were numb with cold, and my toes just wouldn't grip the slick stone. My hands were chilled too, and they started to slide downward.

I lurched to the side. I managed to get one foot back onto the narrow balcony railing, but my other foot slipped off.

That one small motion threw me even more off balance. I lost my grip on the drainpipe completely and plummeted toward the ground.

CHAPTER TWENTY

Somehow, I managed not to scream. My arms and legs flailed wildly, searching for something to latch onto, but my fingers and toes met only cold, empty air.

Desperate, I reached for my magic, trying to use my mind magier power to propel my body toward the palace wall, but I couldn't quite get a grip on my power, and the ground rushed toward me at a dizzying rate. I cringed and braced for impact—

At the last instant, right before I would have slammed into the ground, a shadow darted underneath my body. I landed directly on top of it, knocking it down. The shadow grunted and dropped like a heavy brick.

Thump-thump.

The shadow hit the courtyard, and then I plowed into the shadow a moment later.

The hard, jolting impact knocked the air from my lungs and made my head spin again, but I rolled to my right, dimly wondering what had broken my fall. I slipped off whatever I'd landed on and ended up hitting the flagstones after all. Pain spiked through my ass and rippled up my spine, and a low groan escaped my lips.

Something shifted beside me, and a shadow loomed over me, blocking out the light streaming out of the palace windows. I blinked, and a pair of bright sapphire-blue eyes slowly came into focus.

"Grimley?" I whispered.

The gargoyle leaned down and licked my cheek, his rough tongue scraping against my skin, but not unpleasantly so. "Of course, runt. Who else would save you from falling to your death?"

Joy shot through me, overpowering my pain, and I scrambled up onto my knees and threw my arms around his neck. "Grims! I'm so happy you're here! That you're okay!"

The gargoyle shuffled closer and gently wrapped his wings around me. His love enveloped me, as soft and warm as a fuzzy blanket covering my body. The sensation drowned out some of my aches and pains, and a tight knot of tension loosened around my heart. Suddenly, I could breathe much easier, even though I'd just had the wind knocked out of me. I had been so worried about Grimley flying through Morta. Not that him being at the palace was much safer, but at least we were together again.

I drew back and scratched Grimley's forehead, right in between his two horns, just how he liked. The gargoyle leaned into my touch, his wings stroking down my back.

"I'm sorry I didn't get here sooner," he said in his low, gravelly voice. "It was harder to avoid the strixes and the guards than I thought. Stupid birds. Stupid Mortans."

I smiled, but before I could respond, the *crunch-crunch-crunch-crunch* of footsteps sounded. My head snapped around, and I spotted a couple of fluorestone lanterns bobbing along in the distance. Someone had entered the far side of the courtyard.

I scrambled to my feet, hurried over, and ducked behind some liladorn vines that had twined together to form a large bush. Grimley loped over and hunkered down beside me.

The lanterns grew brighter and closer, and two palace guards stepped into view. The men ambled along, not in any particular hurry, but they were vigilant, shining their lanterns into every corner of the courtyard, their free hands resting on the swords hooked to their belts.

Shall I kill them so that we can escape? Grimley's voice snarled in my mind, and his long tail twitched.

No. I can't leave the palace until I find out more about Milo Morricone's plans for the tearstone.

Haven't you done that already? What have you been doing all day? I flew over a mountain, caught three rabbits, snuck into the palace, and saved you.

I rolled my eyes at his superior, chiding tone. *I've been trying not to rouse suspicion about who I really am.*

And failing miserably, if I was being honest. Reiko Yamato knew exactly who I was, and Maeven also seemed highly suspicious of me, but I didn't mention any of that to Grimley. He would try to get me to leave, and I wasn't going home without knowing exactly what Milo was plotting.

The guards stopped and shone their lanterns at the liladorn bush. I slid my hand into my pocket, clutching the dagger still hidden there. The guards were just doing their jobs, but I would kill them if I had to.

After a few long, tense seconds, the guards lowered their lanterns, walked past our hiding spot, and wandered out the other side of the courtyard.

I exhaled, released my dagger, and reached out with my magic, but their presences quickly faded away. The guards were gone.

"Come on," I whispered. "I need to return to my chambers, and we need to find someplace for you to hide and rest."

Grimley nodded and fell in step beside me as I moved out from behind the liladorn bush and left the courtyard.

To my consternation, dozens of guards were roaming through the grounds, and it took Grimley and me almost an hour to avoid the men, sneak from one courtyard to the next, and wind our way back to the deserted wing where my chambers were located.

Finally, we reached the courtyard underneath my balcony. I glanced up at the other balcony, the one that led into Leonidas's library, but the doors were closed, and no lights shone through the glass.

Disappointment filled me. Leonidas hadn't used his magic to try to contact me while I'd been skulking around the palace, probably because he didn't want Milo or anyone else to sense us using our magic. I would have done the same if our positions had been reversed and he'd been the one trapped in Milo's workshop. But a small part of me had been hoping that he would be pacing in his library, waiting for me to escape, to return. That he would be concerned about me. That he would feel . . . *something* for me, the same way I felt this strange, unwanted *something* for him.

I should have known better, though. A Morricone would never be concerned about anything other than a Ripley's death.

I tore my gaze away from his balcony and pointed at my own. "My chambers are there. Help me up?"

Grimley hunkered down, and I climbed onto his back. The gargoyle flapped his wings, and we shot upward. A few seconds later, I slid down off Grimley's back and onto the balcony. He tucked his wings into his sides and perched on the railing like he was a statue that had been positioned there.

"You're sure that you don't want to leave now?" he rumbled. "We could be out of the city before sunrise."

I hesitated. It was after midnight, and most people were asleep, except for the guards. I could hop onto Grimley's back and let him fly me out of the palace and away from Majesta to the relative safety of the surrounding countryside. I knew that Milo was making tearstone weapons, and his barbed arrow was still nestled in my pocket. I could return to Andvari right now, and everyone, including my father and grandfather, would have to admit that my spy mission and unexpected foray into Morta had been a great success.

But I still had far more questions than answers. Milo might be making weapons and plotting to assassinate his mother, but who were the *true enemies* he'd mentioned? And why did he think tearstone arrows would help achieve his ultimate goal, whatever it was? I couldn't leave Myrkvior until I knew more about Milo's plans. Thwarting his scheme was the best way to defend Andvari.

And I was also concerned about another prince—Leonidas.

Like it or not, he had saved my life, and I had given him my word that I would help him figure out what was going on. At the very least, I needed to stay at Myrkvior long enough to warn Leonidas that he was in even more danger than he suspected, that Milo was planning to kill him and marry off Delmira. The prince and princess had both been kind to me in their own ways, and neither one of them deserved to suffer—or die—just because Milo wanted to be king right now instead of waiting for the natural order of things.

As for whether to tell Leonidas that Milo was planning to assassinate Maeven . . . Well, I didn't know what to do about that. Of course Leonidas already had his suspicions, but part of me wanted to keep quiet and let it happen. That would be one way to finally avenge Uncle Frederich, Lord Hans, and everyone else who had died during the Seven Spire massacre.

Oh, I might not have the satisfaction of actually killing Maeven myself, but it would still be a bloody sweet revenge. Let the bitch suffer the same way I had during the massacre. Let her feel the same fear, pain, terror, and panic I had that awful day. Let her see death slowly, inexorably approaching and realize there was nothing she could do to stop it, nothing she could do to save herself—

"Gemma?" Grimley asked, cutting into my murderous thoughts. "What's wrong? Why are you clutching your pendant?"

I glanced down. My fingers had unconsciously fisted around the gargoyle pendant hidden underneath my dress. The pendant had gone ice-cold against my skin, trying to contain the magic rising up inside me, the raw, brutal power that I yearned to unleash against Maeven.

I exhaled, forced my fist to open, and dropped my hand to my side. The pendant remained ice-cold against my skin, but the chill didn't numb the memories or the white-hot rage still pounding in my heart.

"Gemma?" Grimley asked again.

"I'm fine," I lied. "Just thinking. As much as I would like to, I can't leave. Not yet."

His face scrunched into a frown. "The longer you stay, the more danger you'll be in."

He was right. Every second I stayed at Myrkvior was a risk. I might have made promises to Leonidas, but I had also made them to Topacia and my father, and I had to weigh my own safety against whatever information I might uncover. A compromise, then.

"Give me the day to snoop around and see what else I can find out about Milo's plans. Then I'll sneak out of the queen's birthday ball, and we'll leave."

Grimley's frown deepened, but he leaned forward and licked my hand. "Very well," he grumbled. "As long as you stay out of trouble in the meantime."

"Don't I always?"

He snorted. "Never."

I grinned and scratched his head again. "Well, you're the one who's going to be in trouble if you don't find someplace to hide. See if Lyra can help you. I asked her to watch out for you earlier, and she's probably flying around the palace searching for you. If you're nice to her, maybe she'll find you a quiet tower or parapet to sleep on."

Grimley snorted again. "I can find my own tower. Although the bird is an excellent hunter. Perhaps she could help me track down a rat or two to nibble on," he admitted, a bit of grudging respect rumbling through his voice.

He nuzzled his head up against mine, then drew back, flapped his wings, and shot up into the sky. Another smile stretched across my face. Despite the danger I was still in, things were so much better now that he was here—

Creak.

One of the balcony doors swung open, and a shadow fell over me. I shoved my hand into my pocket. The tearstone arrow was the first thing I felt, so I yanked it out and whirled around to face the enemy sneaking up on me.

The arrow wasn't the easiest weapon to wield, but I gripped it like a dagger and lashed out with it, and the black-cloaked figure scrambled away. I lunged forward, whipping the arrow from side to side and driving the figure back across the balcony.

The figure banged into one of the closed doors, and I charged ahead, preparing to plunge the arrow into my enemy. The figure jerked to the side, and the black hood slipped off its head, revealing a familiar face.

I stopped short, the tip of the arrow an inch away from Leonidas's throat.

He stared at me, wariness filling his eyes. We stayed like that, frozen in place, for several seconds.

I let out a breath, stepped back, and lowered the arrow. "Sorry. I thought you were . . ."

"Who?"

"Milo, Emperia, Corvina, Wexel, Maeven. Take your pick." My eyes narrowed. "Why are you sneaking into my room in the middle of the night?"

"I was worried about you."

The simple admission made something warm and treacherous pool in my heart, but I crossed my arms over my chest, careful not to poke myself with the arrow. "Well, you have a funny way of showing it, leaving me behind in Milo's workshop. It's a wonder I didn't get caught and executed."

Leonidas grimaced. "That wasn't me—that was the liladorn. It has a mind of its own. Sometimes, it . . . interferes, although I've never quite understood why."

He glanced at a nearby vine, a puzzled look on his face. I frowned. Could Leonidas not sense the presence in the liladorn? Could he not hear its voice like I could? Strange. If anyone could communicate with the vines, then it should be the prince. Then again, all mind magiers were different, and no one's magic worked exactly the same way. Still, I found it curious that I could speak to the liladorn, and he seemingly could not.

Leonidas turned his gaze back to me. "It wasn't my intention to leave you behind. The liladorn shut me off from the workshop, then dragged me through the secret passageway and spat me out in the rookery. By the time I made it through the palace and back over to Milo's wing, I couldn't sense your presence anywhere near his workshop. So I took a chance that you had escaped, and returned here to wait for you."

He cleared his throat. "Even if you had gotten caught, I would have protected you. I would never just abandon you."

That warm, treacherous pool in my heart expanded, oozing

down into my stomach and spreading out to other areas. Still, his words reminded me of our childhood encounters. No matter how intriguing I found the Morricone prince, I needed to remember that he had betrayed me back then and he would betray me again now in a heartbeat, if he ever realized who I really was.

Leonidas's gaze swept over my gown, which was torn and dirty, along with the rest of me. "Are you okay?" He frowned. "Where are your shoes?"

"I'm fine. My shoes are in my pockets. I had to take them off to climb down the roof."

He blinked in surprise. "You climbed *down* the roof? Is that how you got out of Milo's workshop?"

"Yes. I climbed up the wall to the window in Milo's workshop and then out onto the roof."

He pointed at the arrow in my hand. "Why do you still have that?"

"Because Milo used the tearstone to make this arrow, and probably many more just like it." I held out the weapon where he could see it.

Leonidas studied the projectile, then let out a low whistle. "That is a nasty design, especially those hooked barbs lining the arrowhead. How long were you in Milo's workshop? Did he say anything about the arrow?"

"Long enough," I muttered, thinking of how the liladorn had trapped me against the wall. "Milo said a few vague things, including something about an old armory. I think that is where he's keeping the other arrows he's made. Do you know where it is?"

Leonidas's face hardened. "I know *exactly* where that is. Did Milo say anything else?"

He was deliberately changing the subject, although I wasn't sure why. Still, I pretended not to notice that he hadn't revealed where the old armory was.

"Milo didn't say anything else important about the arrows. He was much more interested in seducing his paramour."

Surprise flickered across Leonidas's face. "Corvina was in the workshop?"

"Not Corvina—Emperia."

Leonidas blinked, as if he was wondering whether he'd heard me correctly, but then understanding filled his face. "Oh."

"Yes, *oh*. The two of them were getting quite cozy when I slipped out the window."

He started pacing back and forth. "That is troublesome."

"Why?"

He sighed and kept pacing. "Emperia Dumond wants nothing more than to kill my mother and take the throne for herself. And now she's fucking Milo to get him to help her do it." A low, bitter laugh tumbled out of his lips. "Not that she'll have much luck. Emperia might think she's manipulating Milo, but she is the one who will end up being sorry in the end. My brother is far cleverer than anyone thinks."

I hesitated, torn about how much more information to reveal. Leonidas had already guessed most of what Milo and Emperia were planning. I could keep quiet about everything else I'd heard, but I didn't want Delmira to suffer because of my silence—or him either.

"You're right. Milo and Emperia are plotting against your mother. Milo also talked about marrying Delmira off to some lord to shore up his power."

"That doesn't surprise me. And what did my dear brother say about me?"

Leonidas stopped pacing and fixed his fierce gaze on me. I could lie and say that Milo was going to send him away like he was Delmira, but I decided against it. Leonidas might have betrayed me in the past, but he didn't deserve to die at his brother's hand now.

Too many people had already died in royal massacres in my lifetime.

"Milo is planning to kill you, if you put up too much of a fuss about what he does to Maeven," I said.

Another low, bitter laugh tumbled out of Leonidas's lips. "You mean he's planning to kill me regardless, just like he's wanted to all along. I'm surprised he hasn't punished Wexel yet for botching my murder in Blauberg."

For once, words eluded me, and I wasn't sure what to say to ease his pain, or why I even wanted to. Still, I tried. "I'm sorry. About Milo. About your family. That they aren't . . . better."

Leonidas stalked over to the railing, and his hands clenched the stone like he wanted to rip it apart. The moon- and starlight frosted his face, bringing out his handsome features, although it couldn't hide the anger in his eyes or mask the sorrow radiating off him.

"I'm used to it," he said, his voice losing some of its previous heat. "Being a Morricone has never been easy. Sometimes, I think it's only gotten worse since Mother became queen."

"How so?"

"My mother was actually married to Milo's father, a powerful Mortan lord, although he died when Milo was young. But she had a longtime affair with my and Delmira's father. I even think she loved him, as strange as that may sound."

Leonidas shook his head, as if not sure what to make of that thought. Me neither. Maeven loving someone—*anyone*—seemed like an impossibility.

"So Milo is legitimate, but Delmira and I are not. Most of the nobles still treat my sister and me like bastards. They smile to our faces and cut us down with words behind our backs. At least before my mother was queen, no one bothered lying to me, or trying to use me in their courtly games, or fucking with my feelings. Other than Uncle Maximus, of course. But even he was honest about the pain he wanted to inflict on me."

Leonidas's shoulders tensed, and I thought about the horrible scars on his back, the ones he hadn't wanted me to see, the ones he kept hidden beneath his many layers of clothes. That pool in my heart grew warmer, softer, and larger still, and I impulsively crossed the balcony. I started to lay my hand on his shoulder, but I thought better of it. Instead, I placed my fingers on the railing, right next to his.

He stared down at my hand. "You're the only one who does that."

"What?"

"Doesn't touch me," he confessed in a harsh, ragged voice. "Even Delmira and Mother do, from time to time. But not you. Not unless you absolutely have to."

I chose my next words carefully, trying to pick my way across the slippery sheet of emotional ice that had sprung up between us. "You don't seem to like it very much."

"No, I don't. You've seen my scars. You can imagine why."

Yes, I could, and the memory made me sick to my stomach. No matter what had happened between us in the distant past, or the odd tangle of promises, half-truths, and emotions simmering between us now, he hadn't deserved to be tortured like that. No one did.

Leonidas turned toward me. I started to step back, but he reached out and captured my hand, his cool fingers lightly pressing into my skin. I froze, as though the liladorn vines draped around the balcony had rooted me in place again.

"What—what are you doing?" I asked, my voice a breathless whisper.

"I don't like to be touched," he rasped. "But I want to touch you."

Heat flashed in his eyes like lightning strikes, making them burn a bright, beautiful amethyst. Answering heat sparked in my own heart, then swept down into my stomach, and then lower, and lower still, until sharp, throbbing need hammered through my body in time to my pounding heart.

Leonidas's fingers tightened around mine. Neither one of us moved beyond that, but his gaze locked with mine, and I was suddenly, painfully aware of everything about him.

His black hair glinting in the moonlight. The sharp planes of his face. The coiled strength in his tall, muscled body. His warm breath brushing up against my face. The soft scent of his honeysuckle soap. The electric touch of his skin against mine. It all burned into my mind—my heart—like a red-hot brand.

Several seconds ticked by, but we remained like that, hands touching, bodies apart. We stared into each other's eyes, neither one of us daring to say what we truly meant or felt or especially what we bloody *wanted*, even though both of us were mind magiers and could sense the emotions rolling off the other. Interest. Attraction. Desire. And a tangle of hotter, deeper, more intense things that took my breath away.

Part of me longed to surge forward, press my lips to his, and drown in the sea of emotions churning between us. But an equally large part of me feared the idea. Because once I took that plunge, I doubted I would ever recover from it.

Leonidas cleared his throat, shattering the silence. "I'll find out what Milo's schedule is for the morning. Perhaps we can sneak into the old armory while he's busy entertaining some of the nobles."

I should be happy that he was returning to business instead of furthering the madness of the moment, but disappointment washed through me instead. "Of course. Until then."

I started to tug my hand out of his, but Leonidas stepped even closer, and his gaze dropped to my lips, as if he were thinking about kissing me. My body hummed with anticipation, but he didn't come any closer. Instead, he lifted my hand and pressed a soft kiss against my knuckles. The small, gentle, courtly motion was as light and fleeting as a butterfly's touch, but it sent arrows of fire shooting through my body, including one that pierced my heart and stuck fast there, burning, burning bright.

I jerked back, breaking the strange connection between us, lest I do something stupid like throw myself into his arms, despite all the many, many reasons why I shouldn't.

Leonidas's fingers flexed, as though he was thinking about reaching for me again, but he dropped his hand to his side and bowed to me. Then he straightened, his face once again a perfect, blank mask. "Sleep well, my lady."

Before I could return the benign sentiment, he spun around and stalked back inside, leaving me alone on the balcony with my treacherous thoughts and thoroughly wounded, corrupted heart.

chapter twenty-one

I stayed on the balcony until I was certain that Leonidas had left my chambers, then went inside, took a hot bath, and got ready for bed.

I was standing in front of the vanity table, dragging a comb through my hair, when it got stuck on a particularly large tangle. An annoyed grunt escaped my lips, but I kept trying to force the comb through the tangle.

Somewhere around the third yank, a geyser of magic bubbled up inside me. I immediately stopped tugging on my hair, but once again, I was too late to prevent my power from sweeping me away, back into the forest . . .

Young Gemma—Gems—grunted, much like I had just done in my chambers, and lurched to the side, trying to yank her long brown hair out of the clutching grasp of a low-hanging tree branch.

I sighed. I was ghosting again, trapped back in my memories of that day in the woods when the turncoat guards had been sneaking up on Xenia and Alvis.

Gems grunted a second time and finally yanked her hair free. Then she started running again. I followed her.

She darted around trees, leaped over rocks, and skirted fallen logs, her legs churning, her boots sending up sprays of leaves, and her arms slapping away the branches that blocked her path. My heart pounded, just as hers was doing, and a stitch throbbed in my side, but I ignored the remembered pain.

"I see them!"

"Over there!"

"Don't let them escape!"

Shouts filled the air. The guards had already spotted Xenia and Alvis.

Gems staggered to a stop and clutched a tree trunk for support. Memories of the Seven Spire massacre flickered through her—my—mind. The screams, the shouts, the blood spattering everywhere like scarlet rain. Tears gleamed in her eyes, and her legs shook, threatening to buckle.

"No!" she snarled in a fierce voice. "I won't be a coward. Never again."

Gems sucked down another breath and started running again.

Shouts kept ringing out, and flashes of movement appeared through the trees up ahead. Gems slowed and crept forward, glancing around to make sure that no guards were sneaking up on her from behind. She reached the trees that lined the clearing, then sidled forward and peeked around the side of one. I did the same thing, even though I already knew exactly what I would see.

Guards surrounded Xenia and Alvis, who were kneeling on the ground in the center of the makeshift camp.

Xenia had shifted into her larger, stronger ogre form, and her body now bulged with thick, hard muscle. Her coppery *hair writhed around her head like coral vipers, while long, jagged teeth filled her mouth. Black talons had sprouted on her fingertips, and blood dripped off the sharp points and spattered onto the dirt. A dead guard with his throat torn open lay on the ground beside the ogre morph.*

Alvis was kneeling next to Xenia, with a bloody sword lying in the dirt a few feet away from him. The metalstone master must have tried to defend himself, although it looked like one of the guards had knocked his weapon away.

A tall, thin man with dark brown hair, eyes, and skin was stalking back and forth in front of them. "I am Captain Hanlon. We know you're traveling with the girl. Where is Gemma Ripley? Tell me, and I'll make your deaths quick and painless."

Gems shrank back, pressing her body into the tree.

"Talk!" Hanlon roared.

Xenia and Alvis looked at each other. Alvis raised his eyebrows in a silent question. Xenia nodded back at him, then looked up at the captain.

"What a big, strong man you are, chasing a little girl through the woods." A disgusted sneer twisted her face, and she leaned forward and spat on the captain's boots.

Hanlon's cheeks flushed with anger, and he slammed his fist into Xenia's face. Her head snapped back, and she grunted with pain and toppled over onto the ground.

Get up! Get up before he kills you! *Gems screamed the words in her mind, but of course I heard them too.*

Xenia lifted her head. Blood dripped out of her broken nose, but she squinted in this direction. Run, Gemma. Now. As far and as fast as you can.

Gems jerked back in surprise at Xenia's voice sounding in her mind—

An arm snaked around the girl's waist, and a boy yanked her back behind the tree and clamped his hand over her mouth.

The boy looked a year or two older than Gems, thirteen, maybe fourteen. His hair was as black and shiny as polished onyx, while his eyes were a dark, vibrant purple. He was wearing a black cloak over a light purple tunic, but he wasn't carrying any weapons.

Even back then Leonidas Morricone had been handsome, although I had been too angry, panicked, and worried at the time to see it. I frowned, studying him more closely now. Just as I had been too distraught to notice how pale and thin his face was, his torn, dirty clothes, and the tension that radiated off his body like heat from the sun.

"Don't scream," *Young Leo whispered in Gems's ear.* "The guards will hear if you scream. I'm going to let you go now. Don't do anything stupid. Okay?"

He released her, and she spun around, her hands balling into fists.

Who are you? What do you want? *Gems asked the questions in her own mind, but of course they echoed in mine as well.*

To help you, *Leo replied.*

Once again, she jerked back in surprise.

It's okay. My name is Leo. I'm a mind magier. I'm not going to hurt you. *He pointed to the left.* Go that way, and you can escape.

What about my friends?

He shook his head. You can't save them. There are too many guards. Trust me. Run away, and save yourself.

Gems kept eyeing him with suspicion, her hands curling into even tighter fists. Leo stared back at her, his gaze on hers.

In this moment, the Morricone prince seemed so earnest, so concerned, so completely sincere, *as if he truly did want to help her escape.*

No, Gems's *voice whispered in my mind, full of stubbornness.* I never would have made it this far without Xenia and Alvis. I can't just abandon them and let them be killed. What kind of *friend* would that make me? What kind of *person*? I might be a coward, but I'm not a bloody *traitor.*

Frustration filled Leo's face. Cowards get to live, *he snapped, his voice angry and resigned at the same time.* Sometimes, traitors do too.

A branch cracked off to the right, and a turncoat guard appeared. Gems gasped and started to run, but Leo reached out and latched onto her arm.

"What are you doing?" she hissed. "Let me go!"

Leo's fingers clenched around her arm so tightly that I could feel them on mine too, all these years later. Not only that, but magic rolled off him and washed over Gems, fixing her boots to the ground, as though they were mired in quicksand. She couldn't move her feet, no matter how hard she struggled.

Leo gave her an apologetic look, then gestured at the guard. "I found the Ripley princess just like you wanted me to. Here. Take her."

He shoved Gems forward. The invisible force gripping her feet vanished, and she stumbled straight into the guard, who clamped his hand around her arm and smiled, revealing a mouth full of crooked yellow teeth.

"Good job, princeling," the guard crowed. "You finally did something useful. Your uncle Maximus will be pleased. So will your mother. Although I can't believe that Maeven let this girl escape in the first place."

*Gems's gaze snapped over to Leo. "You're a Morricone."
She spat out the name like it was the vilest sort of curse.
"You're Maeven's son."*

Leo didn't respond, but a muscle ticced in his jaw.

*"Come along, princess," the guard sneered. "Time to
watch your friends die—"*

*Gems jabbed her elbow into the guard's gut, then spun
toward him and plucked the dagger out of the scabbard on
his belt. I smiled. Rhea had taught me that move.*

*Instead of stabbing the guard, Gems whirled around,
her hot, murderous gaze focused on Leo. She snarled, lunged
forward, and lashed out with the dagger. Leo scuttled to the
side, avoiding her strike, but he tripped over a dead branch
and tumbled to the ground. Gems snarled again and threw
herself down on top of him. She raised the dagger high, ready
to drive it straight into his heart—*

*The guard grabbed Gems's arm, stopping her from kill-
ing Leo. He knocked the dagger out of her hand and dragged
her off the boy. Gems cursed and struggled, but she was no
match for the guard's strength magic.*

*Leo grabbed the dagger from the ground, then got to his
feet and approached Gems, who shot him a hate-filled glare.*

*"Going to kill me like your mother killed everyone at
Seven Spire?" she asked.*

*A smile tugged at the boy's lips, but it was an odd, lop-
sided, resigned expression. "Nothing as nice as that. I'm
afraid that Uncle Maximus wants you alive."*

Gems sucked in a horrified breath. Me too.

"Take her back to camp," Leo said.

*The guard dragged Gems forward, but she only had eyes
for Leo, who followed along behind them, his face cold and
blank.*

Gems's stunned disbelief slammed into my stomach like

a sword, along with shame that she had been tricked so eas-
ily, but those emotions quickly drowned in the white-hot rage
that boiled up in her heart. The storm crackling inside Gems—
inside me—burned away everything else, including her fear.

"You bastard!" she snarled. "You traitor! You never
wanted to help me!"

Leo remained calm and impassive, although something
that looked like guilt flickered in his eyes, cracking his icy
mask.

"I wish I had lightning magic," Gems snarled again.
"So I could burn you to a crisp."

"Well, then, I suppose it's a good thing you're soft and
weak," Leo replied in a cold voice. "Just like all the Ripleys are."

Gems growled and lunged at him, but the guard tight-
ened his grip on her arm, stopping her. Then the man dragged
her forward again, heading toward the camp . . .

The comb slipped through my fingertips, which were tingling with all that remembered rage, and punched into my bare
foot. The sharp spike of pain in my toes jolted me out of my
memory and back to the here and now.

I staggered over and grabbed the nearest bedpost, clinging to it like a spider desperately hanging on to a fragile strand
of its web. My heart pounded, my breath puffed out in ragged
gasps, and cold sweat slicked my palms. Not for the first time,
I cursed my magic. I had already lived through the encounter
in the woods once, and I had no desire to revisit it or any of my
other memories.

Still, part of me was grateful for the reminder. No matter
how drawn I was to Leonidas, how attractive I found him, or
how wounded he seemed, the Morricone prince had betrayed
me back then, and there was nothing to stop him from doing it
again now as soon as he got whatever he truly wanted from me.

I didn't think I would rest with the memories and magic still swirling through my body, but I went to bed anyway. Exhaustion quickly overtook me, and I dropped into a deep, dreamless sleep . . .

Several loud *knock-knock-knocks* startled me awake the next morning. I sat bolt upright in bed, my mind spinning in a dozen different directions before latching onto one disturbing thought.

Leonidas knew who I really was, and he had sent a guard to capture me just like he had all those years ago in the woods.

My heart galloped up into my throat. I grabbed the dagger hidden underneath my pillow and scrambled out of bed, ready to fight—

One of the doors opened, and Anaka stuck her head inside the chambers. "Sorry to disturb you, my lady, but Princess Delmira asked me to fetch you for breakfast."

I shoved my arm behind my back so she wouldn't see the dagger in my hand. "Of course. Silly me, for oversleeping. Let me get dressed."

Anaka bobbed her head, drew back, and shut the door.

Fifteen minutes later, I stepped out of the chambers wearing a pair of black leggings and one of the light purple tunics from the armoire. My dagger was hidden in the side of my right boot, while the tearstone arrow was nestled in my left one. I didn't dare leave them behind, lest one of Milo's spies decide to search my chambers. Besides, they were the only weapons I had.

Anaka set off down the hallway. Instead of heading toward Delmira's chambers, she led me to a different part of the palace.

"Where are we going? I thought the breakfast was in Princess Delmira's chambers."

Anaka shot me a nervous glance. "The breakfast has been moved to Queen Maeven's dining hall."

Worry bubbled up in my stomach, but I followed the girl until she finally stopped in front of some open doors. Anaka gestured for me to go inside, then scurried away. I envied her escape, but I swallowed my dread, lifted my chin, and strode forward.

The doors led into a modest-size dining hall with a single rectangular table in the center of the room. The only other furnishing was a large midnight-purple banner bearing the Morricone royal crest done in silver thread that covered most of one wall.

"Ah, Lady Armina, do come in," Maeven called out.

The queen was seated at the head of the table, with Delmira and Corvina to her right, and Reiko to her left. I took the empty chair next to Reiko, which was as far away from Maeven as I could get. One more chair perched at the table, next to Corvina.

Maeven glanced at the younger woman. "Are you sure Emperia won't be joining us?"

Corvina smiled at the queen, but there was a sharp edge to her expression. "My mother is feeling a bit under the weather. The excitement of last night's dinner wore her out."

Her words sounded innocent enough, but anger rippled off her, and an image of Emperia kissing Milo flickered through my mind. Despite what she'd told Wexel last night, Corvina didn't like her mother fucking her fiancé. Couldn't blame her for that.

Maeven's lips puckered, as if she didn't believe Corvina's lie, but she clapped her hands together. The loud sound made me flinch. "Let us eat."

Servants streamed into the dining hall, setting bowls of fresh fruit, cheeses, bacon, eggs, and potatoes on the table, along with platters piled high with blackberry pancakes like the ones I'd eaten in Leonidas's library yesterday morning. I filled my plate and concentrated on my food, which was delicious, and washed everything down with a mug of warm, spiced orange cider.

While we ate, Delmira kept up a steady stream of chatter, peppering both Reiko and me with questions about our supposed hometowns, businesses, and more. Corvina chimed in when appropriate, although her comments were more insulting than kind. Maeven remained largely silent, only addressing her daughter from time to time.

The longer the breakfast dragged on, the tenser I became. Soon, I was grinding my teeth at every soft *scrape* of a knife and *ting-ting* of a fork on a plate. What was the point of this meal? Because I seriously doubted Maeven had summoned us here simply to have breakfast.

Beside me, Reiko laughed and talked with Delmira, but below the table, out of sight of the others, she tapped her right index finger on her thigh in a quick, nervous rhythm. Her morph mark had migrated back to her right hand, and the dragon's black eyes had narrowed to slits. The Ryusaman spy was as worried as I was. It was one thing to be an anonymous noble skulking about court, but it was quite another to dine with a queen, especially *this* queen.

Eventually, the food was cleared away, and the purple cloth was removed from the table and replaced with a fresh one. I eyed Reiko, who shrugged back at me. She didn't know what was going on either. Delmira and Corvina also looked puzzled.

Maeven clapped her hands again, and more servants streamed into the hall, pushing two metal carts, which they rolled up to the table next to Reiko and me.

"You ladies both purport to be metalstone masters and jewelers of some renown," Maeven said in a light, pleasant tone, although her smug expression filled me with even more wariness. "I thought it would be entertaining to see what you two can do."

She waved her hand, and the servants removed the purple cloths covering the carts, revealing a stunning array of gemstones. Sapphires, diamonds, rubies, amethysts, emeralds, and more glimmered on purple velvet trays, along with gold and silver settings. A second, lower shelf held tweezers, polishing cloths, magnifying glasses, and other tools.

Reiko smiled at Maeven. "Of course, Your Majesty. Is there something in particular you would like?"

The queen gestured at Delmira. "This was my daughter's idea, so make something for her. I insist."

That last part was most definitely an order. Reiko's smile faltered, but she reached for the closest tray of gemstones. I did the same with my own cart.

For the next hour, Reiko and I worked side by side, while Maeven, Delmira, and Corvina chatted and sipped their cider. While I fiddled with the jewels, I listened carefully to the conversation. When the talk turned to the upcoming wedding, I raised my head and looked at Corvina.

"You must be so excited for your wedding to Prince Milo. Have you set a date yet?" It seemed like an innocent question, but I was hoping that she would slip up and reveal something about her mother's involvement with Milo or her own dalliance with Wexel.

"Well, of course I am absolutely *mad* about Milo, so I would *love* to get married immediately, but my mother insists on a lengthy engagement." Corvina pouted, as though the wait truly did annoy her. "Mother says we won't have time to plan a *proper* wedding otherwise. So Milo and I are planning to get married next fall."

Nothing noteworthy there. A lengthy engagement was typical for a royal couple, if only to have enough time to plan the wedding, just as Corvina had said.

"What about you, Lady Armina?" Maeven murmured, staring at me over the top of her mug. "Is there someone special in your life?"

"I'm afraid not, Your Majesty. I haven't been as lucky as Corvina yet." I smiled sweetly at the queen, who rolled her eyes at my cloying tone.

"What about Leo?" Delmira asked. "He escorted you back to your chambers after dinner last night. Did the two of you have a chance to talk?"

Despite how kind she was, I could have happily stabbed Delmira through the heart with the tweezers in my hand. The very last thing I needed was for Maeven to think I had designs on her son.

I shrugged off Delmira's pointed attempt to play matchmaker yet again. "He was a proper gentleman. Nothing more, nothing less."

"Oh, yes. Leonidas is very fond of taking in wounded things," Maeven murmured.

My fingers curled around my tweezers. Delmira wasn't the only one here I wanted to stab, but I dropped my head and focused on my work again.

"These jewels are all exquisite, Your Majesty," Reiko said, changing the subject. "Some of the finest I have ever seen."

Maeven waved her hand again. "Oh, those are just some baubles I've collected over the years."

"Baubles? Why, I imagine that even Gemma Ripley would be envious of them," Corvina said.

A cold finger of dread slid down my spine at the sound of my real name, and my fingers tightened around the tweezers yet again. Could you actually murder people with tweezers? Probably not, but I was almost willing to try, just to get Corvina to bloody shut up.

"Oh, I doubt my baubles would impress Princess Gemma," Maeven drawled. "What is that dreadful nickname she has?"

"Glitzma," Reiko chirped in an entirely too cheerful voice. "Everyone calls her that because of how spoiled and pampered she is."

Below the table, out of sight of the others, I discreetly lashed out and kicked her ankle. Reiko's eyes widened in pain, but she smirked back at me as though nothing was wrong.

"Spoiled is right. Why, I heard that Princess Glitzma drapes herself in jewels, even when she's just lounging around in bed," Corvina said, a jealous note creeping into her voice.

"Well, I envy Princess Gemma," Delmira chimed in. "It must be so wonderful to be surrounded by so much beauty all the time, and to not have to worry about anything other than picking out pretty gowns and dancing with suitors at balls."

Delmira bit her lip and glanced over at her mother, as if she'd revealed too much about herself, but Maeven ignored her daughter and stared at me.

Another cold finger of dread slid down my spine, and my heart started hammering. Had all this talk of Glitzma jogged the queen's mind? Did she remember the scared girl from the Seven Spire massacre? Did she realize that we were one and the same?

"What do you think of the Andvarian princess, Lady Armina?" Maeven asked.

I fisted my fingers around the tweezers to keep my hands from trembling and gave her a casual shrug. "I don't think much about her at all. She is in Andvari, and we are here in Morta. Why should I waste my time wondering about some pampered princess that I'll never meet? I have much more important things to focus on."

Like making sure I left this room alive.

Corvina shot me a sour look, upset that I was ruining her making fun of me, but I ignored her and stared at the queen. Maeven regarded me over the rim of her mug again, her eyes dark and unreadable. A third cold finger of unease slid down my spine.

"Mmm." Maeven made a noncommittal sound. "I suppose that Lady Armina is right. Who cares about some spoiled Andvarian princess? Especially when we have the much more interesting task of seeing what you two ladies have created. Ready to show off your designs?"

Beside me, Reiko tensed. She might be able to talk about jewelry, but she wasn't very good at making it. She had chosen a simple round gold brooch setting and had arranged several purple amethysts in it, along with green emerald leaves, to create a flower pattern. The design was nice enough, but the execution was messy, and she hadn't properly secured the jewels with the tongs. As soon as she picked up the brooch, all the jewels would fall out of the setting, and Reiko would be revealed as incompetent at best and a fraud at worst.

After that, well, I didn't know what would happen. At the very least, Reiko would probably be expelled from the palace. At the very worst, Maeven could order her thrown into the dungeon—or executed.

Reiko had helped rescue me from the Blauberg mine, so I didn't want to see her get hurt. I also selfishly couldn't take a chance that she wouldn't crack under pressure and reveal my true identity to save herself. So how could I help her?

A servant carrying a tray full of mugs approached the table. I dropped my hand to my side, made a circular motion with my index finger, and sent out a small burst of magic. The servant's dress caught on the edge of the jewelry cart sitting next to me, and she jerked to a stop, the mugs sliding off her tray, tumbling to the floor, and spilling cider everywhere.

Startled by the commotion, Maeven, Delmira, and Corvina all looked at the servant. While they were distracted, I quickly and discreetly waved my hand over Reiko's work tray, concentrating my power on the brooch. In an instant, her design smoothed out, forming a much neater and prettier flower, and the gold prongs curled inward and wrapped tightly around the jewels, firmly anchoring them in place.

Reiko gave me a sharp look, clearly wondering what I was doing.

The servant stammered out a frantic apology and scrambled to clean up the mess. Maeven, Delmira, and Corvina looked at Reiko and me again, and I leaned away from the dragon morph, picked up a cloth, and calmly polished my own design.

"As I was saying, ready to show off your work?" Maeven repeated.

"Yes, Your Majesty," Reiko replied.

She picked up her tray and set it in the middle of the table, so that Maeven, Delmira, and Corvina could all see it.

Delmira clapped her hands together in delight. "It's so pretty! I love the way you curled the emerald leaves around the amethyst petals."

Corvina's lips twisted into a sneer. She wasn't a fan of the design, but hers wasn't the opinion that mattered most.

Maeven leaned forward and examined the glittering brooch. Several seconds ticked by in silence. Beside me, Reiko sucked in a breath and straightened up, awaiting the queen's verdict.

"Very nice," Maeven murmured.

Reiko let out a soft, relieved sigh. The dragon on her hand exhaled as well, and black smoke drifted out of its mouth and skated across Reiko's skin before fading away.

Delmira picked up the brooch and pinned it to her dress. Then she looked at me, as did Maeven and Corvina. I slid my own tray to the center of the table.

Delmira gasped. "Oh! How stunning!"

I had chosen a silver ring setting, and I too had done a floral design—three liladorn vines. I had used pieces of jet to form the vines and thorns, then added a few tiny amethyst shards to represent the lilac blossoms. I'd also done a wavy pattern, as though the three vines were snaking up the wearer's finger.

Corvina leaned forward, far more interested in my design

than she had been in Reiko's, although she soon sniffed her displeasure and sat back. "I suppose that will do, although liladorn wouldn't have been my choice. Horrible weed."

Once again, we all looked at Maeven, waiting for her to pass the final judgment. The queen studied the ring for several seconds.

"How lovely—and unusual. Most Mortan jewelers concentrate on strixes, feathers, and the like, but you took a completely different approach. Well done, Lady Armina."

Her eyes gleamed, and she actually smiled at me, as if something about my design greatly pleased her, although I couldn't imagine what it might be.

Delmira slid the ring onto her finger. "And it fits perfectly. I love it! Thank you! Thank you both so much!"

She jumped up out of her seat. Reiko and I both stood, and Delmira came around the table and hugged us both. She truly was thrilled with our designs.

Maeven also stood, as did Corvina, and the servants stopped what they were doing, awaiting their queen's commands.

"Thank you for a most entertaining breakfast, but I'm afraid that duty calls," Maeven said.

We all curtsied, and the queen swept out of the dining hall.

The second she was gone, Reiko sighed with relief again. Me too. But a small, nagging part of me felt the same way I had last night when Maeven had left the throne room.

That even though the queen was gone, I was in more danger than ever before.

CHAPTER TWENTY-TWO

Corvina flounced out of the dining hall without saying another word to Delmira, Reiko, or me. As soon as she left, one of the servants came over and spoke to the princess in a low voice.

Delmira nodded at the servant, then looked at Reiko and me. "Ladies, I must take care of something. Thank you again for the lovely jewelry. I'll see you both tonight at the ball."

Reiko and I both bowed our heads to the princess and left the dining hall. It was after ten o'clock now, and servants, nobles, and others were moving through the palace. Reiko and I walked along, smiling and nodding at everyone we passed. Finally, we came to a pair of open doors that led into a library.

Reiko glanced around, making sure no one was paying attention to us, then grabbed my arm and dragged me inside. No one was sitting at the reading tables or browsing through the bookshelves, but she still pulled me into a dark, deserted corner.

"Why did you use your magic like that?" Reiko hissed, releasing my arm. "That was a foolish risk to take."

"But?" I challenged.

"But I would have been in trouble otherwise, so thank you." She muttered the last few words, but the dragon on her hand actually gave me a small, grudging smile.

"You're welcome."

Reiko leaned against a bookcase and crossed her arms over her chest. "I must apologize. I underestimated you, Gemma."

"How so?"

"I didn't realize you had so much magic—or that you were a mind magier."

"I don't know what you're talking about." I tried to keep my voice calm, but I could hear the strain in my words.

"You know *exactly* what I'm talking about. You used your mind magier magic to fix my brooch. I know that sort of power when I see it." Reiko gave me a speculative look. "Smart of you and your family to claim that you were only a metalstone master. The Morricones would probably double their efforts against the Ripleys if they realized what you truly are."

"Maeven already tried to kill me once at Seven Spire," I snapped back. "And she doesn't need the excuse of my magic to plot against my family."

Reiko shrugged, neither agreeing nor disagreeing. "Either way, you need to be more careful. Maeven might have been distracted by you tripping that servant, but she is no fool. You should leave the palace before she realizes who you really are."

This time I shrugged, neither agreeing nor disagreeing. "Perhaps I saved you so that you would owe me a favor and help me leave."

Reiko eyed me. "No, I don't think so. You did it simply because you wanted to help me, to *save* me." She shook her head. "You must have read too many storybooks as a child. Being a spy is *not* about saving people. It's about keeping your own head attached to your shoulders."

Xenia had expressed similar sentiments to me over the

years, and she would have heartily applauded Reiko's ruthlessness now.

I hesitated, wondering how to proceed. Despite my snooping last night, I still needed more information about what Milo was plotting—information that Reiko might have, if she was as good a spy as she claimed to be.

"What have you found out?" I asked. "About Milo's plans?"

Her eyes narrowed, and her inner dragon gave me a suspicious look. They were both back to not trusting me again. "You first, princess."

I glanced around, but we were still alone. "I snuck into Milo's workshop last night."

"You and Prince Leo, right?" she drawled. "Skulking around the palace together after dark? How romantic."

I ignored her insinuation. "You might be interested to know that Milo is fucking Emperia Dumond."

"His future mother-in-law?" Reiko's nostrils flared in disgust. "That's a new low, even for a Morricone. Does Corvina know?"

"Oh, she knows, but Corvina has her own affair to manage. She's fucking Captain Wexel."

Interest filled Reiko's face. "Really? Tell me more."

I stared at the dragon morph, wondering how much I could trust her, but she was still the closest thing I had to a true ally here. And if something unfortunate did happen to me, then someone needed to get this information out of Myrkvior and to the leaders of the other kingdoms.

So I told Reiko everything that Milo, Emperia, Corvina, and Wexel had said last night, along with their plots against each other and Maeven too. I also plucked the arrow I'd stolen from Milo's workshop out of my boot and twirled it back and forth in my fingers, making it shift from light gray to dark blue and back again.

Reiko tracked the changing colors, her face creasing into a frown. "Why tearstone?"

"What do you mean?"

"Why make arrows out of tearstone? Why not make them out of iron or some other more common ore? Tearstone is notoriously tricky to work with, and tearstone weapons often shatter, unless they're crafted by a highly skilled metalstone master. Milo didn't go to all this trouble just to make arrows that are going to shatter the first—and only—time they're fired. So what's the point?"

They were all good, troubling questions. "I don't know."

We both stared at the arrow, and I kept moving it back and forth, watching the colors change.

"Give me the arrow," Reiko said in a quiet voice.

My fingers curled around the projectile. "What?"

"Give me the arrow," she repeated. "I have some contacts in the city, some true metalstone masters. They might be able to tell us more about the arrow, and what Milo is planning to do with it."

I arched an eyebrow. "Us? I thought there was no *us*. Just you, the daring, sophisticated spy, and me, Glitzma, the pampered princess playing at being one."

Reiko huffed. "I already said that I underestimated you."

"Is that supposed to be an apology?"

"Given what I thought of you when you showed up at the Blauberg mine? Absolutely."

I gave her a sour look. "Well, I'm glad I could amuse you."

Reiko grinned, and her inner dragon opened its mouth in a wide, silent laugh, although both of their expressions quickly turned serious again. "Give me the arrow, and I promise to return it to you after my contacts have examined it. We need to figure out what Milo is plotting in order to protect both our kingdoms." She paused. "Please."

I looked at her and her inner dragon, but they both regarded me with solemn expressions. I could have tried to read their thoughts, but that would have been a violation of the fragile trust that was struggling to take root between us. So I took a leap of faith. Besides, no risk, no reward, as the old saying went.

I held out the arrow, and Reiko slipped it into her pocket. In return, she offered her hand to me, and I clasped my fingers around her forearm, sealing our missions and our fates together—for now.

Reiko and I looked around to make sure no one had seen us talking, then left the library.

"I'll slip out of the palace and take the arrow to my contacts right now," Reiko said. "What will you do?"

"I have a lead on where Milo might be hiding the tearstone. Maybe I can at least damage the arrows and any other weapons he's made—"

We rounded a corner, and I slammed into someone. I jerked back and started to offer an apology when I realized that I hadn't run into a servant or a random noble.

I'd crashed straight into Leonidas.

The apology flew out of my mind, replaced by a sharp spike of worry. Had he heard me talking to Reiko? Did he recognize her from the Blauberg mine? Did he realize that we'd joined forces? That I was plotting against him?

I stopped short, standing in front of Leonidas, but Reiko kept moving, turning her head, slouching her shoulders, and scurrying right on by him. From one moment to the next, she transformed from a noble lady ambling around the palace to an anonymous servant hurrying about her work. Even I might have overlooked her, if I hadn't seen the smooth transformation for myself.

Reiko was right. She was *much* better at being a spy than I was.

Leonidas started to glance over his shoulder at Reiko, but I loudly cleared my throat, drawing his attention back to me.

Behind the prince, Reiko winked at me, then slipped into another hallway and vanished from sight.

"Lady Armina," Leonidas said. "I thought you might like to take that tour of the palace we discussed last night."

Tour? He must mean the old armory.

"Of course. Thank you, Your Highness."

Leonidas hesitated, then offered me his arm. I too hesitated, but I threaded my arm through his, once again trying not to notice the strength in his muscles or the warmth of his body brushing up against my own. No matter how handsome he was, or how charming he seemed, Leonidas Morricone was still my enemy. My ghosting magic had reminded me of that last night, although certain parts of my body, especially my treacherous heart, didn't seem to be getting the message this morning.

"How was breakfast with my mother?" Leonidas asked.

For once, I decided to give him a completely honest answer. "Stressful."

His small, amused laugh further softened my heart. "Yes, it usually is."

As we walked along, Leonidas pointed out tapestries, statues, and other knickknacks, playing the part of the polite host for all the servants, nobles, and guards that we passed. The more he talked, the more I wished that we truly were just a couple out for a stroll.

Reiko was right. I had read far too many storybooks where love conquered all. Oh, I certainly didn't love Leonidas, but I liked him far more than I should have, especially given all the horrible things his family had done to mine.

Eventually, we moved to a quieter, less crowded section of the palace and then into a deserted corridor. The second we were alone, I forced myself to drop his arm and step away.

"What have you discovered?" I asked.

"Milo has quietly taken over the old armory," Leonidas replied. "No one seems to know exactly what he's using it for, and only he, Wexel, and certain guards are allowed to enter that area. Milo moved into the space while I was gone to Blauberg, which is why I didn't know about it before you mentioned it last night."

"And you want to sneak in there?"

"Yes. Right now. Milo is entertaining some nobles for lunch. We won't get a better chance."

"Then let's go."

Leonidas led me to a large section of liladorn on a nearby wall. He glanced around to make sure we were still alone, then reached out, took hold of a particularly large, curved thorn, and yanked down on it.

Click. Just like in the rookery, part of the wall slid back, revealing a secret passageway. Leonidas stepped inside. I followed him, and the wall slid shut behind us.

Unlike the one in the rookery, this passageway featured fluorestones embedded in the ceiling to light the way. We moved to the far end of the corridor and climbed a set of stone steps that spiraled upward. At the top landing, Leonidas pulled down on another large, curved thorn. That wall slid back, and we stepped through to the other side.

We were back in a regular corridor, but this area was as silent as a tomb. No paintings or tapestries hung on the walls, and not so much as a single chair crouched in the hallway. A thick layer of dust coated the floor, while enormous spiderwebs dangled from the ceiling like gray, silken chandeliers. The air was quite cold, as though no fires were ever lit in this section of the palace. I shivered, wishing I'd thought to wear the purple coat Leonidas had given me.

But the most curious thing was the liladorn. The vines had punched through the stones just like they did in other parts of Myrkvior, but there were more of them here than anywhere else in the palace, except for Delmira's chambers. Perhaps it was my imagination, but it almost seemed like the liladorn was trying to strangle the walls, or at least reclaim this part of the palace for itself.

"What is this place?" I asked, my words steaming out in a faint cloud of frost.

"This wing belonged to King Maximus," Leonidas said in a low, strained voice. "Mother ordered it sealed off after his death. I think she had as many bad memories here as I did."

Another shiver slid down my spine that had nothing to do with the cold. Voices started whispering all around me, the sounds bouncing off the walls and echoing back. The voices quickly grew louder and louder until phantom wails were rending the air, as though we were surrounded by ghosts. But not all the cries were human. Many were sharper and higher and reminded me of how Lyra had cawed with rage when she thought that I'd hurt Leonidas back in Blauberg.

He gave me a sympathetic look. "I can hear the cries too. The sounds are some quirk of the liladorn. The vines and thorns sometimes vibrate with strange noises, especially in this section of the palace."

"Why here?"

"This is where Maximus conducted his experiments on the strixes, where he took their blood and their magic," Leonidas said, his voice even lower and more strained than before. "And where he punished the people who displeased him."

And me too. He didn't say the words, didn't even think them, but they hung in the air between us, as filmy and unsubstantial as the spiderwebs undulating back and forth through the cold, drafty air.

Leonidas cleared his throat and strode forward. I shivered again, but I fell in step behind him. We moved through the hallway, down a staircase, and over to a set of floor-to-ceiling double doors that were cracked open.

I reached out with my magic, but I didn't sense anyone nearby. Normally, that would have comforted me, but not now. If Milo was storing the tearstone here, then he should have at least posted a guard or two. Or perhaps the lack of guards was his strategy to hide the tearstone. After all, why bother to station guards if there was supposedly nothing to protect?

Leonidas slipped through the open doors. I glanced around again, but we were still alone, so I followed him.

The doors led into an enormous room that took up most of this wing of the palace. Stone tables filled with dusty glass tubes and broken jars marched down the center of the room, while books with black, molded covers lined the shelves along the walls. Swords, spears, and other weapons hung in rotten wooden racks, and empty coldiron cages dangled from the ceiling. The space reminded me eerily of Milo's workshop, except for one thing—the blood that covered many of the surfaces.

So much blood.

Puddles of it had dried on the floor, looking like dull brown paint that had been haphazardly spread all over the grimy gray flagstones. Streaks of blood crusted the walls, with more splattered on the cages and all the way up on the high ceiling. I shuddered and hugged my arms around myself. How many creatures and people had Maximus killed? The number must have been quite high for this much blood to still be in here, some sixteen years after the king's death.

"This isn't an armory," I muttered. "This is a slaughterhouse."

Leonidas grimaced, but he didn't dispute my words. "Maximus really did keep weapons in here. After his death, my mother started referring to it as *the old armory*. I think it was her way of trying to forget about all the awful things that happened. Eventually, everyone started calling it that, even Milo and me, even though we knew what it really was."

He stared at a nearby table, which was empty, except for the dried blood dotting the surface. His jaw clenched, his hands fisted by his sides, and his eyes darkened, but I didn't ask what memories were haunting him. I didn't want to add to his pain.

I glanced around the chamber again. "Well, everyone might call it the old armory, but I don't see any new weapons. Are you sure we're in the right place?"

Leonidas nodded. "Yes. Just because we don't see the weapons doesn't mean they're not in here. The palace is riddled with secret passageways, cubbyholes, and rooms, thanks to the liladorn. Or Milo might have left some other clue behind."

We split up. Leonidas took the side with the strix cages dangling from the ceiling, while I headed to the one with the bookshelves.

Up close, the books were even filthier than I'd thought and covered with so much grime and black mold that I couldn't read the titles on the spines. Using the edge of my tunic sleeve, I pulled one book out of its slot and opened it, but the pages inside had molded as well, rendering the volume an indecipherable mess.

"Find anything?" Leonidas called out.

"Nothing. You?"

"Not yet."

I searched my half of the workshop. Broken glass jars, molded books, dust-covered weapons, blood spattered everywhere. I didn't see anything new, although I found myself strangely fascinated—and disgusted—by the objects. Ever since the Seven Spire massacre, I had always wondered what drove someone to hurt other people and creatures to gain just a tiny bit more magic. Or perhaps amassing the magic was the truly thrilling thing, rather than actually wielding the power itself. Hard to say.

I rounded the corner of a table and started to head over to another one when I noticed a small gray object gleaming on the floor. Curious, I went over and picked it up.

It was another arrow.

This arrow was the exact same size and shape as the one I'd given to Reiko, complete with hooked barbs and a sharp, pointed tip.

Why make arrows out of tearstone? Why not make them out of iron or some other more common ore? Reiko's earlier questions whispered through my mind.

Obviously, the purpose of any arrow was to hurt—to kill— and I had no doubt that Milo wanted to murder all his enemies. But I never would have even found out about his plan if he hadn't stolen tearstone from so many places in Andvari, especially the Blauberg mine. Surely, Milo had realized that someone there would notice the missing tearstone sooner or later, but he'd still sent Wexel to fetch it anyway. The crown prince had taken a big risk, which meant that he specifically needed tearstone, and that no other metal, ore, or gem would do.

I started to slip the arrow into my pocket when a lighter patch of floor caught my eye. I squinted. Someone had left a footprint behind in the grime that coated the flagstones.

No, not just one footprint—dozens of them.

A chill skittered down my spine, and I reached out with my magic again. This time, instead of reassuring nothingness, I sensed several people, all hurrying this way.

Leonidas whirled toward me, sensing the same thing. Then we both turned toward the back of the chamber.

Several shadows slithered away from the wall, congealing into guards clutching swords. They advanced on us, with Captain Wexel leading the charge.

It was a trap.

CHAPTER TWENTY-THREE

Wexel headed toward Leonidas. Most of the guards followed him, although a few veered in my direction, grinning and swinging their swords back and forth.

All those long, grueling hours of training and countless sparring matches with Rhea, Serilda, and Aunt Evie filled my mind. I clutched the tearstone arrow a little tighter and dropped my hand to my side, hiding my makeshift weapon from the approaching guards.

Wexel stopped and sneered at Leonidas. "I thought that I'd killed you in Blauberg, but you seem to have as many lives as your bloody strix does." He gestured at the guards. "Well, this time, I brought enough men to finish the job."

More than two dozen men stepped up beside the captain, still swinging their swords back and forth, like they were guillotine blades about to drop.

"You should have kept your nose out of Milo's affairs in Blauberg, and especially his workshop here," Wexel said. "You're not *nearly* as clever and sneaky as you think you are. No one enters Milo's workshop without him knowing about it, and you were all too eager to follow his trail of breadcrumbs right back here."

I silently cursed. Milo must have had some magical trip wire we hadn't sensed. Or perhaps he'd realized that someone had been in his workshop because the liladorn vines had shifted. Either way, it sounded like he had purposefully mentioned the old armory, knowing that Leonidas would come here the first chance he got.

Leonidas drew his own sword from the scabbard on his belt, then stared at the guards. "Sure you want to do this? Attacking your prince is treason. You will all hang for this."

None of the guards flinched at his warning. They were all Wexel's—and Milo's—men.

"The only one who's going to hang is you, Leo," Wexel crowed. "After I kill you, I'm going to stuff you in one of these cages. Maybe Milo will display you in his workshop like Maximus did all those strixes he experimented on."

Leonidas's face hardened, and icy fury filled his eyes.

Wexel looked at me. "I don't know who you really are or where I know you from, but you're no Mortan lady."

Leonidas glanced at me, and I nodded back. We didn't have to send thoughts to each other. We both knew that fighting together was the only way we were going to survive.

Wexel sucked in a breath, probably to taunt us some more, but I cut him off.

"Oh, shut the fuck up," I snapped. "And come and try to kill us, if you dare."

He stabbed his sword at me. "She's mine. I'm going to enjoy sawing her tongue out of her mouth."

The guards nodded, although they kept giving me evil grins. They wouldn't kill me, but they would take great delight in hurting me as much as possible. I tightened my grip on the arrow still hidden in my hand.

"You're making a fatal mistake," Leonidas warned. "I don't have a coldiron collar clamped around my neck to dampen my magic this time."

Wexel laughed. "I don't care whether you have a bloody collar around your neck. This time, I'm going to gut you and make sure you're dead."

The captain snarled, raised his sword high, and charged forward. Leonidas growled, lifted his own blade, and stepped up to meet him.

The guards in front of me grinned again and advanced. They probably thought they were being intimidating, or some such nonsense. Fools. I sprinted ahead, taking the fight to them.

I ducked under the first man's swing, shot back up, and sliced the arrow in my hand across his face. At least, I tried to slice the arrow across his face. The barbs dug into his cheek, and the weapon got stuck in his skin.

The guard yelped and staggered back, jerking the arrow out of my hand, although it remained lodged in his face, as though he were a fish I'd hooked. While he was distracted, I reached down, plucked my dagger out of the side of my right boot, and sliced it across his stomach. That man dropped his sword and crumpled to the ground, whimpering and clutching his guts, which were oozing everywhere.

I twirled the dagger around in my hand and stepped up to face the next guard. I ducked his blow, then whirled past him and punched my blade into his back. As he screamed, I yanked the dagger out, then sank my fingers into his hair, pulled his head back, and cut his throat. He fell to the ground, gurgling and bleeding out.

Across the workshop, Leonidas was battling several guards, along with Wexel, who was using his superior mutt strength to hammer his sword at the prince over and over again.

Leonidas blocked Wexel's blows, then smoothly spun to the side. His long black cloak rippled around his body like a cloud of death as he punched his sword into the chests of first one guard, then another. He skewered a third guard, then spun back toward Wexel. The prince easily avoided another attack and slashed his sword across the captain's arm.

Wexel howled and staggered away. Leonidas cut down another guard and stalked after the captain—

A glint of metal caught my eye, and I instinctively ducked. A guard had snuck up on my left side, and his weapon whizzed by close enough to ruffle my hair. He lifted his blade for another strike, so I snapped up my hand, reached for my magic, and used my power to toss him across the room. The guard hit the wall with a loud, sickening *crack*, then dropped to the flagstones—dead.

That one harsh *crack* echoed in my mind, and I froze, my hand still hovering in midair. Despite all the training I'd done with Rhea, Serilda, and Evie, memories of the attack in the woods all those years ago flooded my mind. The chambers around me flickered as my magic rose up, trying to toss me back into the past yet again.

Another guard yelled and charged at me, and the noise and motion jolted me back into the here and now. I didn't have time to lift my dagger or spin out of the way, so I lashed out with my power again. This guard also flew through the air and hit the wall with a loud, sickening *crack*. That second sound joined the first one still echoing in my ears, and even more memories erupted in my mind, like fireworks lighting up the night sky.

"Not now!" I snarled at my magic, as though it was something that could be scolded into submission, but of course it ignored all my attempts to quash it.

Several more guards yelled, charged forward, and swarmed all around me. The sheer mass and force of the men threatened to push me back, but I planted my boots on the grimy flagstones and held my ground. If they shoved me down to the floor, then I was finished.

Rhea had always said that losing your footing in a fight was one of the worst things you could do, and she'd knocked me down enough times to prove her point. So I gritted my teeth and swung my dagger as hard and fast as I could. The frantic *bang-bang-bang* of metal hitting metal rang in my ears and rattled my whole body.

I couldn't kill all the guards with just my dagger, so I reached for my magic again. But my power suddenly felt as slippery as an eel, and it squirted out of my grasp and sank into the sea of memories still churning in my mind. I growled with frustration, sliced open another guard's stomach with my dagger, and whirled around, trying to give myself more space to manuever.

Across the workshop, several dead guards lay at Leonidas's feet, although a few were still standing, along with Wexel.

Leonidas's eyes locked with mine, as though he was checking to make sure I was still alive, the same way I was doing to him. Then his gaze flicked past me. "Watch out!"

Before I could react, a guard grabbed my shoulder, spun me around, and slammed his fist into my face. Pain exploded in my jaw, my head snapped back, and my feet flew out from under me. I landed hard on my ass on the floor, and the remaining guards quickly formed a tight ring around me.

"Not so tough now, are you?" one of them sneered.

That man reached down, grabbed my arm, and hauled me to my feet. I was still gripping my dagger, but the guards closed in all around me, trapping my hand down against my side. In an instant, their fingers started digging into my arms, back, hips, whatever they could reach.

She has such soft skin . . .

Never had a noble lady before . . .

She won't be so pretty when we get through with her . . .

The guards' horrific, lecherous thoughts slammed into my mind, and my gargoyle pendant blazed as hot as the summer sun against my chest. I latched onto that heat, along with the answering rage boiling up inside me.

So much *rage*.

The rage roared through me like a wildfire scorching everything it touched. But it burned too fast, too hot, too bright, and I couldn't control it. My feelings mixed, mingled, and merged together with the guards' cruel intentions until suddenly, one enormous storm of emotion was churning, crackling, and crashing inside me. I had to do something to release it, to release all the terrible, unspeakable things that the guards were still thinking, that I was still feeling.

So I screamed.

I screamed with rage and pain and fear and frustration and everything else I had been feeling ever since I had first woken up in the palace, in Morta, so very far away from my home and everyone and everything I loved.

I screamed and screamed and screamed.

With each new wave of sound, magic poured out of me, and not just out of my hands like usual. No, this magic surged out of my entire body, like a tornado blasting across a plain and sweeping away everything in its path. In an instant, the storm of power knocked all the guards away from me and sent them flying across the room.

But my magic didn't stop there—*I* didn't stop there.

Tubes, jars, books, swords. Everything that wasn't nailed down blasted off the tabletops and out of the bookcases and off the weapons racks, zipped through the air, and slammed into the guards who had attacked me. Even a couple of the strix cages broke free from their ceiling chains and crashed to the floor. The flying debris pelted the guards, making them hunker down on their hands and knees to keep from getting glass and books and spears smashed into their faces.

My scream went on . . . and on . . . and on . . . until my throat grew scratchy and my breath finally ran out.

I staggered back, staring at the destruction I'd caused. All the guards were huddled on the floor. Most of them were dead, but the ones who were still alive were buried in glass, books, and other debris.

I wheezed and clutched my tunic, my fist closing around the gargoyle pendant hidden underneath the fabric. For once, the pendant didn't feel hot or cold. It was simply resting against my chest, as innocuous as any other piece of jewelry. I kept clutching it, though, pretending it was as heavy as an anchor steadying my internal ship in that relentlessly stormy sea, just like Alvis had taught me.

My wheezing eased, and I slowly came back to my regular self. I kept a tight grip on my magic, though, ready to unleash my power if any of the guards attacked me again. Part of me *wanted* them to rise up, just so I could cut them down—just so I could hurt them even *worse* than how they'd wanted to brutalize me.

Gemma? Gemma! Grimley's worried voice filled my mind. *Are you okay? Why are you using so much magic?*

The gargoyle must have sensed my intense outburst through our bond. *I'm fine. Some guards attacked me, but I got the better of them.*

I'm on my way.

NO, I replied in a stern voice. *You need to stay hidden. I'm fine. If I need you, I'll call for you.*

Grimley grumbled his displeasure, but his presence retreated to the back of my mind—

Boots crunched through the glass that littered the floor. I whirled around and raised the dagger still clutched in my other hand.

Leonidas stopped and held his arm out to his side, as if I were a rabid animal he was approaching. I cringed. He was the very *last* person I had ever wanted to see me like this—utterly enraged and thoroughly, murderously out of control.

Then again, I supposed it didn't matter, since he had seen me like this before, when I'd tried to kill him in the woods. I just hoped he didn't connect me to that girl, for so many reasons.

Leonidas lowered his hand and eased up beside me. "Are you okay?"

His tone was soft and neutral, with no hint of judgment, but it made me cringe again. Even though I didn't want to, I forced myself to release my gargoyle pendant, along with my magic. Then I wiped the cold sweat off my forehead, hoping he wouldn't notice how badly my hand was trembling.

"Of course." The lie slid easily off my lips. My magic might not always work when or how I wanted it to, but my tongue always did.

Leonidas looked out over the shattered glass, tattered books, and other debris littering the floor. I thought he might murmur some inane platitude about how I'd only done what was necessary to save myself, nothing more, nothing less, but he remained silent. Even if he had uttered the words, he would have been wrong.

I had done *more*, and I wanted to do *more* still. Even though my enemies had been defeated, I still longed to unleash more magic, more power, more death and destruction and chaos.

I *never* wanted to be like the Princess Gemma who had cowered under a table, too afraid to help the people being slaughtered around her during the Seven Spire massacre. But I had never learned how to balance those memories and the accompanying fear, guilt, grief, and shame alongside my mind magier magic. At times, using my power felt like too much of a temptation, which made me even more frightened—of myself.

I could literally kill people with a thought. I had done it as a child, more than once, and I had bloody *loved* doing it again right now.

Part of me had reveled in the pain and fear flooding the guards' faces and sensing their panic and terror when they realized that I was going to hurt them, that I was going to kill them, and there was *nothing* they could do to stop me. For a few, brief shining moments, hurting the guards had drowned out my own fears and had made me feel strong.

In some ways, I thought that made me even more of a monster than Maeven was. At least the queen had never been afraid, and she was *always* in control. Me? I was a mess of roiling emotions, and my internal ship careened from one wave to another with no clear course in sight.

But standing here mooning about my feelings was a useless exercise, so I drew in a deep, steadying breath, then looked over at the guards. Half a dozen men were moaning and groaning on the floor, but one person was missing.

"Where's Wexel?" I asked.

"He escaped," Leonidas replied. "He was losing our battle, so he shoved another man in front of him, then ran away, just like he always does when a fight doesn't go his way. Wexel bolted before you unleashed your power, so he didn't see you destroy the workshop."

He shrugged, as though the captain's escape was of no further concern. Well, I was certainly concerned about it, but we had a more immediate problem.

I gestured at the guards. "What are you going to do with them?"

The men were still down on the floor, clutching their heads, ribs, and more.

Leonidas stepped forward, his gaze swinging from one man

to the next. They all grimaced and ducked their heads, unable to meet the eyes of the prince they had betrayed.

Anger radiated off Leonidas, burning as hotly as my own rage had. Sometimes, I forgot he had the same sort of magic that I did, although he always seemed to be in complete control of his power—and especially his feelings. He would probably summon some guards loyal to him, or at least to Maeven, and have these traitors thrown into the dungeon.

Leonidas studied the guards a moment longer. Then he snapped up his hand, reached for his magic, and sent all the broken shards of glass flying at the men.

Thwack-thwack-thwack.

Thwack-thwack-thwack.

Thwack-thwack-thwack.

One after another, the sharp shards of glass punched into the arms, necks, and chests of every guard who was still alive. Blood sprayed everywhere, adding a fresh coat of gruesome scarlet paint to the workshop. None of the men had a chance, and most of them died without making another sound.

I stood there, eyes wide, completely stunned.

When it was over, and the last guard had fallen to the floor, Leonidas released his magic, and a few final bits of glass *tinkle-tinkled* against the flagstones like macabre wind chimes tolling out a dirge for the men he'd just killed.

Leonidas turned toward me, his face eerily calm. I had seen that same expression on him before, when the turncoat guard had dragged me away from him in the Spire Mountains. And more recently, when he had knocked out Conley and his crew in the mine.

"Why did you do that?" My throat was still scratchy from my screams, so my voice came out as a harsh, ragged whisper. "Why did you kill your own men?"

A cold light filled his eyes. "Those weren't *my* men. They sealed their fates when they sided with Wexel. The fewer enemies I have in the palace, the safer I will be."

He hesitated, as if he wanted to say more, but I didn't dare try to skim his thoughts. I wasn't sure I would like what I might hear.

Leonidas stepped even closer to me. He stretched out his fingers as if he were going to cup my cheek, but I jerked back. His face hardened, and his hand plummeted to his side.

"The fewer enemies you have in the palace, the safer you will be as well," he said. "These men saw what you could do. They knew you were a mind magier."

I sucked in a breath. "You killed these men because of *me*?"

A small, humorless smile curved his lips. The dark, grim expression only made him look more handsome, despite the flecks of blood that covered his face like ruby shards. "I brought you here, and I won't be the reason that you die. If any one of these men had blabbed about what they saw, Milo would have come for you at once."

"I didn't ask you to do that. I *never* asked you to do that. I can take care of myself."

He frowned, as though my words puzzled him. "Why would you ever have to ask? I would *never* let any harm come to you. Not if I could prevent it."

"Why not?" I whispered, desperately wanting to know and yet dreading the answer.

Leonidas hesitated, as if he were going to tell me, but then that eerie, calm expression settled on his face again. "We can't stay here. Wexel will return soon with more guards. Or worse, Milo."

He moved past me, leaving me standing in the middle of the ruined workshop, staring down at the dead guards that we'd both had a hand in slaughtering.

CHAPTER TWENTY-FOUR

Leonidas was right about one thing. We couldn't stay here, so I followed him out of the workshop, up the stairs, through the secret passageway hidden in the liladorn, and back to the main part of the palace. He led me through several side corridors, avoiding the busier common areas, and we made it back to my chambers without incident.

By the time Leonidas waved his hand to open the doors, I had gotten over my shock, although questions kept swirling through my mind. I glanced around, wondering if Wexel might be lying in wait for us, but the area was empty.

Despite the blood, dust, and grime covering my torn, ripped clothes, I trudged over and sat down on the bed. Soiling the blankets was the least of my worries right now.

Leonidas prowled around, stopping at the balcony doors. His eyes grew distant, and his magic swirled through the air, as soft as feathers sliding across my skin. *Lyra* . . .

I didn't hear the strix's response, but everything must have been okay, because Leonidas blinked and released his power.

"What do we do now?" I asked. "Leave the palace?"

Despite the rapidly escalating danger, I didn't want to leave. Not until I knew *exactly* what Milo was plotting to do with whatever tearstone weapons he'd made. But Xenia had always claimed that the most important part of being a spy was knowing when it was time for a strategic retreat—or keeping my head attached to my shoulders, as Reiko had said in the library earlier.

Leonidas shrugged. "We don't do anything."

"What do you mean we don't do anything?" I shot to my feet and threw my hands up into the air. "The captain of the royal guards—*your* royal guards—just tried to kill us! Inside your own palace!"

He shrugged again. "Today isn't the first time Wexel has tried to murder me at Myrkvior. He has never liked me, not even when he was a young guard serving King Maximus, and he absolutely *despises* Lyra because she almost killed him once in defense of me. Wexel picked Milo's side a long time ago, and the captain delights in destroying anyone that he or my brother perceives as a threat or an enemy. Unfortunately for me, I top both of their lists."

"You're really not going to leave?"

Leonidas's eyes glittered with a cold light. "I'm not going anywhere. This is just as much my home as it is Milo's."

I ground my teeth in frustration. His stubbornness was going to get us both killed, so I tried another tactic. "What about Maeven? Surely, the queen will want to know that her captain tried to kill her son."

A bitter laugh spewed out of Leonidas's mouth. "Mother prefers to let her children and other relatives settle these sorts of . . . disputes amongst themselves, just like she did when she was the head of the Bastard Brigade. Even if I told her what was going on, she wouldn't help or intervene. She would just sit back and watch and congratulate the winner in the end, just like she's done ever since I was a boy."

My heart ached for him. Mothers were supposed to love and protect their children, not throw them into the deadly gladiatorial ring of palace politics and see if they managed to survive.

I would never, *ever* admit it to anyone, but part of me understood Maeven's actions at Seven Spire. She might have chosen to engage in wholesale slaughter, but she had also been trying to improve her kingdom's fortunes. She'd had a goal and a reason for her actions, no matter how despicable they were. But not helping your own son, even when he was battling your other son . . . Well, that was just heartless.

Leonidas must have seen the worry on my face, because he came over to me. "Trust me. This is how things are done here. Milo set a trap for us, but it failed. He'll retreat, at least for now, and I'll take the usual steps to protect myself—and you too. In the meantime, we'll all pretend like nothing is wrong and that we aren't all plotting to kill each other."

I shuddered. "Pretending nothing is wrong is even worse than your brother trying to murder you."

"It is what it is, and we are who we are," Leonidas replied, his voice as cold as I'd ever heard it. "Milo isn't going to change, and neither am I."

Thwack-thwack-thwack. The sharp, wet sounds of those glass shards plunging into the guards' bodies whispered through my mind. He had killed all those men with no hesitation and no mercy. Perhaps Leonidas was more like Milo—like Maeven—than I'd realized.

I thought of the rage that had gripped me, and how I'd wanted to use my magic to rip the guards to shreds, even after they were wounded and no longer a threat. Maybe I was also more like Milo and Maeven than I wanted to admit. I shuddered again.

Leonidas hesitated, then dropped to one knee, reached out, and took my hand. He wasn't wearing his usual gloves, and he stroked his thumb over my skin, as if he were trying to bring some much-needed warmth back to my ice-cold fingers.

I stood there, torn between tearing my hand away and wrapping my fingers around his. Despite everything that had happened, and all the awful things we had done, part of me was still desperately, crazily attracted to him, and I had to fight the urge to cup his face in my hands, lean down, and press my lips to his.

Hot sparks flared in Leonidas's eyes, as if he were sensing my treacherous thoughts. His thumb stilled, and his hand tightened around mine, as if he were going to stand up and draw me into his arms. I didn't know what I would do if that happened. Probably kiss him like a fool.

But the moment passed, and his grip slowly loosened. Regret pinched my heart, and once again, I had to force myself not to reach for him.

"Don't worry about Wexel and Milo," Leonidas said. "I can handle them. Besides, I promised not to let any harm come to you. If you believe nothing else I've said, then believe that. Please?"

His last whispered word made me shudder for a third time, but this motion was not one of fear or revulsion—more like a last-ditch effort to stop myself from doing something supremely stupid.

"I suppose I don't have any choice but to believe you," I replied, not sure how to respond to the hot sparks still flaring in his eyes and the answering heat simmering in my own veins.

The sparks dimmed, as though my obvious lack of trust disappointed him. "One day, I hope that you'll believe me because you know it's the truth," he said, his own voice hoarse with all sorts of emotions I didn't want to hear right now.

Leonidas leaned forward and pressed a soft kiss to my knuckles, just as he had on the balcony last night. His lips scorched my skin, and the heat of his touch blazed all the way down into my bones, like a wildfire I couldn't extinguish no matter how hard I tried. My fingertips tingled, but not from any magic this time. No, this sensation was my own desperate, foolish yearning for him.

Still, the unwanted sensation helped ground me. Leonidas could spout all the pretty promises he wanted, but he would turn me over to Maeven in a heartbeat if he knew who I really was. Letting myself feel *anything* for the Morricone prince was a path to certain disaster, and I had already taken far too many steps in that dangerous direction.

I flexed my fingers and tugged my hand out of his. The sparks died in Leonidas's eyes, and he stiffly climbed to his feet.

"Try to get some rest." His face was carefully blank, his voice flat and remote again. "It won't be long until it's time for the ball."

He bowed to me, then left the chambers, waving his hand to shut the doors behind him. I stood there and watched him go, wishing my traitorous heart wasn't already longing for him to return.

I waited until I was sure that Leonidas was gone, then trudged into the bathroom, stripped off my ruined clothes, and washed the blood, dirt, and grime off my body. I dressed in a fresh tunic, sat down at the vanity table, and combed my hair, trying not to notice how my hands were trembling.

Making myself presentable helped rein in my emotions and gave me some time to think. Events were rapidly spiraling out of control, but I still needed to accomplish some things before I left Myrkvior.

So I put the comb down, grabbed the silver compact Leonidas had given me, and pressed it up against the mirror. "Show me Dominic Ripley."

The familiar silver light and ripples appeared, although the mirror quickly smoothed out, showing my father's study. He must have been waiting for me because he lunged into view a few seconds later.

"Gemma! Are you okay?" Father asked, worry creasing his face.

"I'm fine. Being here has been . . . stressful."

Before he could ask me any more questions that I didn't want to answer, I told him everything I had learned, including the fact that Milo was making barbed arrows out of the stolen tearstone. I didn't mention having breakfast with Maeven, or Wexel and the guards attacking Leonidas and me, or me lashing out with my magic. That information would only add to my father's worry.

He frowned. "Why would Milo make arrows out of tearstone? Why not just make them out of regular iron?"

"I don't know. Reiko asked the same questions."

His frown deepened. "Who is Reiko?"

I told him about the Ryusaman spy. When I finished, Father actually brightened. "I'm so glad you found a friend."

I didn't know if Reiko and I were *friends*, but I didn't dissuade him of the notion. "Reiko took one of the arrows to some metalstone masters. I need to track her down and see what she found out."

"Well, I hope she learned something useful, but you've both done enough. Now that we know Milo is making weapons, specifically arrows, we can prepare. We can figure out the rest of his plot later. You and Reiko need to leave Myrkvior as soon as possible. Bring her to Glitnir, if she wants to come. We'll protect her. Just come home, Gemma. Please. Before it's too late."

Leaving now felt like admitting defeat, at least as far as my pride was concerned. But given Wexel's attack, it was highly unlikely that I would be able to learn any more about Milo's plot. Leonidas might think he could protect himself and me from another assassination attempt, but I had my doubts. I might have risked my life by staying here and swimming in the dangerous waters of Myrkvior, but the tide had turned against me, and now it was time to head back to shore, lest I drown in my own blood.

And even more troubling was this . . . *warmth* that I felt for Leonidas. This bloody *softness* that made me forget everything that had happened between us as children, and everything his family had done to mine. Leonidas might seem like an ally, a friend, maybe even something more, but he was still a Morricone, and I was a Ripley, and we would always be natural enemies, just like strixes and gargoyles.

"Very well," I said. "I've learned as much as I can. It's time to leave."

"When?" Father asked.

"Tonight. I'll slip out of the palace during the queen's birthday ball. Everyone will be celebrating, and Grimley and I should be able to leave Myrkvior undetected."

Father nodded, although worry creased his face again. "I'll tell Topacia of your plans so she can be on the lookout for you in Blauberg. Be careful, Gemma. I love you."

"I love you too. I'll see you soon."

I leaned forward and pulled the compact away from the vanity-table mirror, breaking the connection. My father's face flickered, then vanished, and I was left staring at my own reflection, trying to figure out exactly how I had gotten here, all tangled and twisted up inside, and so very far off course from where I had started.

CHAPTER TWENTY-FIVE

I still had things to check on before I escaped from Myrkvior, so I stuffed my dagger back into my boot and left my chambers.

I went to the rotunda in the center of the palace and hid in the shadows on the second-floor balcony, studying everyone moving through the area below. Servants, mostly, rushing to and fro with platters of food, trays filled with crystal goblets, and crates bristling with wine bottles, getting ready for the ball. The guards seemed bored by the hustle and bustle, and none of them looked like they were scanning the crowd, searching for me.

Leonidas seemed to be right about Wexel and Milo retreating after their trap had failed to kill us, but I still skimmed the guards' thoughts.

Hope I get a chance to dance with Karina tonight . . .

Maybe I can steal a bottle of wine while no one's looking . . .

Can't wait for this stupid ball to be over so things calm down . . .

Well, that made two of us.

None of the guards was thinking anything sinister, so I went downstairs. I scurried across the rotunda, following along behind some servants. None of the guards here seemed to be loyal to Wexel and Milo, but it was in my best interests to remain as invisible as possible.

I went to the library where I had last seen Reiko this morning, but she wasn't there. Frustration filled me. We should have made plans to meet before the ball and exchange information, but maybe I could still find her.

I stopped a passing servant. "Have you seen Lady Reiko? Do you know where her chambers are?"

He shrugged. "Not recently, my lady. I don't know if she is staying at the palace, but you might check the Hall of Portraits. Lots of nobles go there."

He told me where it was, then hurried away. I doubted Reiko cared about seeing portraits, but it was the only lead I had, so I headed in that direction.

The Hall of Portraits was exactly what its name implied—a large, wide corridor with gold-framed portraits and other paintings lining the walls. Despite what the servant had said about it being a popular spot, the hall was currently empty. More frustration filled me, but I didn't know where else to look for Reiko, so I wandered through the corridor.

Most of the portraits were of Mortan kings and queens. I recognized many of the names from my history lessons, and almost all the royals had the distinctive Morricone golden hair and dark amethyst eyes. I stopped in front of a portrait of King Maximus. Perhaps it was my imagination, but the king had a sour look on his face, as though his image was perpetually disgusted by the fact that he had been murdered in real life. Served the bastard right.

Up ahead, I spotted a portrait of Maeven, although it was much farther down the hallway, as though whoever had hung it didn't want to place her smiling face right next to the sour one of the brother she had killed. A much larger landscape separated the two siblings, so I stopped in front of it.

At first glance, the painting seemed like an ordinary piece, one that showed a large gathering of people on a grassy lawn filled with tables, as though they were at a luncheon. But the longer I stared at the landscape, the more I realized that it wasn't a happy, benign scene chronicling some distant piece of Mortan history. Instead of smiling and sitting upright, people's eyes and mouths were frozen open in pain and terror, and they were slumped over the tables, with crimson blood oozing out of their chests.

The painting depicted the Seven Spire massacre.

I shouldn't have been surprised. After all, that had been just as important a day in Morta's history as it had been in Andvari's and Bellona's, and many paintings featured battles and the like, no matter how bloody and gruesome the scenes were. More than one picture and tapestry at Glitnir depicted gargoyles savagely tearing into Andvarian enemies.

Despite my sick shock, I drifted closer to the painting, studying every little thing about it. Truth be told, it was an eerily good likeness. The position of the tables, the bodies littering the lawn, the bright blue sky above it all. The artist had captured the massacre in vivid, if horrific, detail.

Only one thing was missing—Everleigh Blair.

The Bellonan gladiator queen wasn't depicted anywhere in the painting, even though she had survived the massacre. Aunt Evie had foiled Maximus's plot to start a war between Bellona and Andvari, so of course she wouldn't be included in an image designed to celebrate the Morricones' seeming victory.

A figure in the bottom corner of the painting caught my eye. Blond hair, purple eyes, purple gown. It was Maeven, smiling wide, with purple lightning crackling around her lifted hand, as though she was waving to anyone who peered at the image. She was the only person who wasn't dead and covered in blood.

I shuddered and started to turn away when my gaze landed on another figure, this one in the center of the painting. That looked like . . . No, that *was* my uncle Frederich lying dead on the ground with the other Andvarians. I could tell by the dagger sticking out of his chest and the tiny gargoyle crest done in black thread on his gray tunic.

Once again, I started to turn away, but my gaze snagged on yet another figure—myself.

In the painting, a girl was peeking out from underneath a table. Unlike the other figures, Gems wasn't dead and bloody, but her mouth was open in a silent scream, and her hands were clapped over her ears. The image was eerily similar to what had happened in real life, and a stark, visual reminder of my cowardice.

Cold, familiar, stomach-churning waves of guilt and shame crashed through me, and the screams of everyone who had died echoed in my ears. Tears stung my eyes, and my breath caught in my throat. I stepped back, trying to get away from the awful image, and bumped into someone behind me.

I moved to the side and turned around. "Excuse me—"

My apology died on my lips. I hadn't bumped into a servant or a guard or even a noble.

I had run into Queen Maeven.

I stood there, dumbstruck. It was as though Maeven had stepped out of the painting, out of my nightmarish memories, and right into the hall. I didn't know what to do, I didn't know what to think, and I especially didn't know what to *feel*, other than white-hot rage at the bitch for murdering my uncle and countrymen and for causing me and so many others so much pain.

For a mad, mad moment, I thought about unleashing my magic, about using my power to toss her across the corridor and snap her back against the far wall, just like I'd done to the guards in Maximus's workshop. My gargoyle pendant grew ice-cold, pressing into my heart like a frozen arrow, but the chill didn't drown out the power or especially the rage rising inside me—

A flash of movement caught my eye. Three guards had entered the hall. They were staying at the far end, giving us some privacy, but they all had their hands on their swords, ready to rush forward and cut me down if I made any threatening moves.

Once again, I couldn't kill the queen—not without dying myself.

Frustration pounded through me, but I forced myself to draw in slow, deep, steady breaths. Every time I exhaled, I pushed a little more of my rage and magic down, and my pendant slowly warmed back up to a more normal temperature.

Part of me admired Maeven's caution, even though it was thwarting me now. If nothing else, the queen seemed cognizant of the fact that she had enemies within her own palace. I wondered if she realized that Milo was one of those enemies. Probably. I imagined that very little of what went on at Myrkvior escaped her notice.

Maeven stepped up beside me, studying the painting with a critical gaze. She hadn't dismissed me, so I turned back to the piece, focusing on the liladorn vines curling through the gold frame, rather than the gruesome images on the canvas.

"Maximus had this painting commissioned shortly after the Seven Spire massacre," Maeven said.

I didn't respond. I doubted I could speak right now without screaming curses at her.

"He claimed the painting was to commemorate my greatest triumph," she continued. "But he hung it up next to his own portrait, as though all my hard work assassinating the Blairs was his own personal doing. Maximus was *always* taking credit for my successes while denying his own failures. But I suppose that's the way of kings and queens. My brother was just a bit more boorish and graceless about it than most."

She shrugged, as if her brother's actions were of little consequence, but anger scorched off her, like heat waves rising off a roof in the summer sun.

Maeven faced me. "What do *you* think of the painting?"

I wanted to scream that it was one of the most grotesque things I had ever seen and that I didn't want to look at it another bloody *second*, but I wasn't Princess Gemma, massacre survivor, right now. No, right now, I was Lady Armina, a noble who was supposedly loyal to the Mortan throne. I put on that persona like a cloak, wrapping it tightly around myself, thinking about what Lady Armina would say, and not the guilt, shame, and disgust pummeling Princess Gemma's heart.

"I think it's a waste."

Maeven frowned. "What do you mean?"

"All those people dead seems like a waste. Isn't it better to rule over your enemies rather than kill them?"

The queen eyed me, as if my words had surprised her, but after a few seconds, a small chuckle escaped her lips. "Yes, I suppose that it is."

Her face hardened. "Although there is something to be said for just killing your enemies outright and being done with them."

Her gaze drifted over to her brother's portrait, and images flickered in my mind, as bright and fast as lightning strikes. Maeven striding into an arena packed with people. Staring at King Maximus. Plunging a dagger into his chest. Her remembered joy bloomed in my heart, along with a much more surprising emotion—relief.

Maeven always seemed so cold, confident, and in control. I never *dreamed* that she had ever been uncertain, scared, or wary enough to feel relief. It made her seem much more human, something I had a hard time reconciling with the gleeful monster who stalked my memories.

Maeven moved away from the massacre landscape and wandered over to her own portrait. She still hadn't dismissed me, so I had no choice but to follow her. This image must have been commissioned soon after she had become queen, because she looked at least a decade younger in it than she did in real life. She was also smiling wide and wearing a crown.

At first glance, the silver crown was quite pretty and utterly feminine. But the longer I stared at it, the more I noticed the diamond vines, jet thorns, and amethyst spikes of lilac snaking through the design, turning it into a tangle of liladorn. The shiny curls of metal and the wicked gleam of the jewels added a powerful, sinister air to the crown, while the faceted amethyst spikes looked sharp enough to cut your fingers if you tried to touch them. Much like the liladorn—and Maeven—would cut you in real life if you dared to displease them.

"I was so happy the day I sat for this portrait," she murmured, and I wasn't sure if she was talking to me or to herself. "I thought I had finally gotten everything I had ever wanted."

Killing your brother and taking the throne for yourself was probably enough to brighten even the most murderous royal's day.

"You look quite stunning in the portrait." That was the most benign thing I could think of to say.

Maeven laughed again, but it was a low, bitter sound. "I *was* happy—for a while. But Everleigh Blair was right. Being queen was far more difficult than I had imagined, and it remains so. Certain nobles have never accepted me as their queen, and some of them still plot against me, even to this day."

I wondered if she was talking about Emperia Dumond, but I kept my mouth shut. If Emperia managed to kill Maeven, then so be it. I had no interest in helping the queen survive the coup being orchestrated by Milo and his paramour. Not after seeing the massacre painting.

"But I am still here, despite all the plots against me," Maeven said. "And I plan to sit on my throne for many days to come."

She swept her hand out in a wide motion, as if she was gesturing at the palace as a whole and everyone inside it. "As for the rest of this, all the nobles and their plots and schemes, well, they're all just children playing capture-the-crown."

Capture-the-crown was a popular game for both children and adults throughout the kingdoms. Paper crowns were placed on a circle of chairs while music played. When the music stopped, everyone rushed forward to grab a chair and place a crown on their head. The person who didn't manage to snag a seat or who tore their crown was eliminated. Then a chair was removed from the circle, and the game continued until there was only one person, one chair, and one crown left. I used to love playing the game before the massacre, but I had despised it afterward.

Maeven swept her hand out again. "'Round and 'round the nobles go, all of them fighting each other when they should be focusing on their true enemy—me."

I frowned. "What do you mean?"

"If the nobles were to ever band together, they might—*might*—be able to remove me from the throne, perhaps even kill me," she said, her voice eerily calm as she discussed her own potential murder. "But everyone wants to capture the crown for themselves, so they will never think to work together. That keeps me safe from all of them. It's easy enough to play the nobles against each other to get exactly what I want. I've gotten rather good at it these last sixteen years. I've had to, in order to survive. Everleigh should be proud of me. I've learned her long game quite well."

Grudging admiration filled her voice when she mentioned the Bellonan queen, although she quickly fell silent again. I wondered why Maeven was being so candid with me, a total stranger.

This talk was far better suited for Delmira, some advice from a queen mother to her princess daughter. Or perhaps she was trying to use it as a song of seduction, a way to lure Lady Armina to her side by promising that they would dispatch their enemies together. By her own admission, Maeven was playing some game, although I didn't know how keeping her crown involved me.

"Leonidas is quite taken with you."

I blinked at the abrupt change in topic. "Oh . . . I wouldn't say that. He has been very kind, but I doubt he thinks of me in that way."

She huffed. "I doubt he thinks of you in any *other* way, given how attentive he has been to you over these past few days." She tilted her head to the side, studying me like a strix would eye a mouse it was about to gobble down. "What *is* it that my son finds so interesting about you?"

"I do not know, Your Majesty."

I didn't dare tell her about the attraction that continuously sparked, snapped, and sizzled between Leonidas and me, and I certainly couldn't tell her about how we had saved each other's lives, despite being natural enemies. I doubted she would understand the idea of helping someone you should be striving to kill. I still didn't quite grasp it myself.

"Regardless, Leonidas admires you, and his opinion means a great deal to me. Out of all my children, he has always been the most loyal."

Maeven kept staring at me. Her words seemed innocent enough, but I couldn't shake the feeling that she was saying something else entirely, speaking in some secret language she thought I understood. But I had no idea what she really meant. Right now, all I wanted was to escape from her.

"You have also been quite kind to Delmira."

"Delmira is easy to be kind to," I replied.

That much was true. She was far too tenderhearted to be a Morricone, but I supposed every family had its black sheep.

"Yes, she is kind," Maeven murmured. "It will probably get her killed one day, when she is queen."

I frowned again. Delmira was third in line for the Mortan throne. She would *never* be queen. Milo was the heir, and Leonidas was the spare. The best Delmira could hope for was to marry someone she could tolerate, since her marriage would most likely be used to further ingratiate the Morricones with the remaining nobles who opposed their rule.

"I will not forget your kindness to my daughter," Maeven continued. "She is still wearing that ring you made. Interesting that you chose a liladorn design for Delmira. Most people wouldn't have thought of that."

Once again, I had no idea what she truly meant, so I offered up another benign platitude. "I thought it suited the princess. There seems to be more liladorn vines in her chambers than anywhere else in the palace."

Maeven's eyes sharpened, as though I had just said something extremely interesting, although I couldn't imagine what it might be. "I have some other business to attend to, but I look forward to seeing you at my birthday ball, Lady Armina."

"I will be honored to attend, Your Majesty." I curtsied, but Maeven gave me an impatient wave, telling me to rise.

The queen swept past me, heading toward the three guards still stationed at the end of the corridor. She didn't look back, but I felt like she could see me anyway, standing in the middle of the Hall of Portraits, wondering what long game she was playing—and when she might decide to kill me.

PART THREE

QUEENS

CHAPTER TWENTY-SIX

left the Hall of Portraits and roamed through the palace, trying to find Reiko, but none of the servants had any idea where she was. Frustration filled me, but I moved on to the other things I needed to do in order to leave Myrkvior.

First, I went to the palace kitchen, found Anaka, and asked her to bring some food to my chambers. Next, I stepped out onto the balcony Leonidas had shown me that overlooked the marketplace as well as the palace gates. I stood in the shadows and watched the guards, but there didn't seem to be any more men stationed here than usual. The same thing went for the rotunda and the rest of the palace. Good. No additional guards meant that Grimley and I would have an easier time slipping out.

By the time I had finished studying the guards' positions and returned to my chambers, Anaka was waiting there with platters of sandwiches, sweet cakes, and more. I thanked the girl for her service and gave her several of the amethyst hairpins from the vanity table. Anaka's gray eyes widened, and she curtsied and stammered out her appreciation. I hugged her, then sent the girl on her way.

I ate some of the food, but I stuffed the majority of it in a black leather satchel I found in the back of the armoire. It shouldn't take Grimley more than a couple of days to fly us back to Blauberg, but it wouldn't hurt to take some food, in case we ran into trouble. I also folded the purple riding coat Leonidas had given me and added it to my pile of supplies, since it was by far the warmest garment I had.

After that, there was nothing to do but wait—and worry.

Two hours before the queen's birthday ball, a knock sounded on my door, and Anaka led me to Delmira's chambers. The princess had already donned a gorgeous lilac-colored gown that brought out her amethyst eyes. Her black hair was swept up into a crown braid that arched across her head, and berry balm stained her lips a blackish purple. Her only jewelry was the lila-dorn ring I'd made, and the symbol suited the princess, just as I'd told Maeven.

"Are you as excited about the ball as I am?" Delmira asked.

Not at all, but I smiled as though nothing was wrong. "I wouldn't miss it."

She clapped her hands, and servants rushed forward, showing me gown after gown, along with shoes, jewelry, and more. Normally, I would have loved getting ready for a royal ball, but the last thing I wanted to do was celebrate another year of Maeven's cursed life.

An hour later, I was swathed in a dark blue velvet gown with a high neck and long sleeves trimmed with silver thread, along with matching blue heels. One of the servants had twisted the front of my hair into the same crownlike braid that Delmira had, although the back of my short locks remained loose. Dark gray shadow and liner rimmed my blue eyes, while scarlet berry balm coated my lips.

My gargoyle pendant was safely hidden under the gown, and my dagger was nestled in my pocket, along with the silver compact Leonidas had given me. I should have left the compact in his library, but I would probably never see him again after tonight, and part of me selfishly wanted something to remember him by.

"You look stunning!" Delmira pronounced when the servants finished with me. "Leo will definitely notice."

She winked, and I forced myself to smile again. "I'm sure you're right."

The princess dismissed the servants and told them to enjoy the ball, then threaded her arm through mine and led me to the throne room. We stopped at the entrance, and I blinked, dazzled by the sight before me.

The throne room had been quite impressive during last night's dinner, but the servants had transformed it into something truly magical for the ball. Enormous strixes made of purple paper dangled from the ceiling, as though they were hovering in midair. Purple fluorestones had been set into the strixes' eyes, making them glow and bathing the room in a soft haze. Purple and silver ribbons wrapped around the columns, along with tiny purple, silver, and white fluorestones. More colored fluorestones curled around the second-floor balcony railing before streaming up the walls and covering the ceiling like a blanket of shimmering stars.

"Isn't it beautiful?" Delmira asked, pride rippling through her voice. "I designed the decorations myself."

"It's stunning." I might not like being in the heart of Morta, but I could appreciate its dark, dangerous beauty.

Now that we were at the ball, I needed to find Reiko and warn her about Wexel and Milo. Then I could return to my chambers, grab my supplies, summon Grimley, and finally escape from this wretched place.

I started to slide my arm out of Delmira's, but she tightened her grip. "Come! Let's greet the guests."

She smiled brightly at me, just like she always did, but the expression didn't quite reach her eyes, and she seemed a bit . . . nervous. Perhaps she was worried about the ball going smoothly. I certainly wouldn't have wanted to disappoint Maeven on her birthday.

Either way, Delmira dragged me around the room, introducing me to one noble after another. The names and faces blurred together, and the nobles were far more interested in currying favor with their princess than they were in talking to me. After about twenty minutes, a woman engaged Delmira in a fierce debate about the differences between the colors lilac and lavender, and I was able to slip away from them.

I headed toward the most remote, deserted corner I could find, which, strangely enough, was close to a table full of wrapped presents the nobles had brought for Maeven. Unfortunately for me, the spot was also deep in the throne room, far away from the open doors and the escape they represented.

"Leaving so soon?" a familiar voice drawled.

I turned to find Reiko gliding toward me. She was dressed in a long, flowing gown covered with gold sequins that glimmered like mirrors. The gold pendant shaped like a flying dragon she had worn to dinner last night hung from a chain around her neck, while a matching gold ring stretched across all four fingers on her right hand. Her black hair was pulled back into a fishtail braid that was tied off with a green velvet ribbon. Gold shadow and liner rimmed her green eyes, and her lips had been painted a deep scarlet.

Reiko stopped and peered at me over the rim of her crystal goblet. "Why are you so worried?"

"How do you know I'm worried?"

"You have this little wrinkle between your eyes. You'd better smooth that out before it sticks. Pampered princesses aren't supposed to have wrinkles."

I rolled my eyes. "Neither are glamorous dragon morph spies, but you seem just as worried as I am."

She frowned. "How do you know *I'm* worried?"

I made a little circle with my index finger. "Because you have that same wrinkle between *your* eyes."

Reiko lifted her hand as if to rub away the telltale mark, then scowled when she saw my sly smile. So did the dragon on her right hand. They didn't like being teased.

She huffed and took a sip of punch before getting down to business. "I took your arrow to my metalstone master contacts in the city. I barely got back in time for the ball."

"And?"

She shook her head. "None of them had any idea why Milo would make arrows out of tearstone. The stone itself doesn't necessarily make arrows any tougher or stronger than regular iron ones. Of course tearstone can absorb and deflect magic, but that doesn't seem like a good enough reason to craft it into common arrows."

Worry churned in my stomach. I couldn't stop Milo's plot if I didn't have all the pieces to the puzzle. Still, Reiko had held up her end of our bargain, so I decided to do the same.

"Leonidas and I went to a workshop that used to belong to King Maximus, but it was a trap, and Captain Wexel was lying in wait for us, along with several guards. They tried to kill us, but we killed them all instead, except for Wexel, who escaped."

Reiko's eyes narrowed. "You seem upset about that. Why? Was that the first time you've ever killed someone?"

A harsh, caustic laugh spewed out of my lips. "Even after everything that's happened, you still just see me as Glitzma, don't you? A pampered princess incapable of doing anything more strenuous than picking out gowns and jewels to wear."

Her face remained blank, but her inner dragon winced in confirmation.

"No, today wasn't the first time I killed someone," I continued, my voice even more caustic than my laugh had been. "I gutted some of the guards with my dagger. Then I used my mind magier power to throw others into a wall hard enough to snap their spines. And for the finishing touch, I screamed and inadvertently unleashed a wave of magic that tore through the workshop like a tornado, picking up and destroying everything in its path."

Reiko frowned. "Why are you so upset about that? Those men were trying to kill you. It was self-defense."

"I'm not upset about killing the guards. I'm upset because I lost control of my magic—*again*." The last word left a bitter taste in my mouth. "My magic *never* seems to work right when it counts, when it really *matters*, when people's *lives* are at stake. It either tosses me back into the past, or pours out of me in unstoppable waves, or paralyzes me, rendering me utterly *useless*."

My voice dropped to a ragged whisper. "Just like it made me useless during the Seven Spire massacre."

"I see." Reiko's voice was soft, but no judgment flashed in her gaze. Instead, to my surprise, she reached out and gripped my hand, and her inner dragon gave me a sympathetic look. "You weren't useless during the massacre. Magic or not, nothing you could have done would have stopped what happened."

I shook my head. "*No*. You don't understand. I *heard* Maeven thinking about the massacre before it happened. But instead of warning my uncle Frederich, I was frightened, so I ran away. And then when the turncoat soldiers attacked, I didn't do anything—not one damn *thing*. I could have used my magic to help people, to protect them. But instead, I hid under a table while my countrymen were slaughtered. I'm nothing but a bloody *coward*. I know it, and now you know it too."

I started to yank my hand out of hers, but Reiko tightened her grip, and anger flared in her eyes.

"I didn't say that. I would *never* say or think that, and neither should you. Not for one bloody *second*. You were, what, twelve when the massacre happened? You were just a child, Gemma."

"That's no excuse," I muttered.

Reiko dropped my hand and poked me in the chest, right over my heart. "You don't *need* an excuse. You weren't the one who decided to slaughter a royal family. That was Maeven and Maximus. Nothing that happened on that day is your fault. Hasn't anyone ever told you that?"

My father and grandfather had, countless times, along with Rhea. So had Xenia and Alvis. And Uncle Lucas and Aunt Evie. But I had always felt like they were telling me what I wanted to hear and not what they truly *believed* deep down in their hearts. Maybe that was irrational, especially since I could hear their thoughts and sense their emotions, but then again, nothing about my feelings about the massacre, or especially about my magic, had ever been *rational*.

"As for not being able to control your power . . ." Reiko's voice trailed off, and she shrugged. "I don't have an answer for that. The only thing I can say is that it's *your* magic. The power might be your own version of an inner dragon, but it belongs to you and you alone. *You* decide what to do with your magic—no one else. Maybe sometimes you need to take a look back into the past. Or freeze up. Or even be completely, utterly out of control. That doesn't make you weak or defective or a coward. It makes you human, Gemma, just like the rest of us."

It was perhaps the strangest encouragement I had ever received, but one that was surprisingly effective. Her no-nonsense tone and words actually made me feel a little better, like I wasn't as much of a coward or nearly as out of control as I'd thought.

"Thank you," I said in a soft voice.

"You're welcome." Reiko grimaced and shifted on her feet. "You might be amused to know that a servant informed me earlier that Queen Maeven is not interested in my jewelry designs and that I am to leave the palace first thing in the morning."

She let out a rueful laugh. "Pretending to be a miner was easy enough, but you were right. I should have learned more about making jewelry before I tried to pass myself off as a metalstone master."

I cupped my hand around my ear as though I hadn't heard her. "What? What did you say about my being right?"

Reiko rolled her eyes. "You heard me just fine, princess." She took another sip of her punch. "So what happens now?"

"I'm going to slip out of the ball, leave the palace, and never look back. You should do the same." I paused. "You should come with me—to Andvari."

She blinked in surprise.

"I told my father about you," I said, rushing to fill the awkward silence that had sprung up between us. "He's happy to offer you protection at Glitnir."

"In exchange for what?" she asked in a wary voice.

"Of course, my father would love to hear everything you know about the Morricones and Andvari's other enemies." I cleared my throat. "But he mainly wants you to come because he thinks that you're my friend."

She blinked again, as though *friend* wasn't a word she was used to hearing. "Friend, eh? I would have said *rival*."

I snorted. "Of course you would."

Reiko studied me over the rim of her goblet again, considering my offer. After a few seconds of silent contemplation, she shook her head. "I have my own queen to report to. One royal is enough to deal with. I don't need to add a king to the mix."

Disappointment filled me, but I understood. Reiko had her kingdom and people to protect, just as I had mine. "Either way, I'm going to miss our talks."

"Me too," she murmured. "Good luck, Gemma. Perhaps our paths will cross again someday."

"I hope so."

I held out my forearm to her, and she clasped it just as she had done in the library earlier. We both let go, although she pressed something into my hand. Reiko nodded to me, then melted into the crowd.

I opened my fingers. The tearstone arrow from Milo's workshop glittered in my palm. She had returned it to me, just like she'd promised. I smiled and slipped it into my pocket.

A bargain made, and a bargain kept.

Now that I had warned Reiko, nothing else was keeping me here, so I moved away from the column, heading toward the open doors in the distance. I was only about fifty feet away from them when I felt a familiar presence behind me, as soft as a feather tickling the back of my neck. I stiffened and stopped, right there in the middle of the ball, but he didn't approach me, and somehow, I knew that he wouldn't, not unless I turned around.

That old, familiar battle raged inside me. Past betrayal versus current attraction. Attempted childhood murder versus adult salvation. And a whole tangle of other things that I couldn't put names to, not without giving them even more strength and power. The battle was over in an instant, if it had ever truly been one at all. More like a slow, inescapable, inevitable slide toward doom and destruction.

I turned around.

Leonidas stood in front of me.

The sight of him stole my breath, as quickly and easily as a thief plucking a jewel from a lady's necklace. His black hair gleamed underneath the colored fluorestones, as did his amethyst eyes, which were so dark they almost looked black. A long, formal midnight-purple coat with silver buttons shaped like flying strixes stretched across his broad shoulders and outlined his muscled chest. The Morricone crest was stitched in silver thread over his heart, but for once, I ignored it.

Leonidas gave me a low, deep bow, then straightened and held out his hand. "May I have this dance?"

Whispers surged all around us. Several people had seen the prince approach me and were avidly watching us. I glanced over at the open doors that were so tantalizingly close. Despite my need to escape, I couldn't *not* dance with Leonidas. That would attract even more attention, which was the last thing I wanted.

And you want to dance with him anyway, a treacherous little voice whispered in the back of my mind. I ignored it too.

Instead, I smiled, stepped forward, and placed my hand in his. "I would be honored to dance with you." I paused. "Leo."

Satisfaction flared in his eyes, and he tightened his grip on my fingers. Leonidas led me over to the center of the room, which was being used as a dance floor, and I stepped into the warm, strong circle of his arms. He curled one hand around my waist, lightly holding me, while his other hand cupped mine. He wasn't wearing gloves, and the feel of his skin against my own made me shiver.

And then we danced.

The musicians played a classic Mortan waltz that started at a slow, dreamy pace. For the first section, Leonidas and I stared into each other's eyes, and one sensation after another cascaded through my body, like a series of locks opening on a treasury door. Each release further lowered my defenses and brought me even closer to him.

The light press of his fingers against mine. The heat of his hand soaking through the fabric of my gown. His breath kissing my cheeks. The soft aroma of his honeysuckle soap wafting over me. But most of all, I felt *him*, the soft, feathery, electric presence that was uniquely Leonidas. It wrapped around me like a warm, comforting cloak, flowing and ebbing right alongside my own presence, my own power, my own magic.

It was one of the most thrilling things I had ever experienced.

The waltz ramped up into a much faster reel, and Leonidas and I started whirling, twirling, and spinning with the music. Together, apart, and back again. Every time we touched, more passion simmered in my veins, and every caress of his hand against my own made my fingertips tingle. Every time I whirled away, I felt the aching loss of his presence, although it vanished the second I twirled back into his arms.

I was vaguely aware of other people leaving the dance floor to watch us, but for once, I didn't care that everyone was staring. All that mattered was this dance. It was the last moment I would ever have with him, and I wanted to remember it always.

Everything else could wait, even my escape.

Finally, the music slowed and softened, falling back down into the initial waltz pattern. Leonidas held out his hand again, and I stepped back into his embrace. He gripped me more tightly this time, as though I were made of the same soft, dreamy notes as the music, and he didn't want me to slip away. I gripped him back just as tightly. I didn't want to lose him either.

The music eased to a stop, and Leonidas lowered me into a deep dip. The last notes whispered away, but we remained frozen in place, staring into each other's eyes. Heat shimmered like lightning strikes in his gaze, and he pulled me even closer. Desire sizzled through my body, burning so bright and hot I thought sparks might start shooting out of my fingertips, even though I wasn't a lightning magier—

Someone started clapping.

I flinched, as did Leonidas. I had been so wrapped up in him that I'd forgotten where we were—and exactly how many people were watching us.

He straightened and pulled me up. He dropped his arm from around my waist, although he kept holding my hand. The unexpected touch both surprised and pleased me.

I glanced around. Nobles and servants ringed the dance floor, along with several guards, and Leonidas and I were the center of attention. Worry snaked through my stomach. Those guards hadn't been here earlier.

The nobles and servants parted, and Maeven stepped into view, still clapping as she stopped at the edge of the dance floor.

Her stunning gown was the darkest purple imaginable and looked as soft as a velvet cloud wisping around her body. A silver choker studded with amethysts circled her throat, while matching bracelets and rings were stacked up on her wrists and fingers like usual. All the gems practically dripped with her lightning magic. The same silver liladorn crown I'd seen in her portrait earlier perched on her head, and the tangle of diamond vines, jet thorns, and amethyst spikes of lilac seemed to reach all the way up to the paper strixes dangling from the ceiling.

Still clapping, Maeven glanced over at Milo, who was standing on the opposite side of the dance floor. The crown prince was wearing a short, formal midnight-purple jacket trimmed with gold thread, and the Morricone royal crest once again covered his chest.

Emperia and Corvina were standing on either side of Milo, both wearing scarlet gowns, with rubies glinting in their auburn hair.

I kept glancing around the throne room. Delmira was hovering next to Maeven, a worried look on her face, and she kept twisting her liladorn ring around and around on her finger.

Finally, I spotted Wexel, who was also wearing a formal dark purple jacket with a small Morricone crest done in gold thread over his heart. The captain was standing close to Milo, with several guards flanking him, but far more guards were stationed on the other side of the room, behind Maeven. Cold dread trickled down my spine. What was going on?

Maeven finally stopped clapping. "What a wonderful performance. The two of you move so well together. Then again, I would expect nothing less, given the many lessons you've both had."

That cold dread trickled down my spine again, turning into a larger stream of worry. How could Maeven possibly know how many dance lessons I'd had?

Beside me, Leonidas let out a soft, resigned sigh. So much emotion was packed into that one, small sound, and he dropped his head as though struggling to contain his feelings. He let out another sigh, then lifted his head, his face once again schooled into a blank, remote mask.

What's going on? I silently asked him.

He looked at me. *I'm sorry, Gemma.*

The sound of my own name slammed into my heart like the sharpest sword. *Gemma*—he had called me Gemma, which meant he knew exactly who I was. When—how had he figured it out?

Leonidas released my hand and stepped away from me. Cool air swirled in between us, slapping me across the face. He'd known who I really was, yet he had let me prance around and pretend to be someone else. Anger, embarrassment, and shame burned in my cheeks, while bitterness cloaked my heart. I wasn't a princess. I wasn't a spy.

I was nothing but a bloody *fool*.

Maeven stared at me, a pleased smile curving her lips, then looked out over the nobles, servants, and guards gathered around the dance floor. Her gaze lingered on Milo, Emperia, and Corvina, then flicked over to Wexel. I reached out with my magic, and I finally skimmed a thought from Maeven's mind.

Fools.

It was only one word, one thought, but it was filled with so much smug satisfaction and malevolent glee that it made me want to vomit. Maeven knew all about the plots against her, and this was her moment to play capture-the-crown—and win yet again.

"Thank you all so much for coming to my birthday ball," the queen purred, more smug satisfaction leaking into her words. "I can't believe it's been sixteen years since I took the throne. Here's to sixteen more!"

The guests clapped politely, as did the servants, although Wexel and his men kept their hands on their swords. Wexel eyed the second, larger group of guards, who glared right back at him, their hands also on their weapons.

Maeven waited until the applause died down before addressing the crowd again. "Some of you haven't always been pleased with my rule. Some of you think I've gotten soft and weak in recent years, but I assure you that is *not* the case."

She aimed her last few words at Milo, who grimaced at the pointed barbs.

"Many of you have brought me presents tonight. For that, I thank you," Maeven said. "But I wanted to break with tradition, and give you all a gift as well. Something that wouldn't have been possible without my son's assistance. Leonidas, please step forward."

Leonidas strode over to stand by his mother's side. He looked at me again, his face even colder and more distant than before, as though we were total strangers, and he was more statue than man. No, he wasn't a statue, he was a bloody *weapon*, one that had cut me to shreds. I had just been too stupid to see and feel the sly blows, and now he was going to deliver the killing strike.

"On my orders, Prince Leonidas has been investigating various plots against me, against you and Morta and everything we hold dear," she continued, once again staring at Milo.

The crown prince's lips pressed into a tight, thin line. He hadn't thought that his mother knew about his machinations, but it was obvious now that she did. Anger stained his cheeks, and magic shimmered in his eyes, making them burn a dark, dangerous purple.

Emperia remained glued to Milo's side, but Corvina sidled away from her fiancé.

Worry creased Wexel's forehead, along with a fine sheen of sweat, and he glanced back and forth between Milo and Maeven.

"During his investigation, Leonidas uncovered the identities of numerous spies, several of whom are here tonight," Maeven continued.

My heart sank. I glanced around the throne room again, but I didn't see Reiko anywhere. Maybe she had already left, but if not, I needed to warn her.

Reiko! I sent the thought out as far and wide as I could. *Maeven knows you're a spy. Get out of the palace. Now!*

Something flickered in my mind. It might have been surprise, but it was gone in an instant, like smoke wisping through the air, and I couldn't tell if she had heard me.

"Normally, I would have spies executed at once, but Leonidas came up with a much better suggestion. Isn't that right?" the queen purred again.

"I promised to bring you a grand birthday present. I thought a spy would be a good start. How do you like it?" Leonidas stabbed his finger at me.

Even though I knew they were coming, his words still slammed into my heart, burning as hot as a magier's lightning. My hands fisted in my skirt, although I managed to keep my face as cold and impassive as his still was.

"Her?" Milo sneered. "*She's* your grand present? Your big reveal? So what if she's a spy?"

Instead of rebuking her son for interrupting, Maeven's

smile widened. Milo didn't realize it yet, but he'd just lost his seat in this twisted version of capture-the-crown.

"Oh, she's much more than just a mere *spy*," Maeven said. "Show them."

Leonidas snapped up his hand and sent out a wave of magic. He took me by surprise, and I grimaced, knowing I was too late to block his attack. Only it wasn't an attack. Instead of punching me in the stomach or slapping me across the face, an invisible hand yanked the silver chain around my neck out from underneath my gown.

My gargoyle pendant thumped against my chest, out in the open for everyone to see.

"See that pretty gargoyle hanging around her neck? The Ripley royal crest, the symbol of Morta's enemy, should be as familiar to every one of you as it is to me." Maeven swept her hand out at me. "Let me introduce you all to Gemma Ripley, the crown princess of Andvari."

CHAPTER TWENTY-SEVEN

Shocked gasps rang out, and everyone stared at me, surprise filling most of their faces.

Most, but not all.

Of course Maeven wasn't surprised, and neither was Leonidas. But there was one other person who wasn't shocked by my true identity—Delmira.

Her face was pale, and she kept twisting her liladorn ring around on her finger. Worry blasted off her, but not so much as a flicker of surprise. I remembered how nervous she had seemed earlier and how she had dragged me around the throne room, instead of letting me drift away. Delmira had also known my true identity. I wondered if Leonidas and Maeven had told her or if she'd figured it out on her own.

The princess hadn't betrayed me nearly as badly as her brother had, but a surprising amount of hurt spiked through me all the same. I really had thought we were friends. Delmira tried to smile at me, but her expression wilted under my icy glare.

Milo, Emperia, and Corvina looked as stunned as everyone

else, as did Wexel. At least I'd fooled some people here. Unfortunately for me, I was still going to die.

The captain moved his lips, as if muttering a curse, then took his hand off his sword. He jerked his head, and the men lurking behind him stood down as well. Milo noticed the motions and shot the captain an angry glower, but Wexel shrugged in return. He was smart enough to know the tide had turned and that any attack against Maeven would fail now. The queen was thoroughly, completely in command again.

"So what if she's Gemma Ripley?" Milo said, still trying to undermine his mother. "She's nothing more than Glitzma, a spoiled princess. Hardly a threat to any of *us*."

More than a few agreeing murmurs sounded.

Maeven arched an eyebrow at her son. "This *spoiled princess* managed to dine at my table and walk the halls of Myrkvior as if she were one of us, which is something no other Ripley has ever done. Why, who knows what schemes and secrets she's discovered over the past two days? Perhaps even some of *yours*, Milo."

A muscle ticced in his clenched jaw, although I thought his upset had more to do with Maeven's mockery than any supposed secrets I might have learned.

"You ignore Gemma Ripley at your own peril," Maeven continued. "Then again, you've always had a tendency to underestimate your enemies. It's going to be the death of you someday, my dear boy."

Milo stiffened, and a red flush stained his cheeks, although I couldn't tell if he was more angered or embarrassed by the queen's dismissive words.

I'd thought the Morricones would immediately kill me if they realized who I was, but I should have known better. Instead, Maeven had unmasked me at her birthday ball to put her treacherous son back in his place and show the nobles how cunning and clever she still was, and it had worked like the proverbial charm. Goodwill and admiration surged off the nobles, and several of them smiled, nodded, and toasted her with their drinks. Maeven tipped her head in return, the devious sparkle in her eyes glittering even more brightly than the crown on her head did.

I closed my own eyes, blotting out the smug triumph on Maeven's face. *Grimley. I'm in trouble. The Mortans know who I am.*

He responded immediately, *I'll come get you! Hang on, Gemma!*

NO, I replied in a stern voice. *I don't want you to get captured too. I couldn't BEAR it if you were hurt because of me, because of my foolishness.*

I don't care what happens to me. I'm getting you out of here—one way or another. Grimley's fierce promise boomed through my mind, and a strong fist of love squeezed around my heart.

Despite the situation, a smile curved my lips. *And I love you for that. But I won't be able to escape this mess. Goodbye, Grims. I love you so much. Always remember that.*

Gemma, wait—

I grabbed hold of my magic and blocked the gargoyle, putting up a wall between our minds. His voice quieted to a dim rumble, although I couldn't stop the fist of love that kept squeezing my heart over and over again. The warm, comforting sensation gave me the strength to endure what was coming next. I opened my eyes, lifted my chin, and faced my enemies.

Smug Maeven. Worried Delmira. Angry, embarrassed Milo. Nervous Wexel. Emperia, Corvina, and the rest of the sneering nobles.

Finally, I looked at Leonidas, whose cold features perfectly mirrored my own hard expression. I didn't bother sending a thought or asking why he had exposed me. He was a Morricone, and I was a Ripley. That was explanation enough for everything. Even though I'd warned myself over and over to remember that, I had let our connection—attraction—cloud my judgment, and now

I was going to pay the price. On the bright side, he would never betray me again, since I would most likely be dead within the hour.

"Take her," Maeven ordered.

Guards moved forward, ringing the dance floor. My magic rose up, and my gargoyle pendant went ice-cold against the front of my gown, but I didn't reach for my power. There were too many guards, and Maeven and Milo could easily strike me down with their lightning.

"With pleasure," Wexel growled. He gave me an evil grin, then stepped forward and slammed his fist into my face.

Pain exploded in my jaw, my head snapped back, and I hit the floor. Somehow, I swallowed the groan rising in my throat and lifted my head.

My gaze locked with Leonidas's, and his cold, empty amethyst eyes were the last thing I saw before Wexel punched me again, and everything went black.

A steady, continued wrenching sensation in my arms jolted me awake. At first, I didn't know what was causing the pain, but then I realized that I was hanging limply in between two guards who were dragging me through a hallway.

I tried to lift my head, to fight back, but given the pain pounding through my skull, I couldn't quite manage it, and all I could do was stare down at the purple rugs on the floor. They zipped by one after another as the guards dragged me along. All that damned Mortan purple blurred together, increasing the ache in my mind, as well as the magic rising up inside me . . .

The rugs vanished, but my gaze locked on something else that was the same shade of purple—the tunic of the turncoat guard who was dragging Young Gemma through the woods.

I was ghosting yet again, but this time, I didn't mind the trip back to the past. It was preferable to whatever Maeven had planned for me in the present.

So I followed along and watched the guard strong-arm Gems into the campsite clearing and throw her down in front of Alvis and Xenia, who were still kneeling on the ground.

"Gems!" Alvis cried out. "Are you okay?"

Before she could answer, Captain Hanlon stepped up and slammed his fist into Alvis's face. The metalstone master toppled over onto his side, groaning with pain.

"Alvis!"

Gems reached for him, but the guard who'd forced her into the clearing twisted his fingers into her hair and hauled her upright, the motions sharp enough to bring tears to my own eyes.

What a sad little creature you are.

A voice filled Gems's mind. She glanced over at Young Leo, who was standing at the edge of the woods.

He stared at her. You're a mind magier just like I am. I can *feel* how much power you have, even more than I do. And yet, you just stand there while your friends are about to be slaughtered. I was right before. You *are* soft and weak.

Leo's face remained calm and blank, despite his cruel words. Gems growled and lunged toward him, but the guard yanked her back.

Captain Hanlon gestured at the other guards. "Now that we have the girl, kill the man and the woman—"

Xenia snarled and swiped out with her talons, ripping open the stomach of the guard closest to her. Beside the ogre morph, Alvis pushed himself back up onto his knees and lunged for the sword lying on the ground. He grabbed it, then swung the blade, catching another guard across the knees and making that man scream and tumble to the ground.

Xenia and Alvis both surged to their feet and stood back-to-back. Xenia extended her bloody talons, while Alvis clutched his sword, but they were outnumbered at least six to one, and they weren't going to survive the fight. Everyone else in the clearing knew it, and so did they.

Regret rippled off both of them, especially Alvis. I lost Everleigh, and now Gemma too. I should have done better. I should have done more. I should have fought harder.

Xenia's lips twisted into a fierce, silent snarl. Fucking traitors. I'll kill as many of them as I can. Maybe I can kill the one holding Gemma, and she can escape into the woods. Maybe Gemma can live, even if Alvis and I can't.

Soft and weak. *Leonidas spoke again, his voice dripping with even more disdain than before.*

Gems flinched as their thoughts crowded into her—my—mind, and her angry, panicked gaze zoomed back over to Leo again.

"Why are you doing this?" she yelled. "What did we ever do to you?"

Because you're too soft and weak to stop us, *he replied in a cold, matter-of-fact tone.* Soft and weak . . . soft and weak . . . soft and weak . . .

He kept chanting the words over and over again in his mind, taunting her.

"Shut up!" Gems screamed. "Shut up!"

Her hands clenched into fists, and rage rolled off her in palpable waves, along with the faintest tremors of magic. Something like satisfaction gleamed in Leo's eyes, and he kept right on chanting, his voice louder and crueler than before, until it boomed like thunder in my own mind.

"*Kill them!*" Captain Hanlon ordered again.

The guard tightened his grip on Gems's hair and hauled her backward. She kicked and flailed and thrashed, but the man easily pulled her along with his strength magic.

"*No!*" she screamed. "*No! No! No!*"

But no one listened to her, and Hanlon and the other guards advanced on Xenia and Alvis, who were still standing back-to-back. Leo continued to watch from a safe distance, although he grimaced and kept up his chanting, hammering Gems with his words over and over again. He also clutched his stomach, and sick misery pulsed off him, as though he didn't like what he was doing. I frowned. I had never noticed that back when this had been actually happening.

"*No!*" Gems screamed again.

One emotion after another blasted off her and punched into my own chest. Fear. Dread. Pain. Shame. Frustration. Rage. They all mixed and mingled together, swelling into this one feeling, this one singular energy that bubbled up in my—her—heart. Gems couldn't hold it back—she didn't want to hold it back—and it all erupted out of her mouth in one loud, violent scream.

The sound and the emotions and the power poured out of her, and I found myself screaming right along with her. We screamed because Uncle Frederich was dead. And Lord Hans. And everyone else on the Seven Spire lawn. We were alive, and they were dead, and we screamed because it wasn't bloody fair.

"*Shut up!*" the guard yelled.

He tried to clamp his hand over Gems's mouth, but she snapped out and sank her teeth deep into the web of flesh between his thumb and index finger.

The guard yelped, tore his hand out of her mouth, and staggered back. Gems whirled around to face him. The guard *growled and charged at her, but she lifted her hand, instinctively pulling on all the invisible strings attached to his body.*

Gems clearly didn't know what she was doing, but somehow, she managed to toss the man through the air. His back cracked into a nearby tree trunk, and he dropped to the ground. His head lolled to the side, and his sightless eyes fixed on her in a shocked accusation.

Gems's eyes widened. She had killed him. She—I—had never killed anyone before. Her stomach rumbled ominously, and I clenched my own stomach, trying to quell the nausea roiling there.

A hand clamped down on Gems's shoulder and spun her around. Captain Hanlon drew back his fist to punch her—

Suddenly, the captain flew backward through the clearing. He too slammed into a tree and tumbled to the ground—dead.

Gems whirled around.

Across the clearing, Leo lowered his hand to his side, although magic kept pouring off him. Not so soft and weak after all. Good. You just might live through this.

Why did you save me from your own captain? *Gems asked.*

Leo's eyes glittered, and a faint, resigned smile tugged at his lips. Because I know what it's like to be hunted.

Another guard rushed toward Gems, drawing her attention. She raised her hand, pulled on those strings of energy, and tossed him into a tree as well. He too was dead before he hit the ground.

Yet another guard rushed at her, his speed magic making him impossibly fast. Gems scrambled back, but she wasn't going to be able to get out of the way before he hit her—

The guard screamed and arched back. Xenia yanked her talons out of his side, then reached around and tore his throat open. Blood sprayed all over Gems, making her shriek in surprise, and that man pitched forward and hit the dirt.

Alvis limped up beside Xenia, clutching a sword. Despite being outnumbered, he and Xenia had killed all the guards, and the men's bodies littered the ground like bloody, tattered leaves.

"Are you okay?" Alvis asked. "Are you hurt?"

"I'm fine," Gems replied.

Xenia stepped over the guard whose throat she'd torn open, slapped her hands on her hips, and glared down at the girl with her bright amber eyes. She was still in her larger, stronger morph form, and blood covered her face and teeth and dripped off her long black talons.

"I told you to run," she growled.

"I did run—straight into trouble," Gems replied.

I grinned. Even back then, my mouth had had a mind of its own.

Xenia's stern face softened at the girl's black humor. "This was only one patrol. We need to leave before more of them come pouring out of the woods."

Alvis hurried over, scooped three knapsacks up off the ground, and slung them over his shoulder, while Xenia went from one guard to the next, rifling through their pockets and taking all the coins and anything else she found interesting.

A flicker of movement caught Gems's eye, and she whirled to her right.

Leo was still standing at the edge of the clearing.

Gems's hands clenched into fists. You didn't even stand and fight with your own people. That makes you even more of a coward than I am—and a traitor.

Leonidas shrugged. As I said before, traitors get to live. And now, so do you.

Her eyes narrowed. I should come over there **and kill
you myself.**

*Another one of those small, humorless smiles flickered
across his face.* You probably should. At least if you killed
me, my death would be quick. Uncle Maximus won't be
nearly so kind, especially after he hears about this.

*Leo dropped into a perfect bow, then vanished into the
trees. Gems opened her mouth to tell Xenia and Alvis that
the Morricone prince was escaping . . . but no words came
out. Instead, she just sighed and let him go.*

To this day, I still didn't know why I'd done that.

"Gemma?" Xenia called out. "What are you doing?"

*"I was just . . ." The girl cleared her throat. "Making sure
no more guards were sneaking up on us."*

*Xenia's eyes narrowed, as if she could hear the lie in
Gems's voice, but she didn't call the girl out on it. "Well, let's
get out of here before more of them show up."*

*Xenia took her knapsack from Alvis. Gems also grabbed
her knapsack and hoisted it onto her shoulder. Xenia headed
toward the far side of the clearing, with Alvis following along
behind her.*

*Gems glanced back over her shoulder, but once again all
she—I—saw were trees. Leonidas Morricone was gone, so the
girl hurried into the woods after her friends . . .*

A hot, electric presence filled my mind, yanking me back
into the here and now and making my fingertips tingle in warning. Someone with magic was nearby—someone very dangerous.

I blinked a few times, but instead of more purple rugs, all
I saw was a haze of dull gray under my feet. Flagstones, maybe?
My head was spinning so badly that I couldn't quite tell.

A finger hooked under my chin and forced my head up,

making it spin again. Slowly, the world righted itself, and amethyst eyes came into view. My traitorous heart lifted, thinking that Leonidas was here. Then the man leaned down, coming into focus. His golden hair gleamed under the lights, and an ugly sneer twisted his face.

Milo Morricone was looming over me.

CHAPTER TWENTY-EIGHT

I jerked back, but there was nowhere for me to go.

Clank-clank-clank.

I glanced up. My arms had been spread out wide and chained to the ceiling, while my feet were anchored to the floor, so that my body formed a five-pointed star. I yanked on the chains, but the thick, solid links didn't budge, and the shackles clamped around my wrists felt like circles of hard, unbreakable ice stuck to my skin. I reached for my magic, but it seemed weak and far away, like a limb that had gone to sleep and was stubbornly refusing to wake up. I bit back a curse. The shackles were made of coldiron, which was dampening my power.

My gaze darted around. I expected to see dungeon walls, perhaps some bars lining the front of a cell, but tables full of broken weapons, books, and papers surrounded me. My heart sank. This was so much worse than a dungeon.

I was back in Milo's workshop.

Milo snapped his fingers in front of my face, making me jerk back again. "You're awake. Finally. I was starting to think Wexel had knocked you senseless for good."

He drew back. A flicker of movement caught my eye, and I looked past him.

Maeven was standing by the open doors, surrounded by three guards. Delmira was there too, although she was staring down at the floor, as if she didn't want to see what was going to happen next. Wexel hovered in the corner by himself, his back to the wall and his hand gripping his sword, as if he was expecting trouble at any second.

Leonidas wasn't here, and I cursed myself for looking for him.

"So you're the great Gemma Glitzma Ripley," Milo said. "You don't look like much of a princess. I thought you were supposed to be some storied beauty, always swathed in silks and dripping with diamonds."

The nickname angered me, and I seized on to the emotion, letting it drown out my dread. No matter what happened, I would *not* cower in front of my enemies.

"What can I say?" I drawled. "The Mortan coffers aren't *nearly* as rich as the Glitnir ones are. Why, I've had to make do with rags and paste here."

Milo casually reached out and slapped me. The solid *crack* of his hand hitting my cheek rang out like a thunderclap. Pain exploded in my face, reigniting the dull throb from Wexel's earlier punches, but I swallowed the groan rising in my throat.

"Insult Morta or her coffers again, and I will saw out your tongue with a butter knife," Milo said.

"So what's it to be?" I asked, determined not to let him see my dread. "What sort of torture do you have planned?"

He grinned. "Mother did say that I could have some fun with you."

"How kind of her," I replied in a dry tone, looking over at Maeven.

The queen stared back at me. Her cold amethyst eyes were devoid of emotion, but a small smile played at the corners of her lips, and I felt a wave of smugness ripple off her, despite the coldiron shackles stifling my magic. She might have captured me, but I got the sense that her long game—whatever it was—was still playing out.

"Just a mild bit of torture," Maeven said. "Don't damage her too badly. She's no use to me dead."

Milo sneered at his mother the same way he had at me. "You wouldn't have said that sixteen years ago. You would have fried this Andvarian bitch to a crisp with your lightning in the throne room for everyone to see."

Maeven shrugged. "Older and wiser and all that." Her face hardened, and magic crackled in her eyes. "Do *not* disobey me in this, or there will be consequences—ones that you won't enjoy any more than Gemma is going to enjoy what you do to her. Do you understand me?"

Milo gave his mother a wary look. "Yes."

"Yes, what?" Maeven's voice was pure ice.

A muscle ticced in Milo's jaw, but he tilted his head to her ever so slightly. "Yes, my queen."

His words slithered out as a low, angry hiss, but Maeven didn't seem to mind her son's obvious lack of sincerity and fealty. She eyed him a few seconds longer, then motioned at the three guards. To my surprise, they took up positions along the wall. Apparently, the queen didn't trust her son not to kill me. How considerate of her.

Maeven left the workshop. Delmira scurried after her, still not meeting my harsh, accusing gaze. The doors closed behind them, leaving me in the workshop with Milo, Wexel, and the queen's three guards.

Milo ignored the captain and the guards and circled around me. He did that several times before stopping behind me. A cold finger of unease slid down my spine. Something rustled, and a faint, ominous *creak* sounded. What was that—

Agony exploded in my back.

The pain was so sudden, so intense, so blindingly shocking and searingly white-hot that I couldn't even scream. All the air dribbled out of my lungs, and I scrambled to get it back. I managed to suck down a surprised breath—

The pain came again.

And then again. And again.

Dully, in the back of my mind, I realized what was happening.

Milo was whipping me.

The crown prince stood behind me, out of my line of sight, and every soft *creak* and then resounding *snap* made me flinch. Sometimes, he cracked the whip against the flagstones, or an empty table standing nearby, or my back. There was no hurry in his attacks and no pattern to them either, but the worst part was not being able to *see* them coming, not being able to brace myself for the whip slamming against my skin and peeling away another strip of my flesh.

Desperate, I reached for my magic, trying to do something, *anything*, to stop it, but the coldiron shackles dampened my power. All I could do was stand there and take the blows, each one so hard and vicious it stole my breath, leaving me unable to scream out any of my pain.

Finally, the whipping stopped.

Red-hot ribbons of fire seared my back from top to bottom, as though coral vipers were writhing through my skin, biting and poisoning me over and over again. Blood also trickled down my back, adding to my misery. The steady stream of it matched the tears cascading down my cheeks. My breath puffed in and out in choked, ragged gasps, and I struggled not to whimper.

Milo stepped in front of me, holding a long whip. The handle was made of ordinary black leather, but the whip itself was a shockingly bright orange-red. Just looking at the vivid color made the ribbons of fire in my back burn a little hotter.

"Do you like it?" he purred. "I stole this from Uncle Maximus's workshop years ago. I used to sneak in there as a child and watch him play with the people who displeased him. Sometimes, if I was lucky, he would let me play with them too. That's when I first learned what true power *really* is—having your enemies helpless before you." He cracked the whip against the floor to punctuate his gruesome point.

So Maximus had had a hand in warping Milo. I wondered what Maeven had thought about her brother teaching her son how to torture people. If she'd been horrified by the idea. If she'd tried to stop it. Or if she simply hadn't cared.

"Maximus had an extensive collection of whips, but this one was always my favorite. It's made from the skin of coral vipers. The whip's magic is designed to make you feel like your skin is on fire, even more so than it would anyway from the sting of the actual wound. Just like coral-viper venom makes people feel like their blood is boiling inside their veins."

He expertly twirled the whip around, and I couldn't stop myself from shuddering.

"The wounds can be healed, but supposedly not even the most talented bone master can get rid of the scars that the whip leaves behind," Milo continued in a light, conversational tone, as if he were talking about how sunny it was and not about the horrible torture he had just inflicted on me. "Leonidas would know. Uncle Maximus used this whip on him all the time. Sometimes, if I was very, very good, Uncle Maximus would let me use the whip on Leonidas too."

I thought of how ashamed Leonidas had been for me to see the scars on his back. How he wore layer after layer of clothing like a suit of armor. How he didn't like to be touched. How he was always so gentle and careful with me. My breath escaped in another ragged gasp, and more tears streamed down my face, but this time, they weren't entirely for myself.

"Those truly were magnificent times." Milo's eyes gleamed, and a smile slithered across his lips, as if he was remembering all the terrible things he'd done to his own brother—and now to me too.

I was going to kill Milo Morricone.

I didn't know how, I didn't know when, but I *would* kill him. Even if it was the last thing I ever did, even if I died in his horrid workshop in the next five minutes, I was going to find a way to fucking take him with me. My silent vow didn't ease the pain in my back, but it gave me something else to focus on besides my own misery.

"What's the matter, Gemma?" Milo mocked. "Strix got your tongue? You were full of witty remarks earlier, but now you're so strangely silent. I wonder why that is?"

He tapped a finger against his lips, as if contemplating his own question. "I suppose it's because I've beaten all the wit right out of you. Why, you're nothing but a broken doll now."

If I'd had the breath for it, I would have laughed in his face. Yes, Milo had beaten me, whipped me, wounded me terribly—but he had not *broken* me. The Seven Spire massacre had broken me, but this pompous, arrogant, sadistic prince would *not*. I added that vow to the cold, murderous one already beating in my heart.

"If only your people could see you like this," Milo sneered. "You're a bloody, blubbering mess. They wouldn't call you Glitzma now."

He drew back his arm, as if to snap the whip against the front of my body, maybe even my face, but one of Maeven's guards loudly, deliberately cleared his throat. Milo shot the man an angry glare, but he lowered the whip. No matter how much he wanted to hurt me, he didn't want to risk his mother hurting him in return. He was even more of a fucking coward than I was.

Milo motioned at the three guards. "Do something useful. Put her on the table."

I was hoping that Maeven's men would ignore his command, but the guards stepped forward. Two of them held me upright while the third man unhooked my arms from the chains dangling from the ceiling, although he left the coldiron shackles clamped around my wrists.

I frowned. Why wasn't the guard putting a coldiron collar around my neck like the one Wexel had used on Leonidas in Blauberg? Maybe the Mortans didn't realize what kind of magic I had. Princess Gemma was thought to be a metalstone master, and I had never shown anyone at Myrkvior my true mind magier power, except for Leonidas and Reiko. A spark of hope ignited in my chest. Perhaps I could use this oversight to my advantage—if I stayed alive long enough.

The third guard undid the chains from around my feet. Then the other two guards dragged me over to an empty table, picked me up, and laid me down flat on it. To my surprise, the stone actually had a cooling effect on my back, and tears of relief leaked out of my eyes as some of my pain eased.

The guards spread my arms and legs out into that five-pointed-star position again, then chained my limbs down to the table. They stepped back, and Milo loomed over me. I yanked on the chains, which had a bit more give than the other ones, but I couldn't do much more than wriggle helplessly, like a worm caught in a strix's beak.

Milo drew something from his pocket, then held it out over the table where I could see it. A tearstone arrow glinted a dull gray in his fingers. "You have such a keen interest in my arrows that I thought I would show you what they can truly do. Would you like that, Gemma?"

He smiled at the growing horror on my face. "Oh, yes. I thought you would."

Milo leaned forward and drove the arrow all the way through my right hand.

Flesh ripped. Muscles tore. Bones broke. Pain exploded in my hand just like it had in my back. Only this time, I had enough breath to scream. And scream. And scream . . .

"What do you think, Gemma?" Milo said, when my cries finally died down. "Will my arrows help me destroy my enemies?"

I didn't have the breath to answer him. More tears streamed out of my eyes, and my hand throbbed and pulsed with every frantic beat of my heart.

Milo grinned, moved around the table, and held another arrow out where I could see it. Then the bastard grinned and drove that one through my left hand.

More pain, more screams, more tears.

He waited for me to get my breath back before he spoke again. "You're probably wondering why I went to so much trouble to steal tearstone just to make arrows out of it. Let me show you."

Milo lifted his hand. I tensed, thinking he had yet another arrow to drive through my body, but purple lightning flared on his fingertips. He gave me another cruel smile, then flicked his fingers, shooting small bolts of lightning at the arrows embedded in my hands.

Tearstone was known for its ability to deflect magic, but Milo's arrows didn't do that. Instead, they acted like lightning rods, absorbing his magic and then shooting it out into my wounds. In an instant, my hands felt like they were on fire and being electrocuted at the same time, and the sensation zipped up my arms and out into the rest of my body. I screamed and screamed, but I couldn't stop the searing agony of his magic . . .

I must have passed out, because the next thing I knew, Milo was looming over me again. His lightning was gone, and he was studying me with a curious expression, as though I were a bug trapped in a jar that he was going to scorch with a magnifying glass—again.

He gave me another wicked grin. "And now, for the really fun part—my favorite part."

All my strength was gone, and all I could do was stare at him dully, wondering what new horror was coming next. Milo grinned again, then reached down, took hold of the arrow in my right hand, and yanked it out.

I hadn't thought anything could hurt worse than the coral-viper whip peeling the skin from my back, the arrow punching through my hand, or the tearstone conducting his lightning through my body.

I was wrong.

The hooked barbs lining the arrowhead dug into my skin, ripping and tearing and chewing through my muscles, tendons, and bones, and doing as much damage as possible.

More pain, more screams, more tears.

Milo held the arrow up where I could see it. My blood coated the weapon, turning the tearstone such a dark blue that it almost looked black.

"Oh, don't worry, Gemma," he said, seeing my horrified expression. "I don't have Uncle Maximus's mutt ability to absorb magic from blood, so I have no interest in drinking yours. Although it is rather amusing to watch it spurt out of your body."

He tossed the arrow onto an empty table across from the one I was lying on. The *clank-clank-clank* of the projectile sliding across the stone made me shudder.

"And lucky for me, I still have one more arrow to go," Milo purred.

He took hold of the second arrow and ripped it out just as brutally as he had the first one.

More pain, more screams, more tears.

Then everything went black, and I finally, mercifully, passed out.

One moment, I was drifting along in the sweet black void of unconsciousness. The next, I was standing by the table, staring down at my own tortured self. I sighed. Thanks to my severe injuries, I was ghosting again. Terrific.

One of the workshop doors creaked open. I glanced in that direction, although my real-world body didn't move. To my surprise, Delmira slipped into the chamber carrying a small basket.

She glanced around, but Milo, Wexel, and the guards were gone, and I was the only one in here. Delmira shut the door behind her, then rushed over to me.

"Oh, Gemma," she whispered. "I'm so sorry. I never meant for any of this to happen."

A few tears dripped off her cheeks and spattered onto my right hand, and a little jolt of power, of magic, pulsed through my wound. Even stranger, it eased my pain, just a bit.

Delmira wiped her tears away, set her basket down, and started pulling items out of it. A bowl of water, a tin of salve, white bandages. Not what I'd expected.

The princess cleaned the wounds in my hands, then opened the tin and dipped her fingers into the salve inside. She talked to me the whole time she worked, the way that people sometimes did to sick loved ones. She must have thought that I could hear her. If she only knew.

"This is liladorn salve." Delmira smeared a light purple cream all over my injured hands. "I made it myself from a recipe I found in an old book in the palace library. It will close and heal your wounds, although they will probably still scar."

The purple salve started glowing with a faint, almost translucent light, but Delmira didn't seem to notice it, and she kept rubbing the concoction all over my hands. Cool, soothing tingles rippled out of the salve and soaked into my skin, and the soft scent of lilac filled my nose. I wondered how much magic was in the salve—and how much of it was Delmira's own doing.

My bones straightened, my tendons realigned, and my muscles pulled themselves back together. A few minutes later, the ugly wounds in my hands had healed to bright red scars, as though someone had painted crimson starbursts onto my skin.

"I begged Mother to let a bone master heal you, but of course she refused," Delmira continued talking. "She *never* should have let Milo torture you. Sometimes, I don't know who is the bigger monster—Mother or Milo."

She slathered a final layer of liladorn salve onto my hands, then bandaged them. Next, she turned me over onto my side, grimacing at how the chains clanked. Her lips pinched together as she saw the whip wounds on my back, but she cleaned and bandaged those as best she could through my tattered gown.

"I used to bandage Leo's wounds after Uncle Maximus hurt him," Delmira said, still talking to my body. "Uncle Maximus was always jealous of Leo's mind magier power, and he would have Leo brought to his workshop. He claimed that he was teaching Leo about magic, but we all saw the marks on Leo's back, and we knew that Maximus was really trying to take Leo's power for his own. He never succeeded, but Leo still suffered terribly. My uncle had a whole collection of whips, and he used them all on Leo. Milo too, from time to time. And me, once."

Her voice dropped to a whisper, and she stared off into space, as if remembering that horrible event. Delmira shuddered and rolled me onto my other side so she could reach the rest of my wounds.

"Of course Mother tried to stop it, but Uncle Maximus

shipped her off to Seven Spire. He said it was so she could spy on the Blairs, but we all knew that he wanted to get her out of the palace. She thwarted him, though. She sent Leo and me away from Myrkvior before she left for Bellona."

Surprise filled me. I had always assumed that Maeven had *wanted* to go to Seven Spire, that she had been eager to orchestrate the massacre, but that didn't seem to be the case.

"You must hate Mother and Milo and probably me too," Delmira continued. "Not only for tonight, but also for what happened to you during the Seven Spire massacre. And rightly so. But please don't hate Leo. He truly does care for you. I can see it in his face whenever he looks at you and hear it in his voice whenever he speaks about you. Mother just twisted the situation around to her own advantage, the way she always does."

Bitterness dripped from her voice, and misery flooded her face, as though she was speaking from personal experience. What cruel thing had Maeven done to her own daughter to provoke such a reaction?

"Leo didn't realize that Mother knew who you really were until she called him out in front of everyone at the ball," Delmira continued. "She trapped him, and you too. And you've both suffered for it."

My eyes narrowed. Leonidas was suffering? How?

Delmira finished tending to my wounds, laid me back out flat on the table, and returned her supplies to her basket. Then she leaned forward and smoothed my hair back from my face. "I wish I could do more for you. I should have told you to flee the palace the second I saw your gargoyle pendant. I recognized it at once. Plus, I've heard so many wonderful stories about Princess Gemma Ripley, the queen of fashion and style and everything else beautiful in Andvari."

A wistful look twisted her face. "You were so kind to me, even though you probably didn't want to be. We could have been friends if things had been different. If I had been braver, stronger."

She laid her hand on my forehead, and her pain, conflict, and anguish trickled down into my body. Despite everything that had happened, my heart softened. She was a good person trapped in a bad situation who was just trying to survive.

Delmira removed her hand, gathered up her things, and snuck out of the workshop, but she didn't leave me alone. As soon as she vanished, a familiar presence filled the air.

I stiffened and glared into the shadows in the far corner. "I know you're there. I can feel you oozing about. Like pond scum."

"Pond scum?" a voice murmured. "I was hoping that I would at least merit a physical form. Perhaps a coral viper."

"Well, you certainly are a snake," I hissed back.

A sigh sounded, but a figure slowly stepped forward—Leonidas.

Oh, it wasn't the *real* Leonidas, but rather his ghostly presence, just as my own essence was still hovering outside my body. He hesitated, then eased a little closer, although he remained in the shadows on the opposite side of the table from me.

Leonidas stared down at my body. A muscle ticced in his jaw, and he ran his hand down his face, as if the motion would wipe away the awful sight before him. Several seconds passed before he slowly raised his gaze to mine. Rage crackled in his eyes, making them burn bright and clear, despite the shadows cloaking his face, but it was *nothing* compared to the rage hammering in my heart, pounding through me even stronger than the lingering pain of my wounds.

"I'm going to kill Milo for this," he snarled.

"No, you won't." My voice was even colder and harsher than his was. "*I'm* going to kill him. And you too, you lying, duplicitous bastard."

He flinched as though he could actually feel the icy venom in my words. Maybe he could with his magic. I bloody hoped so.

Still, I had questions, and this was probably the only chance I would ever have to get answers, so I set aside my rage—for now. "How long did you know who I really was?"

Leonidas sighed again, but his gaze stayed steady on mine. "I always knew. From the very first moment I saw you in the clearing in Blauberg. I immediately recognized you—and your magic." He paused. "After all, you never forget the first girl who tries to kill you."

I didn't know whether to feel vindicated that he remembered me as vividly as I did him or disgusted that I hadn't realized he'd known who I was all along. Either way, I was still a fool.

"If you knew who I was, then why did you save me from the mine?"

"Because saving you was the right thing to do," he replied. "I would have done it regardless of anything else, even if you hadn't saved me from Wexel first."

"But why bring me here?" I demanded. "Why let me spy on your family? Why pretend like we were . . . partners?"

My voice hitched on the last question. It wasn't the one I truly wanted answered. No, I wanted to know why he had kissed my hand on the balcony, and then again in my chambers. Why he had danced with me in the throne room, and all the other times he had touched and looked at and spoken to me as though he actually *cared* about me, as though I were truly *special* to him. But I'd be damned if I'd ask any of those questions—not a single bloody one—no matter how much my heart yearned for the answers.

"I really did bring you to Myrkvior so that the bone masters could heal you. I didn't want to trust your well-being to someone I didn't know, especially given how . . . important you are." His voice hitched just like mine had.

"And then I insisted on staying, just like a fool."

"I hoped that if you stayed that it might ease tensions between Morta and Andvari. I wanted you to see that we aren't all vile and corrupt," he replied. "That all Mortans are not evil. That my family wasn't all bad. That even though I'm a Morricone, that I'm not all bad either."

"Your family? Not all bad? *Look* at what your brother did to me." I gestured down at my own unconscious body. "And don't even get me started on your mother. Princess Gemma Ripley survived the Seven Spire massacre, remember? I saw what Maeven did to the Blairs. She orchestrated the murders of *children*. She is a fucking *monster*, just like you are."

Leonidas opened his mouth to speak, but I cut him off.

"Your mother might be a monster, but you're even *worse* than she is," I hissed. "Everyone knows what Maeven did at Seven Spire, and she had the audacity to murder King Maximus in front of an arena full of people. But you? You brought me here and pretended to be considerate and honorable and fucking *noble*. Well, guess what? Your plan worked, and I did see the Mortans as people instead of monsters, especially Anaka and Delmira. You made me feel things for them."

For you. I didn't say the words, but they hung in the air between us like a dark, ominous storm cloud.

Leonidas flinched again, but he didn't look away from me. "I didn't think anyone else would recognize you. You had cut and dyed your hair, and no one in Myrkvior had ever seen you in person before, besides my mother. Even on the off chance that someone did recognize you, I was confident I could protect you."

"Well, your confidence was sorely misplaced."

He didn't dispute my point. He couldn't.

"How long were you going to let me stay here?" I demanded. "How long were you going to let me risk my life on the slim chance that Maeven wouldn't recognize me?"

"I was going to sneak you out of the palace tonight, but Mother must have realized what I was planning. She summoned me to her chambers right before the ball began and told me that she had a way to fix everything and to stop Milo's plot against her. She said that all I had to do was follow her lead during the ball." Leonidas paused. "And that if I didn't, then she would be very displeased—and take her anger out on Delmira."

Maeven had threatened her own daughter to get her son to cooperate? Just when I thought the queen couldn't surprise me anymore, she achieved a higher level of cruelty.

"I'm sorry, Gemma," Leonidas murmured, his voice a harsh, ragged whisper. "So very, very sorry. More than you will ever know. I promised to protect you, and I utterly failed. I will *never* forgive myself for letting this happen to you."

Rage continued to hammer in my heart, but the colder, more logical part of me could appreciate the impossible situation he'd been thrust into and even understand his reasoning. If I'd been forced to choose between my father and a man that I . . . mistakenly cared about, then I would have chosen my father, just as Leonidas had picked Delmira over me.

"I didn't want it to come to this," he continued. "After the ball, Mother promised me that you wouldn't be hurt. She swore that you would be imprisoned, nothing more. I thought I could release you from the dungeon and smuggle you out of the palace."

"You didn't think Maeven would have me tortured?" I shook my head. "That makes you either naïve or stupid. At this moment, I'd say both. Either way, I'm suffering the consequences."

Once again, he didn't deny my accusation. Instead, his face twisted into a grimace, and he clutched his ribs, as though he were in pain.

My eyes narrowed. "What happened to you?"

"Nothing," Leonidas muttered, dropping his head and turning away from me.

But it was most definitely something, so I rounded the table and planted myself in front of him. The prince sighed, but he lifted his head and stepped forward, so that he was finally standing in the light.

Leonidas had been tortured—again.

He had two black eyes, plus a broken nose. I hadn't noticed his injuries before, due to my own anger and the shadows cloaking the workshop. He kept clutching his ribs, as though it hurt to simply breathe, and he only wore a thin tunic, instead of the formal jacket he'd sported at the ball.

I eased to the side. His black tunic hung in tatters on his back, and long, thin, angry red marks crisscrossed his skin— the same marks I had seen on my own back when Delmira had healed me. I lifted a hand to my mouth, trying not to be sick.

A humorless smile split Leonidas's battered face. "Mother had me . . . restrained when I objected to you being brought to Milo's workshop. Wexel decided to teach me a lesson for disobeying my queen. So did Milo."

So Maeven had had him imprisoned, Wexel had beaten him, and Milo had whipped him, just like Maximus used to. Once again, my treacherous heart softened, but I shoved the feeling aside. Leonidas Morricone had done nothing but use and betray me, and I would not be fooled by him again.

I started to step away, but he reached out and touched my arm. It was the softest, lightest, gentlest touch imaginable, no more than a brush of his fingers against the sleeve of my ruined gown, but somehow, it hurt worse than all of Milo's torture.

"Don't you *dare* touch me," I snarled, jerking away. "Not even here, in my dream."

"*Our* dream," he insisted. "*Our* world. Don't you remember how we used to talk to each other as children?"

I didn't respond. That had come later, after our first encounter in the woods. When he had been back in Morta and I had been home in Andvari. More painful memories I didn't want to dwell on.

"We used to talk all the time. At least until you put that damn necklace on." Leonidas stabbed his finger at the gargoyle pendant still dangling from the chain around my neck. "You bottled up your power for the last sixteen years. Why? Why would you ever do that?"

"You know why," I muttered. "You saw what I did to those turncoat guards in the woods all those years ago. How I killed them with a wave of my hand. With a bloody *thought.*"

"Ah, so you were afraid of your power. All this time, I thought you just didn't want to speak to me anymore." He frowned. "But why would you ever be afraid of your own power?"

Anger and frustration surged through me. He didn't understand. He would *never* understand. We might both be mind magiers, but Leonidas Morricone could turn himself to pure ice, when need be, and nothing seemed to scratch the surface of his cold, cold heart.

Me? I could lie, and fight, and kill, but I still *always* felt too much, whether it was my own fear of being paralyzed—or the twisted joy I took in inspiring that same paralyzing fear in others. There was no balance, no silence, no fucking *calm* in my stormy mind and heart.

"Gemma?" Leonidas asked again. "Why are you afraid of your own power?"

"Because I can't *control* it," I snapped. "I can't control my magic any more than I can control how I bloody feel about you."

My confession boomed out as loud as a thunderclap. As soon as the words flew off my tongue, I wished that I could take them back, and I once again cursed my own foolishness, my own weakness. Even now, after everything that had happened, I still couldn't hate Leonidas.

I just . . . *couldn't.*

Perhaps that made me even more naïve and stupid than he had been.

Leonidas eased toward me. He didn't touch me again, didn't even try to, but he stood as close to me as possible. My hands balled into fists, but I lifted my chin and glared at him. I would not back down, and I would not run away. Not from him.

Never again.

I would burn the softness in my heart and bury his corpse in the hot, smoking ashes.

"I'm so sorry, Gemma," he repeated in a low, strained voice. "For everything you've suffered because of me. I know I can never make this right, but I'm going to try my best. Starting right now."

"What do you mean—"

Before I could react, Leonidas put his hand in the air in front of my heart and twisted his fingers. An answering *wrench* ripped through my chest, and I gasped and staggered back.

For a moment, I thought he had crushed my heart with his magic, that he had *killed* me, but then he drew his hand back, and the pain in my chest eased.

I gasped again. A black, writhing mass flickered along his fingertips, with streaks of purple lightning shooting through it, as though he were clutching a miniature tornado in his hand.

Leonidas gave me a grim smile, then shoved the black mass into his own chest, into his own heart. He screamed and crumpled to the floor.

I couldn't stop myself from falling to my knees beside him. "Leo! What did you do?"

He looked up at me, his face twisting with pain. "Milo . . . isn't the only one . . . who read Maximus's journals," he said, gasping for breath. "My uncle . . . wrote quite a bit . . . about his experiments . . . about inflicting pain . . . and taking it away . . ."

He lay on his back, still gasping for breath, but his words

made me realize that I actually felt . . . *better*. The stinging, shocking, burning pain in my hands and my back was finally, fully gone. Somehow, Leonidas had taken the pain of my injuries into his own body so that he would suffer them instead of me.

"Why did you do that?" I demanded. "Why would you willingly hurt yourself?"

"It's the only way . . . to help you . . . save yourself . . ." he rasped.

He tried to smile, but his eyes fluttered closed, his head lolled to the side, and his body went slack and still on the floor.

I blinked. From one moment to the next, he vanished, and I was all alone in Milo's workshop again, with only my unconscious body on the table for company.

I surged to my feet and spun around, looking for him. "Leo! Leo!"

But he was gone, and he didn't return no matter how frantically I called for him or how much my weak, traitorous heart yearned to see him, just a moment more.

CHAPTER TWENTY-NINE

Sometime later, I woke up again—in my own body this time. I was still chained to the table in Milo's workshop, but I felt much better and stronger than before, thanks to Delmira's liladorn salve and Leonidas . . . doing whatever he had done. Taking my physical pain away, if not the emotional wreck he had made of my heart.

I cautiously flexed my hands. No sharp, stinging pain bloomed in my palms, although my skin was tight and itchy, and a dull ache rippled through my fingers. I wasn't completely healed, but I was in far better shape than before. Leonidas had kept his word—at least about giving me a chance to escape, if nothing else.

So I lifted my head up off the table and glanced around, trying to figure some way to remove the shackles still clamped around my wrists. A long, simple bolt ran through a hole on the top of each shackle, holding it together. If I could knock the bolt out, then the shackle would pop open. All I had to do was free one of my wrists, and then I could sit up and remove the second bolt.

I reached for my magic, wondering if it would feel as numb

as before, but whatever Leonidas had done had reawakened my power, and it came to me much more easily, although it still wasn't as strong as normal. Still, I gripped it tightly, then focused on the bolt on the shackle on my right wrist, trying to use my magic to slide it through the hole. But the coldiron blocked most of my power, and I couldn't so much as wiggle the bolt.

Frustration filled me, but I forced myself to keep thinking. I might not be able to move the bolt with my magic, but maybe I could use my power to get some *other* object to slam into the bolt and slide it free. I glanced around the workshop again, but all the hammers, pliers, and other tools were too far away and simply too heavy to float over here with my limited supply of magic. My gaze moved over to the tables surrounding me, but none of the glass jars, broken weapons, or books were the right shape, size, or weight to do what I needed done.

My heart sank, and I started to smack my head back against the table in vexation when a couple of gleams caught my eye—the two tearstone arrows Milo had stabbed through my hands.

They were lying on the table directly across from me, about six feet away. My blood had dripped off the arrows, leaving the weapons strangely, pristinely clean, although the tearstone was now midnight-blue instead of its previous starry gray. Disgust roiled through my stomach, but I pushed the emotion aside, grabbed hold of my magic, and focused on the arrows.

I could sense the invisible strings of energy wrapping around the arrows, but thanks to the coldiron shackles, I couldn't quite get a grip on them. Sweat beaded on my forehead and trickled down my face, but I ignored the drops, as well as the salty tears of frustration leaking out of my eyes, and kept concentrating.

All that mattered was grabbing hold of one arrow—*just one*. So I drew in a deep breath and slowly let it out. Then I raised my right wrist up off the table as high as it would go. When I had the angle right, I turned my head and focused on one of the arrows.

More sweat slid down my face, but no tears. I didn't have time for tears or frustration or any other useless emotion—just ruthless determination. So I redoubled, tripled my efforts and focused on my magic, on reaching out and grabbing hold of that invisible string of energy on the tip of the arrow. Then, when I had a firm grip on it, I imagined yanking back on that string, aiming the arrow exactly where I wanted it to go, and shooting it through the air—

Thunk!

The arrow zipped off the table and hit the shackle. The projectile slammed into the center of the bolt and punched it all the way through the slot. The shackle dropped from my wrist and clattered against the table, along with the arrow. A wide grin spread across my face.

I had done it—I had freed myself.

I sat up and removed the other shackle from my left wrist, along with the ankle chains. The second the coldiron dropped from my skin, the rest of my magic came rushing back. I exhaled in relief. I had never been so glad to feel my power, no matter how uncontrollable it might sometimes be.

The tearstone arrow was lying on the table beside the shackles, so I scooped it up. Then I grabbed the second arrow from the other table with my magic. It zipped through the air and into my hand, and I slid both arrows into my pocket. I had come too far and suffered too much to leave them behind.

A silver gleam caught my eye. The compact Leonidas had given me was also sitting on the other table. I used my magic to grab it and stuffed it into my pocket as well.

Once that was done, I reached for that wall in my mind, the one I had put up between Grimley and me, and tore it down. *Grims? Are you there?*

Gemma! he responded immediately. *Where are you? Are you okay?*

In Milo's workshop. I'm in one piece, more or less.

I'm going to kill the Mortans for hurting you. His fierce growl filled my mind. *Starting with Leonidas. No matter how much his stupid bird has been helping me.*

His dark, vicious promise made me smile, although the mention of Leonidas and Lyra twinged my heart.

Forget the Mortans. We need to escape. Can you get up on one of the rooftops without the strixes seeing you?

He huffed. *Of course I can.*

Good. I'm going to slip out of Milo's workshop and find you. And then we're going home.

I'll be ready.

I pushed our connection to the back of my mind and swung my feet off the table—

One of the workshop doors creaked open. I didn't have time to hop off the table, and there was nowhere to hide anyway, so I did the only thing I could—I wrapped the chains around my wrists and lay back down on the table, as though I were still shackled and helpless.

Maeven strode into the room, followed by Emperia. The noble lady left the door open behind her, but no guards appeared in the hallway beyond. The two women must have wanted to lord their triumph over me in private. My hands tightened around the chains. It was going to be the last bloody thing they ever did. Milo might not be here for me to murder, but killing Maeven and Emperia would be an excellent start to avenging myself against the Mortans.

I rolled my head to the side as they approached me. Emperia was smiling wide, but Maeven's earlier smugness had vanished, and her expression was surprisingly neutral. The two of them stopped and stared down at me.

"I still can't believe *this* is Gemma Ripley," Emperia sneered. "I thought she would at least be pretty, given all the songs about her. 'The Bluest Crown' certainly makes her sound like a great beauty, but she's rather ordinary. And her metalstone magic feels exceptionally weak. Rather like Delmira's magic."

Maeven's nostrils flared with anger. She didn't like Emperia maligning her daughter's seeming lack of power. "Yes, well, this *is* Gemma Ripley, and you're a fool to underestimate her. Just like you've been a fool about a great many things."

Emperia faced the queen. "What do you mean?"

Maeven dropped her hand to her side. Something silver glinted in her fingers, and she gave the noble lady a cold, thin smile. "Perhaps this will make my point."

She snapped up her hand and plunged a dagger into Emperia's chest.

I gasped and jerked back on the table, rattling the chains. Out of all the things I thought might happen, Maeven killing Emperia was not one of them.

Emperia opened her mouth to scream, but Maeven clamped her hand over the other woman's lips, muffling her cries.

"Did you really think I didn't know that you were fucking my son?" Maeven hissed. "Encouraging his ambitions? Using him to plot against me?"

Emperia let out another muffled cry and swayed on her feet. She lifted her hand, but only a few tiny hailstones sputtered out of her fingertips before falling harmlessly to the floor.

"I've known about your plot with Milo for *months*. I had hoped that Corvina was aligned with you and that I could eliminate both of you at once, but your daughter has her own plans. She is a teeny bit smarter than you in that regard." Maeven spoke in a calm voice, twisting her dagger even deeper into Emperia's chest. "For *years*, you have undermined me at every turn, thinking that *my* crown should have been yours. But I killed Maximus to earn it, and I'm killing you now to keep it. For myself and especially for Delmira."

Maeven smiled at Emperia again, then ripped the dagger out of the other woman's chest and shoved her away. Emperia staggered back, hitting the table where I was still lying. I rolled away from her, letting go of the chains and dropping off the opposite side of the table. Then I popped back up and onto my feet.

Emperia stared at Maeven. Her mouth kept opening and closing, but no words came out, only a few bloody coughs. Then her eyes rolled up in the back of her head, and she tumbled to the floor.

Maeven turned toward me, still clutching that dagger. "You freed yourself already. Good. It will help sell my story."

"What story?"

She tossed the dagger down onto the table. "That you managed to get free and murder Emperia. How sad that a spoiled, pampered princess like Gemma Ripley was able to kill such a strong weather magier as Lady Dumond. But I suppose that's what Emperia gets for coming in here alone and foolishly interfering with my prisoner."

My eyes narrowed. "You lured Emperia in here so that you could kill her and use me as your bloody scapegoat. Just like you blamed the Seven Spire massacre on Captain Auster all those years ago. You should have thought of a new plan. You're becoming predictable."

Maeven shrugged. "Why come up with new plans when the old ones still work so well?"

I ground my teeth, hating her cool logic. "Let me guess— you're going to kill me now so I can't tell anyone what you did." My bandaged hands clenched into fists. "Well, that's not going to happen."

I snapped up my hands, reached for my magic, and threw the chains on the table at her. But Maeven summoned up her own purple lightning, blasting the metal to pieces.

I ignored the flying metal, lunged forward, and grabbed the dagger off the table. The weapon was much lighter than I expected and slid into my hand with an easy familiarity. I glanced down at it. My snarling gargoyle crest glittered in the hilt.

I silently cursed. Maeven had killed Emperia with *my* dagger to further incriminate me. She really had thought of everything. My fingers clenched around the hilt. Well, I could kill her with the blade just like she'd murdered Emperia with it.

I hurried around the table, but Maeven moved in the opposite direction so that it remained in between us. She raised her hand, and purple lightning crackled on her fingertips. The two of us stood there, facing off across the table. She gave me an amused smile. I snarled and bared my teeth in return.

Maeven flicked her hand, and a bolt of lightning zipped out of her fingers and slammed into some glass jars on another table. The subsequent explosion *boomed* through the workshop.

In the distance, a voice rang out. "What was that?"

"I think it came from Milo's workshop!"

"This way, men! Hurry!"

I tensed, recognizing the last voice as Wexel's.

"You're not killing me tonight, Gemma," Maeven purred. "Not with your mind magier power or that dagger or anything else."

I silently cursed again. By throwing those chains at her, I'd shown Maeven what I truly was, if she hadn't already guessed.

"You might—*might*—be able to murder me if you were at full strength, but you've been severely injured." Her lightning burned a little brighter and hotter in her hand. "And I have not."

I snarled again with anger and frustration, but I held my position. I was still weak from Milo's torture, and she would easily fry me to a crisp.

"You have two choices," Maeven said. "You can stay here and die trying to kill me, or you can attempt to escape. The guards are still a few corridors away. If you leave now, you might make it out of the palace. As for what happens after that, well . . ." She shrugged. "You'll never know unless you try."

"Why are you doing this? Why are you giving me a chance to escape?"

"I told you that I would not forget your kindness to Delmira."

A harsh laugh erupted out of my lips. "You don't care about *kindness*."

"No, but like it or not, I need you, Gemma Ripley. So does Delmira." Maeven paused. "And Leonidas most of all."

Her soft words ripped into my chest, as though she'd stabbed me the same way she had Emperia. That traitorous softness trickled into my heart again, but I shoved it away.

"Leonidas can die a cold, miserable death for all I care."

"It wasn't his fault," Maeven replied. "I lied to him. Now, he should have known better than to believe me, but Leonidas has always been a bit naïve that way. Always wanting to believe there is still a sliver of good left deep down inside me. He's wrong, of course, but he can't quite let go of that hope. He really would be better off if he didn't love me at all."

Her words and obvious concern for her son, however twisted, proved his point, although I doubted she would see it that way.

In the distance, more shouts rose up, but still I hesitated, desperately wanting to kill Maeven for everything she'd done, for how skillfully and easily she'd manipulated me and everyone else at Myrkvior. The queen was right. She had learned from Everleigh, and she had fully mastered the Bellonan long game.

"Fly, Gemma," Maeven purred, another smug smile stretching across her face. She'd won this round, and we both knew it. "Fly away, as fast as you can."

Cursing, I had no choice but to do as the queen commanded.

I tightened my grip on my dagger, then fled out the open work-shop door.

I sprinted out into the hallway. At the far end of the corridor, Wexel jogged into sight, along with several guards.

"The prisoner has escaped!" he roared. "After her!"

I bolted in the opposite direction. Despite Maeven's machi-nations, Wexel and the guards would kill me if they caught me. So I ran, ran, ran, as fast as I could, darting down hallways, ca-reening around corners, and shoving through doors. But I was physically and mentally exhausted, and the guards were not, and their shouts and footsteps quickly grew closer and louder.

They were gaining on me.

I ran through some open doors, stopped, and turned around to make a stand. Wexel sprinted toward me, his sword clutched in his hand and an evil grin on his face, eager to cut me down. I lifted my dagger and reached for my magic, determined to at least kill the captain before the guards swarmed me.

Right before Wexel would have reached me, the double doors abruptly swung shut, leaving him and the guards trapped on the other side. A wide, heavy iron bar anchored to the wall also swung down and dropped across the doors, blocking them from this side. I reared back in surprise. How had that happened?

A flicker of movement caught my eye, and I glanced up. Leonidas was standing next to the second-floor balcony railing. Delmira was there too, her arm around his waist, supporting him.

Leonidas looked even worse in real life than he had in his ghostly form in the workshop. His skin was pale and sweaty un-derneath the black bruises, and he was swaying on his feet, as though he was about to collapse.

Somehow, despite his injuries, Leonidas had found the

strength to block the door with his magic, to stop Wexel from killing me. I might have felt gratitude, perhaps something else, something far deeper and much stronger, if I'd had the time or space for any emotion other than determination right now.

Go, Leonidas's weary voice sounded in my mind. *I'll delay them as long as I can.*

I stared at him a heartbeat longer, then started running again.

Desperation spurred me forward, and I sprinted through corridor after corridor, and up first one flight of stairs and then another, steadily climbing higher and higher through the palace. As I ran, all the doors swung shut and locked behind me, falling into place like dominoes in a child's game. I had left Leonidas far behind, and his magic had vanished, but the doors kept swinging shut—thanks to the liladorn.

The vines twisted and writhed as I hurried past, shoving the doors closed one after another. *Helping,* that presence whispered in my mind.

Thank you, I replied, and ran onward.

Wexel's frustrated screams and the guards' answering shouts soon grew faint, but I didn't stop running. Instead, I reached out with my own magic.

Grims! I'm on the fifth floor. West section. Guards are chasing me. I'm going to find a window and climb outside.

On my way! he replied.

I reached a crossway and slowed down long enough to orient myself. I wasn't too far from Leonidas's library, and I remembered walking past a row of floor-to-ceiling windows near there, so I hurried to my right. Sure enough, I rounded the corner, and the windows came into view, along with something, or rather, someone else.

Milo.

I skidded to a stop.

The crown prince stood in the hallway, a ball of purple

lightning sizzling in his hand. Fury sparked in his gaze, matching the crackle of magic on his fingertips. "You're not going anywhere, Glitzma—"

A large shadow punched through the glass, shattering the whole row of windows. Milo shrieked in surprise and stumbled away, covering his head with his arms to protect himself from the flying debris.

Lyra landed in the hallway, putting herself in between Milo and me. The strix winked at me, then let out a loud squawk, flapped her wings, and hopped to the side, as though she was turning to face an enemy. One of her wings stretched out wide and clipped Milo, knocking him down to the floor.

"You stupid bird!" he hissed. "Get out of my way!"

Lyra ignored his yells and kept hopping around, as though she was searching for an enemy to fight. I started to run away when another dark shadow zoomed through the opening and landed in front of me.

Grimley.

My heart soared, and a wide grin stretched across my face.

"Gemma!" he rumbled. "Let's go!"

I stuffed my dagger into my pocket, darted over to the gargoyle, and climbed onto his back. Then I leaned forward and wrapped my arms around his neck, hugging him tight. *I have never been so glad to see you in my entire life!*

I love you too, runt! Now let's get out of here!

Milo scrambled back up onto his feet and shoved Lyra out of the way. Another ball of lightning popped into his hand, and he reared his arm back to throw his magic at us, but Grimley growled, charged forward, and spun around.

Thwack!

The stone arrow on the end of the gargoyle's tail sliced across Milo's cheek, drawing blood and making him scream and stagger back. The sight filled me with malicious glee.

Hold on tight! Grimley roared.

I leaned forward again and grabbed the bases of his wings. The gargoyle galloped toward the shattered windows and threw himself and me out through the jagged opening.

For a moment, we hung in the cold night air, strangely weightless. Then we started to fall, but Grimley pumped his wings over and over again, and we zoomed upward.

A startled squawk sounded behind us, and I glanced back over my shoulder. A couple of strixes were streaking through the air toward us, quickly gaining ground—

Lyra surged into view beside us. She let out a wild, fierce cry, and the other strixes peeled away, coasting back down toward the rookery.

Thank you. I sent the thought to her.

You're welcome. Then she too peeled off, disappearing into the night.

I faced front again and tightened my grip on Grimley's wings as the gargoyle soared over the palace walls, flying us away from Myrkvior.

CHAPTER THIRTY

Grimley flew us out of Majesta, before his strength gave out late the next morning. I was exhausted too, but I used my magic to make sure the old, decrepit barn Grimley had landed next to was deserted before we slipped inside. We curled up in some moldy hay bales and slept for the rest of the day.

That evening, around sunset, we left the barn. A nearby farmhouse was also deserted, although the people who had lived there had left behind some clothes, along with some canned apples and a few other forgotten things in the pantry.

While Grimley went out hunting, I got enough water out of the well to clean myself up and changed into a gray tunic, along with matching leggings. I also stuffed my feet into a pair of old black boots, even though they were half a size too small and pinched my toes. When Grimley returned, I gobbled down some canned apples and a hunk of dried-out cheddar cheese while he tore into the rabbits he'd caught.

After dinner, I mounted Grimley again and opened the silver compact Leonidas had given me. I still had it, along with my gargoyle pendant, my dagger, and the two tearstone arrows. I used the compact's compass to figure out which direction to go, then Grimley took off and flew the rest of the night, avoiding the strixes in the area.

We landed again the next morning, this time taking refuge in a small, damp cave and once again scrounging for food. As soon as Grimley had rested enough, we took off again, trying to put as much distance between us and the Mortans as possible.

But it wasn't working.

I didn't have to use the compact's Cardea mirror to know that Milo and Wexel were chasing us. I could *feel* the Mortans behind us, slowly but surely closing the gap. But I was exhausted, and Grimley even more so, and together, we did the best we could.

Every once in a while, a faint, familiar flicker would float through my mind, as soft as a feather tickling my skin. Leonidas was with the other Mortans, although I had no idea if he was helping or hindering Milo and Wexel in their relentless quest to hunt me down. Probably both, knowing him.

The next day, Grimley and I finally made it to the Andvarian-Mortan border. I wanted to weep when the Spire Mountains came into view, even though we were still several miles away from Blauberg. The air grew steadily colder the higher we climbed up the mountains, and I shivered, since only thin layers of grubby rags covered my body. Milo was right. If my people could see me now, they wouldn't call me Glitzma anymore, but that didn't matter.

All that did was making it home.

We followed the sun up into the air, but my worry grew, despite the bright rays shining down on us. That creeping presence was growing stronger behind us. The Mortans were closing fast. Grimley must have sensed them too, because he pumped his wings harder.

We had just reached the top of Blauberg Mountain when the strixes screamed behind us.

I glanced back over my shoulder. Several strixes were streaking through the sky in an arrow-shaped formation. Milo was leading the charge, the tip of the arrow, with Wexel to his right, and more guards flying along behind them. Three strixes lagged behind the main pack, although I couldn't make out who was riding them.

"The Mortans are right behind us!" I yelled.

"Hold on!" Grimley yelled back.

The gargoyle shot up over the top of the mountain, then tucked his wings into his sides, streaking down the rocky slope as fast as he dared. Behind us, a wild cry went up. I glanced back over my shoulder again.

One of the strixes had tried to follow Grimley's steep dive, but the creature had misjudged the distance and clipped the top of a pine. Its rider went flying through the air to his death. The strix managed to stop its own freefall, although it still slammed hard into the ground.

"It's working!" I yelled. "Keep going!"

Grimley tucked his wings even tighter against his sides, dropping lower and going even faster, until it felt like we were falling down the mountain, rather than flying. Grimley came dangerously close to the tops of the trees, and the sticky scent of pine sap filled my nose.

Another wild shriek rang out. A second strix and its rider were down, this time felled by a rocky ridge that jutted out at an odd angle from the landscape.

But Milo was still right behind us, and he snapped his hand up. "Fire!" he screamed. "Shoot that bitch out of the sky!"

The other riders steered their strixes forward and out to the sides, forming a solid line in the air with Milo and his bird. Then the riders raised their crossbows and let loose a volley of arrows.

"Watch out!" I screamed.

Grimley swerved from side to side to side. The Mortans' arrows whizzed through the air like a swarm of pointed bees, but he managed to avoid them all.

Down below, the plaza in front of the mine came into view. It was just after noon, and the miners were outside eating lunch. They looked up, along with the merchants and shoppers, all of them startled by the shrieks of the strixes and the arrows dropping from the sky.

Grimley kept going, streaking downward like a falling star. At the last instant, right before we would have slammed into the ground, the gargoyle snapped his wings open, halting our rapid descent. Even then, he still plowed into the flagstones, his feet skidding out from under him. I gritted my teeth and held on to his wings, trying not to get thrown off.

We ended up in front of the gargoyle fountain in the center of the plaza. Somehow, I managed to unclench my fingers from around the bases of Grimley's wings and slide off his back. My legs were trembling, but I forced myself to crouch down beside him.

"Grims? Are you okay?"

"Tired . . ." He panted for breath. "So . . . tired . . ."

The gargoyle tried to get to his feet, but he couldn't manage it and flopped back down onto his belly.

A shadow loomed over us, blotting out the sun. My head lifted. Milo was hovering in the air above us. He raised his hand, then brought it down.

One by one, the strixes landed in the plaza in front of Grimley and me. Milo, Wexel, and the guards quickly dismounted, drew their swords, and advanced.

The Mortans had finally caught up to us.

Grimley tried to get to his feet again to protect me, but I put my hand on his head.

"Stay still and rest. You've done more than enough."

And he truly had. I would have been dead a dozen times over if not for his love, friendship, and loyalty. Death was coming for me anyway, and I would meet it head-on. So I got to my feet, lifted my chin, and marched forward, stopping in front of the Mortans.

Milo and Wexel stepped up to face me, while several guards spread out behind them. Everyone else stayed frozen in place. The miners eating their lunches, their sandwiches halfway to their lips. The merchants with their hands hovering in midair, showing off their goods. The shoppers clutching the wheels of cheese, bolts of cloth, and other items they'd been admiring. None of them moved.

"Gemma Glitzma Ripley," Milo called out. "You've run out of time and space."

Everyone remained frozen, although shocked whispers surged through the crowd.

"Is that Princess Gemma?"

"No! It can't be! Glitzma would never look like that!"

"What are the Mortans doing here?"

I waited until the murmurs died down before I responded to Milo's taunt. "We're not in Morta anymore. You're on Andvarian soil now. Do you really want to attack me and start a war right here in front of everyone?"

Milo glanced around, as if he was just now noticing all the other people. A bright, fanatical light burned in his eyes. "I've *always* wanted to start a war, Gemma. I'm happy to do it here. Why, there's no *better* place. I'll kill you, your people, and claim your mountain and all its tearstone for my own. Then no one will be able to stop me from implementing my plan."

That light burned a little brighter and hotter in his eyes. "I am the future king of Morta, and Andvari and all the other kingdoms *will be mine*."

He waved his hand, and two guards wearing gold visored

helms stepped forward. One of the guards raised a crossbow to shoot an arrow at me. I reached for my magic, ready to send the projectile spinning away—hopefully, straight into Milo's heart, if I could manage it.

Right before that guard would have pulled the trigger, the second one surged forward, grabbed the crossbow, and smashed it into the first man's face, making him tumble to the ground. Then that second guard spun around, pointing the crossbow at the other Mortans and backing up until they stood beside me.

"What the fuck are you doing?" Wexel yelled.

"Helping my friend," a muffled voice replied.

Friend? My heart lifted.

The second guard ripped off their helm and tossed it aside, revealing their features. Black hair, green eyes, a mischievous smile. Reiko grinned at me, as did her inner dragon, which was on her neck again. I grinned back at them.

"You!" Wexel snarled. "How did you get here?"

Reiko shrugged. "Gemma warned me that Maeven knew I was a spy, so I hid in the palace. Once I heard that Gemma had escaped on her gargoyle, and that you were chasing her, I stole a strix from the rookery and followed. You and your merry band of idiots never even looked to see if someone might be trailing along behind you."

"You win," I said. "You are most *definitely* the better spy."

Reiko's grin widened. "I know."

"It doesn't matter," Milo snapped. "There are only two of you, and more than three dozen of us. We'll kill you both, along with anyone else stupid enough to get in our way, and then take what we want. And do you know what the best part is, Gemma?"

"What?"

Another sneer twisted his face. "My mother, sister, and brother are here to witness my triumph."

Milo gestured to his right. I'd been so focused on him, Wexel, and the guards that I hadn't noticed that several other strixes had landed on the refinery rooftop.

Maeven was sitting atop one of the strixes, as was Delmira. The queen seemed as calm as ever, although the princess's face was twisted into a worried squint. Off to their right were three guards surrounding another figure.

Leonidas.

The guards were clearly watching the prince, and metal gleamed around his neck, as though he was wearing a coldiron collar again, although I couldn't be sure, given the distance between us. Leonidas was not quite a prisoner, but he obviously wasn't free either. Neither was Lyra, judging by the angry looks she kept shooting the guards and their strixes.

"Leo won't be able to interfere and save you this time," Milo said. "I don't know why he ever bothered to help you to start with."

Neither did I. Or maybe I did and just didn't want to admit the reason to myself. Or that I was thinking about trying to save him in return, despite everything that had passed between us.

Milo raised his hand and curled his fingers into a fist. Everyone tensed. Me, Reiko, Grimley, Wexel, the Mortan guards, the miners, and other Andvarians in the plaza.

"Time to die, Gemma." Milo dropped his fist. "Kill them all!"

The Mortan guards lifted their swords and charged forward, heading straight for Reiko, Grimley, and me.

CHAPTER THIRTY-ONE

All around the plaza, people screamed and scrambled back, trying to get out of the way. I yanked my dagger out of my pocket and held my position, waiting for the Mortans to advance.

On my right, Grimley got to his feet. The gargoyle had finally gotten his breath back, and a low, terrifying growl rumbled out of his throat, even as he pawed at the ground, his talons ripping through the flagstones.

On my left, magic rippled through the air, and Reiko morphed into her other, larger, stronger form. In an instant, she grew several inches taller, and the muscles in her arms, back, and legs bulged against her stolen guard's uniform. Razor-sharp teeth sprouted in her mouth, her green eyes grew even brighter, and her long black hair started flickering like ebony flames around her head. Her nails lengthened into long black talons, while a few hot green sparks flashed on her fingertips. Not all dragon morphs could summon up fire, although it seemed like Reiko could.

A guard rushed at me. I waited until he was in range, then spun past him and sliced my dagger across his back. He screamed and tumbled to the ground. He tried to get up, but I punched my dagger into his back, once, twice, three times, killing him. I transferred the dagger to my left hand, then wrested the dead man's sword out of his grip. With a weapon in both hands, I turned to face my enemies.

Hacking, slashing, whirling, twirling. I called upon everything I had ever learned about fighting from Rhea, Serilda, and Evie, and I spun this way and that, cutting down every Mortan who came near me. Beside me, Reiko swiped out with her talons, ripping open a guard's stomach, while Grimley lowered his head and rammed his horns into another man.

I cut down another guard and whirled around, ready to fight a new enemy, when I spotted Milo standing about ten feet away. I tightened my grip on my weapons and charged forward. He grinned and watched me come. I screamed and raised my weapons high, determined to kill him.

But it was a trap.

Right before I would have shoved my sword into his gut, Milo snapped up his hand and blasted me with his lightning. I managed to dodge most of the magic, but one of the bolts clipped my shoulder and spun me around. Hot, electric pain exploded in my right arm, and I lost my grip on my stolen sword, which tumbled away across the flagstones. I snarled, but I whirled around and faced him again.

Milo charged forward. I lashed out with my dagger, but he avoided the blow and punched me in the face. Pain exploded in my jaw, and I staggered away. Milo grabbed the front of my tunic, yanking me back toward him.

"You're pathetic!" he hissed. "I can't believe that you survived the Seven Spire massacre. You're not worthy of that ugly royal crest."

Milo reached down and broke the silver chain around my

neck, tearing my gargoyle pendant off my chest. Then he reared his hand back and threw it away.

"No!" I let out a choked scream.

Desperation filled me, and my gaze locked onto the pendant as it zipped through the air. I had to get it back—

Milo snapped up his hand and hit me square in the chest with his lightning.

The blast of magic threw me back ten feet. I crashed into one of the merchant carts filled with bolts of cloth, lost my grip on my dagger, and fell to the ground. Part of the cart splintered under my weight, while the top of it landed against the ground at an angle, creating an odd sort of table over my head, with scarlet fabric draping over one side.

"Gemma! Gemma!"

Reiko and Grimley both shouted at me, but they were surrounded by Mortans, and they couldn't come help me. They were barely keeping themselves alive.

Milo shot off another bolt of lightning, this time targeting the gargoyle fountain in the center of the plaza. The stone figure exploded, and sharp shards of shrapnel zipped through the air and pelted the miners, merchants, and shoppers still gathered around us.

"Kill them all!" Milo yelled. "No one escapes!"

Chaos erupted in the plaza. People screamed and ran away, trying to escape from the charging Mortans and their slashing swords. The strixes also moved forward, hopping along the ground, lashing out with their beaks and raking their talons across the merchants' carts, reducing the wood to kindling. Yells, cries, and shouts tore through the air, along with the strixes' high-pitched shrieks, and the coppery stench of blood filled my nose.

All of that was horrific enough. But without my gargoyle

pendant, I couldn't block out the thoughts and feelings of every-one around me, and they all stabbed into my mind one after another, just like the Mortans were stabbing their swords into whomever they could reach.

Gotta run! Hide! Get away!

Hurts so much!

No! No! No!

The confusing, babbling thoughts and the accompanying fear, panic, pain, terror, and dread instantly overwhelmed me. I clapped my hands over my ears to muffle the actual, audible screams and shrieks, but that didn't stop the thoughts and feel-ings from pummeling my mind. Tears streamed down my face, a choked sob escaped my lips, and I rocked back and forth on the ground, still halfway under the splintered cart.

I wasn't seeing the plaza anymore. No, the shouts, the screams, and the stench of blood had taken me right back to the Seven Spire massacre. Suddenly, I was twelve years old again, watching the turncoat guards slaughter everyone around me.

A miner screamed and crumpled to the ground right in front of me, a sword sticking out of his chest, but in my mind's eye, it was Uncle Frederich, stabbed through the heart with a dagger. Another miner screamed, felled by Milo's lightning, but to me, it was Lord Hans, burned alive by magic. More lightning clipped the shoulder of a woman running past me, so close that I could feel the electric sting, which morphed into Xenia being battered with magic as she tried to spirit me to safety.

The sensations and the similarities went on and on and on, until I was all tangled up in my own mind, not sure what was real and what was a nightmarish memory. I drew my knees up to my chest, still rocking back and forth, and back and forth, des-perately trying to find some way to steer my tiny internal ship through the massive tidal waves of fear, panic, and pain that just kept slamming into me one after another.

"Gemma!" Reiko yelled, trying to wade through the chaos to get to me. "Gemma!"

A guard rushed up and stabbed Reiko in the side with his sword. She screamed and spun around, raking her talons across his face. He yelped and stumbled back.

Reiko slashed her talons across his throat, killing him, but another guard came up behind her and punched her wounded side. She snarled and staggered forward. Her boots slipped on a piece of the fountain rubble, and her legs flew out from under her. She hit the flagstones hard, her arms and legs splayed out at awkward angles.

Reiko's pain spiked into my mind, and the hot shock of the wound in her side stole my breath. More tears streamed down my face, but my mind kept spinning and spinning, and I struggled not to vomit as the roiling sea of thoughts and emotions kept cascading over me.

A Mortan guard charged toward me. I watched him come with wide eyes, wondering if he was real or if this was just another awful memory. The man grinned and raised his sword high. Too late, I realized that he was real. I lifted my hand to try to fend him off, although I knew that I wouldn't be able to manage it—

An arrow-tipped tail slammed into the guard, knocking him away from me. Suddenly, Grimley was there, peering under the cart at me, just like Everleigh Blair had done all those years ago during the massacre.

It's okay, Gemma, his rough, familiar voice sounded in my mind. *Breathe. Just breathe. Your magic doesn't control you—you control it. Remember?*

The gargoyle's low, rumbling tone cut through some of the overwhelming thoughts and emotions. I sucked in a breath and forced myself to breathe, in and out, just like he said. The steady rhythm helped to clear out some of the screaming cobwebs cloaking my mind.

Grimley smiled, sensing that my paralysis was easing, then leaned down and licked my cheek, his rough tongue scraping across my skin—

A bolt of purple lightning zipped through the air and hit the gargoyle, knocking him away.

"Grims!" I yelled. "Grims!"

He slammed into the base of the fountain, and his pain jolted all the way down my own spine. Grimley snarled and tried to get to his feet, still determined to fight, but his paws slipped, and he was too badly injured to manage it. He looked at me, his dazed eyes meeting mine.

Run, Gemma! Save yourself!

My head snapped back and forth. The guards were still cutting down everyone in sight, while their strixes kept destroying the merchants' carts. With Reiko and Grimley down, the Mortans had free reign of the plaza, with Milo standing in the center of the destruction, grinning widely as he shot bolt after bolt of lightning out at the panicked people. He wasn't even trying to kill the miners, merchants, and shoppers. No, he was just toying with them, making them run back and forth and straight into the guards' swords.

Suddenly, another memory, another voice filled my mind, rising up above all the others—*I should have done more. I should have fought harder.*

Alvis had said that to himself in the woods when he thought that he and Xenia were going to be killed by the turncoat guards.

His voice vanished, replaced by Xenia's. *Fucking traitors. I'll kill as many of them as I can . . . Maybe Gemma can live, even if Alvis and I can't.*

The two of them hadn't even known me before the Seven Spire massacre, but they had still risked their lives time and time again to save mine. And how was I repaying their bravery, their courage, their sacrifice? By once again being a scared little girl cowering out of sight while Reiko, Grimley, and my people fought, bled, and died.

Well, no more—*no more*.

Despite the screams and shouts still ringing through the plaza, and the louder chorus of fear, panic, and pain buzzing in my mind, I crawled out from under the remains of the cart and staggered up and onto my feet.

Run, Gemma! Run! Grimley's voice filled my mind again. *You can escape, but you have to go right now!*

He was right. There was an opening in the madness. I could slip out of the plaza, sneak through one of the alleys, and escape. But I wasn't going to do that. I wasn't going to let innocent people—*my people*—die. Not again. Not without doing everything in my power to help them.

No, I told the gargoyle, and myself too. *I'm not running. Never again.*

Then I turned and waded deeper into the fight.

All around me, the audible screams and shrieks continued, along with the silent ones in my mind, creating a crashing cacophony of sound, but I shoved it all to the back of my brain. The noise, the pain, the fear and dread and stench of blood clouding the air. I ignored it all and focused on myself, on my power, on my magic.

I had always thought of my mind magier power like a storm brewing in my mind. One that came and went, ebbed and flowed, intensified and lessened just like actual storm clouds in the sky. Something I had little control over and preferred not to think about or use unless absolutely necessary. Well, it was definitely necessary now, and I dove headlong into that storm in my mind, plunging down, down, down into its depths like never before.

It was difficult, so very, very difficult, but the noise, chaos, and commotion in the plaza slowly receded, even as my magic grew in commensurate measure. Not only could I feel my own power bubbling up inside my body, but I could feel the energy in everyone and everything around me, from the whistle of the guards' swords through the air, to the bulge and strain of the miners' muscles as they tried to defend themselves, to the water still gurgling in the ruined fountain. In an instant, I could sense all that and so much more.

A Mortan guard charged at me. I reached for my magic and yanked on those invisible strings of energy. He flew through the air and slammed into the cart that Milo had thrown me into, completely splintering the wood with his heavier weight.

Another guard charged at me, and I tossed him aside as well. And then another. And then another. One by one, they all sailed through the air, away from me and the innocent people they were trying to kill.

Blocking out everyone's thoughts and feelings and still using my magic at the same time was much, much harder than I'd thought it would be. More than once, my resolve wavered, and I almost drowned in the sea of noise and emotions roiling around in my mind. But the harder I concentrated, and the harder I fought, the easier it became.

And I realized something important, something that so many people had tried to tell me, something that I should have known all along. My magic might be a storm, but it wasn't caused by *other* people's thoughts and feelings. Not really, not fully. No, that storm of emotion was all *mine*. *My* power, *my* feelings, *my* love and pain and rage.

I was the true storm.

Unpredictable. Uncontrollable. Unstoppable.

"The princess is pushing them back!"

"Rally to her!"

"Gemma! Gemma! Gemma!"

One by one, shouts rang out, and people's fear receded, washed away by something much, much stronger—hope. That hope buoyed my own spirits, my own magic, and I strode forward, heading toward the Mortans instead of away from them. The miners, merchants, and shoppers grabbed the dead guards' swords and went on the offensive, attacking the rest of the Mortans.

I had just tossed another guard through the air when I spotted a flash of purple out of the corner of my eye. I whirled around.

Milo was standing in front of me, a disgusted look on his face. "You're a fucking mind magier, just like Leonidas is. No wonder he's so fascinated by you." A cruel smile curved his lips. "I wonder what he'll think when I kill you."

My gaze cut to the left. In the distance, on the refinery roof, Leonidas was still sitting atop Lyra, both of them looking tense. His gaze locked with mine, and I remembered what he had said to me in the woods so long ago.

You're soft and weak . . . soft and weak . . . soft and weak . . .

Leonidas had chanted that at me over and over again. Not to hurt, mock, or tear me down, like I'd thought back then. No, he'd been trying to enrage me, to get me to embrace my mind magier magic, to use it to save myself, and Xenia and Alvis. And I realized something else that I should have known all along. My magic might not always work the way I wanted it to, but I *always* had the power to act, to fight, to battle until my last breath.

"Time to die, Glitzma," Milo sneered.

He hurled another round of lightning at me. This bolt had more magic than all the others, and I could see it growing and growing as it streaked toward me. But instead of trying to get out of the way of the killing strike, I reached for my own magic, snapped up my hand, and curled my fingers into a fist, yanking tight on all those invisible strings of power.

The lightning bolt stopped in midair, inches away from my heart.

I stared at the mass of magic hovering in front of me. The lightning kept spitting, hissing, and crackling, like a coral viper trying to twist, turn, and wrench its way out of a gargoyle's mouth. Milo was by far the strongest enemy I had ever faced, and he was just as powerful in his magic as I was in mine. Sweat poured down my face, and my entire body shook from the strain of holding back so much hot, deadly, electric force.

"You think you can stop me? Never!" Milo yelled.

He hurled another bolt of lightning at me. Then another one, then another one.

Somehow, I managed to grab on to all those invisible strings of energy, and I stopped each and every bolt, although they all kept dancing and crackling in front of me, like wayward kites I was trying to wrestle in a tornado.

Surprise flickered across Milo's face, and he actually took a step back, as if he couldn't believe that I was holding on to so much magic at once.

I should have done more. I should have fought harder. Once again, Alvis's voice echoed in my mind, quickly followed by Xenia's. *Fucking traitors. I'll kill as many of them as I can. Maybe Gemma can live, even if Alvis and I can't.*

I was fighting harder than I had ever fought, but the battle wasn't won yet, so I gritted my teeth and tightened my grip on all those strings of magic. I drew in a breath to steady myself.

Then I screamed and threw every last one of Milo's lightning bolts right back at him.

CHAPTER THIRTY-TWO

Milo's eyes widened, and he lurched to the side. He managed to avoid most of the lightning, but one of the bolts punched into his right hand, making him scream. He whipped around and tossed another bolt at me, but I threw that one back at him too, punching the power through his left hand.

The crown prince screamed again and clutched his hands to his chest, his skin burned, blackened, and smoking from his own power.

I held up my bandaged hands and waggled my fingers at him. "Now we're even," I hissed.

Milo snarled and raised his hand to try to hit me with his lightning again, but Wexel grabbed the prince's arm, jerking him back.

"Let's go!" Wexel yelled. "Before she kills us all!"

Milo tried to lunge at me again, but Wexel kept dragging him back toward a waiting strix. My hands curled into fists, and I stepped forward, determined to kill them both—

A lightning bolt slammed into the ground at my feet, shattering the flagstones and making me stagger back.

My gaze darted to the left. In the distance, on the refinery roof, Maeven held up her hand, more purple lightning crackling on her fingertips.

That's enough, her voice snapped in my mind. *You've made your point. You don't have enough magic left to fight me too. Don't do something stupid and make me break my promise to Leo not to kill you.*

Rage roared through me. I wanted to keep going until I killed Milo, and then Wexel, and finally Maeven, but she was right. I had used up most of my magic, and I was barely standing. I didn't have enough power left to block her lightning. So as much as I hated it, I stopped and looked at Milo again.

Wexel had gotten the crown prince up onto the strix, and he had mounted another creature. They were the only two Mortans left alive, although it seemed as though all the strixes had survived. Silence dropped over the plaza, and no one moved.

"Let this serve as a warning to Morta!" I yelled, although my voice was more of a hoarse, broken rasp than a strong, commanding tone. "If you, Milo Morricone, set one foot in Andvari ever again, then I will kill you! And all who are with you! Is that understood?"

Somehow, the silence grew quieter, tenser, and even the injured seemed to stifle their moans.

"Is that understood?" I yelled again, louder than before.

Milo glared at me, hate boiling in his eyes. Beside him, Wexel's face was equally red and angry. Milo opened his mouth, probably to spew curses at me, but a smooth, silky voice cut him off.

"Understood," Maeven called out.

I stared at the Morricone queen. To my surprise, a satisfied smile slowly spread across her face. Why was the bitch smiling? I had escaped her clutches and beaten back her son. She should be trying to murder me, not grinning like I'd done her some wonderful favor.

Maeven respectfully tipped her head to me. "Well done, Gemma. All hail the new gargoyle queen."

My frown deepened. Why would she call me that?

Maeven made a sharp motion with her hand. Wexel nodded back at her, and his and Milo's strixes shot up into the sky, along with the creatures the dead Mortans had been riding. Delmira stared at me, her face pale, but her strix also shot up into the sky. The three guards followed her, along with Maeven. That left Leonidas and Lyra alone on the refinery roof.

A small smile flickered across his bruised, battered face. *I always knew you were magnificent.*

Despite the distance between us, I could hear the ring of truth in his words, and I couldn't stop the spurt of pleasure that filled my heart.

Now your people know it too. They will never call you Glitzma again.

I glanced around. He was right. Everyone in the plaza was staring at me with a mix of awe and wonder—and a touch of fear.

I looked back at Leonidas, not sure what thought to send to him. High above, a strix screamed out a warning cry. Somehow, I knew that it was Maeven's creature and her way of ordering her son to leave. Leonidas's dark amethyst gaze locked with mine again. Then Lyra flapped her wings, and the two of them sailed into the sky.

Leonidas Morricone might be gone, but he would never be far from my thoughts—for better or worse.

I stared up into the bright blue autumn sky, but the strixes quickly climbed the mountain and vanished over the peak. The Mortans were gone—for now.

Once I was sure they weren't coming back, I limped across

the plaza. The miners, merchants, and shoppers were slowly climbing to their feet, as well as checking on the injured, but I staggered over to the broken fountain.

Reiko had propped herself up against the base, and Grimley was lying beside her. I crouched next to my friend, who had shifted back into her human form. Blood stained the side of her purple tunic, but she gave me a pain-filled smile.

"It looks worse than it is," Reiko replied. "I'll be fine after a round or two of healing."

One knot of tension in my chest loosened. I looked at the gargoyle. "Grims?"

"I'm okay," he rumbled. "Just a little sore and scorched, but I'll be fine."

The other knot loosened, and I sat down in between them. Reiko leaned her shoulder against mine, while Grimley shuffled over and put his head in my lap. I scratched right in between his horns, just as he liked.

Five minutes later, Reiko, Grimley, and I were still sitting by the fountain when a familiar figure dropped to a knee in front of me.

Topacia stared at me with wide eyes. "Gemma! Are you okay?"

"More or less."

Topacia turned to Javier, the bone master, who was standing beside her. "Heal Princess Gemma at once!"

Javier stepped forward, but I waved him off. "I'm not hurt as badly as others are. Take care of the worst of the wounded first."

Topacia opened her mouth, but I stared her down. "That's an order."

My friend and guard bowed her head. "Yes, Your Highness."

Topacia stood up and started yelling out orders to Javier and the other bone masters who had rushed to the plaza, along with the royal guards. The injured were healed, while the dead were carted off to be buried.

An hour later, I stood by the ruined fountain and watched while Topacia and the Andvarian guards loaded the last of the dead miners, merchants, and shoppers onto wagons. The slain Mortans were still in the plaza, although they too would soon be loaded up and taken away. The sound of the wagon wheels *creak-creak-creaking* dug into my mind like daggers, making my heart ache and my stomach churn with guilt.

"It's not your fault," Reiko said.

The dragon morph had been healed and was standing beside me, watching the proceedings. Grimley had also been healed and was lying in a nearby sunspot, napping and recovering his strength.

"Yes, it is," I replied in a bitter tone. "I was a fool to think I could just waltz around Myrkvior and no one would recognize me. I was a fool to think I was a spy instead of a princess."

"I would argue that you're a very good spy," Reiko countered. "You did what no other Ripley has done in centuries—you visited Myrkvior and survived."

Despite the grim situation, I snorted out a laugh, but my merriment quickly faded away. "Regardless of my spycraft, or lack thereof, these people—*innocent people*—are dead because of me."

Reiko shrugged. "Perhaps. But I'm alive because of you. And so is Grimley and everyone else in the plaza. You didn't ask the Mortans to come here. They invaded your kingdom, your city. And you made them pay for that."

She might have been right, but her words didn't ease my sorrow, shame, and guilt. If only I'd actually gone on that shopping trip to Svalin, then none of this would have ever happened. I wouldn't have been injured in the mine. Leonidas wouldn't have taken me to Myrkvior. Milo wouldn't have tortured me. Maeven wouldn't have used me. And I wouldn't have led the Mortans back here to attack my people.

And you never would have seen Leo again, that treacherous little voice whispered in the back of my mind.

I shoved away that unwanted thought and focused on Reiko again. "Come back to Glitnir with me."

She frowned, as did her inner dragon. "What? Why?" Suspicion filled both their faces. "Does Prince Dominic still want to pump me for information? Or do you want me to spy for Andvari?"

"Well, you are a master at it, remember? As good as Lady Xenia herself."

Reiko gave me a sour look, but her lips twitched up into a smile, and her dragon laughed silently on her skin.

"You're right. I could use a spy of my own, instead of trying to do everything myself." I paused. "But what I could use even more is a friend."

Reiko tilted her head to the side, studying me. "And what exactly would I do at Glitnir?"

I shrugged. "Haven't you heard? Princess Gemma Glitzma Ripley is known for her hospitality. There will be at least a few shopping trips and royal balls and other equally frivolous things."

Reiko barked out a laugh. "Good. I could use a few frivolous things after all this danger and drama."

"So you'll come home with me?"

She threaded her arm through mine. "Absolutely. You need someone around to watch your back besides Grimley."

I smiled at her, despite the guilt and sadness filling my heart. Then we stood there, arm in arm, watching while the rest of the bodies were loaded up and taken away.

CHAPTER THIRTY-THREE

Three days later, I was back home at Glitnir.

I was in my father's study, watching Reiko play kronekling, a card game, with Father, Rhea, and Topacia. They were laughing and talking, while Grimley was stretched out in his usual spot in front of the fireplace, snoozing and soaking up the heat from the crackling flames. Grandfather Heinrich was also here, dozing in a chair, his reading glasses sliding down his nose, and an open book stretched out across his lap. The normal, happy scene warmed my heart and made it ache at the same time.

"A crown for your thoughts?" a low voice asked.

Alvis came over to me, holding a mug of hot chocolate. I was standing in the corner, also holding a mug of hot chocolate, although I wasn't drinking it.

"I was thinking how grateful I am to be here."

It was the truth. All the things I had taken for granted before had new meaning now, even something as simple as a quiet evening with my friends and family. I appreciated it all much more now—and I realized just how easily Milo Morricone could destroy it.

"I've been studying those tearstone arrows you brought back from Morta," Alvis said, as if picking up on my dark thoughts.

"What do you think Milo plans to do with them?"

Alvis frowned. "I'm not sure. But if Milo has found some way to get the tearstone to channel his magic, then it can't be anything good. Just those two arrows by themselves could be turned into powerful weapons. And if he has enough tearstone to make thousands more of them . . ."

He didn't say anything else, but I could hear all the awful things he was contemplating.

Alvis must have seen me wince as his thoughts intruded on my own. "I can make you another pendant. A larger, stronger one to help you block out the thoughts again. To keep you from getting paralyzed like you have in the past."

I had told him how everyone's fear and panic during the Blauberg battle had overwhelmed me, just like it had during the Seven Spire massacre.

I shook my head. "No. I used your pendant as a crutch for far too long. It made me feel safe, secure, protected, and I wanted to hold on to that feeling for as long as possible. But I'm not a little girl anymore, and it's time to grow up. It's time that I stopped hiding from my magic, and my memories too."

Alvis squeezed my arm. "You grew up the day of the massacre, Gemma. You will be a wonderful queen, and you will protect Andvari from the Mortans, just as Everleigh has defended Bellona from her enemies."

"Do you really think so?" I whispered.

He smiled. "I know so."

Alvis held out his mug, and I *clinked* mine against his, that one soft note drowning out all the noise, commotion, and doubt in my heart, at least for this moment.

Thirty minutes later, I said my good nights to everyone and left the study. I'd been in so many meetings with Father, Grandfather Heinrich, Rhea, and our advisors this past week that I wanted some quiet time to myself, so I went to my chambers. I stood out on the balcony for several minutes, breathing in the chilly night air and the floral perfumes drifting up out of the Edelstein Gardens in the center of the palace.

When I was calm again, I closed the balcony doors and stepped back into my chambers. I was going to soak in a hot bath when the freestanding Cardea mirror in the corner began rippling with a bright silver light.

I tensed. He had been calling out to me every night since I had returned to Glitnir. He must be able to sense that I was back home, the same way that I knew he was back in Myrkvior.

So far, I had avoided the mirror, but no longer. So I stepped in front of the glass and waited. A few seconds later, the mirror stilled, and a familiar figure appeared on the other side.

Leonidas.

His injuries had been healed, and no trace of Wexel's beating remained on his face, although he probably had some new scars on his back from Milo's whipping, and even deeper marks on his heart from Maeven's betrayal. The cold, malicious part of me hoped that those marks pained him just as badly as his duplicity had hurt my own heart.

Delmira's liladorn salve had gone a long way toward healing my own wounds, as had Leonidas's pulling the pain out of my body and shoving it into his own. The Glitnir bone masters had managed to remove the coral-viper whip marks from my back, but ugly pink scars still marred my hands, both front and back.

Yaleen, my thread master, had offered to make gloves to

conceal the marks, but I'd refused. I wasn't a pampered princess any longer, and I wasn't going to cover up the scars and hide from what had happened. I had done that with the Seven Spire massacre for too long. No more.

Just as I wasn't going to hide from Leonidas any longer.

"Hello, Gemma," he said. "You look well."

"So do you," I replied in a neutral tone.

The two of us fell silent, once again staring at each other and not saying what we really thought or felt.

"How are things in Myrkvior?" I asked.

A humorless smile lifted his lips. "Tense. And in Glitnir?"

"Also tense."

He nodded. "You might be interested to know that Milo has been holed up in his workshop ever since we returned."

I snorted. "No doubt he's working on a new weapon to try to kill me."

"Yes," Leonidas replied. "I haven't been able to find any trace of the tearstone. Milo must have moved it out of the palace. I'm sorry, Gemma. If I knew where it was, I would tell you."

"Would you?" I challenged.

"Of course." He kept his gaze steady on mine. "I will never lie to you about anything. Never again. I promise you that."

A spark of foolish hope flared in my heart, but I quickly, ruthlessly extinguished it. "And I will not trust you. Never again. I promise you *that*."

He grimaced, and we both fell silent.

"You don't have to worry about the tearstone anymore," I said. "I will deal with Milo when the time comes. And Maeven as well, if she dares to interfere again."

Leonidas nodded again. "As is your right. I'm sorry, Gemma. So sorry. For everything that happened. For everything that you suffered because of me. If I could go back and change it, I would. I never should have brought you to Myrkvior."

"Why *did* you bring me to the palace?"

"You know why."

"I thought you promised not to lie to me anymore," I snapped.

He grimaced again, but his gaze remained locked with mine. "I brought you to the palace because I always remembered the girl from the woods."

"You never forget the first girl who tries to kill you." I echoed what he'd said in Milo's workshop.

A small grin curved his lips. "It certainly made you memorable."

"Why *did* you save me in the woods that day? Why did you kill your own captain? Especially after I had just tried to kill you?"

His grin faded away. "Because I knew what Uncle Maximus would do if he got his hands on you. I wouldn't have doomed anyone to that fate. Plus, I thought that if I helped you escape, that it might make up, just a little bit, for everything Mother had done at Seven Spire, for all the horrible things she had done to you. Foolish, I know."

Perhaps. But at least he had tried to do the right thing, which was more than most people would have done, especially given our families' bloody history.

Leonidas cleared his throat. "But you weren't just the girl who tried to kill me. Mostly, I remembered the girl that I talked to for months afterward. The one who was a mind magier just like me. In many ways, you were the only friend I ever had, besides Lyra and Delmira. But then you went away. I always wondered why."

"Because I was afraid of you and my power and everything else," I confessed, unwanted emotion thickening my voice. "Alvis made me that gargoyle pendant, so I blocked you out, along with my magic and everything that happened during the Seven Spire massacre."

What a strange pair we made, him yearning to remember

those times, and me trying so desperately to forget them. Perhaps that was one of the reasons why we were so drawn to each other.

"I did something similar after the Regalia Games. I still have nightmares about the tidal wave that Uncle Maximus used to try to kill Queen Everleigh." A shudder rippled through his body.

As much as I hated to admit it, the two of us were far more alike than different, including how haunted we were by our pasts.

"Was any of it real? When we were on the balcony the night we snuck into Milo's workshop? Or in my chambers after Wexel attacked us in the old armory? Or on the dance floor during the ball?" The questions tumbled out of my lips before I could stop them.

Surprise flickered across Leonidas's face, although it quickly vanished, replaced by something much brighter and hotter, a promise of magic and fire that made desire sizzle through my veins. "If you were here right now, then I would show you how real it was."

The low, husky vow in his voice sent a shiver skittering down my spine, even as that desire in my veins flared up to new heights.

"If I were there, then I would shove my dagger into your heart," I snarled.

He arched an eyebrow at me. "Now who's lying? I thought we weren't going to do that to each other anymore."

"I made no such pledge—and I'm not lying."

His eyebrow arched a little higher, but then his face turned serious. "I truly am sorry, Gemma. I hope that you can forgive me someday. I bungled everything so very badly."

Yes, he had bungled things, and I wasn't sure I could ever forgive him—or especially myself for being such a blind, stupid fool. So I changed the subject. "There is one more thing I want to know."

"What?"

"Why did your mother call me the gargoyle queen? What did she mean by that?"

Leonidas's brow furrowed in thought. "Obviously, the Ripleys are known for their connection to the gargoyles, but I think she meant something else by it. Something more. I don't know what, though." He paused. "But you seem to have made her . . . happy."

I threw my arms out wide. "I killed her guards and drove back her son. Why would any of that make Maeven *happy*?"

"I don't know, but she's already scheming something else. She's been in her personal library all week, studying old books about courtly etiquette. Part of me doesn't want to know what she's plotting."

Part of me didn't want to know either. Whatever it was, Maeven's new scheme would most likely be sly, complicated, and put me in mortal danger again.

Leonidas stepped closer to the mirror. "I have something for you."

He held his hand up to the glass. A silver chain was wrapped around his fingers, with a bejeweled disk dangling off the end—my gargoyle pendant.

My breath caught in my throat. I'd found my dagger in the debris, but I hadn't seen the pendant since Milo had torn it off my neck and tossed it aside during the plaza fight. "How did you get that?"

"The night of the fight, we camped on the Mortan side of the mountain. I snuck back over to the plaza and used my magic to fish it out of the rubble."

I frowned. "Why would you do that?"

"Because it's *yours*," Leonidas replied. "Milo already took so much from you. I didn't want him to have this too. Here. I'll send it through the mirror to you."

I froze as the mirror started rippling, and Leonidas's hand stretched through the glass and out into my room. My gaze dropped to the pendant. He was right. It *was* mine, and I wanted it back. So I stepped forward and wrapped my fingers around the snarling gargoyle face.

He let me pull it and the chain out of his hand, but when I started to step back, he reached out and curled his fingers into mine. I froze again, both enjoying and hating the heat of his skin against my own.

Leonidas stroked his thumb across the scar on the top of my hand, bringing more and more heat to my body. For a mad, mad moment, I thought that he might step all the way through the mirror and come to me, here in Andvari, into my bedroom. That he would keep his promise and show me how real this attraction between us was. Part of me ached for him to do that and more—so much more.

But the other part of me remembered his betrayal. I would not be a fool again. So I iced over my heart and yanked my hand out of his.

Disappointment flickered across his face, but he didn't reach for me again. Instead, he drew his own hand back through the mirror, so that he was standing on the other side again.

Leonidas dropped into a low, formal bow. Then he straightened, his gaze burning into mine. "Until we meet again, Gemma."

He waved his hand, and that bright silver light flared once more. A moment later, he was gone, and the mirror was cold and still again.

I let out a breath and raised the necklace up to the light. Leonidas had cleaned the dirt and grime off the pendant and had fixed the broken chain. I rubbed my thumb over Grimley's snarling face, then went over to my writing desk, placed the gargoyle pendant on the corner of the wood, and sat down.

Several books were piled on the desk, along with papers, maps, and more from the Ripley royal library. Ever since I had returned to Glitnir, I had been trying to find out everything I could about tearstone, its magical properties, and how it could be used as a weapon. I might have sent Milo running back to Morta, but he was far from defeated.

Maeven was right. We were all playing capture-the-crown, although the stakes were much, much higher than in any child's game. The last part of the old Andvarian song chimed through my mind.

> *But for those who conquer*
> *their fear and capture the crown,*
> *that lord or lady has the power*
> *to tear their enemies down.*

Capture the crown, and you could tear down the throne that went with it. Well, my eyes were firmly fixed on the Morricone throne. So I opened a book and pulled it closer, reading through the passages and trying to find a weakness that would let me destroy my mortal enemies.

ACKNOWLEDGMENTS

My heartfelt thanks go out to all the folks who help turn my words into a book.

Thanks go to my agent, Annelise Robey, and my editor, Erika Tsang, for all their helpful advice, support, and encouragement. Thanks also to Nicole Fischer, Rhina Garcia, Naureen Nashid, Angela Craft, and everyone else at Harper Voyager and HarperCollins.

And finally, a big thanks to all the readers. Knowing that folks read and enjoy my books is truly humbling, and I hope that you all enjoy reading about Gemma, Grimley, and their adventures.

I appreciate you all more than you will ever know.

Happy reading! ☺

THE GARGOYLE QUEEN SERIES CONTINUES MAY 2022!

READ ON FOR A SNEAK PEEK!

Reiko grumbled some more, but she climbed onto Fern. I did the same with Grimley. Then, with a whisper of wings, the gargoyles took off.

I leaned over Grimley's back, admiring the vibrant gardens below. White crushed-shell paths shimmered like opalescent ribbons twining around the lush green lawns, while gray stone arbors draped with pink, purple, and blue wisteria stood next to the enormous oaks that gave Oakton its name. The wind whistled through my hair, bringing with it the delicate scents of the colorful blossoms that populated the flowerbeds, as well as that crisp, earthy tang that was uniquely fall. The cerulean sky was clear of clouds, and the late-October sun added some pleasant warmth to the brisk day.

I was never happier than when I was on Grimley's back, sailing through the sky, the landscape laid out before me like a carpet at a queen's feet. And perhaps best of all, way up here, there was no dining hall full of condescending nobles, gossipy servants, and bored guards silently judging me in their own minds, where they thought I couldn't hear them. These days, I appreciated the quiet more than ever, especially given all the unquiet in my own mind. So I tilted my face into the wind, breathed in deeply again, and enjoyed every single moment of our flight.

It didn't take the gargoyles long to zoom past the stone walls that bordered Eichen's estate, along with the nearby town of Haverton. People were walking and shopping in the plazas below like usual, and no one seemed to notice us pass by overhead. Then again, they had no real reason to, since gargoyles flew over the town all the time to hunt for rats, rabbits, and more in the countryside.

We quickly left the town behind as well, and Grimley and Fern flew for about thirty more minutes before I spotted an odd shape on the forest floor. Below, through the trees, the remains of a campfire stood in a stone pit in the middle of a clearing, like a black bull's-eye on an archery target.

I pointed out the spot to Grimley. *Over there. That might be what we're looking for.*

On my way.

Grimley flexed his wings and veered in that direction. But instead of landing in the clearing, he flew past it. I might be taking a risk by investigating the rumors, but I wasn't about to land right beside the fire pit. That was just asking for trouble, especially since I didn't know how many Mortans might be lurking.

A few minutes later, Grimley spiraled down, down, down and landed in another, smaller clearing. Fern and Reiko also glided to a stop beside us.

I slid off Grimley's back. As soon as my feet touched the ground, I pulled my dagger out of its scabbard and scanned the area. Beyond the clearing, the woods stretched out as far as I could see, and my breath steamed faintly in the chilly air. Given the high elevation of the Spire Mountains, fall had already come and gone here, and many of the trees were bare, although a few were still swathed in brilliant scarlet, gold, and citrine leaves like noble ladies draped in colorful ball gowns.

No one was moving through the trees, converging on our position, so I glanced over at Reiko, who was still sitting atop Fern.

"You can let go now," Fern chirped in a helpful voice.

Reiko flinched, as though the gargoyle's bright tone had startled her, but she slowly released her white-knuckle grip on the bases of Fern's wings and slid to the ground.

"Problems?" I drawled.

Reiko shook her head, and some of the sickly green tinge faded from her face. "Nope." She shook her head again, as if pushing away the rest of her nausea, then drew her sword. "Let's go find the Mortans."

We left Grimley and Fern in the clearing to hunt and headed deeper into the woods.

Reiko and I moved from one tree to another, careful to step on as few dried leaves and dead twigs as possible. We were still making far too much noise, but we didn't encounter anyone, and we quickly reached the clearing I'd glimpsed earlier.

The fire pit was much larger than it had appeared from above, and the scent of charred wood hung in the air like an invisible, smoky cloud. I reached out with my magic, searching for flickers of thoughts and spurts of feelings, but the surrounding area was silent and still. I nodded at Reiko. Together, we stepped into the clearing.

I strode over, crouched down, and put my hand in the blackened detritus of the fire. The gray ash was still wet, indicating that someone had been here recently. I glanced around, looking for crusts of bread, stray bits of cloth, loose coins, or anything else someone might have accidentally dropped, but nothing had been left behind—except boot prints.

Several boot prints grooved into the soft, muddy ground

around the fire pit, indicating that at least half a dozen people, maybe more, had recently tromped through this area. My heart picked up speed. This *had* to be a Mortan campsite. No one in Haverton would have any reason to be this far out in the woods, especially not this many people at once.

Reiko also eyed the boot prints. "Whoever was here cleaned up after themselves fairly well. The next hard rain would have washed away all traces of them."

I got to my feet and wiped the ash off my hand. "Let's track them, and see if the rats lead us back to their nest."

Together, with our weapons in our hands, we headed out the far side of the clearing and even deeper into the woods.

The Mortans might have doused their campfire and picked up their trash, but they hadn't bothered to hide their trail, and Reiko and I were easily able to follow the boot prints, broken branches, and scuffed leaves over the hilly, rocky terrain.

I was about to crest yet another ridge when Reiko lifted her hand, stopping me. She held her finger up to her lips, then pointed at her ear. Most morphs had heightened senses, including hearing.

I reached out with my magic, and a couple of presences sputtered to life in the back of my mind, like matches flaring in a dark room. "We've caught up to them," I whispered.

Reiko nodded. We stepped off the faint trail we'd been following, then crept forward, quickly and quietly climbing to the top of the ridge.

This ridge made a wide, sweeping curve to the left before sloping down into another, much larger clearing. At the base of the ridge, a square opening had been carved into the rocks and shored up with wooden beams. No light spilled out of the black hole, but it was clearly man-made.

I pointed out the opening. "That must be the old tearstone mine."

Reiko stabbed her finger at the ground. "And judging by how thoroughly the grass has been trampled, several people have been here recently."

She had barely finished speaking when two men stepped out of the mine entrance. We fell silent, watching them.

The men strode through the clearing and stopped next to a couple of flat, waist-high boulders that looked like table leaves that had been pushed together. The men were both wearing black tunics, leggings, and boots. No crests or symbols adorned their clothes, but their purple cloaks, along with the swords on their belts, marked them as Mortan soldiers.

My heart quickened with equal parts worry and excitement. The rumors were true. The Mortans *were* here.

Each man slung a black leather satchel down onto the flat boulders and rifled through the contents, causing several soft but distinctive *tink-tink-tinks* to ring out. I might be a pampered princess, but mining was one of Andvari's main industries, and I knew the sound of rocks—ore—rattling together when I heard it.

"You're sure this is all of it?" one of the men asked, his voice floating up the ridge to Reiko and me.

The second man nodded. "Yep. We got every last piece. Let's go."

The first man hoisted his satchel onto his shoulder and headed toward the far side of the clearing. The second man hurried to do the same, but he didn't close his bag all the way, and something slid out of the top and dropped to the ground. Another distinctive *tink* rang out, but the second man rushed after his friend without a backward glance. My eyes narrowed, but I couldn't see whatever he had dropped.

The men left the clearing and disappeared into the trees beyond.

Reiko and I held our positions on the ridge. She scanned the woods, while I reached out with my magic. Other than the two

men, I didn't sense anyone else in the immediate area. I nodded at Reiko, and we followed the curve of the ridge down to the
clearing.

I stepped inside the mine opening, scanning the dust-
covered ground, as well as the walls, just in case the Mortans
had strung up some trip wires. But the area was clean, so I went
in a little deeper. All I could see were a few feet of rough-hewn
rock walls before the mine's yawning darkness swallowed up
the sunlight, but the smell of freshly dug earth filled the air,
indicating that someone had been working in here recently.

My gaze landed on a small pile of rubble close to the entrance.
I crouched down to get a better look, but it was just a mound of
rocks, many with jagged, blackened edges, like they were shards
of burnt, shattered glass rather than solid stone. Odd. Maybe
Milo had used his lightning magic to blast tearstone out of the
mine, although I didn't see any scorch marks on the walls. Either
way, something about the burnt stones made me shiver. I slid
one into my pocket to study later, then got to my feet.

The last time I'd been in a mine was a few weeks ago in Blauberg, when Conley, the corrupt foreman, had shoved me into a
chasm to hide the fact that he was stealing and selling tearstone
to the Mortans. I stared into the darkness in the back of the
mine, but instead of seeing total, absolute blackness, memories
flooded my mind.

The cool air rushing over my face as I fell. My body slamming into a stone ledge jutting out from the side of the chasm.
The bones shattering in my left arm and leg. White-hot agony
exploding in my wounds. The chill of death slowly creeping
over me. And then a shadow looming over me, slowly morphing
into a man with dark amethyst eyes—

"Gemma," Reiko called out. "Come look at this."

Her voice jolted me out of my memories, although it didn't
stop all that remembered pain from pounding through my body,

hammering right alongside my racing heart. Perhaps it was all the trauma I'd endured in Myrkvior, but ever since I had returned home, my magic had been flaring up in new, unexpected ways, including all these unwanted glimpses of the recent past that kept intruding on my present.

I wiped the cold sweat off my forehead with a shaking hand. Then I schooled my face into a calm mask and strode back out into the clearing.

Reiko was crouched down by the two flat rocks the Mortans had used as a table earlier. She plucked something out of the grass, then straightened and held it out to me.

The jagged shard was about the size of a small dagger. I rolled it back and forth in my fingers, watching as the rock, the ore, shifted from light gray to dark blue and back again.

"It's definitely tearstone. The mine must not have been as played out as Lord Eichen claimed during the luncheon."

"Either that, or Eichen is working with the Mortans," Reiko suggested.

Surprise shot through me, and I opened my mouth to automatically defend my countryman, but Reiko stared me down.

"First rule of being a spy—anyone can betray you at any time. Even someone you think is a staunch ally."

She was talking about Eichen, but another man's face filled my mind—the same handsome face with the same dark amethyst eyes I'd seen in my vision. In some ways, Leonidas Morricone haunted me far more than any injuries I'd received in the Blauberg mine.

I shoved those memories away and considered Reiko's point. "Eichen could be working with the Mortans, but it's highly unlikely. He has plenty of power and money, and he's never shown any interest in trying to wrest the throne away from my grandfather. Plus, one of Eichen's sisters was killed by Mortan bandits a few years ago. He has no love for them."

Reiko nodded, accepting my conclusion.

I rolled the tearstone shard back and forth in my fingers again. "We should follow the Mortans. They might have a camp set up in the woods. Maybe that's where Milo is storing the stolen tearstone and the weapons he's made with it."

Reiko's eyebrows shot up. "It could still be a trap. Us just *happening* to see two Mortans outside an old mine and one of them just *happening* to drop a piece of tearstone is highly suspicious."

"I know, but it's—"

"Worth the risk," she finished.

I gave her a sour look. Reiko grinned back at me, as did her inner dragon, then jerked her head. "Let's go, princess."

Reiko headed toward the far side of the clearing. I nestled the tearstone shard in the side of my boot so that I wouldn't lose it, then pictured Grimley in my mind.

We've found the Mortans. We might need you and Fern.

Grimley answered me almost immediately. *We're done hunting. We'll be there soon.*

Quietly, please. We don't want to spook the Mortans.

You might like sneaking around, but I prefer a more direct approach.

Really? Is that what you told the Glitnir glass masters last week when you, Fern, and the other gargoyles were flying around doing barrel rolls and you accidentally smashed through the windows in Alvis's workshop?

Glass shouldn't be so bloody fragile, he grumbled.

I grinned, released my magic, and headed after Reiko to keep tracking our enemies.

Reiko and I crept through the woods. We didn't speak, but Reiko clutched her sword a little more tightly, and her worry throbbed like a splinter embedded deep in my heart. I adjusted my grip on my dagger and tried to ignore her worry, along with my own.

Another faint trail ran through this section of the woods, although the dirt was so hard-packed that I couldn't see any boot prints or tell how many people might have passed this way. Reiko and I stayed within sight of the trail, creeping from one tree to the next.

We walked for the better part of a mile before the trail led into another clearing that was even larger than the one in front of the old mine. Wide, flat rocks jutted out from the surrounding steep ridges like stone bleachers, making the whole area look like a rough, unfinished gladiator arena.

I didn't see the two Mortans, although the trail led through the center of the grassy clearing before winding its way past the rocks and up the opposite ridge. The surrounding ridges were too steep to climb without a rope, so the Mortans still had to be following the trail.

"How close are we to the Mortan border?" Reiko asked.

I pointed to the opposite ridge, where a four-foot-tall gray stone obelisk had been driven into the ground beside the trail. I couldn't see it from this distance, but I knew that the Ripley snarling gargoyle crest was carved into the arrow that topped the obelisk. "See that stone?"

Reiko squinted in that direction. "Is that a trail marker?"

"Yes. It's also a warning that we are exactly one mile from Morta. The obelisks along the actual Mortan border are painted solid purple and have the Morricone royal crest carved into them, so that people know when they cross from one kingdom into the other."

"We're too close," Reiko muttered. "Especially if this is a trap."

Given my recent disastrous trip to Myrkvior, I would have been quite happy to never set foot in Morta ever again. But finding where Milo Morricone was storing the stolen tearstone might help us stop his plot before more lives were lost.

"What is your magic telling you?" Reiko asked. "Picking up any thoughts?"

I concentrated, scanning the clearing and the ridges again, but I didn't hear so much as a whisper of thought, and I didn't sense anticipation or any other strong emotions. "No one's hiding in the grass to stab us in the back. As for what's on the other side of that ridge, well, I can't tell without getting closer."

Reiko twirled her sword around in her hand. "Then let's get closer." She grinned. "After all, it's worth the risk."

I rolled my eyes. "Are you going to mention that every time I want to do something dangerous?"

Her grin widened. "Absolutely."

I huffed with annoyance, but we left the woods and stepped into the clearing. We moved through the knee-high wild grass as quickly and quietly as possible, but the longer we walked, the more unease filled me. I still didn't sense anyone nearby, but the clearing and surrounding woods seemed unnaturally still and quiet. No birds twittered in the trees, no squirrels rustled through the underbrush, even the breeze had stopped blowing. The utter lack of noise and motion was unnerving.

A shadow flitted by overhead, momentarily blotting out the afternoon sun. I glanced up, thinking it was Grimley or Fern, but the shadow's shape was sleeker and more streamlined than those of the blocky gargoyles. The shadow vanished over a ridge before I could get a good look at it, but a presence flickered through my mind, as soft and light as a feather tickling my skin. I frowned. That felt like—

A faint *creak* of leather sounded, and a man stepped into view beside the trail marker at the top of the ridge. I froze, as did Reiko, who let out a soft, muttered curse. The two of us were completely exposed in the clearing, and there was no way he didn't see us.

The man was a few inches over six feet, with short black hair, hazel eyes, and bronze skin. His body was thick, strong, and muscled, and he clutched a sword with the easy familiarity of a seasoned soldier. Even though it was only midafternoon, heavy stubble had already darkened his square jaw. Most people probably would have thought the man handsome. I might have too, if I hadn't known how cruel, petty, vindictive, and vicious he was.

Just like the two Mortans we had seen earlier, this man was also wearing a purple cloak over a black tunic, leggings, and boots. A fancy cursive *M* surrounded by a ring of strix feathers—the Morricone royal crest—was stitched in gold thread over this man's heart, marking his importance and position.

Wexel, the captain of the Mortan royal guards, who was loyal to Milo Morricone.

Wexel sneered at me, then lifted his sword and brought it down in a sharp motion. Several more *creaks* sounded, along with the steady *scuff-scuff* of footsteps, and more than a dozen men appeared, lining the top of the ridge, all of them clutching crossbows.

My heart sank, and I cursed my own foolishness. Reiko had been right.

It was a trap.

ABOUT THE AUTHOR

Andre Teague

Jennifer Estep is a *New York Times*, *USA Today*, and internationally bestselling author who prowls the streets of her imagination in search of her next fantasy idea.

She is the author of the **Crown of Shards**, **Elemental Assassin**, and other fantasy series. She has written more than forty books, along with numerous novellas and stories.

In her spare time, Jennifer enjoys hanging out with friends and family, doing yoga, and reading fantasy and romance books. She also watches way too much TV and loves all things related to superheroes.

For more information on Jennifer and her books, visit her website at www.jenniferestep.com or follow her online on Facebook, Goodreads, BookBub, and Twitter—@Jennifer_Estep. You can also sign up for her newsletter at www.jenniferestep.com /contact-jennifer/newsletter.

READ THE WHOLE
CROWN OF SHARDS SERIES

KILL THE QUEEN
A Crown of Shards Novel, Book 1

Gladiator meets *Game of Thrones*: a royal woman becomes a skilled warrior to destroy her murderous cousin, avenge her family, and save her kingdom in this first entry in a dazzling fantasy epic from the *New York Times* and *USA Today* bestselling author of the Elemental Assassin series—an enthralling tale that combines magic, murder, intrigue, adventure, and a hint of romance.

PROTECT THE PRINCE
A Crown of Shards Novel, Book 2

> **"An exciting new fantasy series full of magic, fierce women, and revenge."**
> **—*Booklist***

Everleigh Blair might be the new gladiator queen of Bellona, but her problems are far from over.

From a court full of arrogant nobles to an assassination attempt in her own throne room, Evie knows dark forces are at work, making her wonder if she is truly strong enough to be a Winter Queen...

CRUSH THE KING
A Crown of Shards Novel, Book 3

A fierce gladiator queen must face off against her enemies in an epic battle in this next thrilling installment of *New York Times* and *USA Today* bestselling author Jennifer Estep's Crown of Shards series—an action-packed adventure full of magic, murderous machinations, courtly intrigue, and pulse-pounding romance.

Queen Everleigh Blair of Bellona has survived the mass murder of the royal family, become a fearsome warrior trained by an elite gladiator troupe, and unleashed her ability to destroy magic. After surviving yet another assassination attempt orchestrated by the conniving king of Morta, Evie has had enough. It's time to turn the tables and take the fight to her enemies.